UNCHAINED

Pure Blood, Book Two

GENAVIE CASTLE

Castle Publications

COPYRIGHT

ISBN: 978-1-962047-14-2 Ebook

ISBN: 978-1-962047-15-9 Print

Cover design by: Genavie Castle

Edited by: EPONA Author Solutions

Printed in the United States of America

ABOUT THIS BOOK
Content / Trigger Warnings

This is the second book in the Pure Blood series. It takes place where book one left off. I strongly recommend reading book one before proceeding, to get familiar with the characters and the story's setting.

As with book one, everything about book two is completely fictional. It contains explicit content suitable for mature readers only. There are multiple love interests, including MFMM scenes, profanity, and violence. Please consider these potential triggers before moving forward:

Mild Bondage scenes

Mild knife play

Dubious consent

Kidnapping

CHAINED, PURE BLOOD BOOK ONE

Summary

A plague has decimated the world's population. The Better Health Federation (BHF) has taken over and is hunting down the Rebels who have not succumbed to their rules.

Elyanna a Pure Blood with mind-bending powers is determined to track down the man responsible for her sister's death. On her journey, she is captured by three men, Hudson, the telekinetic; Axel, the seer; and Xavier, the invisible man. After a rocky start, Elyanna develops a relationship with all three men. Together they storm the enemy's community, and Elyanna gets her revenge. Victory is bittersweet for Elyanna. Lives are lost and a loved one suffers irreparable damage.

Almost two years later, Elyanna is living a peaceful, happy life, with a new baby and surrounded by people she loves. But things are about to change.

Book Two begins the same day where book one left off.

CHAPTER ONE

Elyanna

Roman placed my son, Axel, in my arms, and I followed Hudson into the house.

"Grab what you need, babe; I'll get Axel's things," my husband told me as we went our separate ways at the top of the stairs.

We'd been preparing for BHF to show up ever since the Rebels had taken over Hillside. It was fortunate they hadn't come while Becks and I had been pregnant. We'd had over a year of peace, which was spent nurturing our babies while preparing for war.

I placed my sleeping son in the middle of my bed, threw on a pair of jeans, a tank top, and a leather jacket, then strapped on my sword. A bag of emergency essentials was in a bag near the door, where I always left it. To keep up with Axel's growing needs, I kept a bag of his things in his room. I did, however, keep his baby carrier that had been retrofitted to accommodate my sassy stick and still allow me to carry my kid.

In less than eight minutes, I was ready to go with Axel in my arms.

"I'll see you at Royal Summit, beautiful." My firebug kissed the top of my head and Ax's.

"Wait, where are you going? I thought we were all sticking together," I asked.

"We're taking the chopper. We'll deal with the convoy before they get close," Roman replied, then slipped out the front door.

"No. We need to stay together. Hudson?" I faced my husband. This wasn't the plan.

"Slight change of plans," he said. Hudson wrapped his arms around me and Ax. I sighed with relief. It was never a good idea to separate from loved ones in times of crisis.

"I'm going with them, Elyanna. If we take to the skies, we'll be able to pick them off before they get close. You need to drive down to Summit and stay with the others," Hudson told me.

"Are you fucking serious right now?" I glared at him. "No. You just want to take the Blackhawk for a spin. No, Hudson."

He cupped my face. "Do not argue, El. Not now. Let me do this. We'll be back before you can miss us."

A lump formed in my throat, and I fought to keep my tears from falling. The deep rumble of the chopper's engine forced me to swallow my rebuttal. Hudson had gotten an armed Blackhawk, and Roman had taught him and Xavier how to pilot the damn thing. My men were chomping at the bit to test it, and this was their chance. I wasn't going to win this one. Damn it.

"Come back to me, Hudson Pierce. And bring Roman and Xavier back with you. Unharmed. All of you."

He helped me load Ax into his seat. "See you soon," Hudson said then rushed to the helicopter.

Willing my tears away, I drove to Summit. Axel cried the entire drive. I wasn't sure if he'd known his daddy was going off to kill bad guys or if he was just crying enough for both of us.

Becks and Julia greeted were waiting at the main entrance as we drove into the community. I hopped out of the car and gave them both a hug.

"I can't find my brother," she said, her voice on edge.

"That's because he's with Hawk and Bug." I took Axel out of the car seat and grabbed our bags.

"What? When? How?"

I told her about my run-in with her twin.

She gaped and then bit her lip. "Using his gift to hide in my car?!

That sneaky little shit! Are you okay?"

"Xavi didn't hurt me, Becks. He seemed different, but not in a psychotic 'I'm going to kill you' way."

"Shit," she said again. A deep furrow creased between her brows. "I . . . I don't know what to say."

"There's nothing to say. We'll deal with it when they return." I glanced at the cloudless blue sky.

"Well," she shrugged her shoulders. "Let's get you settled then. We can rewatch *Friends*."

The cottage I'd given birth to Axel in was still ours. Hudson, Roman, and I stayed at Summit once in a while, and the residents hadn't complained. Not that they would. They supported Hudson and me in all things. The main building of Royal Summit could easily accommodate two hundred guests, and there were about twenty-eight residents. Every resident had ample living space and plush accommodations. It was designed to be a five-star resort, after all.

Hudson and the other men still did what they needed to keep Royal Summit, Gator Springs High, and Briar County Penitentiary as one unified community. We had the least number of residents, while Gator had the most. The high school was a forty-five-minute drive, and Briar was almost two hours away. The location of each community had proven to be ideal, as we had set up lookout points, allowing us to watch the highways for incoming vehicles. Typically, there weren't many cars on the road, aside from our daily patrols or trade between the communities or visitors from Hillside.

For us to have gotten a warning of a BHF convoy was a godsend. Hudson wanted to keep BHF away from our residences as much as possible. His idea was road patrols, the occasional helicopter tour, and, when needed, attacking before they attacked us. I was grateful for his insight and diligence. He'd had everyone within the three communities preparing for this day since we'd helped Hillside. He was a brilliant strategist, and I, like the rest of the community, trusted his judgment. Still, as his wife, I worried.

It had been hours since they'd taken off. Johnny, Becks' husband, would alert me if something had gone amiss. A communication hub had been set up in the main building of Summit. The communities were able to communicate via radio, and I knew Hudson would report any news to Johnny. Maybe I should just go in and check.

"Stop fretting," Becks said from her end of the couch. "They're fine and will be home before you know it."

We settled into the cottage to watch *Friends* after the kids went down for a nap. In the lodge, our primary residence, we'd found an extra DVD player and a massive collection of DVDs. It wasn't like streaming movies and shows like we did pre-plague, but it was a form of entertainment we enjoyed. My thoughts were occupied with my men; I hadn't been paying attention to the screen at all.

I sighed. "I thought I was supposed to be the mind reader."

She smiled and turned her gaze toward me. "You are, but I can feel you thinking. It hasn't been that long."

"Five hours is long," I retorted.

"You know how your husband is. He's probably doing a tour of the entire state. If it makes you feel better, we can go see my husband as soon as the kids wake up," she told me.

On cue, Julia wailed, and then Axel followed a minute later.

We tended to our children and then headed up the paver path past the gardens to the main building. There was an expansive courtyard between the cottage and the main building, and more buildings were scattered around the property that I hadn't explored yet. I was told Xavier lived in one.

"Where's Xavi's place?" I asked.

Beck pointed toward her left. "That way. On the other side of the main building. I believe it was supposed to be a barn or horse stable. He's set it up like the studio he had at Gator. There is a workshop on the bottom where he works on cars, and on top is a loft where he sleeps. He still doesn't like being around people."

She gave me a devilish smile. "Why, do you want to peek at his secret hideout?"

I laughed. "I have a feeling you already did that."

"Of course I have. He's my twin. I have to keep tabs on him." She shrugged.

"You did not?!"

"I was worried about him after the whole Luther thing. He's gotten a little better, but it's like he's reverted."

"Reverted to what?" My eyebrows raised.

"Uh, forget I said anything. Oh! Look who's home," she said.

Hudson, Roman, and Xavier strolled toward us, wearing boyish grins. My heart swelled in my chest.

"I told you everything was fine." Becks winked at me. "I'll see you in the dining hall for dinner. I'm going to check on my husband."

"Thanks, Becks! I love you," I called out. "And this conversation is not over!"

She waved me off and kept walking.

Roman took Axel from my arms, while Hudson picked me up and spun us in a small circle. He pressed a wet kiss on my lips before setting me on my feet. "Hi." He grinned. The gleam in his eyes and his playful demeanor melted my concerns. My men were home safely, and they were happy.

"Did you have a good day playing with your new helicopter?" I asked him.

"It was so badass!" He smiled so big that I thought he might be high. In some ways, he was.

"You should have seen it, El! Explosions everywhere," Roman exclaimed. "It was exhilarating. I've never fired a gun like that."

"Oh my god. You two shouldn't be so thrilled about blowing up shit."

"But we are!" my men said it simultaneously.

Their exuberance was infectious, and I was grinning alongside them as they recounted what had happened. I was happy my men were happy and we were safe until I realized Xavi had taken off with his sister without saying hello. One step forward and three steps back.

CHAPTER TWO

Elyanna

BHF had been bombarding our communities with continuous attacks. Not even a month later, another BHF convoy was spotted on the road, heading toward Summit. Hillside had been hit twice, and Briar had dealt with a large group of invaders as well.

Hudson had set up road blockades along specific points on the highway to keep BHF from getting too close. His plans weren't foolproof yet, but we were getting there. Near the blockade, hidden within the woods, was a hunting tower that the men had built. It rose twenty-four feet in the air. I was sitting in said hunting tower, which gave me the perfect view of the blockade while still being hidden amongst the pines. The mile or so of distance was just far enough for me to use my gift and get a read on whomever was in the convoy. That was the hope anyway.

I'd been waiting in the tower long enough to become bored. Hudson was down at the blockade with other men, waiting out the trucks that had been spotted via a chopper patrol.

We now had two choppers in each of the three communities. The men and a couple of women had been taking lessons from Roman and Johnny on how to fly the birds, and Hudson had set up a random schedule for the communities to do an aerial patrol. Between the road and the occasional helicopter patrols, we monitored the roads between the three communities and the highways leading to and from us. Our communities had been growing since we'd taken over Hillside, which meant we had the manpower to protect ourselves from BHF. This tactic had saved our bacon more than once.

So why had I been roped into this mess? My husband thought it was a great opportunity to test the range of my gift in an unfamiliar setting. Of course, he was right, since it had been easy at the Summit, where I was familiar with the area and the people. I was even able to do two miles at Gator Springs. Briar was different because of the thick cement blocks. I didn't have the range to cover Hillside, which was our largest community, spanning over fifty miles from one end to the other. Here at the tower, I could see my handsome husband through the binoculars.

How are you holding up, baby? Hudson asked through the radio.

Bored. No wonder I'm not a hunter, I replied.

He chuckled.

Next time, I'll remind you to bring a book. Not much longer, babe. I hear a truck approaching.

I peered out of the binoculars and waited. Five minutes later, a single SUV rolled up. One man. Hmmm . . . Weird.

I used my gift and got nothing but buzzing bees. Shit.

Hudson, I can't get a read on his thoughts.

I watched my husband drag the man out of the SUV by his collar. He hit the man with the butt of his rifle, and the guard went limp.

Climb out of your tower, peaches. We're done here.

Finally.

Yes, sir.

Climbing into the tower was a piece of cake. Hudson was so impressed with how quickly I'd made the assent that he felt comfortable leaving me alone. I was proud of myself. Going down was a different story. Morning dew made the metal rungs slippery, and my clammy hands didn't help. I hadn't been afraid of heights until I'd begun my dissent and made the mistake of looking down. Shit.

Deep inhale, El.

I continued my downward climb, one slow step at a time.

"Hurry it up, woman; we don't have all day."

Xavier's snarly voice startled me, causing me to slip, and knocking the radio off my belt in the process. The radio dropped and my body followed. My arms flailed, and my stomach flipped as trees zipped past me. I squeezed my eyes shut as I plunged to my death.

Strong arms caught me with a thud. I flung my arms around Xavi's neck.

"You saved me! Thank you." My pulse raced.

For a moment, he held me close, and I snuggled into the crook of his neck, savoring his warmth and unique manly scent of pine and motor oil. *I missed you.* His body stiffened, and he released me dropping me unceremoniously to the mud.

Asshole.

"Hawk's waiting." He walked away.

I stood, wiping my muddy hands on my jeans, glanced at the broken radio, and then looked up at the tower. *Well, at least he saved me from breaking my neck.*

"Any day now," Xavi said.

He was back to being a dick again. Surprise. Not. I caught up to him.

We walked in silence, and I absently opened my gift to scan the area.

Xavi slammed me against a tree, knocking the wind from my lungs.

"Never use your gift on me," he snarled, pressing a knife to my neck.

"I'm sorry! Habit. I was just scanning the area," I sputtered.

The blade bit into my flesh. Xavi's eyes were feral.

"I'm not sure what's a bigger turn-on, the thought of my cock in your pussy or watching you bleed." He licked his lips.

He pressed his knife deeper into my skin.

"You won't hurt me. You just saved my life." My voice sounded confident, but in truth, I wasn't. Xavi was such a wildcard when it came to me.

He kicked the inside of my heels, spread my legs apart, and wedged himself between my thighs. His thick erection ground into my belly.

Here we go again.

He leaned in and his mouth latched onto my neck, sucking and licking the injury he'd caused. Xavi was drinking my blood.

His actions should have been alarming. I should have been pissed off. I should have fought back. But no, my traitorous cunt had different ideas. I arched into him.

"Are you wet for me, Elyanna?"

"No!"

He regarded me with a devious smirk, his lips red with my blood. He plunged his other hand down the front of my jeans. His fingers found my slick entrance.

"You're a fucking liar." His mouth latched onto my neck while he jammed a finger into my pussy.

His knife bit into my flesh while he fingered me. We were broken, Xavi and I. My brain was saying no. My body was saying hell yes. The situation was so messed up, and yet . . . I. Fucking. Moaned.

"My sweet girl loves a little knife play." He trailed the tip of his blade down my chest. The sound of my t-shirt tearing echoed through the woods. A sharp sting bloomed over the top of my breast.

I rocked into his palm as he laved over the new wound he'd caused.

He put his knife in its holster and said, "Cream all over my fingers, baby."

"Xavi," I moaned his name.

Suddenly, he withdrew his hand from my pants and clamped my mouth shut. "Not a fucking word."

My eyes snapped open. Xavi's face wore a deranged expression. I heard the familiar click of a gun cocking back, and then *BOOM*.

My ears rang. Xavi shoved me to the ground and disappeared. I couldn't access my gift. I couldn't hear a thing except the damn ringing in my ears.

Feeling vulnerable, I crouched beside the tree, searching the area. Xavier was nowhere to be found. Trees and shrubs were shaken by an unknown disturbance. A man several feet away dropped to the ground in a bloody heap. Another man was thrown into a nearby tree. BHF guards. We were being attacked.

I drew my sword, rose to my feet, and spun in a small circle.

My sassy stick flew from my hand, and I was shoved against the tree. Xavi dropped his gift. He mouthed something I couldn't hear.

I pointed to my ears and shook my head.

He drew away from me and began speaking into a comms device.

Xavi was covered in blood, and he wore a satisfied grin on his face. I scanned the woods and noticed more bodies. The unhinged lunatic had saved me. Again. Maybe he still loved me. Maybe not. If there was anything I could be certain about at that moment was, whatever demons existed in Xavier's head had been sated by bloodlust.

I stared at the man who had once been my light-hearted Ghost. Worry began to ebb into my consciousness when Hudson nearly bowled me over.

"Are you okay?" His voice sounded muffled, as his gaze traveled the length of my body and then flicked up to meet mine. Fury and concern in his emerald depths.

I looked down at my blood-covered clothes and shook my head.

"Not mine." I pointed to my ear. "Ringing. I can't hear anything."

He fixed Xavi with an accusatory glare and positioned my body behind his. I placed my hand on Hawk's back and felt him relax. Xavi merely shrugged and gestured to the fallen soldiers. I followed his hand gestures, taking notice of one man several feet away with his guts strewn across the ground. I turned my head fighting the urge to gag and gathered my sword. A second later, Hudson took my hand and led me out of the woods.

I glanced at Xavier, who stood in the middle of the woods, bloodied and smiling from ear to ear.

CHAPTER THREE

Elyanna

"No!" Ax grumbled with me. "Da-da and Bug!"

My son was willful and gave me a helluva time getting into bed.

"Get under the covers, and I'll call them." I pulled back the sheets while he climbed into bed.

Using my gift, I reached out to Hawk. *Your son wants you and Bug.*

We'll be up in a minute, Hawk replied.

"No momma!" Ax complained.

"They're on their way. Give them a minute," I replied.

"No!! Asks them," He pouted.

"I did. Mommy has magic," I told him. I may not be able to do storytime voices, but I could do magic. So could Hawk and Bug, but Ax didn't know that yet.

"Oooh magic." His eyes were big and round.

"Magic is for big kids." We hadn't made any decisions as to when we'd tell him about our gifts. It was possible he'd inherit them from us. Hudson's parents were both telekinetic, so we assumed he'd have the same. He hadn't exhibited any gifts and so we'd decided to cross that bridge when we came to it.

"Big." Ax patted his chest.

I smiled. "Yes, you are, love."

"Magic momma," he whispered.

"Not tonight, maybe tomorrow," I told him.

Hudson and Roman entered the room.

"Momma's magic!" Ax exclaimed.

The men laughed. "She sure is." Hudson pecked my cheek.

"Apparently, I don't have enough magic to read bedtime stories," I retorted. "Have fun."

I exited the room and stood outside the door, eavesdropping.

Hudson and Roman were the best storytellers. They made sound effects mimicking cars or trains, and their voice variations were perfect. They could have made a killing narrating books back when that was a thing.

It warmed my heart to see them entertaining our son. I wished I'd had a video camera. Ax was growing up fast, and these moments were precious.

I settled onto the living room sofa with a book Becks loaned me. She'd collected a nice selection of romance novels over the years. It was a welcome distraction, which I needed, especially after dealing with the convoy earlier in the day. The first time I'd had to use my gift to sentence so many lives to death wrecked me, and it never got easier. I had to remind myself repeatedly that if I hadn't taken them out, then they'd have come after innocent people, like my son and my goddaughter, Julia. That steeled my resolve, and I had no remorse.

You made the right decision, El. Your family and so many others are safe.

Soft lips and a warm, masculine scent woke me. "How long have I been out?"

"Not long, thirty minutes. You want to go upstairs?" Hudson said.

"No. I'll get up and prep Ax's breakfast for tomorrow." I rose to see Roman, my firebug, sitting on the loveseat across from me.

"I'll do it. Relax." He patted my shoulder and sauntered off.

We were in our home, the mountain lodge I'd claimed a couple of years ago. The original owners never showed up, and we assumed they perished, just like ninety percent of the population.

"You did good today, El," my firebug said. "How are you holding up?"

"Fine," I replied.

After the ringing in my ears stopped, I questioned the driver using my gift. He was a new BHF recruit and was told to drive to a certain spot, let the other soldiers out, and continue down the road. Another vehicle would arrive after him and collect the others.

The other truck arrived within minutes, and I used my gift. Their mission was to attack Gator Springs. I lashed out with my gift and had twelve guards dead within minutes.

"Liar," he scoffed.

I smiled, then went to sit on the floor between his massive thighs and placed his hands on my shoulders.

"Are you looking for a massage?" he asked.

"Yes, please," I said.

He chuckled. "Anything for you, my queen." His warm, strong fingers kneaded the tension away from my body. I groaned.

"You protect our people, Elyanna. Without you . . ."

"I know," I cut him off. "I know. I would rather it be three dozen enemies than one of our people. It's just . . . pointless. The population has already been annihilated, and still, we're fighting against one another. Shouldn't we be living in peace?"

"I don't disagree, however . . . people are just people. From the beginning of time, mankind craved power and control. It is inevitable. Especially now; it has been almost nine years, and people are still afraid. Haunted by ghosts from past mistakes and afraid of phantoms of the future, it's an endless cycle of fear. And when there is fear, people generally follow the most powerful."

"Who might that be?" I asked. We'd taken out Luther, the man whose list of bad deeds ran miles long. He had been responsible for my sister's death. He'd been kidnapping and experimenting on children. Presumably, he had also engineered the virus causing the plague. And he was the only person who was a mind-bender like me. He was a powerful force, but not the big bad. There was someone else in charge, and whomever that was, he had been sending troops after us continuously for the last month.

"Thinking of taking out the man in charge?" Roman asked.

"Or woman," I muttered.

My firebug chuckled. "If anyone could take down BHF, it's you, sweetheart. But I don't think your husband would go for that one."

"Go for what?" Hawk strolled into the living area, grabbed a pillow, placed it on my lap, and stretched out on the floor.

"Your wife wants to go after the head cheese at BHF," Roman told him.

"I do not," I replied. "Not really, anyway."

"That's a no, El." Hudson tilted his head to look at me with narrowed eyes.

"Fine. I wouldn't know where to begin anyway." I thought about it for a moment and wondered if anyone knew. I hadn't rooted around in the enemy's minds long enough to seek out that information. Interesting. Perhaps I needed to dig deeper next time.

"Ouch!" My husband pinched my thigh. "Hudson! What the hell did you do that for?" I swatted his arm.

"You're planning something dangerous." He chuckled. "The answer, sweet love, is no."

"I'm not planning anything. Just thinking," I replied.

"Sit still." Roman nudged my shoulder.

"Does anyone know who's in charge of BHF? I mean, there has to be someone in charge, right?" I asked. "I've never sought that information from our enemies."

"According to Samson, the higher-ups are all in the Arizona desert." Hudson kissed the spot he pinched on my thigh.

Arizona . . . Something about that location niggled at the back of my head.

I leaned over to look into Hawk's face. "Why didn't you tell me that?"

"Do you want a massage or not?" Bug asked.

"Yes, I do. Please continue." I straightened and began running my fingers through Hudson's hair. "Answer me, Hawk. Why didn't you tell me?"

"I didn't realize you wanted that information." Hudson rubbed his cheek along my thigh.

"I didn't either," I admitted. "This constant killing seems pointless. There aren't many of us left."

"You have a point." Bug kneaded my shoulders. "But it's too dangerous."

"That's only because we don't know what we're up against," I replied.

Hudson sat up to face me. "You're not going to let this go, are you?"

"Well, no. Not really. I'm not saying I'll storm the castle, but I'd like more information. I'd like to know more about the person who is trying to control whoever is left on the planet."

He placed a chaste kiss on my lips. "If I get you the info you seek, will you leave it alone?"

"Okay." I kissed him back.

Bug groaned. "And that's my cue to leave."

Roman kissed the back of my head and exited the living room. I almost felt bad.

My firebug had been a surprise for me and Hudson. We'd welcomed him into our lives and he easily fit right in despite the run-ins we'd had with him before the Luther fiasco. Axel's passing left a hole in our lives, especially for Hudson. Rome's steady presence and quiet protectiveness helped us heal. Roman had never been Axel's replacement and never would be. But he was always there. A constant shadow, always protecting me and my son. Aside from the occasional massage, chaste kisses, and hand-holding, he never asked for more, and I never pushed. Did I want more from him? I wasn't going to lie; Roman was easy on the eyes, and he had a seductive side to him that was impossible to ignore.

I asked Hudson how he felt about me welcoming Roman into our bed. My husband loved me and would let me have him if I wanted to, but I wasn't getting that vibe from Rome and wouldn't force him into something he didn't want. Maybe he wasn't into girls. Or maybe I wasn't his type.

"I think you two will need to discuss this intimacy thing. Or lack thereof," Hudson said as though reading my mind.

"Discussion? There's nothing to discuss," I said.

He leaned away from me. "You're kidding me, right? You give him a raging hard-on every time he's around you."

"But he never . . ." My voice trailed off.

"Makes the first move?" Hudson asked. "He won't. He respects you too much, and I think he's afraid of what will happen if he crosses that line. He doesn't want to lose you. There's no doubt in my military mind that that man is in love with you."

"He is not."

"Yes, he is. It may have started as friendship or his way of repaying you for saving him from Luther. But that is not the case anymore and hasn't been for a long while. I see the way he watches you. It's never creepy; it's always endearing and protective. I like it. I appreciate having him around. He loves you and Ax as much as I do."

"Have you and he talked about me?"

"Not in that sense. No." He replied.

"Well, maybe he wants to talk to you about it first," I said.

"I am happy to ask, babe. If that's what you want."

"You know I love you, Hudson. You're all the man I need," I told him.

"Elyanna, you choosing Xavi or Rome does not bruise my ego in the least bit," he said with conviction.

"Why is that?" I asked.

He regarded me with a sly smile. "Baby, I own you. Your heart, body, and soul are all mine. Your relationship with Rome and Xavi only exists because I allow it. I can intervene, and will, if the need arises, but I promise you, bodies will hit the floor."

He ran his thumb across the faint wound on my neck from Xavi's blade. It'd happened hours ago but it was shallow and my gifted genes were already healing the damage. He kissed it gently then murmured in my ear, "Do I need to intervene, Elyanna?"

His gentle touch, contrasted with the intensity of his words and sent tantalizing shivers through me. I remembered to breathe. "No," I croaked.

Hudson was the type of man who sat back and waited for people to come to him. If he came to you, it meant you were so fucked. If he went after Xavi or Roman, it would not be pretty and that wasn't a scenario I wanted. I loved them, all three of them. It would wreck me if Xavi or Roman were taken from me. And although Hudson wouldn't flinch if he had to take either one of them out, it would tear him to pieces inside.

"No, Hudson." I cupped his face and kissed him lightly. "We'll be okay."

"I don't want either of them hurting you. The situation with Xavi has gone on much too long as it is. And there's this." His tongue flicked over the scar. "Tell me about what happened. Xavi gave me his version. I want to hear yours."

The situation with Xavi was a ticking time bomb. Was I still in love with him? Yep, no doubt, even though he despised me. He either wanted to kill me or have sex. If he wasn't glaring daggers at me, he completely ignored me. The incident in the woods was different. He saved my life. Twice. The intimacy part was also odd. It was intense. And wild.

"I liked it," I blurted.

Lust filled my husband's eyes. Without saying another word, he picked me up and carried me upstairs.

CHAPTER FOUR

Elyanna

"You have everything?" Chef Loretta asked me.

I loaded a box full of groceries into the trunk of the car. "Yeah, I got it. Thanks, Chef. You're welcome to come over."

"No, thank you. I have plans with my girl," Chef said.

"Ooooh. Date night with Dr. Carla." I wiggled my eyebrows at her. "How's that going?"

"It's only our second date, but . . . I'm hoping to move our relationship into something more." She blushed. "I have a very special dinner planned at sunset, overlooking the valley."

"Well, I don't know her, but I know you. And she's a lucky lady. Have fun!" I waved and then got behind the wheel.

I drove around the Royal Summit community and stopped at the main entrance, where Becks was waiting with our kids.

"Momma!" Ax exclaimed. I picked up my son and wrapped him in a hug.

Becks put Julia in one of the car seats, and I did the same with Ax.

"They are going to be fast asleep by the time we get to your place." Becks clicked her seatbelt.

I glanced at the kids in the rearview mirror and smiled. Both toddlers were nodding off to sleep.

"It's nap time." I drove out of the parking lot.

"Thank God," Becks and I said simultaneously.

Toddlers were a handful. Ax and Julia had a lot of energy, and the two together were Tasmanian devils.

Thirty minutes later, Becks and I were busy in the kitchen. After settling the kids in Ax's room for their nap, we began preparing dinner.

"So, what's going on with Samson?" Becks asked.

"Curiosity, on my part." I put the venison dish in the oven. Chef Loretta prepped dinner for the group that was gathering at my home for dinner. She created everything, and all I needed to do was place a few dishes into the oven and assemble the others.

"I was thinking about BHF and how little we know about whomever it is that's running things."

"Huh? Interesting. I figured it was some politician from the old days. Or some rich dude. You never peek into their minds for that information?" she asked.

"No, and it bothers me. These soldiers keep showing up, and they're all following orders. Sure, it is possible they hate all rebellions and are willingly killing and capturing people. But the population has dwindled, and we keep killing each other off. It sucks."

Becks hugged me. "I'm sorry you always have to kill the bad guys, El."

"Me too. I'd rather it be them than one of us, but there must be another way. Hudson said Sam may have more intel on the subject since he worked for BHF as one of the top commanders," I said.

"You're not thinking about going after them, are you?" Becks popped a cherry tomato in her mouth and hopped on the kitchen counter.

"No. Not at all. But . . . the info might be useful."

An hour later, my husband, Bug, and our guests arrived. Johnny, Becks' husband, and Dr. Jeff were in attendance. Joining us from the Hillside community were Sam and his wife, Mel, and Sheridan, head of security. Xavier was present as well.

My stomach clenched at the sight of Ghost. Aside from the incident in the woods, we always avoided each other. We hadn't had a civil conversation since Luther and discussing what transpired seemed like a losing battle. With so many people in the same room, Hudson and Roman were confident he'd be on his best behavior. And from the way he'd behaved in the woods, I was confident he wouldn't harm me. Glares and scowls were given, and as expected, he kept his distance.

"Drink." Becks handed me a glass of wine. "My brother will come around."

"You've been saying that for months." I gulped the wine. "Maybe I should just give up."

"Don't give up on him, El. He's struggling with whatever Luther did to his head. He's making progress. A year ago, having dinner in the same room was a definite no, and now look at us."

"Right," I agreed. She made a valid point. Overall, we were making progress. It was slow, painful progress, but it was something.

Chef Loretta had prepped a delicious, roasted venison, with roasted potatoes and a fresh salad, plus a pie for dessert. I was grateful for her help. Roman did most of the cooking in our house since I sucked at it, and Hudson wasn't much of a cook, either. There were a few simple dishes I could throw together to keep my kid fed, which worked for me. Cooking had never been my thing, even pre-plague, when I'd been married. I was a boxed mac and cheese kind of cook. Occasionally, I tried to make more of an effort in my luxurious kitchen. The lodge we lived in was huge and operated on all natural resources, gas, and solar-powered electricity. We had fresh water with a triple-filtration system and produce grown in the gardens. My men hunted for meat or fish. It was simpler than the days before the plague. Still, it was lavish in comparison to how many rebels lived.

The conversation was casual during dinner. We didn't discuss BHF once, which was not a bad thing. The new world order was a sore subject.

After the meal, we gathered in the gaming room. It housed a bar, a pool table, and a flat-screen television, which didn't work unless someone turned on the DVD player. Most of the time, my men preferred to leave it off.

Hudson and Johnny were keeping an eye on the kids who had

woken just before dinner, and I was behind the bar fixing a vodka martini for Bug, while Sheridan, Mel, and Dr. Jeff sat at the bar counter talking about something happening at Hillside. Dr. Jeff had been at Hillside for a week, working in their hospital. Hillside had the only working hospital available to Rebels. Their community had grown exponentially since the rebels took over. News had spread and people came looking for help. Our three communities continued to grow as well, but the harsh winters kept people away. Hillside was much more amenable for all seasons. If we could take the entire Royal Summit community with us, I'd be willing to move there. Although leaving the majestic mountains behind wouldn't be my first choice.

Mel was telling a story, I'd tuned out. I wasn't purposely being rude, I was more interested in Sheridan. I met Sheridan when I was going after Luther. He'd been the head of the security team in the tower. The tower was where the directors lived in their posh penthouse apartments while the medical team conducted experiments on the children in the basement.

I had used my gift on Sheridan for an hour, if not longer, where he'd divulged pertinent information about Hillside and Luther. I'd met him a time or two since, and he hadn't shown any signs of recognizing me. Out of curiosity, I peeked into his head while mixing the martini. There was nothing—not even a flash of recollection of my presence that night.

I decided to press my luck.

"So, Sheridan, what's your story? How did you become head of security at the tower and all that?" I asked while keeping my gift open.

"Originally from New Mexico, I was doing border patrol. When things started to go sideways, my supervisor recommended me for a position with BHF. I got hired and moved my family to California. Wife and three teenagers. The plague took them while we were traveling across the country." Sorrow flashed in his eyes, and the memories came rushing back to him.

His loss squeezed my heart, and I sucked in a sharp breath.

Sheridan shook his head, and his mind pushed the memories back, shutting them off like he had hit a switch. "Um, so yeah, I made it to Hillside and rose through the ranks. Fewer people meant less qualified individuals for the job. It was easy to do. It wasn't my finest moment working for those assholes, but until you and Hawk came along, there weren't any other options."

Still no recollection of meeting me. Nice. I retracted my gift, relieved and impressed with myself. I'd never analyzed a mind that I'd previously used my powers on. It gave me comfort to know I hadn't scarred Sheridan's brain the way Luther had done to Xavier.

"Sorry to bring up painful memories," I told him.

"It's okay, El. Everyone knows your story. It's only fair you know mine." He smiled. "What are you making back there?"

"A vodka martini, which means vodka, and more vodka. I can't make a casserole to save my life, but I make a mean martini. Would you like one?" I replied, grateful he changed the subject.

"Sure. Why not? Thanks for hosting us. This is a sweet setup. How'd you find it?"

I slid over the cocktail and began working on another for Bug. "Well, that's an interesting story. It all started with a mission gone wrong."

Roman came to stand behind me, resting his chin on my shoulder. "Did you just give away my martini?"

I laughed. "I'm making you a new one; give me a second."

The guests gathered around the bar as I told the tale about how I found the lodge.

Later that night, we were seated in the living room, just me, Hudson, Sam, Bug, Sheridan, and Xavier. The rest of our dinner guests had either gone to Royal Summit or were asleep upstairs in one of the guest rooms. It surprised me that Xavier had insisted on staying.

"So, you were curious about BHF?" Sam asked, looking at both Hudson and me.

My husband nodded. "El brought up a valid argument after our last confrontation with the convoy they sent. We know the basics, which are to take out the rebellion encampments and bring back the gifted as hostages. As you well know, BHF has been sending soldiers continuously for the last couple of months, even though their soldiers never make it back. Yet they keep sending them. We'd like to know more about who we're dealing with."

Sam scrubbed a hand down his face. "It's not just one person, like with Luther. It's a group of gifted people. The last I'd heard, there were almost fifty of them."

Well, shit. We had four sitting in the room, plus Dr. Jeff and Becks, who had already gone to bed. Six of us weren't enough to deal with that many, or even half that amount.

"Who's in charge?" Xavi asked.

"I don't know exactly, but they call him the Godfather. Supposedly, he's the first gifted person ever reported."

Hudson's body went rigid against mine; his jaw clenched, but he remained silent. My husband knew who this Godfather was, and judging by his body language, he didn't want to deal with the man.

CHAPTER FIVE

Hudson

I slumped in the chair beside my son's bed. The rise and fall of his chest comforted me. It was my job as his father to ensure Ax slept soundly every night of his life. Well, maybe not his entire life, but until he could care for himself. The plague changed everything, making the world a dangerous place. It would toughen him up. In time. For now, the best I could do was keep him safe as long as I could.

Sam's revelation about the Godfather reverberated through my brain. Elyanna was right; we needed the information. But now, what do we do with what we learned? The question became a heavy weight I carried with me. I hadn't had a decent night's sleep since. Could it be the same person? It had to be. I recalled the warning I received from Alexi, my classmate at Leadership Academy for the Gifted.

Watch your back. The headmaster is alive. He goes by the Godfather now.

I'd gotten the message about a year before the plague hit. Around the same time, Axel had been in the hospital, where we became obsessed with the beautiful patient in the room next to his. Elyanna.

Alexi disappeared after that. All of my classmates had. I wondered if they had become a part of the Godfather's crew. That would suck if they were. My classmates had been top-tier gifted, packing a lot of punch. There weren't that many of us, but there were other schools for the gifted around the world.

Fifty gifted were too many for us to deal with. Why would they want the rest of us? They had plenty of power. The population was nearly nothing. What more could they want? Corruption was limitless, it seemed. The more power they wielded, the more they wanted. Why? To create more gifted? I didn't have the answers; the only thing I did know was that living a quiet life in the country wasn't going to work. It had been three weeks since we'd been attacked, but Hillside was being hit a couple of times a week. If that continued, I'd have to lead a team to provide aid. They'd do it for us.

A part of me wanted to go to BHF's headquarters and knock on the asshole's door, but I had a family now and so many others to take care of. Preparing to fight seemed like the best option for everyone. Yet, waiting for the enemy to show up did nothing to ease the constant tension riding my shoulders. The price of freedom was costly, and we had already lost so much. And I refused to lose anyone else, least of all my wife and son.

Ax rolled over. *I miss your namesake, son.* If Axel, my best friend, were alive, we could rely on his gift of foresight. I relied on him for years; his visions made it possible for us to sit back and relax. If nothing dire came to him, we had the luxury of time. Maybe depending on him all those years had dulled my instincts. As it was, I couldn't decide which route to take, and I'd been reticent to rely on the team I had.

I propped my elbows on my thighs and covered my face with my palms.

Hudson - age fifteen -

"Hudson Joshua Pierce." The headmaster glanced at my file. "Telekinetic."

He slapped the file on his desk and glared at me.

"Do you know why you're here?" he asked.

"I went off campus when I wasn't supposed to," I replied.

"No." His intense glare bore into me. "Unlike your professors, I don't care about your studies or extracurricular activities. I am a busy man with no time to deal with adolescent tantrums. The only thing I care about is each student honing their gifts and becoming a valuable member of our cause. Do you think you've mastered your gift?"

I nodded.

"Show me."

Using my gift, I floated a few books from his shelf to his desk.

"Child's play. Is that all?" He scoffed.

My mother's warning rang in my head. Keep the extent of your power hidden, Hudson. Never let anyone know how powerful you are.

I let a heavy tome hover over his desk and began tearing the pages one by one while allowing each piece of paper to spin in the air.

A staticky sensation washed over me, making my skin prickle. The book I'd been manipulating with my gift was snatched from my grasp and slammed into my face so hard that I blacked out.

When I came to, my jaw ached and my left eye throbbed. The headmaster peered down at me.

"Good, but not impressive."

My body was hoisted into the air and crashed into the concrete wall. An invisible force wrapped around my neck and squeezed. I clawed at my neck, desperate to breathe.

"Only the most powerful can make the rules, Hudson. And you are not powerful. I am. Next time I hear about you stepping out of line, I will gut you."

I startled awake with an anguished grunt. The ruckus roused Ax, and he began to whimper.

"Shh . . ." I patted his back. It didn't help. He began to cry. Shit. I lifted him into my arms and bounced. "It's okay, kid. You're okay. Shh, you're going to wake your mom and Uncle Bug."

Sure enough, El walked through the room, bleary-eyed.

"Hi," she said, resting her cheek on Ax's back and wrapping her arms around us.

"Sorry to wake you, peaches. I got this; go back to bed."

She mumbled something I didn't catch.

"Momma." Ax reached for her. I released him into her arms and guided them both to sit on my lap in the chair beside his bed.

"Did you move the recliner?" she asked me.

"Yeah, I like this angle better. I'll return it to its proper place in the corner later."

"It's fine." She settled between my legs, making herself comfortable, and Ax nestled against her breasts.

Elyanna tilted her head and rubbed her nose along my jaw. "Couldn't sleep?"

"Just restless."

"Wanna talk about it?" she asked.

The words were right there. My mouth just wouldn't spit them out. What was it about my time at the academy that made it so difficult to talk about? Aside from my parents, I hadn't told anyone about the many incidents I'd encountered with the headmaster. The first time in his office was one of many. I was a stubborn little shit and wanted to prove myself. After enduring months of abuse, I had enough and called my parents. My mother arrived to find me with a swollen face, a black and blue torso, and welts around my neck. It was homeschooling for me until I went to college and then joined the military. I stayed in touch with a few classmates over the years; Alexi had been one of them. *Where are they?* I hadn't cared until Samson mentioned the Godfather.

"I don't know where to start," I finally said.

"May I ask you a question?" I could see the whites of her eyes. She was wide awake now, and she had me cornered. We were going to sit in this chair until I opened up.

"Of course," I replied.

"Umm . . ." She exhaled audibly. "Do you know the Godfather?"

How did she know that? She could have used her gift. But if she did that, she would already know the answer. Then again, using her gifts on her ex-husband had caused the couple plenty of problems. Elyanna didn't want that for us.

"I didn't use my gift, Hawk. I told you I wouldn't. Unless you want me to."

"I know you don't use your gift on me, babe, even though you're welcome to," I said. "The answer to your question is yes. I think I do know him. He was the headmaster at the boarding school I'd gone to as a child."

"Was he . . . abusive?" she asked.

"Yes."

"What kind of gifts does he have?"

"He's like me. Telekinetic."

"Oh. Wow, that's not good."

"You could take him," I told her.

She released a light chuckle. Ax squirmed in her arms. Elyanna ran her fingernails along his scalp, which settled our son. After a moment, she gracefully rose and placed him back in bed.

"Come to bed with me." She held out her hand.

The man in me viewed her invitation as something more, something intimate. But I knew better. Elyanna wasn't going to let the topic go, even now at one in the morning. I grasped her hand and let her lead me into our room.

CHAPTER SIX

Hudson

"Be good, little man." I kissed Ax's head and strapped him into his car seat.

"Need anything from the Summit?" Roman asked.

"Nah, thanks, man. I think we'll head down later. You coming back?" I shook Roman's hand.

"Yep. In a few hours. I'll give you and the missus time to get reacquainted." He waggled his brows.

"Whatever." I punched him lightly on the bicep and headed back into the house where the missus was still asleep.

We were fortunate to have Rome with us. He was the perfect bodyguard, nanny, and a good friend. I had no idea what I'd do without him. He cared for Elyanna and Axel, and he would often give us these small moments of privacy. It didn't happen often, but El and I didn't hesitate to take advantage of the time. We needed to do something special for the firebug. Even after all this time with us, he wasn't vocal about himself. Aside from what I knew about him when he was leading a rebellion faction of his own, we didn't know anything else. And he never shared. He seemed content to be a part of our lives.

Elyanna was still asleep, and I didn't want to wake her yet. We'd stayed up for hours talking about the Godfather situation and my time at the academy. The world had changed so much since the plague that we never talked about the past beyond meeting her in the hospital. Our respective childhoods didn't seem to matter. What schools we went to, childhood pets, favorite holiday memories—none of it mattered. The only thing rebellions concerned themselves with was surviving. Elyanna made me realize my situation was different. I had experience with other gifted people and the headmaster, aka the Godfather. After talking things through with her, I realized my history could help us win the war that was sure to come.

I went into my home office to check in with the other communities. We had set up a radio system that allowed us to communicate with Gator Springs High, the penitentiary, and Hillside. The comms system wasn't anything like we had in the old days with emails, cell phones, and texts, but it was something. It was a good thing some of us still knew Morse code and were able to teach the others. Especially the kids. In time, we'd get back to fast ways of communicating, but I suspected that was decades, if not another century, off.

Almost an hour later, I peeked in on Elyanna. The way Ax and El slept so soundly each night made me proud. It made me feel like I was doing a good job of keeping them safe. Not that El needed protecting because she could hold her own, but I did everything I could to make sure she was well cared for, safe, and didn't have to worry about anything. A part of me wanted to give her more time to rest, just because she could, but the man in me wanted his woman.

I slipped into bed beside her, snuggling into her warm body. She sighed, her arms wrapping around me. I traced the belly chain I'd given her as a gift and ran my palm over her stomach, missing the roundness she'd had while carrying our son. Stretch marks feathered over her soft skin and I kissed the trail, which started below her navel and went down to her pelvis. Every inch of her was so beautiful.

Elyanna mewled and stretched her limbs like a cat lounging in the sun. A smile splayed over my lips as she began to respond to my touch.

As much as I wanted to keep going south, I changed directions and crawled my way up to Elyanna's lips.

"Good morning, sweetheart." I captured her lips with mine and slid my tongue through her mouth. She tangled her fingers through my hair and pressed our faces closer together.

"Glad you're awake," I said when we came up for air.

"Hudson," she moaned. She tilted her head to the side, granting me access to her neck. I nipped and sucked the sensitive skin; her pulse raced, and she parted her legs for me.

I pushed up her camisole and sucked on her nipples. Her skin heated under my touch. She tugged on my t-shirt. "Clothes off," she said.

I sat up to undress. Before I could kick off my jeans, El got on all fours and took my cock into her mouth, making me hiss.

The mirrored closet door gave me the perfect view of her juicy cunt. I fisted a handful of her silky, golden hair and yanked her head back. Her eyes watered as she peered up at me through her lashes.

"You like that?" My voice was deep and raspy.

She nodded and swirled her tongue all over my tip.

"Play with your pussy while I fuck your mouth."

El did as I asked. She swallowed and opened up her throat while her fingers spread her pussy lips, giving me the perfect shot of her slick entrance.

"Fuck yes, that's it." I thrust into her mouth. "That's it, love. Finger that pretty pussy."

We moaned together. I was close to shooting my seed when something in the mirror caught my eye. It was there, then gone. I growled.

I pulled El off my cock. "Come here, baby. Turn around and sit on my cock." I sat on the edge of the bed in front of the mirror.

Elyanna straddled my lap, her back to my chest. I moved her hair to one side and focused my gaze on our reflection. "Look how beautiful you are when you take my cock." I fondled her full tits, pinching her hard nipples. She sheathed my cock with her cunt, one slow inch at a time. Where was a fucking camera when I needed one?

She rocked her hips, and her walls choked my dick. I strummed her clit. El tossed her head back, groaning wildly. "That's it, baby, come all over my cock."

She came. I bit the inside of my cheek, holding off my release.

Before she had time to catch her breath, I slipped her off my cock. "On the bed," I told her.

El scrambled onto the mattress.

"Spread your legs, babe." She did as I asked. I used my gift to gather the chains we liked to play with. I entwined the chain around her ankles and then anchored them to the bedpost. Then I gathered the other set of chains to bind her wrists above her head.

I dove face-first into her dripping cunt. She tasted of my cock and her juices. Delicious. Her body quivered, and she arched her back, another orgasm cresting.

I released her pussy before she could come. She glared at me, panting. I lined up at her tight entrance and slid home. Our lips collided. I slammed into her with brutal thrusts. My balls tightened. Her cunt clamped down on my cock with her release. I couldn't hold back and didn't want to. I bit her lower lip as my release burst out of me. A trickle of metallic liquid flooded my mouth.

Her chest heaved with every breath and sweat dripped down my spine. I rolled off her and snuggled into her side, appreciating how her nakedness fit perfectly against mine. I glanced at our reflection. Something moved at the end of the bed. Son-of-a-fucking-bitch.

"Stay put, please," I whispered.

"What's wrong?" she asked.

"Trust me."

In a split second, I used my gift to strip the top sheet from the bed and wrap it around the intruder.

Xavier released his gift as he fought with the sheet. Motherfucker.

"Xavier? What's going on?" El asked.

With my gift, I bound his legs with the sheet, then picked up my jeans from the floor, tied them around his neck, and pulled. He gasped for air.

"Get a good show, asshole?" I climbed off the bed and stomped out of the room, dragging his body behind me.

"Hawk?! What are you doing?!" Elyanna called out. "Get back here and unchain me!"

The metal rustled as she tugged on her restraints. "Hudson!! Don't hurt him!"

I ignored my wife's pleas and dragged a gasping Xavier downstairs, passing Roman on my way.

"Dude, put some clothes on. Wait? What?" He glanced at the writhing body in the sheet. "Xavier?"

Roman's gaze whipped from me to Xavier. "Oh, fuck, did he just?" He glanced upstairs.

"Hudson, get back here!" Elyanna's cries reached us.

"Do not set her free. I need a minute to deal with this," I told him.

I grabbed a pair of sweats and a t-shirt from the laundry room, shrugged them on, and continued dragging Xavi until we reached the garage.

"Seriously, Hawk, you can't just kill him," Roman said.

"Fuck yeah, I can." I loosened the jeans around his neck.

"No, Hawk! This isn't the way," Roman argued.

"Either leave or shut the fuck up and let me teach this fucker a lesson!" I punched Xavier in the face.

"How fucking long have you been creeping around my house and watching my wife?" I snarled.

"Fuck you. She's not just yours." Xavi spat. "She fucking loves me too, asshole."

"She did until you abandoned her because you couldn't get over your fucking hangups. You've been snarling at her for over a year, Xavi. Do you realize how that makes her feel? Your actions make her feel like this bullshit is all her fault!" I wound my arm back.

"Go ahead, take your cheap shots at me while I'm tied up." He raised his chin.

Happy to oblige. Asshole.

CHAPTER SEVEN

Roman

Hawk storming through the house, with his dick swinging and a writhing body wrapped in a sheet trailing behind him was not what I expected when I returned home. And it was a sight I wouldn't forget anytime soon. The telekinetic was furious. Muscles flexed, skin flushed and covered in sweat. He looked like an angry Greek god.

As soon as he released the noose around Xavi's neck, I left the garage to let them sort their shit out. It was a long time coming, and Hawk had every right to be pissed.

My focus was on Elyanna. She was screaming her head off, demanding to be released. What the fuck did Hawk do?

I found El bucking like an animal. Her wrists were chained above her head, and her legs were splayed apart. Her pussy was flushed and wet, and, oh my fucking god, beautiful. My breath hitched at the sight of her.

"Firebug," she pleaded.

I approached the bed, one slow step after the other. My eyes were glued to her exposed core. It dripped with cum. Hers and Hawks. Blood rushed to my cock. I couldn't look away. It was rude, and I should have been more respectful and averted my gaze, but fuck, I wanted her so . . . fucking . . . much.

I stood at the foot of the bed, openly staring. I palmed my cock and licked my lips.

"Roman?"

The sound of her voice snapped me out of my trance.

I blinked rapidly. "Sorry, umm . . ." Fuck, I'm such an asshole. I moved to her side, doing everything I could to keep my eyes on her face.

"Firebug." El's voice was husky.

"You are so fucking gorgeous. I am powerless." I couldn't control my eyeballs, as my gaze roamed the length of her body. She rolled her hips, and her breathing changed.

"I . . . umm . . . I like the way you're looking at me right now. But this might not be the right time to explore this . . ." Her voice trailed off.

Somehow my shoes had come off, and I was on the bed next to her, with my face hovering dangerously close to hers.

"Rome . . ."

"No. I'm your firebug, always."

She smiled, then craned her neck to nuzzle my face. "Firebug. I want this. I want you. But . . ."

"I know, your husband is trying to kill your other husband." We all knew she was still pining after Ghost, even though he was a royal asshole to her.

"Please don't let Hawk kill my Ghost."

I grazed my lips along her jaw. She parted her lips. I dared a glance down the length of her to find her pumping her pelvis. "Fuck, angel. I'm dying to touch, taste, and ravage you whole."

Her back bowed, and the hard tip of her nipple brushed my arm. I sucked in a breath. If I didn't get out of the room, I was going to whip out my cock.

"Key, El," I croaked out.

"Hawk."

Dammit.

I closed my eyes and counted to five.

"I'll go make sure your husbands are still alive." I scooted off the bed. She glanced at my crotch and licked her lips. Fuck me. She wasn't making this any easier.

I leaned in to claim her mouth, then changed course and pressed my lips against her forehead. On instinct, I ran my nose down the side of her face, along her neck, between her breasts, and down to the sweet spot between her thighs, taking a deep inhale. She smelled delicious. I drank in her pretty, wet, pink flesh with my eyes, savoring the sight of her. So perfect. The naughty angel tilted her pelvis. Juices dripped from her opening. I was dying in place. I wanted to taste it. I wanted to touch. Just once. Taste or touch. Taste or touch.

"Firebug, please," she mewled.

"Please, what, angel?" My gaze flicked to hers. "Taste or touch?"

"Both," she said, giving me a sly smile.

I released a deep chuckle, and that tight hold I'd had on my restraint loosened just enough for me to reach between her legs. I slid a finger between her folds and dipped into her depths. Her cunt contracted around my digit. I was so turned on I couldn't see straight.

A loud bang from downstairs had me withdrawing from her sex. Hawk and El's cum coated my finger. I sucked my finger and groaned.

"That's so hot," Elyanna gasped.

I placed a kiss on her lips. Her tongue greedily delved into my mouth, seeking the juices I had just sucked off my digit. I wanted more. I reached down and stabbed a finger into her cunt. She cried out.

Another bang from downstairs. Idiots.

"I'll send Hawk to take care of you." I released her and hurried out of the room, sucking on my finger as I went.

Hawk and Ghost were exchanging blows in the garage. Hawk hurled a hammer at Xavier. He'd disappeared, and the hammer was wedged into the wall. Xavier reappeared behind Hawk and placed him in a chokehold. Hawk executed a hip-toss, slamming Xavier onto the concrete floor. I winced. Xavier struck out and connected with his chin.

"Enough!" I shouted.

Both men paused. I pushed them apart. Hawk swung around my body, and I shoved him away.

"Get in the Jeep, Xavier! I'm taking you to Summit," I told him. He huffed but did as I asked. "Enough, Hawk. Go take care of your wife."

His nostrils flared, and his gaze narrowed.

"What?" I snarled.

He leaned in and sniffed. My dick was still hard, and I didn't care if he noticed.

"Did you just?" He glared.

"No. But if you ever leave her compromised like that again, without a key, I will fucking kill you."

I walked away.

He shoved my back. "Be honest, asshole."

I stepped into him. "No. I wanted to. But no. I restrained," I sighed. "One touch. That's it."

His nostrils flared, and his eyes raked over my body. My cock pulsed.

"We'll deal with this later. Get that fuck face away from my house." Hudson turned on his heel. I watched him walk away. My body desperately wanted to explore what just happened with both Elyanna and Hudson.

I slumped into the driver's seat with Xavier bleeding beside me. His face was swollen and bruised. That had to hurt. I shrugged. He was gifted; he'd heal.

"Learn your lesson?" I asked. Not because I cared, but because I needed to get El and Hawk out of my head. My balls were blue, and my shaft strained against my jeans.

"Fuck off," Xavier responded.

"You're an idiot," I muttered.

"You don't know what it's like!" he spat.

"No. I don't. Why don't you explain it to me?" This time, I was curious. It had been nearly two years since Luther. During El's pregnancy and Axel's first year, we'd kept him far away from them. We thought he'd just get over it, but if he was creeping around the house, it had gotten worse.

"I can't shut it off. The memories I have of her are all about her betrayal and deceit. The desire to kill her is so fucking strong!" He punched the door.

"Then stay the fuck away. Why are you creeping around the house? Why are you watching her and Hawk fuck?"

"Because I want her. I want to fuck her just as much as I want to kill her." He hit the door again. "And because she's beautiful. I can't stay away. I love to look at her," he said in a softer, melancholic tone.

"I know how that feels," I mumbled.

Xavier snapped his gaze toward me, then grimaced. Hawk worked him over good. I almost laughed. Served him right.

"You're in love with her, too. Of course." He crossed his arms over his chest.

Not just her. Hawk, too.

"Listen, if you want to mend the broken bridge, you need to make an effort. Talk to her. Work your shit out. Hawk is right; she blames herself every day for your issues. And it's not her fault," I told him.

"My memories tell me she's the one responsible for torturing me!!"

"Your memories are wrong! She got you out of there and saved your sorry ass!"

"That's all I have!"

"Well, make fucking new ones!" I snarled. "If you can't forget the falsified memories, create new memories with her. Start fresh!"

That shut him up. We drove the rest of the way to Royal Summit in silence.

I parked at the main entrance and glared at my passenger. He made no move to get out, so we sat there for a few minutes, which was fine with me. There were things I needed to sort out in my head before going home to El and Hawk. What transpired between me and El crossed a boundary I'd worked so hard to maintain. I wanted to leap, but I wasn't sure if I was ready to open that door.

It was complicated. I was complicated.

And then there was Hawk. I tasted his cum from El's sweet pussy. The thought of our fearless leader sent butterflies afloat in my stomach. *Stop it, Roman.* The couple had welcomed me into their home and their lives. I was going to ruin the perfect situation because I was me. A bisexual fire-starter starter in love with El and the two men who loved her. El was polyamorous. Hawk was not. He got off on watching his woman get wild and that was it. And then there was Xavier. That man was sexy as sin but a fucking moron when it came to El.

"He's not that way, you know?" Xavier said.

"Who is not what way?" I replied. There is no way he knew what I was thinking.

"It's obvious to everyone how you feel for El. But I notice things. And I've seen how you look at him when you think no one is looking."

"Fuck you."

"Fine. Just saying. He won't judge you. He loves El; if being with you makes her happy, he will accept you as you are. Just don't expect more. Trust me. I know."

"You don't know shit. How about you worry about yourself!" I was angry. Not because he was speaking the truth. But because he'd been watching me. *Had he noticed me watching him, too?*

"I'm trying. But fucking El . . . she's manipulative. Always twisting my thoughts and inciting me to react in ways that suit her."

"What the actual fuck are you talking about? Elyanna keeps her distance so she doesn't set you off. She is kind to you whenever you're in the same room. She doesn't treat you like the asshole you are. What do you want her to do?" I argued. The fucker was begging for another ass-kicking.

"Dr. Carla pointed out that this is all part of her plan. It's manipulation, man."

"No, it isn't. You need a new fucking therapist." I fumed. What the hell was the head doc feeding him? "Xavier, you're not a stupid man. You can make your own decisions. I suggest you listen to your instincts and not rely on the shrink. If nothing else, talk to your twin. Do you believe Becks would be best friends with a manipulative bitch? Think about it."

Xavier eyed me, not saying a word.

"I need to check on the kid," I told him.

"Thanks, man." He held out his hand.

"We're not friends, Xavi. You need to make amends with El before that can happen." I opened the door and exited the car.

CHAPTER EIGHT

Hudson

The frosty exchange between El and Roman made me grind my teeth. Fucking firebug. Elyanna glanced my way and winked before walking away with Ax in her arms. My son waved at me and then turned his attention to his mother. I was a lucky son-of-a-bitch. Time to deal with one of the assholes who was making my woman unhappy. El told me not to intervene but I'd had enough.

"Roman," I called out and gestured to the office door. I entered the vast space, which had been a ballroom in Royal Summit. We converted a lot of the rooms to fit our needs. Since we didn't live here, I didn't need a designated office. Those were reserved for residents like Becks and Dr. Jeff. The space I used as an office was also a meeting space with a large conference table. We brought over a few chalkboards from Gator Springs High, which came in handy since PowerPoint was a thing of the past. We were still able to use computers to some degree. We had electricity, laptops, and such; we just couldn't upgrade software like we used to. Pen and paper worked fine, but those would run low soon. As far as I knew, all manufacturers were non-existent. For now, we made do with what we had.

"I'm ready to take off when you are, boss." Rome strolled into the office behind me.

"You're not going," I said.

"Excuse me?"

"You heard me, Rome. You need to fix things between you and El by the end of the day," I told him.

He raised one eyebrow and had the nerve to ask, "What? What are you talking about? There's nothing to fix."

"Bullshit. You know exactly what I'm talking about. You've been weird around us since I caught Xavier lurking in our bedroom." I gave him a stern glare.

"I . . . I uh." He slumped into the seat opposite me.

I waited while he collected his thoughts. His skin was ashen, and the lines on his forehead appeared deeper than usual. I knew this was going to be a tough conversation for him, but I didn't care. His actions or lack thereof, were hurting my wife. It had been a week, and BHF attacks had become more frequent. We didn't have time for hurt feelings. And I refused to go easy on him.

"She told you everything," he finally said.

"Of course. I'm not bothered by what happened, Rome. I am fucking pissed about how you've been treating her since."

"I'm conflicted. You don't . . . you don't understand," he muttered.

"Wrong. I understand everything. If this is about me, let's have it out."

He gaped at me. Tongue tied again. Jesus.

"I love Elyanna and Ax more than anything. And you do, too. For almost two years now, you've been by her side, caring for her, and Ax. And because of the love and care you have shown for the two most important people in my world, I appreciate you. To be perfectly honest, you were a total asshole when you led your rebellion group and I wanted to kill you. Now that I've come to know you, I don't hate you and I like having you in our lives. You are important to me and my family. We all love you."

Something flashed in his eyes—hope.

"But, intimately speaking, my wife is all I want and all I need. Yes, I like watching her with other men. Not all, but with Axel and Xavier, it was exciting and hot. It's my kink. And I loved those men. It's been hard to lose them both. And then came you. She loves you; maybe she hasn't said it yet, but she does. I am willing to accept you in her life and our bed. The question is, is what we can give you enough? I won't be able to give you the physical connection you desire. You need to decide."

"What if it isn't enough?" He couldn't even look at me.

"Then I want you out of my house by tonight."

"What?" His eyes went round with disbelief.

"You heard me. I'm tired of you and Xavier hurting her. Your refusal to even talk about what happened is killing her. Just as much as Xavier's reluctance to move forward. I'm done with you two making her feel as though she's done something wrong when none of it is her fault. It's not her fault that you are attracted to men and women. It's not her fault that Luther scrambled Xavi's memories. But it is your fault for not talking about it and letting her stew in self-doubt for the past week. I'm done. That goes for both of you."

I blasted my power into the corner of the room, slamming an invisible Xavier into the wall. I held him against the wall with my gift.

Roman jumped out of his seat and cursed.

"This fucker never learns." I scowled at Xavier. "Am I clear, Roman?"

"Yes. I'll umm . . . I need some time." He exited the room.

"You have until the end of the day!" I shouted.

I released my gift, causing Xavier to crumple to the floor.

"You're such an asshole." He rubbed his shoulder and then stood.

"And you're a fucking pervert." I glared at him.

"I was in here first," he argued.

I slammed my fist on the table. "Dammit! I'm so fucking sick of your bullshit! Why are you using your gift if you weren't trying to be sneaky?"

"It wasn't like that! I was waiting . . ."

"I don't want your lame excuses, Xavier," I cut him off. "You heard what I said to Roman. The same goes for you, too. Make amends with Elyanna."

"I'm trying!"

"Trying is for losers. Fix it."

"Or what?" He raised his chin. "It's not like you can kick me out."

"Are you sure about that?" I sneered.

He ran his hand through his hair, tugging at the short strands.

Fucking asshole. Fuck this place.

The other leading members of the community walked in, Roman among them.

An hour later, we ended our meeting with a plan to head to the prison to make a pick-up and drop-off. I usually let the others handle these types of things, but I needed to get away from Xavier and Roman. But first, Elyanna.

CHAPTER NINE

Elyanna

hat did I do? I asked myself the same question over and over ever since Roman had seen me naked. He'd been so strange around me—distant. It seemed like he was attracted to me. No, it did not seem like he was. His massive erection was a clear indication. Wasn't it? I was so confused. I had asked him if he wanted to talk about it, and he'd said there was nothing to talk about. And he always found an excuse not to be alone with me. *What did I do?*

"El?" Becks asked. "Earth to Elyanna? Hey!" Becks shook my shoulder. "What is going on with you? You're on another planet."

"Sorry, just thinking," I told her, realizing we'd reached Ax and Julia's classroom. It wasn't a school; it was more like a babysitting service. Our children were the youngest in the Gator and Hillside communities. Adults, teens, and the other children loved spending time with the two toddlers. It was a great way for our kids to socialize with others, and it gave me and Becks some girl time.

"Are things still awkward with Bug?"

I nodded. "And Xavier. I haven't seen him since."

"My brother will come around." She insisted. "He's just lost."

"Sure," I replied, but didn't believe it. I'd hidden from Xavier for months after the Luther incident to give him time to come around. When he discovered me in the garden, eight and a half months pregnant, he came around, then lost himself again. It was always the same. One day everything was fine; the next, he wanted to kill me. I'd hoped the situation in the woods would change things between us, but it hadn't. It was a repeat performance. He wanted me. And then he went back to hating me again. It was getting old.

Becks and I joined the kids in coloring books, reading, and playing games.

Elyanna! Hudson's voice rang in my head. I stood abruptly, eyes wide. He was pissed.

"Stay with the kids," I said to Becks, and I ran out of the office.

The main building of Royal Summit was a sprawling five-story solid concrete monstrosity with off-grid power and plumbing facilities. The elevators worked, but Dr. Jeff, the brainiac, had said it took too much energy, so the residents only used the elevators on days when heavy items needed to be moved, which was rare. The residents used the stairs daily and were used to them. The classrooms were on the third floor, where there were adjoining junior suites. It gave the teachers a small kitchenette to fix lunches and snacks for the kids and separated the kids by age group or study. It was a brilliant system and provided plenty of exercise.

I jogged down the stairwell and ran into Hudson half-way. I jumped into his arms. "Hudson?! What's happened?"

"Nothing. Nothing, babe. I didn't mean to scare you." He held me in his arms, my legs wrapped around his waist.

"Nothing? You sounded upset."

"I'm sorry; I was. Am. Doesn't matter. I'm heading out."

"I thought the others were going to the prison." I scanned his face.

"No. Not this time. It'll be a quick run. We're taking the chopper. I'll be back by sundown."

I waited for him to say more. He pressed his forehead against mine and huffed. "Everything I do is for you and our son."

"I know," I whispered.

"I may have to make some hard decisions soon. Decisions you may not like."

I drew away from him and caressed his jaw. "Xavier and Roman."

He nodded. "Dammit." I hugged him close.

"Sorry, El."

"Don't be. It's time," I said. "Thank you for making the hard decisions that I can't.'"

"Always. Come on, I have time. There has to be an empty room on this floor." Hudson set me on my feet and led the way to find us some privacy.

I adjusted my clothes as Hudson walked me back to Ax's classroom, where he said his goodbyes to our son. Our toddler wanted to take a ride in the helicopter, and I almost said yes, but Hudson insisted he'd return faster without the little one.

A moment after he left, Roman walked in, his eyebrows drawn together in a tight arch.

"What's wrong?" I whisper-asked him.

"Nothing. Everything's fine." His voice was an octave higher than usual.

"Hmm. You may want to tell your face that. You look like you're trying to hold in a fart." I waved my finger in front of his face.

He chuckled and his posture relaxed. "It's fine. Do you have a minute?"

"Sure, they're moving to the garden." I jutted out with my chin. During spring and summer, the teachers prepped lunch and took the class outdoors. Typically, Becks and I stayed through the morning session and then walked with the class to the gardens and let them have lunch with the other kids while she and I did girl stuff.

"I'll walk down with you," he said. Ax and Julia stretched their arms out to him, and he carried the two toddlers down the stairs.

On our way to the gardens, I ran into Hudson again. "Change of plans, babe. We're leaving at first light," he told me.

"Okay, are we staying at the cottage?"

"Yes, I'll arrange for dinner there." He kissed my cheek and pointedly ignored Roman.

Dammit. This sucked.

"Do you need me for anything, boss?" Bug asked him.

"Nope." Hudson walked away. "Tick-tock, Rome."

I stared at Hudson's retreating back and then glanced at Bug. The firebug scrubbed a hand down his face.

Men were complicated. Why did I think a reverse harem situation was a good idea?

"Let's walk, El; Ax will be fine with the others."

He was. My son was busy playing with the other kids.

I waved at Becks and moved to follow Bug, who was scanning the crowd. I followed his gaze, then asked, "Is everything okay?"

"Yeah, uh. Have you spent much time with Dr. Carla?" he asked.

"No. Why?" Xavier's doctor was elusive. I'd met her once and seen her at gatherings, but we'd never had a conversation. "I hear she's dating Chef."

"Hmmm . . ." He motioned for me to follow him. "Be careful of her. And if you get a chance, I'd recommend doing your thing." He tapped on his temple.

"Okay, that's weird. Why?"

He shrugged. "Just something Xavier said the other day."

"Is that what this is about?"

"No." He didn't offer another word.

We meandered through the gardens toward our cottage, which had been designed to be the yoga pavilion. It was much smaller than the lodge, yet it was cozy. If Xavi hadn't been an issue, I wouldn't mind living in it full-time. It was closer to Becks and Julia. And I liked being near everyone else in the community. Xavier was an issue, though. Hudson was right. Soon, drastic decisions needed to be made. I couldn't continue walking on eggshells around Ghost for the rest of my life. I didn't want to leave Becks, though, and I couldn't ask her twin to leave her either. And if that wasn't enough, Bug was being weird.

Bug held the cottage door open for me. I walked through the door and began opening the windows to let fresh air in. "Something to drink?" I offered.

He declined. We didn't have much, but it seemed like a conversation that needed alcohol. The lodge had a beautiful wine cellar that was full. We drank a bottle a week and hadn't made a dent in the stock. The cottage had brandy. It wasn't my fave but it was something.

I flopped on the couch next to Bug, a full glass of liquor in hand.

"Okay. I'm listening."

"Did Hudson tell you? About me?"

"Um. No. Not specifically. Why?"

"This is hard for me to talk about." He rubbed his hands back and forth on his jeans. Tiny ember sparks ignited.

My eyes widened. Bug didn't notice. Christ. Roman was a lot of things. Nervous wasn't one of them.

I placed my palms over his wrists. "Stop, Bug. You'll burn down the cottage."

The denim was charred in some places, and the scent of smoke lingered in the air.

"Shit!" He wiped his hands together.

He took my glass of brandy and swallowed the contents in one gulp. He winced.

"That shit is gross," he mumbled.

"You're stalling."

He breathed deeply.

"I um. I . . . I love you, Elyanna. I didn't think I was capable of the emotion. But I am. I love you and Axel so much. And also Hawk." His voice croaked when he said my husband's name.

His eyes flicked to mine, then he stared at the ground. I figured he did. We loved him, too. He knew that. What was I missing?

"I hid my sexuality all my life," he said.

It took me a beat until I got it. Oh shit. I had no idea. How the hell did I miss this?

"My family was religious, and it was expected of me to have children and all that. As much as I love women, I love men, too. I hid my relationships—well, not my relationships. My hookups. When the plague hit and I started my rebellion community, I wanted to come out. But couldn't. I wanted to be fearless and tough, like Hawk. I pulled it off, but all it did was make me angry. I hated myself. Hated people. I just wanted to fight all the time. So I did."

"Being with you and Hawk makes me so happy, El. I don't want it to end. I love you, and I want you so damn much." He choked on his words, and his eyes watered. "But, with you, I can't explore this other side of me."

My heart broke for my firebug. I cupped his cheeks.

"Oh, firebug." I pulled him in for a hug. "I'm sorry, I didn't know."

What an impossible situation to be in! He wanted us—me and Hudson. But Hudson he couldn't have. Not in the way he hoped for. My husband loved Roman as much as I did. But Hudson was hetero, and I couldn't ask him to change his sexual preferences any more than I could change Roman's. Fuck my life.

I held him for a moment, then sat back on my side of the couch. "So. Where do we go from here?" I asked.

"We?"

"Yes, we. Just because we can't be in a romantic relationship, it doesn't mean we need to go our separate ways."

"Elyanna, I can't. I love you. I want you. Being near you and not being with you is killing me. I may never have the life I envision, but I'm afraid if I stay I may end up hurting you and Axel down the line and I don't want that. I think it's better for all of us if I leave now."

His words ripped my heart from my chest. Two years of him always by my side, caring for me and my son, and now he was leaving us.

A dam broke behind my eye sockets. "Okay. I understand."

Roman's presence was missed at dinner. He had decided to move to the resort immediately. I understood, and so did Hudson. Neither of us wanted him gone, but we couldn't give him what he wanted, even though Hudson offered.

"I'll be with him if you want," Hudson said while I cried on his shoulder.

"Stop it. He doesn't want a man to have sex with. He wants a man to love him as much as he loves him. There's a difference."

"I know, baby. I'm trying to make this easier for you." He rubbed small circles on my back. "I'm sorry I had to force the issue."

"You knew?" I sat up to face him.

He nodded.

"Since when?"

"I'm observant, El. I suspected it a long time ago but brushed it aside, thinking it was just my ego. Sometimes he looks at me the way he looks at you. And the day we caught Xavier in our room, he stared at my crotch a little longer than usual."

"Why didn't you tell me?" I asked.

"I didn't know for sure until this morning. I prodded the information out of him because I knew something was up. He's been awkward around us since that day, and you were taking it to heart like it was your fault. I wasn't going to let that stand. With Xavier being an ass for so long and now your firebug, I had enough and unleashed. On both of them."

"Does this mean I'll get a visit from Xavier next?"

"Probably. He needs to get over his shit, or I will send him away."

I gasped. "Becks is going to hate me."

"She's going to hate me. But I don't care. Let her. We've been coddling his ass for too long. If he can watch you get naked and have sex, he can man up and leave behind the thoughts Luther implanted."

"I don't think it's that simple, Hudson. He's been traumatized. And Bug mentioned I should be wary of Dr. Carla. I have a feeling she's not helping him."

"Well, I don't know much about the head doc and will look into it when I return. Still, the facts remain; Xavi using his gift to sneak into our home, and watch us having sex has crossed a line. I won't tolerate this type of behavior."

Hudson made a valid point. How long had Xavi been spying on us? On me?

"Oh, before I forget. Get up; I need to show you something." He got out of bed, and I followed, stewing over what the future would look like without Bug and Ghost.

CHAPTER TEN

Elyanna

I'd gone for a run while Ax was in daycare. We'd gotten up when it was still dark out to see Hudson off. He got in the chopper with Roman and Johnny. It was bittersweet seeing Bug so soon after our separation. Out of habit, he kissed me and Ax. Hudson grimaced but didn't say a word. At least they were still working together.

I was braiding my hair when I noticed something off in the reflection. Shit, Hudson was right. The straight edge of the nightstand wavered out of focus. The movement was so subtle that I would have missed it entirely if Hudson hadn't told me what to look for. Xavier was spying on me again.

The desire to toss my brush at him was so strong I clenched the handle. I couldn't perceive him with my gift when he was in ghost mode, and my aim was never good to begin with. Fuck it. I threw the hairbrush anyway.

"Ouch! Stop throwing things!" Xavier released his gift. He was sitting on my bed, rubbing his shoulder.

"Stop? Seriously?! You're in my house! How long have you been here? Did you watch me shower?" I clutched the towel wrapped around my body.

"No." His gaze dropped to the ground. Fucking liar.

I lunged at him, swinging furiously. I got in one good hit to his chin before he overpowered me and flipped me onto the bed. Xavi smirked. I kneed his groin. It wasn't the right angle, but the hit was enough for me to roll out from under him. I slid off the bed and snagged the knife under Hudson's side of the bed. And I lost my towel in the process.

Xavier eyed me appraisingly. The fucker.

"Get out of my house!" I snarled.

"Or what? You'll stab me?" he goaded. He stepped toward me, his eyes glued to my nakedness.

I backed away.

He lunged. I stabbed, hitting air. Xavier caught my wrist and squeezed; my fingers released the knife.

"Let me go, Xavier," I said through clenched teeth.

He pressed me against the wall and pinned me with his muscular frame. Xavier had a slender build in comparison to my other men, but he still had a lot more muscle and power than I did. Where was my sword when I needed it? In the bathroom, where it shouldn't be. My life with Hudson had made me soft.

With one hand, Xavi gripped my wrist above my head, then placed his knee between my legs, spreading them apart. His half-hooded gaze was filled with lust. Before Luther, Xavi had never been into rough play; he was a little devious because of his gift, but this dominant side was unexpected, and despite myself, I liked it.

Dammit, Elyanna. Focus.

He ran the tip of his nose along my jaw to my ear. Heat flooded my core, and moisture pooled between my legs.

No, no, no.

I stomped his foot. He yelped. I shoved him away from me and ran to get my sword.

I unsheathed my sassy stick and swung behind me.

He wasn't there.

"Get out of my house, Xavi. I won't ask again." I tiptoed out of the bathroom and into the living area. He was nowhere to be found.

"Cheater," I muttered.

For the next five minutes, I prowled around my house naked with my sword out. I must have looked like a lunatic. After a full ten minutes, I decided to give up my hunt and got dressed.

I clasped my bra and slid up my panties when my sword was snatched from the dresser, thrown into the hallway, and the bedroom door slammed shut.

I launched myself over the bed, only to be pulled back into a hard, invisible chest—a thick, calloused hand wrapped around my neck. I clawed at it, digging my nails into his flesh. His grip tightened. I gasped for air.

"Stop. Fighting. Me," Xavier growled.

I stopped clawing, and he loosened his hold. "Xavier. Enough," I croaked.

"What did you call me?"

"Xavi."

His hand tightened around my throat. "Wrong again."

"Ghost," I gasped. "Enough."

"No. I think you like this." His hot breath fanned over my cheek. His free hand traveled across my torso to the waistband of my panties. "Look at yourself."

We were in front of the mirror. My chest was heaving as an invisible force contracted around my neck. Slowly, my panties rolled down my waist. My body quivered in response.

Children's laughter floated in from the open window.

Xavier chuckled. "We'll play again later." He kissed my cheek and was out the door in seconds.

Later that day, Becks and I sat in my living room drinking wine while the kids napped after lunch.

"Spill," Becks said.

I looked at the coffee table, the chair, and the floor. "Where?"

"Not a wine spill, you ninny. Tell me what's bothering you. And don't you dare say nothing. You've been in your head for the last week. What has my brother done now? Or is it still the not doing?"

I took a deep breath. There was so much to share, and a lot of it had to do with Xavier.

"I love him and always will. But I will be the first to say to him and everyone else that I vehemently dislike the way he's treated you. It's not right. If I could fix it for you, I would," Becks added.

She reached out and grasped my hand. "You're my best friend, El. I know you love him and would never do anything to harm or hurt him. This has gone on for a while, and enough is enough. I want you to know that you can trust me with anything. Even when it comes to him."

Her voice, her words, and even the look in her eyes told me she was being genuine. And I needed to talk to someone, so I told her everything.

"Holy fucking shit balls. Wow. I knew things were off. This . . ." She drained her wine with one gulp and refilled her glass.

"I'm sorry to unburden my troubles on your lap." I sighed.

"Don't be, El. I'm not sorry you told me. There's um . . ." She paused, her face pinched. "I tried to tell you about this before. It's an awkward conversation, and I don't know everything."

Becks cleared her throat. "So, when we were teenagers, Xavier went through a strange phase. My parents insisted that it was best if I didn't know the details. And for Xavi's sake, I went along with it. He and I talked about it, sort of. He was embarrassed, so I told him he didn't need to tell me. We left it at that. I never understood. I just knew he'd sneak out at night and come home . . . different. As adults, things changed. He went into the military, and his gift was widely accepted and used. Then he got married. When he finally told his wife about it, she freaked, and I think you know that story."

I nodded.

"Well, I noticed he got a little different then, too. Now, with you, his behavior is strange again, and I don't know what this means."

"Different how?" I asked.

"Using his gift to, you know, lurk in the shadows," she replied.

"Shit. Is this how he's going to be now?"

"Not sure. I hope not. Maybe Luther did something to trigger it. Can you use your gift to find out?"

"Hell no." I shook my head. "Never. He doesn't trust me as it is. If he finds me rooting around in his brain, he will kill me. I don't want my son to grow up without a mother. Never going to happen."

"What will you do about Firebug?" she asked.

"There's nothing I can do about that either. He wants a life I can't give him. I have to let him go."

"Well, you'll always have me." She scooted closer to me on the couch and draped an arm around me.

I leaned on her shoulder. "Don't leave me, Becks. I need you."

"I need you, too."

Becks and I had dinner with the rest of the community in the dining hall. Interestingly, Dr. Carla was absent, and Chef was tight-lipped about her date.

After dinner, Becks and I went to her office to speak with our husbands, who were still at the penitentiary. They were unable to return as expected but promised to be home first thing in the morning.

Ax wasn't impressed with my storytelling abilities, but three pages in, he was fast asleep. Maybe my narrating abilities bored him to snores. I went to bed wishing I'd taken Becks up on her offer to spend the night at her place. The house was small, but it seemed cavernous with my men gone. Family life had changed the independent rebel who had traversed across the country on a motorcycle. I missed that girl.

I smooshed my face into the pillow, inhaling Hudson's manly scent. As soon as my eyes closed, I imagined his broad shoulders and every muscular ridge of his chest and torso. It didn't take much for desire to overwhelm my senses. Hudson had a way with my body that set me aflame with just a look. My fingers sought the wetness between my legs. I rolled onto my stomach and ground my pelvis into my palm, applying the perfect pressure to my clit. Ghost entered my thoughts. His invisible touch heightened my arousal. And his dominance made me groan. I slid a finger between my pussy lips and found my entrance. Hudson. Ghost. Firebug. Visions of my three men swam in my head. I wanted them. All of them.

I fucked myself with my slender finger, wishing for the thickness only my men could provide. I humped my palm, chasing my release.

Something thick slid in beside my finger. I scrambled to sit up, but a heavy body pressed me further into the mattress.

"Did you miss me?" Ghost rasped. "No need to reply. Your wet pussy has already answered my question."

He slid his finger in and out of my core.

"Ghost!" I gasped. "You need to leave."

"Why? You like having me here . . . between your legs." He flipped me over, but he wasn't there. Not visibly. Not even a silhouette of the man. Only the dark shadows of my room hovered over me, but Ghost's touch was there. Hot and rough on my skin.

He spread my legs apart, and the stubble on his cheek scraped my knee. I could have fought him off. Should have. My brain had taken a vacation, and my body responded to his intrusive touch.

"I've been watching you, sweet, sweet Elyanna. I've seen you undress and shower. I watched you fuck your fingers when your man was not home. Such a greedy, insatiable cunt you have."

His dirty words and invisible touch drove me mad. I reached for him and grasped cotton. I tugged on the material, pushing it over hard muscle and smooth skin. Ghost chuckled. A swish of fabric fell on the mattress. The weight of him pressed upon me.

"And I especially love watching you get fucked." His lips roamed over my skin, nipping and sucking. "I love how you take Hawk's huge dick in your mouth, in your pussy, in your ass."

I mewled. He sucked on my nipples. "You're so perfect while he's railing you. Your cunt always so wet as you take all of him. I'm addicted, and you are my drug."

His cock pressed at my entrance. "How does that make you feel, knowing that I've been watching you come all over his cock? Does that turn you on? Or does it turn you on more to have an invisible cock fucking you?"

He sank his length into my depths.

"Oooh, Ghost!" I moaned.

"You feel so fucking good, El. I've been dying for this. Dying to be inside you." He pumped his hips wildly.

Ghost's lips found mine. He breathed into me, rough and ragged. His thrusts unrelenting. He released his gift and stared into my eyes.

His gaze filled with love and desperate need. He ground himself deeper into me, searing my insides with his cock, branding me with his love. I wrapped my arms around his neck, and my release burst through me. Ghost came with a guttural moan and then he collapsed against me.

"Forgive me, Elyanna. For everything I did. For Axel. I can't forgive myself for killing him. I know it's not my fault. It's not yours either. It's just easier to blame you. Forgive me. I'm not whole yet. But I'm trying. Don't . . . don't forsake me. Not yet. Please." He feathered kisses all over my face.

CHAPTER ELEVEN

Xavier

Elyanna slept like an angel. She was an angel. She believed in me. And for her, I would try to be better. It wouldn't be easy. It never was. No one understood. How could they? I never spoke about my demon.

Yes, my demon. I was two different people in one body. The good man everyone knew and loved. And then there was the deviant. The demon I'd kept hidden most of my life.

I blame my gift and my awkward teenage body. I'd been a lanky kid with a face covered in pimples. Becks got the looks and the bubbly personality. I got social ineptitude and a target on my back for bullies to pick on. High school had been unpleasant and soon the respect and humility teachings that had been ingrained in me as a child faded into the background and something sinister took root.

My parents taught me to hide my gift and to use it only for good. I did as they asked until I snapped. The bullying had gone too far. I haunted the biggest bully in school. For three nights straight, I hid in his room and slapped him around a few times. He went crazy. And I had never been happier. The bullying stopped. But my deviant nature had risen. What was a teenage boy to do with all that power? I couldn't help myself. I began to use my invisibility gifts to sneak out at night. It was all fun and games to start with. I'd steal candy from the corner store. I snuck into bars and stole a couple of beers. Then my sexual awareness grew. Like any curious teen, I explored and soon found others who introduced me to a salacious lifestyle. They were older, but that didn't matter to me. Both men and women found my scrawny body beautiful. It was wrong on many levels, but I was accepted and liked and that meant everything to me.

After almost a year of debauchery, I'd been caught—or saved. My parents sent me to a military school, which helped. The strict schedule, the rules, and the acceptance of my gift tempered the darkness, and the good-natured boy took charge again.

Throughout adulthood, I had an occasional outing. One wild night a month to sate the demon. It was enough until I got married. My wife hated my gift. She forbade me to use it or even speak of it. After a while, my demon bucked and needed to be set free. My wife knew. Too many nights out did not go unnoticed, and I didn't care. It was either let loose once in a while or hurt someone. The way I saw it, if I let my dark side out on my terms, it was only a detriment to me.

After the plague, we'd been overwhelmed with survival, and I used my gift constantly. All was well until Luther. He must've seen what I'd hidden in the depths of my psyche and cut the chains. For months, it had been constant angst. I was angry and had no outlet. I worked harder. Trained harder. Nothing worked. Not even my dick. I would have fucked any willing pussy or ass had I been able to get hard.

Filled with rage, I stomped around the Royal Summit grounds and found Elyanna in the garden. She was radiant, and that pissed me off. I was suffering with anger and guilt, and she was glowing and gorgeous. I wanted to tear out her throat. And then I glimpsed her swollen abdomen, and that confused me further. The sight of her incited rage in me and made me want to love her at the same time. I couldn't decide. Hawk wisely hid her and the baby from me for months. I was unstable, and my demon was restless again, demanding to see her. No one would tell me where she lived, and when she came to visit Becks or Dr. Jeff, I was conveniently busy or away on an assignment. Hawk was clever. But my demon was a deviant beast. I got smart, used my gift, and hid in Becks' car when she went to visit El at her lodge.

And that was day one of my stalking her.

It had started innocently enough. I watched her do chores, practice her sword work, and play with her son. I even watched her sleep. I wasn't kidding when I told her she was my drug. Everything she did mesmerized me and settled my demon.

The first time I watched her undress, I immediately looked away. It was indecent to look without an invitation. The good man in me knew that, but the darkness chiseled away at my resolve, and soon I found myself timing my schedule around her bath time. I watched her undress, shower, bathe, and touch herself. She was glorious.

Hudson came home from Hillside one night, and the two were like rabid animals. They went into a fucking frenzy, and I could not remove myself from the room. She was exquisite. Sweat covered her body; her pussy was wet, and her skin flushed. I couldn't look away. Didn't want to. How Roman lived under their roof without going mad was insane. Hawk and El fucked like champions, at least twice a day.

My addiction grew, and I made myself at home in their basement. The house was so big, they didn't notice my presence. My control over my gift grew, and I got into a routine. Nightly, I'd hide in one of the cars as they drove Ax home from school. And in the morning, I'd watch the fuckfest and then jog down the mountain to the Summit. No one noticed, and my demon was sated.

I'd been living in the lodge and watching them for a couple of weeks. Every time I gripped my cock and exploded all over my hand. The couple was entranced by one another; they didn't even notice me. Until a week ago. Fucking Hudson. Not sure how he found me, but he did. He kicked my ass good, and he was right to do so. He'd given me an ultimatum: make amends with El or leave the community. Maybe that was the best. But no. Despite everything, I loved her and would die before giving her up.

If it weren't for Hudson's ass-kicking and those three words Roman had said to me, I could have lost her forever. *Make new ones,* the fire-starter said referring to my convoluted memories of Elyanna. And here I was, day one of making new memories with her and it had been so worth it. I'd have to thank Rome one day. Maybe with a good blow job. He'd be into it. Maybe.

I dipped my hand between El's legs and lightly stroked between her folds. Wetness coated my fingers, and she released a soft groan. My cock was hard again, so I threaded my crown into her opening.

"I love you," I said as I slipped into her tunnel. Her walls closed in around me, and she moaned. I fucked her until I was spent, dozed off, and then woke with the desperate need to fill her again and again.

Sometime later, I jolted awake, my heart hammering in my chest. A wave of panic rolled up my spine as I scanned the unfamiliar room. Elyanna rolled over, her blonde hair luminescent in the waning moonlight. The sight of the beauty amped up the fear already stirring in my gut, and I clamped my hand over Elyanna's mouth. Her eyes flicked open wide with fear.

"Wake. Up. Now," I snarled. "And don't say a fucking word."

CHAPTER TWELVE

Elyanna

A thick hand covered my nose and mouth, stifling my breath. I blinked rapidly to find asshole Xavier was back.

"Wake. Up. Now. And don't say a fucking word."

I opened up my gift and was ready to lash out when he added, "Get dressed and grab as many weapons as you can. I'll get the baby."

He rushed out of the room, and I hurried to get dressed, choosing comfortable leggings and a matching sports bra.

"We're not going to a fucking fashion show, El. Move your ass," Ghost snapped.

He already had Ax wrapped in a blanket and his to-go bag on his shoulder.

I hurried to get dressed, grabbed a hoodie, and strapped my sword to my back.

Ghost was by the front door, peering to his left and then right.

"How many guns do you have?" he asked.

"One." Then I grabbed another pistol hidden near the door. "Two. What's going on?" I asked.

"Shut it!" he said through clenched teeth. "Listen."

I strained my ears and heard nothing for a beat and then a faint rumbling. "Is that?"

"Forget it, come on." He ran toward the main building. The sun hadn't crested over the horizon yet, and the mountainside cast a silvery glow.

In the building, Ghost ran down the hall, went behind what was once a front desk, and hit something under the counter. A resonant gong went off. The lights flicked on. And I heard rumbling from the floors upstairs.

"Elyanna! Focus. We've got company." He tossed a two-way radio to me. "Call your husband. Now!"

I fumbled with the radio with shaky hands. Footsteps came down the grand staircase. Ghost barked out orders. I tuned them out, trying to reach Hudson.

- *Hudson, come in.*

I waited a beat.

- *Hudson, goddammit, answer me!*

- *El? Baby? We're on our way. Is Xavi with you?*

- *Yes, he's woken the residents.*

- *Good. He'll take care of you. Be safe.*

- *How long, Hudson?*

- *Fifteen minutes out. I love you.*

The line went dead, and I froze. Uncertainty filled my belly.

Ghost gripped my chin between his fingers forcing me to meet his gaze.

"We got this, El. I won't let anything happen to you or Ax, but for now, the baby is going with Aaron."

"Momma." Ax reached for me. I took my son into my arms and kissed his little head.

"Be brave, little man," I said. Tears welled in my eyes as I handed him to Aaron, Becks' eldest son. Ax cried, his little arms outstretched toward me.

"I got this, Aunty El." He took off and led the children downstairs.

Becks hugged me. "El!"

I hugged her back, grateful for the distraction. Aaron and Ax were already out of sight. I blinked away the tears while everyone who could wield a weapon readied themselves.

Ghost cupped my face. "You with me?"

I nodded. "Yep, fight mode on."

He pressed his lips to mine.

"Xavi, we got movement," someone shouted.

Ghost instructed everyone to their designated spots, guarding the entrance and exit. We waited.

The sound of trucks approached. Our group fell silent.

"Everybody get back!" Xavier shouted a moment later.

I spared a glance out the window and saw several vehicles rolling into the parking lot.

In the bed of a truck, a gunner stood with a rocket launcher aimed at the resort.

Oh, fuck no.

I clamped onto the soldier's mind and tore him apart. The rocket went wide and tore into the side of the building. The residents screamed. Chaos broke out behind me. I tuned them out and focused on the intruders. I opened my gift and let it loose. Bodies fell.

I swayed on my feet.

"El, come on, they need us out back." Becks tugged at my elbow. I followed her to the courtyard area behind the resort. BHF soldiers encroached onto the Summit grounds. There were so many, I couldn't believe my eyes. How did they get here unnoticed?

I didn't have time to find out; everyone fired at will. I got into the fray, saving my gift. Guns were not my thing. I couldn't keep track of the other residents or the enemy. I hid behind a concrete planter. Cement shards and dust sprayed around me.

"Cease fire," someone called out.

Silence.

I peeked over the planter. BHF bodies were strewn over the lawn.

"El!" Ghost shouted. I raised my head a little higher.

He ran toward me, kneeled, and pulled me to his chest.

"I need help," Jeff called out. "Let's get the wounded inside."

Ghost took off, and I followed. I found Becks; she was shaken, but there was not a scratch on her. We helped Dr. Jeff sort out the wounded.

Thumping in the distance caught my attention. My focus snapped to the sky. A helicopter approached. I sighed.

"Johnny," Becks said.

We held hands and watched our husbands inch toward us. Time slowed. A fireball arched into the sky, aiming toward the chopper. The missile connected with the helicopter, and it exploded on impact. Becks broke free from my grasp, screaming at the top of her lungs. I fell to my knees. My heart shattered.

Time sped up. Gunfire rained around me. "Xavier!" someone shouted. "Behind you!"

My head whipped to my left. Xavier was in the middle of the court-yard, checking bodies. A BHF guard was five feet behind him. Something hit his back. He arched and then crumpled. I screamed and ran toward him. Two soldiers scooped his body and ran as a truck blazed onto the lawn.

I opened my gift just as something stung my arm. I glanced at the dart and then darkness.

Water was splashed across my face. I sputtered as the world around me came into focus.

"El. Wake up," a desperate voice pleaded. "El!"

"I'm up. I'm up." I sat upright, groggily. "Doc?"

"Yes, yes. It's me," he said. "Thank God, you're awake."

"What happened?"

"BHF came. Kicked our ass. Took the men this time and left me with the wounded."

"The children?! Hudson? Ghost? Bug?!" I sat up.

"Easy, El. They shot you with a tranquilizer. Becks shot the fucker, and the rest took off, taking Xavi and a few of our men with them. Ax is fine."

I pushed off the cot. "I need to see my son."

"El," he warned.

I wobbled on my feet. Nausea threatened to set me on my ass. "What?!"

He handed me a glass of water. I drank in small sips.

"Julia's gone."

CHAPTER THIRTEEN

Elyanna

"Where's Becks?!" I forced myself to walk out of the medical exam room.

"She's with the kids. El, wait. We need to figure things out," Jeff pleaded.

"Becks!!" I shouted.

"Elyanna, stop. We need help. The leaders of the community are gone. If we don't come up with a plan, people will panic," Jeff said.

"We're beyond panic mode, Doc." I braced my hand on the wall as I searched for Becks.

"I know that. We still need a plan," Jeff persisted.

"El?!" Becks' voice rang from across the hall.

"Becks!" I hurried to her, ignoring the wave of nausea running through me.

She met me halfway, and we hugged. Both of us were in tears.

"I'm sorry about Julia," I said. "I'll get her back. Don't worry."

"Elyanna, you can't leave," Jeff pleaded. "We need you here."

"Like hell I can't!" I told him. "Take care of Axel for me," I said to Becks.

"We need you!" Jeff said.

I followed his gaze and saw the bedraggled faces of women and children.

Shit.

Okay, okay, okay. What would Hudson do?

"Any BHF survivors?" I asked Dr. Jeff.

"We didn't check," Becks replied.

"Fuck them," A woman I recognized but whose name I had forgotten spat.

"I need answers. Arm yourself; if you find a BHF soldier alive, shout. Take anything valuable off the bodies—weapons, cash, even vests. I need two people out front; the rest of you check the bodies in the back."

The residents split up.

"Ms. El, what about me?" Aaron asked, a sleeping Axel in his arms.

I kissed my son and hugged Aaron. "Stay indoors with the kids for now, please. I don't want them to see outside."

He nodded, and I went in search of a live person to gather information from.

Out of thirty soldiers, six were alive. Out of the six, only one had information that made him worth saving.

"Patch him up and keep him sedated," I said to Jeff.

Royal Summit was a graveyard. It was an awful sight, and there wasn't much I could do about it. All our men were either wounded, dead, or gone. Hudson, Bug, and Johnny were presumably in the chopper that had exploded. I'd been trying to contact Hudson via radio, but there was no answer. I refused to believe he was dead. Jeff offered to head toward the crash. He couldn't leave though; there were people at the Summit who needed him.

Xavier and other members of the community had been abducted. And Dr. Carla had gone missing, taking Julia with her. Because of Dr. Carla's involvement, we presumed Royal Summit was compromised. Aaron thought it weird that she'd chosen to follow the kids to the basement instead of protecting the community with the adults. He asked her about it, and she told him that she was a doctor, not a fighter. An hour or two later, Ax had called for Julia, who had gone missing. Dr. Carla was also gone.

After the fight, Chef was found in her room with a knife sticking out of her stomach. Fortunately, it was a shallow wound, and Jeff assured us she'd be fine. Chef had overheard Dr. Carla speaking to someone about the kids via the radio. When she asked the doctor about it, the doctor laughed it off and then stabbed her. Chef passed out and awakened when the alarm went off. We searched Dr. Carla's room and found several items linking her to BHF: radio, weapons, and correspondence. How she exchanged letters with her contacts was still a mystery.

Becks was beside herself. "Why?! Why my child?!"

"Mom. I think she would have taken them both if she could have," Aaron offered.

I blinked in surprise.

The teenage boy's words were meant to comfort his mother, but they made my stomach flip.

Rebellion trucks pulled up. Reinforcements. I sighed with relief. I'd contacted the leaders of the high school and the penitentiary communities to tell them what happened. Gator High was the closest, and our residents would be moving there until we could get Summit back to livable conditions. A group of men from Gator would be joining Dr. Jeff to search for any survivors of the helicopter crash.

As the community gathered their things, I pulled Becks aside.

"Do you know about the farm?" I asked her.

She nodded.

"I'm taking Axel there to stay with Faith and Roy," I said. Hudson and I had come up with a plan in case something happened to both of us, and we agreed that the farm would be the safest place for him.

"I'm taking my kids there, too," Becks said. "I'm going with you, El. You're not searching for my daughter without me."

"I'll get her back. And Xavi, too," I vowed.

"I'm going with you!" Becks stood.

"No. You can't. I work alone on this. It won't be an easy journey, Becks. Your boys need you here." I glanced over my shoulder. "Aaron?"

"I'm here," the kid replied.

"I need to borrow your bike," I told him. I'd given him Baylor when

I'd gotten pregnant. It wasn't a proper ride, and Becks' eldest son had taken a keen interest in it. "I'll return him safe and sound," I promised.

"Her. He's her now. Her name is Bella," Aaron told me.

"Oh, okay." Who knew my bike was gender-fluid?

"Elyanna!!" Becks snapped. "I'm going with you, and we're not taking a motorcycle. Where were you going to put Jules when you found her?"

She had a point.

"She's my daughter, El! And Xavier's my twin. And my husband is . . ." Becks gasped for breath. "I have to do something."

"It's okay, Aunty El. I'll look out for the other kids. I promise. Mom should go with you," Aaron pleaded.

"Elyanna, we're ready. Are you following us?" Troy, one of the Gator High leaders, asked.

"No. I'm going after my goddaughter. The Salinas family is coming with me," I told him.

"Me and a few men will come with you," he replied.

"No. I'm good, Troy. Watch over the others."

Chris, the big man who never spoke, pulled a notepad and pen from his jacket pocket and wrote something.

I'll go with you.

"No."

YES!!!!

"No, Chris. You have to go with Dr. Jeff. Find Hudson. Please."

The big man crossed his arms over his chest and glared at me. I mimicked his position.

A minute later, he caved, and we went our separate ways. Jeff and company went to find Hudson, Johnny, and Bug. Troy and the survivors went to Gator High.

Becks, her kids, Axel, and I reached the farm by late afternoon.

A few years ago, I needed help with a flat tire and stumbled onto a farm owned by Faith and her husband, Roy. They fixed the flat tire and provided me with food and shelter. In exchange, they wanted me to find someone who had been taken by BHF.

Since then, Hudson and the crew had worked out a trade agreement with the couple. They had a working gas line, livestock, and an abundant garden. During the last two years, my men helped to fortify their bunker. The farm was our safe house in the event shit hit the fan and only a select few knew about it. The natural resources and its underground accommodations made it a better option than the lodge.

"Thank you, Faith. I owe you one. A big one." I pulled the elder woman in for a one-armed hug.

"Don't think nothing of it, dear. Your family has helped us in more ways than we can repay. We will be fine. Go, find that baby girl and bring her home."

I glanced at Becks. "Are you ready?"

She took a deep breath and nodded. I cradled my son, inhaling his scent. "Julia Momma," he whined.

"I know, son. I know. Mommy and Aunty Becks will bring her home. You stay here with Aaron, Jonah, and the others. Okay." I kissed his hair.

"No. I go!" He fussed.

Tears spilled over my cheeks. I rocked him back and forth. In moments, he was asleep, and I laid him on a makeshift bed. It killed me to duck out while he was sleeping. It was awful leaving him at all, but my best friend and her daughter needed me. And if he was the one that had been taken, Becks would be leaving her kids behind for me.

"Don't worry, dear. He'll be safe here. Your men built this for a reason. There's plenty of fresh water, produce, and canned food. We are well stocked for years. And no one knows it exists except your men and Becks' husband," Faith offered.

I nodded, said goodbye to the others, and walked away with a heavy heart.

Roy waited for us in front of the store.

"I gassed up the vehicle and stocked it for ya," he said. "Added food, blankets, and extra ammo. Get going before your passenger wakes."

Becks and I thanked him and began our journey to the desert.

CHAPTER FOURTEEN

Elyanna

"E l," Becks nudged my shoulder. "It's time."

Becks had taken the first driving shift while I napped. Using my gift had expended my energy and I needed to recharge to deal with our passenger. The soldier I'd gathered information from had been sedated and would wake again soon.

I glanced at the back seat to make sure he was still out.

"Just as we discussed," I told Becks.

She nodded.

I smacked the guard on his head. "Hey! Wake up, man! Your turn to drive."

Becks got out of the car and moved to the backseat.

"Where are we?" he asked. He'd be groggy for a time, but he'd be able to drive until we reached the next gas station.

When I rifled through his brain, I'd gotten the fastest route to BHF's headquarters in Arizona with the least amount of BHF stations. There were several roads to get there and I could have used my gift at every station but that would have been too taxing. With the soldier under my control, he'd drive through each checkpoint with ease, be able to speak the lingo with any guards we came across, fill up gas, and buy us essentials. Once we got to the city, we'd have to go it alone and he'd have to die. It would have been too difficult to convince others that a lowly soldier was waltzing into BHF's headquarters asking questions. As it was, he'd wake up thinking we were men and comrades he was familiar with.

"Almost home," Becks answered. "We've taken our shifts, now it's your turn."

They changed places. Becks gave me a wink, adjusted her helmet to cover her face, and pretended to sleep. I'd instructed her to say as little as possible. We didn't want our guide to learn too much about us.

Ian Loxley, our designated driver, got us back on the road. He fidgeted with the stereo system which didn't work and snarled. "With all the resources BHF has you'd think they'd at least put some tunes in these trucks."

"Witnessed the spoils have you?" I asked.

"Oh yeah. Most of the citizen encampment is gross. But the FC has it all, it's nice," he said. "Well, you know. You've been."

I hadn't. I'd only seen the city through his thoughts. I weaved an intricate pattern into his mind. Leaving his memories intact, I implanted a perception of what Becks and I looked like and our roles in BHF. He thought Beckham and Elliot were trainees on our first rebellion mission. Our commanders were killed on the front lawn at the resort, and we found him dying in the back of the resort, which he'd been. We escaped the rebellion encampment, patched his wound, and headed back to report to the headquarters. This lie was probable in his head thus making it easier for me to manage. To maintain this farce all I needed to do was reinforce the thoughts and images in his head which was easier to do versus having to manufacture an entire story.

"Only the guard station. What's FC like?" I replied.

"Oh, right, new recruit. All the newbies go through the recruiting center and that is where we work and live. It's fine, though. We're on the other side of the wall and I'd been told there are even service women. Haven't seen one yet but looking forward to it. Federation City itself was made for the Gifted and all the pre-plague rich people, it's more exquisite than you can imagine."

I shrugged.

"Don't believe me?" With his finger, he made the sign of the cross on his chest. "God's truth I've seen it myself . . ." he continued.

Ian went on and on telling us stories about his experiences in FC. I tuned him out. I'd seen most of what he was regaling through his thoughts. My own wandered to the past.

During the last few years of the pre-plague era, a group of billionaires partnered to create a master-planned community called Pleasanton, located in the Sonoran Desert. It bordered southwest Arizona and southeast California. The company hit social media hard. It was purported to be the first self-sustainable master-planned development. It was a live, work, and play concept with the added benefit of being able to obtain food grown in the community.

I'd been in college at the time when this began. Like others in my generation, the idea of living in a green self-sustaining community was appealing. My parents thought it was a cult. I rolled my eyes at them as most children do when disregarding the wisdom of their elders. Not that it mattered. The astronomical cost made living there a pipe dream, even for our upper-middle-class family.

To entice buyers, the developers had planned to include every comfort such as retail, restaurants, and entertainment. If that wasn't enough, hospitals, law enforcement, and schools were also part of the allure.

Every structure in the master plan was designed to run on solar power and diesel generators. Pleasanton was an instant hit. The custom lots sold in minutes and construction began. The list of residents building custom homes consisted of celebrities, athletes, politicians, and any number of worldwide dignitaries who could afford the lavish price tag.

Since the community couldn't run itself, smaller single-family residences had also been built for families who wanted to live a green lifestyle. The price ranges well exceeded what most middle-class families could afford and still, those homes were soon sold out.

Apartments and townhomes had become available to those working within the community. By this time I was married and in my last year of nursing school. A representative for the soon-to-be-built hospital had visited my school, recruiting medical staff. If selected for employment after graduation, a home for purchase would be available to me at a fraction of the cost. I was ecstatic. So was Tyler, my husband. It seemed like a fun adventure.

I filled out the paperwork and broke the news to my family over Sunday dinner. My sister was excited. My mother was sad at the thought of me moving away. My father was furious. As I told the family of all the benefits of working at a state-of-the-art medical facility and owning a self-sustaining home, my father slammed his fist on the table and said. "No! I forbid you to move to Pleasanton."

My father was a teddy bear. I was his eldest daughter and we were always close. He never in all of my life raised his voice the way he had that night. After his outburst, he excused himself from the table and the rest of us ate in silence.

He reappeared a little while later, with gruff instructions. "Everyone in front of the television," he said.

He fiddled with his phone, pressing on buttons then turned to Tyler, "Put this on the big screen."

Tyler set up the screen share functions, and Daddy pulled up an email.

"This is from Bob Costa. His construction company has been building residential properties."

My father was a general contractor. He owned a construction firm that specialized in commercial buildings. He hadn't had massive projects like Pleasanton, but he made a decent living. Being upper-middle-class Americans, we still were unable to afford the studio apartments in the upcoming green community and at the time I couldn't understand why he wasn't happy for me.

The video showed the development in the early construction phases. Structures were up here and there, and I could tell it'd be years until completion.

"Here's the interesting stuff," a male voice said as the video panned to a wall.

Although Daddy had taken us to visit construction sites through the years, I wasn't sure what I seeing. It seemed like a typical wall to me. It was seven feet or so of steel and concrete, which ran along the perimeter of the development. It looked like they were building a fence of what would become a gated community. The videographer walked toward an opening of the wall and showed it from another angle. The wall was thick, approximately three feet deep. As the daughter of a construction worker, I knew the standard minimum of an outer wall was nine inches. They were being extra careful. The camera changed angles again. The wall continued along the perimeter for at least a mile and at its farthest point, it rose in the air at least twenty feet. And they were still building.

My father pressed paused and rounded on me.

"This, Elyanna, is not a perimeter wall. This," He tapped on the screen. "Is a barricade."

I went home and tore up the application. Why were they building a residential community with a fortified barricade?

I never received an answer to that question. Tyler and I never spoke about Pleasanton again. I graduated from nursing school, and we moved to Frisco. Soon after that dinner, the media coverage of Pleasanton changed. We often heard about what a great concept it was, but any pictures of the ongoing construction stopped appearing.

Then the car accident happened, and the plague came soon after. Pleasanton had become a thing of the past until now.

CHAPTER FIFTEEN

Hudson

"Rocket launcher! Jump!" Roman shouted.

"Go, Johnny!" I watched Becks' husband strap on a parachute and jump.

"Let's go, Roman!" I made my way to the open door. The helicopter swerved.

"I'm fireproof, Hawk. Jump!! Now!"

Shit. I wasn't sure about that. I hesitated.

"Now, Hudson!!" Roman barked. "I'm right behind you."

The fire-starter messed with the controls, undid his seatbelt, and stood.

"See you on the ground." I jumped.

Unlike Johnny, I didn't have a chute. But I had my skills. Or so I thought. The world blurred past me; the ground was coming up fast. It was disorienting, and I had a hard time harnessing my gift. My body bounced off a tree branch or five and slammed into a rock, then rolled down the rough terrain until I fell off a cliff, which propelled me into the river. I held my breath.

The impact of the frigid water jabbed my skin with a thousand icicles. I gasped. Agony wrought all over my body as I plunged into the icy depths. Everywhere ached.

I forced my body upward until I broke the surface and then sucked in a lungful of air. The current of the river pulled me, and I latched onto the nearest rock, clawing my way to climb onto the shore, favoring my left shoulder.

"Johnny?" I called out.

No answer.

I scanned the air and saw a plume of smoke in the distance. The chopper crashed.

Roman, you better have survived that, or El will have my ass.

"Hawk!"

I gingerly turned toward the voice. Johnny waved, then jogged to my side.

"You look like shit," he said.

"Dislocated shoulder."

"Easy fix." Without even asking, Johnny grabbed my wrist and pulled, popping the joint back in place.

"Motherfucker! A little warning would be nice," I cursed.

Johnny shrugged.

Breathing deeply, I scrambled to my feet. "We need to check on Roman."

"You think he survived that?" he asked.

"He better, or my wife will skin me alive." I analyzed Becks' husband, tilting my head to the side. "You don't have a scratch on you. How is that possible?"

He flashed a cheeky grin and spread his arms, then spun in a slow circle. "One hundred percent human, baby."

I chuckled, then winced. No wonder Xavi's twin was in love with him. He didn't speak much, but when he did, he was a fucking comedian.

We picked up the pace toward the crash site. Interestingly enough, there was smoke but no fire, as though the fire department had already doused the flames. Roman. This was a good sign as far as the fire-starter was concerned.

"Roman?!" Johnny called out as we searched the area.

I peered into what was left of the helicopter. Nothing but charred ash and a melted console. The comms devices were completely destroyed. If Roman survived, it would be a fucking Christmas miracle.

Johnny and I fanned out, sweeping the area twenty feet from the site. I wasn't feeling optimistic until I noticed a heap of smoldering flesh upon a bed of moss and rock.

"Here!" I called out to Johnny and rushed to Roman's side.

Oh shit. His body was covered in third-degree burns. I was too afraid to check for a pulse.

"Rome? Can you hear me?" I asked.

Skin crackled as he raised his thumb.

"Don't move," I told him.

Johnny came to stand beside us. "Fuck me." He gagged.

I couldn't blame him. Roman was a fucked-up mess. His skin melted around bone and sinew like molten cheese. The worst part was the smell. It was a sickening combination of burned hair, blood, and the acrid scent of plastic. The stench wasn't just pungent. It was thick and almost had a taste to it.

"We need to get him home. Jeff will know what to do," I told Johnny.

"Uh . . . okay. If you think that will help . . ." he started to say.

"It'll help!" I snarled. Roman responded to my questions, which meant he was still very much alive.

"Hold on, Roman. I'll make sure you get the help you need," I said.

"Come on," I prodded Johnny.

In minutes, Johnny and I fashioned a stretcher out of the parachute and branches. From the sun's position and general landscape, we were thirty miles out. We were deep into the forest, not an ideal location for a flare, so we hiked.

It was slow going, carrying the stretcher over the uneven terrain. Johnny and I kept going, moving alongside the river. We had to stop every mile or two. Roman was heavy.

Birds scattered above the tree line. I halted in place and strained my hearing. Footsteps. Loud footsteps. Not soldiers, then. Hikers?

I ushered Johnny to a large boulder sitting between the river shore and the edge of the forest. We laid Roman behind the boulder and crept toward the hikers.

My senses picked up more footsteps. Seven pairs if my instincts were correct. They were breathing heavily and stomping through the forest with a mission.

I signaled Johnny to wait behind and watch my six while I crept closer. Less than a quarter mile away, I caught sight of a familiar bald head.

I whistled. Chris turned his head. The others stopped and looked my way.

"Hawk?! Is that you?"

I breathed a sigh of relief as Jeff trampled through the forest like a baby rhino.

I guided the rescue party to Roman's body. Jeff's eyes widened.

"Fuuck," he muttered.

"You should have seen him a couple of hours ago," Johnny said.

I scanned Roman's body, and Johnny was right. As impossible as it had seemed, Roman's flesh had been healing at a slow but certain rate. His skin didn't appear as melted as it had been. It was still red and raw, but it was as though his flesh was knitting back together. Gifted healed fast, but this was something different. Maybe it was his affinity for fire.

The doctor jabbed a needle into what I presumed was a vein and then hooked up an IV.

"We need to get him home now," Jeff said.

We didn't hesitate. Four members of the rescue team picked up the stretcher, and we jogged back to where they'd left a truck.

As we ran, I asked Jeff, "Elyanna?"

He panted, sweat pouring down his temples. "Fi . . . Fine. She . . ."

"She went after Ju . . . Julia."

Chris tapped my shoulder and handed me a piece of paper.

BHF stormed the resort. Took hostages. Xavier gone. Julia was taken by Dr. Carla. El and Becks went to find Julia.

Of course, she did.

"My son?"

Jeff came to a stop, hands braced on his knees. "Farm."

Relief washed over me. Ax was at the farm. El was playing hero, which was typical of her. Dammit, El. I didn't doubt her skill; I was just worried about my love.

The rescue crew had come in two vehicles, so I instructed the others to keep going.

"You have to keep moving, Jeff. You'll cramp up if you stop now."

"I know that, Hudson Pierce. I am a doctor," he snarled and began running again.

One minute I was sipping a cup of coffee, and the next I was waking up in the med ward of the Summit.

"Jeff!" I growled.

"Shh! We have patients!" Jeff admonished in a whispered shout.

"Did you fucking drug me?" I asked through clenched teeth.

"Of course. You needed the rest. You completely ignored the gash on your head; your body was black and blue. I'm not sorry. You're no good to El and Becks if you can't stand. Besides, it's only been two hours. During that time, I had someone prepare a truck for you and Johnny to go rescue your wives. You're welcome." He stomped away from me.

I swung my legs over the cot and scanned the room. There were several bodies laid out, all with various injuries. Fucking BHF. Johnny was resting on a cot nearby. I decided to let him rest a little longer and went to check on Roman.

Roman looked much better since I'd last laid eyes on him. If I hadn't witnessed his injuries, I would have guessed he had been burned months ago, not a few hours.

"He's healing at an incredible rate," Jeff said.

"How's that possible?" I asked.

"Not sure. I'm guessing it's his gift. I've taken blood and tissue samples. I'll be studying this in detail, I assure you. It's nothing short of miraculous."

"Stop talking about me like I'm not here," Roman said, his voice hoarse and gravelly.

"Just making sure you're still with us," I retorted.

"Don't . . ." he wheezed. "Don't leave without me."

"You're barely fifty percent combat effective, Roman. You're not going anywhere," I told him.

The crazy fucker gingerly sat up with a groan. I stepped back, and Jeff panicked.

"Roman! Don't! As your physician, I demand you lie back right now!!"

"I'm going with you to find Elyanna," Roman rasped.

"Alright, alright. I'm not going anywhere for another hour, at least. Do what the doctor says," I said.

"You better not leave without me." Roman glared. At least most of his face had been spared.

"Fine," I acquiesced. "Rest, I'll get organized." *And leave you behind.*

I let Jeff deal with the snarly patient and made preparations to leave.

Royal Summit was nearly empty. There were no residents left aside from the injured and a few people who had stayed behind to help Jeff. One of the men filled me in on what had happened. Everyone had assumed BHF had taken the others to BHF headquarters in Arizona. That was a fifteen-hour drive, and it had been about seven since they last laid eyes on Elyanna. She had taken Ax to the farm, and by my estimation, she'd been on the road for at least five hours. I had some catching up to do.

My first stop was our cottage, and from the looks of things, El left in a rush. And she hadn't slept alone. Xavier. That made me smile. It was about time that asshole made amends with her.

I rushed through a shower, gathered a few personal things for myself and Ax, and then gathered more items necessary for my mission.

I checked in with Briar and Hillside. Those communities were fine. We hadn't gotten around to providing the farm with radio communication. I had hoped we wouldn't have needed it so soon. Epic fail on my part. I gathered the gear for that, too, as I planned to stop there first.

Two hours later, I found Jeff in his office.

"You're leaving?" he asked, his eyes red with fatigue.

"You need to rest," I said.

"Stop doctoring me, Hawk."

I put my hands in the air. "Fine, I'm just concerned about you. How are the patients?"

"Everyone is on the mend. As soon as they're movable, I'll contact the high school and have them transported."

"Alright, I'm stopping at the farm first, then I'll catch up to El and Becks," I told him.

"Alone?" He quirked his eyebrow.

"Yep, Roman is not fit for combat. And Johnny is human. I'm afraid he'll fight me if I try to leave him at the farm, so I'm sneaking out now. I'll do my best to stay in touch. Good luck."

We shook hands, and I exited the Summit's main building. Johnny was in the driver's seat of the truck.

Shit.

I opened the door. "You're staying with Jeff."

"No, I'm going with you," Johnny insisted. "I'll drive."

I got into the passenger side of the vehicle. "Farm first. And that's where you're staying."

Johnny shrugged.

Thirty-five minutes later, we were on the freeway, and a gruff voice said, "I can't fucking believe you were going to leave without me."

I nearly lashed out with my gift.

"Bloody fucking hell, Rome! What the fuck are you doing in here?!" I glared at the fire-starter stretched out in the back seat.

His skin was still red, uneven, and bubbly in spots. It was gruesome, but a hell of a lot better than the last time I'd seen him. "Does Doc know you're here?"

"No," Johnny replied. "I snuck him out. We have an IV. He's healing. He'll be fine by the time we reach the girls."

"Fucking asshole." I punched Johnny's arm.

He smirked.

I glanced at Roman. "You're staying at the farm, too."

CHAPTER SIXTEEN

Xavier

"This guy doesn't look like much. Are you sure we should bother taking him back?" an unfamiliar voice said. "We should have grabbed the women."

"I agree," another voice replied.

"The other two we picked up are dead, and we can't go back empty-handed. You all know that," an authoritative tone scolded. "Shut up and continue driving."

I chanced a glance and came face-to-face with the dead eyes of a familiar face. Fuckers.

"We should at least stop and throw the bodies out," the first speaker said. "It'll get rank in here if we don't get rid of the dead."

"Plus it's unsanitary," the second speaker added.

"Fine. We'll dump them at the next station," the driver said.

It wasn't long before the truck slowed. I kept my eyes closed and my breathing shallow. The vehicle stopped, and the men moved around. Within minutes, Craig, one of the members at the Summit was pulled away from the truck. *Don't worry, man, I'll avenge you and make sure your family is cared for.*

Minutes later, another body beside me was pulled out of the truck. I waited.

As soon as the doors closed, I used my gift and got out of the vehicle. We were at a BHF encampment. A rather large one. I noticed several buildings and at least two dozen guards milling around outside. Well, I wouldn't be fighting my way out of this one.

I strode closer to the guards, listening to their conversation and gathering intel as I studied the area.

Since the incident with Luther, I'd used my gift continuously. My sister and her kids constantly checked in with me to make sure I was okay. They meant well, and I appreciated their efforts. I was never left alone for very long. Even when I said I needed to clear my head, someone, usually one of the boys, would follow me around. In time, it got stifling, and I needed my space. I began using my gift to hide, and my powers grew. I'd been able to go ghost for almost two hours, versus the forty minutes I'd been accustomed to. And I was able to use it more often without getting tired. Still, it wasn't something I could do all day without repercussions, making every second valuable.

There was a command center in the middle of the encampment where several men and women were speaking. I snuck in and made myself comfortable in the corner as the soldiers discussed their mission. I learned we were a few hours from Royal Summit, at a BHF encampment, and they had been studying our community with the help of someone on the inside. The small hairs on the back of my neck stood. Who the fuck was feeding them information about us?

"Where's the doc?" A man, whose name tag read *Shakir* asked.

"Leaving the kid with one of the nurses. She should be here soon," One of my captors said.

Kid? There were several kids at Summit, three of whom were my kin, and one was mine. Well, not mine. Ax was El's and Hawk's son, but I'd grown attached to the kid as I stalked his mother. Yeah, that sounded crazy. Maybe I was crazy.

I shook off the thought and continued listening.

"Why is there only one kid? We were told there were several," Shakir asked.

Dr. Carla strode into the room. "There are more. I was only able to carry one. Your incompetent soldiers should have brought the rest of them."

I glared at the doctor. The woman who had befriended me for months—almost two years. All that time, she acted as though she cared for me. Like she was trying to help. Fucking lying bitch.

"They were ready, and they outgunned us," Torrence sputtered.

"Excuses. I spent months risking my life for this mission, and you botched it! You won't get another shot," Dr. Carla spat.

"You need to go back," Shakir told her.

"No! My cover is blown, and the kid should be transported to headquarters immediately. I'm gathering my provisions and will be gone in the morning," she replied.

"What's the plan with the Gator rebellions?" Torrence asked.

"Don't know. My guess is they'll be hiding out in one of the other communities. And no, I wasn't privy to that information. I wasn't given a vehicle to come and go as I pleased. I had access to Royal Summit as per my reports. They have gifted there; I told you about them. I don't have anything else to offer."

Shakir straightened his spine and glared at the woman. "Guess you're no longer useful."

"Please. Are you going to drive seven to eight hours with a one-year-old baby girl? Do you even know how to take care of a baby, Captain?" She met his glare.

The bitch took my niece. I was so going to kill her.

Shakir didn't respond.

"I didn't think so." Dr. Carla walked out of the room.

I followed her while using my invisibility gift until we came to a building that was a communal shower house. I didn't want to see the woman naked, so I searched the area for Julia. She wasn't hard to find. She was with a few women who were fawning over her. Julia seemed to have sensed my presence. She looked straight at me. I placed my finger over my lips, telling her to keep quiet, and she mimicked the movement. That was interesting.

In the adjacent room, I found a bathroom and a change of clothes. I changed into BHF gear and then went to find Julia again. My niece was asleep, and Dr. Carla was in the room, setting aside two bags near the door.

"Doctor, your vehicle is right outside when you're ready," a female guard had told her. "Do you need help with anything else?"

"No. Wake me in four hours," Dr. Carla replied as she lay on a cot next to Julia's and closed her eyes.

I glanced out the window to see a Jeep parked outside. I peered into the bags next and frowned. Clothes and papers. Hmmm, I'd need food for Jules.

Since I was wearing a BHF uniform, I roamed the encampment, not bothering with my gift. I came across two of the men who had taken me and followed them into the communal shower area. I snagged a rope that had been lying on the floor and snuck up on one man while he was using the urinal. I wrapped the rope around his neck, strangled him to death, and shoved him into the cleaning closet. The other man had gotten out of the shower as I exited the closet. His mouth hung open, and I threw my knife, which landed at the base of his neck. Before his body hit the floor, I grabbed him and shoved him into the closet with his friend. He'd bleed out eventually, hopefully not before anyone found them. I tossed their personal belongings in a nearby laundry bin, taking anything of value, then continued my perusal of the area. There were four of them that had taken me, and as much as I wanted revenge, there was no time.

I found the cafeteria, shoveled food into my mouth, and packed provisions for the road. It was a good thing I spent time with my sister and her kids. I knew what my niece could eat and made sure we had plenty of everything for the road. No one paid any attention to me.

Quietly, I entered Julia's room to find her and the doctor still asleep. I pressed the weight of my body on the doctor's chest and the tip of my blade to her neck.

"Scream and I slice your throat," I snarled.

Her eyes snapped open. "Xavier! What are you doing here? It's not what it looks like. Please have mercy," she muttered.

"Mercy?" I clamped a hand over her mouth and nose, then sliced her carotid artery. She began flailing. "You kidnapped my niece. A one-year-old. You've been filling my head with lies for the last year and a half. There will be no mercy. I want to watch you bleed. But my niece needs her mother, and I need Elyanna."

She squirmed on the bed, hitting and clawing my arms. Her futile attempts amused me. I tilted my head to the side watching the life bleed out of her eyes. The deviant side of me wanted to make her death gruesome; she certainly deserved a nasty end. But I had Julia to consider.

My niece was awake, staring at me with wide eyes.

Oh shit.

"Bad person," I said.

"Bad," she whispered.

My sister was going to kill me when she learned I'd killed someone in front of her daughter. I ran my hand through my hair.

"Hey, kid. Ready to see your mama?" I asked in a soothing voice.

"Ax!" she exclaimed.

I chuckled. "Yeah, Ax, too. But you have to keep quiet for me, okay?"

She nodded, and I picked her up and the bags Dr. Carla had left by the door. After loading the vehicle, I heard a commotion coming from the far end of the encampment. Perhaps they had already found the bodies. It didn't matter; in minutes, we were taking the back roads out of the BHF encampment, heading home.

CHAPTER SEVENTEEN

Elyanna

I an talked for hours non-stop. I dozed off and woke up when we arrived at a gas station.

"I'm going to fill up and grab some grub," he said.

"Yep. I'll hit the bathroom," I said. *Leave the key*—I pushed the thought into his head.

As soon as his door shut, Becks groaned. "Jesus, that man can talk."

I laughed, then grabbed the key. We couldn't risk Ian taking off on us.

Becks and I went to the ladies' room. One stood outside, guarding the door, and pretended to smoke a cigarette, while the other used the facilities.

We walked back to the truck just as Ian walked out of the store.

"Hey Beckham, take this; I need to drain the pipe." He shoved a bag into Becks' hands.

"I hope he got something reasonably healthy." She peered into the bag. "Hot dogs—six of them. Gross."

I laughed. Life on the road was not glamorous. I'd done it for years. "At least it's not rats-on-a-stick," I teased.

Becks made a gagging noise, making me laugh.

We refilled the tank, ate our hot dogs, and then got on the road again. Ian hadn't shown any signs of fatigue and had offered to drive to the next checkpoint, another four-hour drive.

From the info I'd gotten from him earlier, it would take fifteen hours or so with stops. If we each took five hours, we could do it in one shot. I'd driven two, Becks drove three, and Ian had done six. We were more than halfway there, and I was well rested. I planned to get through the next checkpoint and cut him loose.

Becks sat shotgun, and I stretched out in the passenger seat, listening to him talk about his life with BHF.

He wasn't a bad guy. He was twenty-six, never married, and had no children. His parents and four siblings died of the plague. He joined the BHF and had risen through the ranks to corporal. He was in high school when the plague hit. Aside from his work with BHF, he had no life. I almost felt bad about having to kill him.

"Where'd you get the sword?" Ian eyed me via the rearview mirror.

"Stole it from a rebel," I said. *You won't remember seeing a sword. The only sword you'll remember is a toy you had as a kid.* I pushed the thought into his mind.

"I had a toy sword once. Cheap plastic thing. My favorite toy was . . ." Ian droned on, and I sighed.

That was close, Elyanna.

"Hey! Wake up!" Becks' voice startled me awake.

I sat upright as Ian slowed the vehicle. There was a commotion up ahead. Several BHF vehicles were blocking the road, and about a half dozen guards had been standing sentry.

"What's going on?" I asked Ian.

"Roadblock. Something must have happened at this encampment," he answered. He slowed at the blockade and rolled his window down.

I opened up my gift as Ian began conversing with the guard.

"Where are you headed?" the guard asked.

"Headquarters," Ian replied.

"You need to check in with management before we let you pass," the guard told Ian. "It won't take long; pull into the next driveway and keep going until you see the command center. You'll see the sign."

I rummaged through the guard's mind and learned that someone was found dead and another person was missing, along with an important asset.

Ian did as the guard asked. I pushed a few instructions into his head, having him park on the side of the building away from onlookers, and convinced him that he had been traveling the entire time alone.

"We're going to need another way out of here," I told Becks as soon as Ian exited the car. "They'll inspect this vehicle. Come on."

Becks and I rounded the command center, sticking to the shadows. We crouched near a windowsill and overheard Ian talking to another man. As instructed, Ian told him that he'd been traveling alone. His comrades were dead, and he took the only vehicle to return to the headquarters as per his senior officer's instructions. Whoever he was talking to told him he'd need to wait for clearance before continuing his journey and instructed him to wait in the common area.

I peeked into the man's head and barely refrained from stifling a gasp. Dr. Carla had been found dead at a BHF encampment not far from Royal Summit. She arrived with Julia, and the baby had gone missing. His thoughts indicated that one of the guards had taken Julia to the headquarters in hopes of gaining a promotion. They set up a roadblock, thinking the guard would try to pass on his way to HQ.

Shit. I grasped Becks' hand and squeezed.

From my perusal of his thoughts, I learned the layout of the base and guided Becks to an area that was rarely used.

The building was a storage facility with a surplus of everything. It was the leftovers they stored but never needed. It was as big as a pre-plague convenience store. This facility was stocked from floor to ceiling with toiletries, dried goods, and weapons. According to the thoughts I'd seen in the captain's head, they received shipments from headquarters weekly and rarely used the stuff. The wastefulness was disgusting.

"What in the world?" Becks' widened gaze swept the room.

"Surplus. We should raid this shit. Let's find useful things; restock food and water."

"This way; I see some decent stuff." Becks led the way to one of the shelves.

With our bags stuffed, I pulled Becks toward the exit at the back of the building.

"There's something you're not telling me," Becks said.

I sighed. If Axel had been taken, I'd want to know every detail.

"Dr. Carla was found dead at a nearby encampment. And . . . Julia's missing. The captain has two theories. He thinks she was taken by one of the guards to the headquarters. He was looking for a promotion and thought showing up with Jules was his ticket. The other theory is that she was taken by a hostage who had gone missing. He may have taken Julia home."

Becks' eyes watered. "Okay. Umm . . . What are we going to do?"

"Whatever you want, Becks. Xavi may have her, and he's taken her home," I replied, hoping that was the case.

"I'm not sure, El. If my brother has her, he'll get her to safety." She swiped her face. "But if he doesn't, my baby is being taken to Arizona. What would you do?"

It was a conundrum. I rubbed my temple. The surplus store didn't have radios, and I wouldn't want to risk going into the command center to contact Royal Summit. We wouldn't be able to reach the farm, so that option was out. On one hand, if Xavi had Julia, he'd keep her safe, and we could head back. I wanted to see my son and find my husband. But we were less than five hours from Federation City, and according to Ian, there would be no other BHF stations until we reached the headquarters. It should be an easy drive. And if Julia was there and we headed home, we'd be farther away from her and have to restart this journey.

I explained our options to Becks.

"I hope Xavi has her," her voice cracked. "But I don't want to drive ten hours to the farm and find out she's not there. I'd rather continue. Just to be sure. Are you okay with that?"

"Of course."

"I know it can't be easy being away from Ax and Hudson." Her gaze was focused on the ground.

I pulled her in for a hug. "Becks, I'm with you on this. One hundred percent. I'd make the same choice."

I drew away from her and gave her shoulders a reassuring squeeze. "Let's go find Jules."

We exited the storage room and found a vehicle.

"Are we going to just drive through the blockade?" she asked.

"Not exactly. The captain's thoughts showed me another exit. It's a small road; no one knows about it," I told her.

We found the road, which was more like an off-roading path. It was dark, and the rocky terrain made me glad we'd found a four-wheel drive. If it'd been winter, this was a definite no-go. I clenched the steering wheel and drove slowly. Becks was silent. The tension in the Jeep was thick and unnerving. The road seemed like it would never end. It took an hour to reach the main highway.

Becks patted my arm. I let out an audible sigh of relief.

"We're coming, Julia."

CHAPTER EIGHTEEN
Roman

"I'm staying in the car." My voice was gravelly. Fucking smoke inhalation. At least my skin was healing.

"You're not coming to Federation City," Hudson growled.

"Try and move me from this truck. I dare you," I told him.

"Roman, you're not helpful to Elyanna if you're lying in the backseat recuperating," he argued.

"I'll be fine. You have a thirteen-hour drive."

"You may as well come in," he sighed.

So you can leave me behind? Not a chance.

"I don't want Ax to see me like this," I said.

His eyes raked over my body, and then he got out of the car without saying another word. I must look awful.

I dozed off as soon as both Hawk and Johnny exited the vehicle.

A wave of nausea hit me as the forest spun. My body was jerked around in the helicopter, making it difficult for me to exit. The chopper knocked into tall pines. A thick branch punched through the windshield, barely missing my head. The concussive force from the explosion punctured my eardrums. I called on my fire as the helicopter became engulfed with flames. Heat seared my skin. Pain lanced through every nerve ending. I pushed my gift, forcing my fire to the surface in hopes of shielding my body from the explosive heat. I tried to scream, but my throat burned and my lungs scorched. Pure agony wrought through every cell in my body. This is what all those people felt when I used my fire to burn them alive.

My eyes snapped open, and I sat upright with a groan. Fuck me. I glanced down at my hands and arms. The skin was red, uneven, and angry-looking. I looked like a monster. I was a monster. I'd used my gift on so many people. Now I knew what it felt like. Gingerly, I got out of the truck. Grimacing with every movement. Perhaps Hawk was right. No, I needed to know El was okay. She was mine to protect. And I . . . I loved her.

She was just as much mine as she was Hawk's and Xavi's. She loved me, too. I hoped. I'd rejected her. She was everything to me. And she was willing to accept me into her family, her heart, and her bed. And I basically told her she wasn't enough. That couldn't be the last time we spoke. I had to tell her how much she meant to me. I had to tell her she was enough; she was everything.

I walked around Roy's and Faith's store. My body ached, but the fresh air felt good, and it took my mind off the bad deeds I'd done with my gift. Something moved in my periphery, and then Xavi appeared on my left.

The surprise had me gasping for air. Asshole.

"You look like shit." Xavi rocked a sleeping Julia in his arms.

"Where's El?" I glanced behind him.

"She's not here?" he asked.

"No, she took off with Becks to search for her." I jutted out my chin at Julia's sleeping form.

"Fuck," he muttered under his breath. "Hawk inside?"

I nodded.

Xavi took off. I got back in the vehicle, swallowed a bunch of pills Doc had given me, and fell asleep.

Hours later, the car jostled my body, waking me as we cruised down the road. Xavi was in the passenger seat, and Hawk was driving. No Johnny. I was still feeling groggy, so I closed my eyes as their conversation drew me in.

"I'm glad you finally came to your senses. It took you long enough," Hawk said.

"I'm not . . ." Xavi shook his head.

"I swear to all that's fucking holy, Xavier, if you hurt her again, I will shoot you in the face," Hawk growled.

"It's not that, Hawk. I love her. But fuck. It's hard to explain. I'm not the same."

"You are. You're just . . . you. The real you." Hawk paused.

Xavier angled his body in the passenger seat to fully face him. I couldn't see his face clearly from where I was lying, but I imagined he was puzzled by what Hawk was alluding to. So was I.

"I know, Xavier. I've always known about . . . your dark passenger," Hudson stated in a low tone.

My eyes flicked open. Xavi had a dark side. Aside from how he treated El, I would have never guessed the happy-go-lucky man had a sinister bone in his body.

"Wha . . . What are you talking about?"

"I was your commander, Xavier. I studied your profile before you joined our unit. I know about the things you dealt with during high school. Your psych evals were in your file."

"You never said anything." Xavi stammered.

"There was no reason for me to bring it up. You're a good man, Xavier. Always have been. I'm impressed you didn't let that part of you take over more often. Invisibility is a powerful gift. Dark and seductive in many ways."

"This is... I'm shocked. You never said a word. Weren't you curious?" Xavi sputtered.

"It didn't matter to me what you were doing as long as you did your job and you weren't committing any crimes."

"How do you know I wasn't?"

"I followed you," Hawk replied. "Your wife came to me. Said you were gone at night, doing illegal things. She wanted you court-martialed."

"Why didn't you tell me this, Hawk? You're supposed to be my friend!" Xavier shouted.

Yeah, I was wide awake now.

"Cool your tits. It wasn't an issue. And, like I said, I didn't care. She threatened to go to the colonel. I told her not to and that I would take care of it. I followed you a couple of times. You weren't doing anything illegal. I mean, yeah, you weren't being a loyal husband, but that had nothing to do with your performance as a soldier. I told the colonel that your wife may make waves about your extracurricular activities, and that is when I got the information regarding the plague and our options."

"Oh. That was right before we left Florida. You followed me. To the club?" Xavier's voice was tight.

"Yep. The gay club. If you can't say it out loud, you'll never get over your hangups." Hawk glanced at him.

"I'm not gay," Xavi interjected.

"I didn't say you were."

"And it's not like I want to dick every guy I meet." Xavi's tone was defensive.

"Just me, right? I can't blame you. Everyone does. I'm a sexy moth-erfucker," Hawk snorted.

"How can Elyanna stand your oversized ego?"

"My wife loves my oversized everything. And no, I don't think you're gay, bi perhaps, but who cares? I'm not judging you."

"I'm not bi, either."

"Are you sure about that?"

There was a lengthy pause and someone, I guessed it was Xavi, was tapping nervously on the dashboard.

"No. I'm confused. Yes, I'll admit I'm attracted to men. It's a sex thing. A kink I guess. Ever since Luther, it's like I can't turn off my deviant nature. I always had more control." Xavi turned his head to stare out the window. "Did you tell anyone? Ax? El?"

"Of course not. It's not my story to tell. You may want to talk about this with someone. It will help. Did you talk to Dr. Carla about this?" Hawk asked.

"No. Fuck that bitch. She was playing me the whole time, and I didn't even know it. I sliced her throat, and I didn't feel an ounce of remorse."

Hawk was silent for a beat, then said, "Don't stress about it, Xavier.

I don't care about your past. I care about how you treat El going forward."

"My darkness is out, Hawk, and I don't know how to make that part of me go away. And a part of me doesn't want to. I like how it feels to be free and to let the darkness out to play. It feels good to kill. The sexual side . . . I don't know what to do about that. I don't want to bottle that part of me again. I don't want to harbor any guilt for being who I am."

"Hate to break it to you, but no one is making you feel guilty except you. Only you can free yourself of that guilt you've been carrying around. You can start by being honest with yourself and being honest with El," Hudson said.

Xavi let out a long sigh. "Elyanna is my heart. I'm afraid she'll reject me when she finds out the truth. I am nothing without her. I'm conflicted, Hawk. And that pisses me off. But the thought of never seeing her again is worse. It makes me feral. You can't take her away from me." He scrubbed a hand down his face.

"Do you want to test me? Go ahead. Fuck around and find out. Her safety and happiness come first. You can't have it both ways, asshat. You commit to our family or let her go." Hawk's voice had a sharp edge to it.

"I can't walk away. I won't. Despite everything Luther did to me, I can't survive without El. I will be a dangerous man without her. As weird as it seems, it helped to stalk her."

"Is that why you were hiding in our house?" Hawk asked.

"No! I mean . . . yes. You kept her away from me for so long that I had to know where she was. I became obsessed. Skulking around in the shadows, watching her, sated that desire in me that wants to do unsavory things."

Hawk shook his head. "I don't know how to move forward with all of this but do not hurt my wife. I swear, Xavi, one teardrop and I will end you."

"I don't want to hurt El or Axel. Or you. But with El, it's a love-hate relationship. I hate the memories implanted in my head. I hate being obsessed with her. So I ignore her. But when she's gone, I want to kill everyone. Being around her quiets my inner demons."

"And so what? You're going to ignore her and scowl at her when you're in the same room? Use her body when it's convenient? No fucking way. I won't allow it. I'm sick of this shit. It's gone on too long as it is. Either be honest with her and we work this out together or say your goodbyes. And that goes for you, too, Roman."

Busted. Not that they could blame me for not sleeping through Xavi's shouting. And the discussion was just too juicy to not eavesdrop.

I sat up and grimaced. Xavier turned in his seat to look me over. "Holy shit, you're almost normal."

CHAPTER NINETEEN

Elyanna

The beauty of my gift was it slept when I slept. It was blessed silence unless the person next to me was broadcasting their thoughts.

I rubbed my eyes and then trained my focus on my best friend.

"Are you singing the *Macarena*?" I asked while bringing my seat to the upright position.

Becks jerked in her seat causing the truck to swerve. "Fuck!"

I braced my hand on the dashboard.

"Damn it, El! You scared the shit out of me." She righted the steering wheel.

I laughed. "Were you?"

"Was I what?"

"Singing the *Macarena* in your head?"

"I thought you didn't look into my thoughts."

"I wasn't trying to. You were broadcasting so freaking loudly. Why the *Macarena*? How do you even know the words? No one knows the words to that song anymore." I eyed my friend.

She looked sheepish. "It got stuck in my head."

I laughed again and started doing the dance. "Come on, then. Let's hear it. You sing, and I'll do the moves."

She doubled over, laughing.

"Eyes on the road." I reached over to steady the wheel.

"Ahh shit, I needed that laugh. Now I have to pee." She pulled over to the side of the road.

I opened the door, and a wall of hot, oppressive air punched me in the face. Welcome to the desert. Ignoring the heat, Becks and I did our business on the side of the road. After we were done, Becks stepped toward a cactus and called forth a stream of water.

I raised my eyebrows at her.

"Get over here." She ran her hands back and forth under the water. "Wash your hands, El. Geez."

Smiling I did as I was told. "You have the coolest gift."

She shrugged. "At least it's sanitary."

"Why are we carrying around tons of water bottles, when you can do this?" I asked as she somehow cut off the stream of water with a wave of her hand.

"I thought they were part of the negotiation package if we needed it," she replied, hopping into the passenger seat. "Plus, we had an unwanted companion for most of the journey."

"Correct on both counts," I said as I got behind the wheel. "So, what made you start singing the *Macarena*, aside from sheer boredom?"

Her face morphed from happy to depressed in two seconds. Shit.

"Sorry, you don't need to talk about it unless you want to," I told her.

"Just thinking about Xavi and me when we were kids," she said.

"Good memories, I hope."

She nodded.

"So tell me, why do we pronounce Xavier like X-zay-v-yer, and in short, we drop the X and pronounce it ah-vee?" I asked, trying to steer the conversation to a lighter subject.

She grinned. "My kids asked the same thing. When I was little, I had a speech impediment and couldn't pronounce x's or z's. I started calling him Xavi, and he liked it, so it stuck."

"Aww, that's sweet," I said.

"My brother was a sweet kid. Are you two back together? I've been wanting to ask since I saw you kiss, but between the dead people, my daughter being kidnapped, and then we had an escort. It was never the right time."

"True, true. It's been a shit storm." I sighed. "I want to say yes to your question. However, it's Xavi. Every time we take a step forward, he freaks out, and we slide back another five steps. So, I guess the best way to answer that question is . . . I hope so."

"How did it happen? Did you guys have make-up sex?"

My face heated. "Ummm . . ."

She chortled. "Oh my god, your face is so red! I guess that means yes."

I laughed with her.

"Why are you embarrassed? We've talked about your sex life before, El. Is it because he's my brother?"

"Yes," I admitted. "Seems weird."

"It is a little. Just spare me the details. I have a feeling my bro is into some kinky shit. For a while there, I thought he was into dudes."

That was news to me. I glanced out the window to hide the shock on my face. Is that why Xavi has been so weird around me lately? Great, first Bug, and now Xavi. I wasn't sure what to do with that information.

"Would it bother you if he was?" I asked.

"No. Not at all. I wish he'd be honest about his bisexuality and stop being so sketch." She said it without an ounce of hesitation. "Is that where we're going?"

Her gaze was fixed on the looming monstrosity in the distance. The last I'd heard about the exclusive "green" planned unit development was that they had been building a barricade around the perimeter. From the angle, it looked like a massive stadium.

The truck we'd stolen jerked, sputtered, and then came to a rolling stop. Becks and I looked at one another.

"You don't by chance know anything about cars, do you?" I asked.

"No. Not really, that was my brother's gig. I can change a flat tire if need be." She leaned over to peer at the dashboard. "Is there gas?"

The needle on the fuel tank gauge was in the middle. "Seems so."

"And no warning lights, either. Well, shit. Now what?"

"Guess, we're walking the rest of the way."

"This is going to suck, isn't it?" Becks' voice was soft.

I patted her arm reassuringly. "We got this."

"Right." She didn't sound convinced.

Nor was I. The distance wasn't the issue. We weren't far, just a dozen or so miles outside of the city. It wouldn't take long on foot if it was a straight shot. Plus, the stifling heat was a factor and then we'd have to get through the citizens that lingered outside the city. Every city had citizens who lived on the outskirts. They weren't rebels like we were. They opted to live near the city in hopes of receiving work, food, or healthcare. They lived in meager dwellings, scraping for food. Sometimes BHF had temporary jobs that would offer medicine, food, or room and board as compensation. It was a horrible way to live, but BHF controlled everything. Thus, rebels lived far from the cities and made a life for themselves. If the citizens were caught transacting business, growing food, or doing anything that would show independence, BHF guards would kill them on the spot. Citizens were desperate people, and they'd do anything to survive. I'd hoped we could drive straight to headquarters and bypass all the nonsense.

I tried starting the engine again. Nothing.

I gave a half-hearted shrug, and we gathered our things. "Check your weapons, Becks."

She pulled a pistol out of her backpack.

"You need to keep that handy. Put it in your holster," I told her.

"It's a bit cumbersome," she murmured.

"Becks." I waited for her to look me in the eye. "This is going to be dangerous. These people have been living on the streets for years. Many have lost loved ones. Many are starving. Many are angry. Prepare yourself for the worst."

"I know, El. We traveled across the country, remember," she said.

"There were more of you that time. Things haven't gotten better since then, Becks. It's gotten worse. And we're women. The depraved always think women are easier prey. And sometimes they're right. We have to be vigilant. Weapons on you at all times, and whatever you do, stay beside me, okay?"

She swallowed hard and nodded.

The desert heat was bloody awful. It was late afternoon. The sun beat down on us as we trudged along, searing our skin. Heat waves rose from the asphalt beneath our feet. To make matters worse, we were wearing full BHF gear—all black cargo pants, long sleeves, a bullet-proof vest—and my backpack weighed about twenty-five pounds. It felt as though I was being roasted alive. We left our helmets in the abandoned truck and decided to stay in our BHF gear as a precaution. This close to Federation City, a BHF patrol would likely shoot us down if we were wearing our civilian clothes. At least this way, they'd give us a chance to speak.

Per usual, in an unknown area, I cast out with my mind-bending powers. I hadn't picked up anything thus far, but it had become difficult to focus. Becks was afraid, and she broadcast fearful thoughts like she was speaking into a bullhorn.

"Hey. I'm sorry. I didn't mean to scare you," I told her.

"Don't be. I needed the reality check. It's been a piece of cake so far, and I took our circumstances for granted. I'm sorry. I feel . . . help-less. I'm afraid of what they'll do to Jules." Her voice hitched.

"They won't do anything to her, Becks. We'll get her back before they have a chance," I said.

"I wish I had spent more time around Dr. Carla. With my gift, I could've prevented all this. But that woman steered clear of me. Now I know why."

"Yeah, she did, come to think of it. I always thought she had a thing for Xavi, and that was the reason she kept her distance. I'm glad the bitch is dead," she said.

"So am I," I muttered.

"How much farther?" she asked.

"A few miles. We'll need to find somewhere to sleep before it gets dark."

"No problem, we should be able to find a posh five-star hotel . . . for free."

I laughed. "I'd be down for that. Maybe we can book spa treat-ments, too."

"Oh! I would kill for a massage!" she exclaimed.

"Yeah, sign me up. My firebug left me. I need a replacement."

"Firebug gives good massages, huh?" She wiggled her brows.

"The best. He has strong hands. Combine that with his gift, it was like getting a hot stone massage," I admitted.

"Damn, girl. You have the best life."

"I did. He doesn't love me anymore," I told her.

"He'll come around," she said quietly.

If he, Hudson, and Johnny are still alive. The painful thought lanced through my heart, causing me to lose my footing. Becks placed a hand on my elbow, steadying me.

"They're alive, El. They have to be." She draped an arm around me.

"They have to be," I repeated, leaning on her for emotional and physical support.

CHAPTER TWENTY

Elyanna

Becks and I walked on for a while, both of us lost in thought. It had been a few days since we left the farm, and although I hadn't received confirmation, in my heart I knew Hudson was still alive. I hung on to that glimmer of hope and put one foot in front of the other.

A hot breeze brushed my face, and with it came a foul stench. According to Samson, once the plague hit, BHF took over the green community and blocked the entrance. People from all walks of life came to Federation City in hopes of being let in. The reports stated that thousands of people came from all over the US and Mexico. They squatted around the perimeter, hoping for mercy. Many were denied and died waiting.

Becks wrinkled her nose. "What is that?"

"Humans. Body odor, excrement. Death. Brace yourself; it will get worse." I dug into my backpack, drew out two bandanas, and gave one to her.

"Just what we needed—more clothes." She fastened the cloth around her neck. "Well, you know what they say—at least it's a dry heat."

I laughed. "Dry heat my ass. I'm being cooked alive."

Becks and I chuckled at our situation, which lightened the mood.

We walked on for some time, chatting about everything and nothing. For a moment there, it seemed like we were just out for a stroll. And then the buzzing started. Bees flitted through my mind, buzzing in my ears.

Here we go.

"Becks, we've got company. Just stay calm. Say nothing until I get a read on whoever it is. If they want a favor from BHF, we're soldiers and can promise them the world. If they hate BHF, then we were kidnapped in Nebraska. We killed our kidnappers and took their things. I'll dig into their heads."

"Will you be able to, you know?" She swiped a finger across her throat. "With your mind."

"If I have to, yes. I reserve that tactic as a last resort to avoid detection. If I feel threatened, I won't hesitate. If the person is helpful, I'll gain as much information as I can. If the person is not helpful and non-threatening, I'll make them take a nap."

"You are the coolest chick ever." Her lips spread into a genuine smile.

I chuckled. Less than five minutes later, the buzzing got louder and was approaching faster than any human could walk or run. Bike maybe? And there seemed to be more than one of them.

"Let's take a break," I said loudly.

Becks and I paused alongside a building, using its shadow as shade. I leaned against the concrete wall and took out a bottle of water.

"I need to focus on my gift," I said to Becks with the bottle of water poised near my lips. "There's more than one of them."

She nodded and rolled her head from side to side.

I listened intently and picked up dialogue between two children. It sounded like I was listening to Jonah, Becks' youngest son, speak to one of the other kids at Royal Summit. They were scouting the perimeter of the city. How very interesting.

They hadn't seen us yet, so I led Becks a couple of blocks to our left, where we could surprise them.

We crouched behind a dumpster enclosure and waited. A few minutes later, two kids, about eight years old, rolled past us on scooters and stopped several feet away. They both had long, stringy hair and dirt-covered skin. Their T-shirts were threadbare and hung loosely on their emaciated frames. It was difficult to tell if they were boys or girls. I clamped onto their minds, searching for information. They were alone and on a scouting mission, searching for food. There were more of them. From their thoughts, I counted two others. All hiding in an abandoned building. They survived by staying hidden and scrounging for food. I was glad Becks and I had stuffed our backpacks with canned goods. I relayed the information to Becks, and then we stepped out from the shadows behind the kids.

"Hey," I said.

Both kids stumbled off their scooters and pulled sharpened sticks from their pockets.

"Stay back!" One kid pointed a stick at me. "I'll gut you."

The other kid said nothing; his hands shook as he waved his stick in front of him.

I held up my hands. "We're not going to hurt you."

"Of course not, bitch! We're not afraid of you. Give us your bags!"

"What did you just call me?" I placed my hands on my hips. "That is no way to speak to a lady."

"Yeah, what are you going to do about it?" You ain't my mom."

"No, I'm not your mother, because if I was, I'd swat your behind for using that kind of language." I stepped closer to them, with Becks right behind me.

The mouthy kid rushed me. I snagged the weapon out of his hands and tapped his tummy with the dull end. Then I turned toward the other kid and held out my other hand.

The kid looked at my hand and tilted his head.

"The stick. Give."

He laid it gently in my palm.

"Let's try this again. I'm El. This is Becks. Who might you be?"

"We might put you in a world of hurt." The mouthy kid raised his fists.

I tossed the sticks to the ground. Rule number one for using my gift was to never use it on children. Peeking at their thoughts sure.

Encouraging them to do my will was a no-no, even though sometimes the little shits deserved a nudge in the right direction.

I held fast to my self-imposed rules and turned to Becks. "You're better at this mom stuff. You try."

Becks tried to sweet-talk the kids, which got her nowhere. She gave them a stern gaze, put her mama bear persona on, and delivered a smackdown.

"You two, front and center. Now!" Becks pointed to the ground in front of her.

The children complied.

"Where are your parents?" she demanded.

"Gone."

"Where do you live?"

They pointed.

"By yourselves?" she asked.

They shook their heads. "Our sisters are waiting."

Becks blew out a breath and said gently, "Take us to them."

The children grasped her hands and chattered away while leading us to their hideout, which had been a gas station.

The kids, Max and Beth, were twelve-year-old twins. Their malnourished bodies made them appear much younger than they were. Their siblings, Shelly, ten, and Dana, nine, stayed home while they went looking for food. They were waiting for their mother, who had gotten a job with BHF. How long had it been? The answer they gave us was *moons* ago. A flurry of emotions washed over Becks' face. Even without looking into her mind, I knew what she was thinking and feeling. We were saving these kids, no matter the cost.

I'd suspected they lived in squalor considering the way of the world and our surroundings, but nothing I imagined came close to reality. The gas station, although secure, had no power or plumbing. And the summer heat didn't help. It was suffocating, and the fetid odor made my stomach lurch. Layers of dust and grime covered every surface. The windows were covered with sheets, which helped keep the sun out, but it wasn't enough. In these conditions, it was amazing they'd survived this long.

Their siblings huddled together on large sofa cushions, which were laid on the floor in a section they called the bedroom. The younger siblings wore ribbed tank tops that hung past their knees. They were so thin and frail. My heart ached, and from Becks' watery eyes, the overwhelming sadness hadn't escaped her either. Max and Beth stood protectively near their sisters and introduced us.

They were hesitant at first until we unpacked the canned goods we had in our bags. We gave them everything we had on us, which wasn't much. Between the four of them, the kids shared a can of peaches and two cans of soup. And that was enough to fill them up.

Becks and I offered what support we could. There was a water pump nearby where they would go to refill cups of water. It wasn't enough, but it wasn't like they could carry much, being malnourished as they were. We searched nearby and found containers to fill with water. We helped the kids clean up and made sure they had an excess supply to last until we returned.

A part of me felt a pang of guilt. Our lives at the Summit and lodge were idyllic in comparison to these conditions. We had fresh air, food, and water. Plus clean clothes, blankets, and beds. I missed my son and was eager to return home, but these four little ones couldn't grow up like this. I wouldn't allow it. How many more children lived in these conditions?

We visited with the children longer than anticipated. The children gravitated toward Becks and clung to her. From the thoughts flashing through their minds, Becks resembled their mother.

"You're not soldiers, huh?" Max asked me while Becks told a story to the girls.

"No, we're not. How can you tell?" I replied.

"You're nice. The real soldiers would have taken us to the city and made us slaves," he said.

"How do you know that?"

"Friends. Two were taken. One came out, and then he died. He was given lots of needles." He rubbed up and down his forearm.

"Are there a lot of children that live in the encampment?" I asked.

"Not anymore. Are you going inside?"

"Yes. Do you know a way in?"

He stared off into the distance, pondering my question. I peeked into his thoughts.

He imagined the front gate. Citizens surrounded the area, while armed guards picked random people from the crowd for work.

"Can you find my mom?" Max asked.

"I can try," I replied.

He hung his head.

"Max, if I am unable to find her, I promise I will get you and your sisters out of here and take you somewhere safe."

"You can't promise that."

"I can. And I'll tell you why." I stated. "My goddaughter was taken by BHF. I will find her, and when I do, I will leave the city behind and go home to my son. And if I don't find your mom, then you and your sisters will be coming home with me."

His lips quivered. "Okay. But wait until it's dark."

Max proceeded to tell me about his mother and what she looked like. The physical description was unnecessary. I gathered his mother's appearance through his memories of her. Her name was Cynthia, and like Becks, she had dark hair and brown eyes. That was where the similarity ended. Cynthia had been chosen to work for BHF, and she left Max to take care of his sisters.

Becks had her hands full with the younger girls, and I'd fallen asleep shortly after the sun went down.

"El." Max shook my shoulder. "It's time."

My eyes snapped open, and I scanned the room. The other children were on their makeshift beds, and Becks was nowhere in sight.

"Where's Becks?"

He shrugged his shoulders.

Using my gift, I cast out as far as I could and couldn't locate her anywhere. Unease clawed at my belly. I searched the interior of the gas station and found nothing. Not even a note. If she'd been taken, I would have heard her, and she'd never leave without me. Her backpack was still where she'd left it—next to mine. Slinging my bag over my shoulder, I rummaged through hers while rushing outside. It was so dark I couldn't make out footprints or anything. There was no other indication that she had gone.

I reached out with my gift. There were more people around; it was like being in a beehive.

"Where are the others?" I asked Max.

Before I had fallen asleep, Max had told me there were millions of citizens near the perimeter walls. I almost smiled at the exaggerated number. At most, I'd bet there were at least two hundred people living in the citizen encampment.

Max and his siblings stayed far away from the citizens because his mother had taught him to do so. Children were taken, and it was best to remain unseen. His friend, the one with the needle marks on his arm, had lived with his grandmother. She helped Max when she could. If Becks had been taken, she would be able to find out. Leaving his sleeping sisters behind, Max took me to her.

Abandoned cars, trash, and crumbled buildings made a maze of streets that would be easy to get lost in. Max was an excellent guide, he pointed out markers that would guide my way back to his gas station. Smart kid. Twenty minutes later, he knocked on the door of a tire-less city bus. A woman with gray hair stuck her head out the window. "Max? What are you doing roaming about at this hour? Get in here!"

CHAPTER TWENTY-ONE
Hudson

"If you listened to me in the first place, we would have been there by now," Roman said.

"First of all, you don't know shit. And second, I liked you better when you were injured and silent," Xavi retorted.

"All you needed to do was stay on the main road. But no, you decided to be fancy. And now we've lost hours," Rome complained.

"Hours? Really? Listen to you, drama king."

"You just can't admit when you're wrong, can you?"

"And you just can't shut the fuck up. We're nearly there. Quit whining like a bitch," Xavi snapped.

"Don't tell me to . . ."

"Knock it off!" I roared from the back seat. "You sound like an old married couple bickering about bullshit."

"He . . ." Xavi and Roman began.

"I said shut it! I've heard enough."

Blessed silence filled the car. Xavier had taken the backroads to avoid BHF stations, which hadn't been a bad idea. But Roman had a point as well. We lost a couple of hours. They'd been arguing for the last twenty minutes, or maybe longer. We'd been driving non-stop, each of us taking turns. I'd gotten some shut-eye and woke to hear them arguing.

The moon illuminated the desolate landscape as we crossed the city limits. The sun had gone down hours ago, and it was still hot as Hades.

We'd reach Federation City in less than an hour at this pace. I gazed out the window, wondering how Ax was doing. He was upset when I'd left him at the farm. His chubby face was streaked with tears. It fucking sucked having to leave him behind. He'd thrown a tantrum. His first. And probably not his last. If Xavi hadn't shown up with Julia, I wasn't sure how I would have managed to calm him down. The toddlers cried, held each other close, and eventually fell asleep. It was like they knew their mothers were gone and in some kind of trouble.

Johnny was adamant about coming with us to find his wife until Xavi had returned with Julia. He was reluctant, but he had three kids at the farm who needed their daddy. I was glad he'd decided to stay behind. It made me feel better to have someone there to care for Axel. If he were a couple of years older, I would have dragged my son with me to rescue his mother. Not that El needed rescuing. I had full confidence in her abilities to take care of herself and Becks. El was strong and a good fighter, and her gift was unparalleled; still, she wasn't indestructible. She couldn't take BHF down on her own. But my headstrong woman would try.

A BHF vehicle sat on the side of the road. I craned my neck as we passed.

"Stop." I tapped on the back of the driver's seat.

"You wanna check out that truck?" Xavi brought the truck to a rolling stop. "That's not wise, Hawk."

"Just pull over. That might be the girls' car." I opened the door while the car was still moving.

I jogged to the abandoned vehicle. The area was quiet; faded footprints marred the desert sand. I peered into the windows and gave Xavi and Roman the all-clear signal.

The car beeped when I opened the door. The unique smell of my wife lingered in the air. Faint, but she had been in here. Hours ago, though. I scanned the vehicle's interior. No blood, no sign of a struggle. Tension released its claws on my neck. There were a few empty water bottles. Nothing else. I turned the ignition. The lights flickered, and the engine didn't churn.

"Pop the hood." Xavi tapped on the door.

I did as he asked and then went to check out the back of the truck.

"They'd taken everything; there was no sign of struggle," I told Xavi as he poked around the engine.

"Aside from ambient heat, the engine is cool. It hadn't been turned on for several hours, and everything seems to be working," he replied.

"Maybe out of gas. Come on, we may be able to catch up with them."

We jogged back to the truck, where Roman was waiting behind the wheel.

I got into the front passenger seat and told the fire-starter what we found.

"If they approached the city on foot, it would take them a few hours, longer if they ran into trouble," Roman offered.

I ignored his statement. El could handle trouble. I clung to that thought as Xavi continued driving.

A mile or so from the main entrance, we found a place to hide the truck and got dressed in BHF gear. I glanced at Roman as he dressed. It had been three days since the crash, where the fire claimed nearly every inch of his skin. It appeared as though the crash had happened months ago, if not a year ago. The molted flesh had knitted, leaving behind angry, reddish skin, like a nasty sunburn. It had to hurt. He grimaced as he pulled up his trousers. He still needed time to heal. Who knew what would happen if he aggravated his skin further? The last thing we needed was for him to get some sort of infection.

I tore my gaze away, wondering what would be the best way to keep him out of the fray, and pulled out the notes I'd taken during my last conversation with Samson from Hillside. He had been to the head-quarters and had done his best to relay what I would be able to expect. It had been a radio conversation, so most of what I had was a guessti-mate of what I would have to do.

Roman and Xavi waited for me to give the orders.

"We're splitting up," I began and laid out a piece of paper reflecting a shoddy drawing of what Samson had told me. "This is a best-guess scenario, but this is all we have to go on. There are two known entrances, both heavily guarded. The uniforms will help. I'll take the side entrance where the citizens have surrounded the perimeter of Federation City. There will be hundreds of them, according to Samson." I pointed to the X indicating the southeast access point, then pointed to a larger X on my map. "The main entrance is here. Xavi, you go in with your gift; Roman, you will remain here with the truck. Elyanna has her gift; when she comes out of this place, she'll be using her gift and walking out of the main entrance. Food is scarce, so we each will carry a bag of food to barter with."

"Are you making me stand guard because you're not confident in my ability to fight?" Roman asked.

"I am confident in your fighting skills, my friend. But I'm not confident that you've completely healed. You're nearly there, Roman. A few more hours, and I suspect you'll be back to your old self."

"But," he started.

"No buts. Stay here. Keep an eye out for El and Becks. We stay in touch via the comms systems. Got it?"

His jaw ticked. The need to argue with me rolled over his face. Surprisingly, he managed to keep his trap shut. Xavier nodded, shook my hand, rolled his eyes at Roman, and turned on his heel. I cleared my throat. Xavi stopped, then about-faced, and extended his hand to the fire-starter.

Roman crossed his arms over his chest and glared.

"Stop being petty. Both of you. We're a team. Our women need us; stop acting like assholes," I snarled.

Roman's shoulders sagged a bit, and he shook Xavi's hand. "Good luck."

"See you soon." Xavier disappeared.

I watched the direction I assumed he went and didn't notice a thing. Not even the slightest disturbance in the dirt-covered asphalt.

"Damn, that's a helluva gift," I muttered

"I can still singe his ass," Roman snarled.

"I heard that," Xavi said, his body still invisible.

"Meant you to," Roman quipped.

"Can't believe you openly admitted to checking out my ass," Xavi's voice rang through the still night.

Roman's eyes narrowed, and he was about to open his mouth and deliver what I imagined to be a nasty retort. I shook my head.

"Don't. We're supposed to be in stealth mode," I told Roman. "You good?"

"Go." He nodded. "Find our girl. I'll be here, laying down cover fire."

I broke into a light jog, sticking to the shadows. The city was walled off by solid concrete, which rose fifty feet into the air and encircled the city's center, spanning the length and width of four, maybe five, football stadiums combined.

It'd been years since I was in a city this large, and I didn't miss it at all. All cities were alike in the post-plague world. Citizens surrounded the perimeter of Federation City, and they lived in horrific conditions. The desert heat had to make it unbearable. But people were desperate for basic needs like health care and food. BHF, for all their snobbishness, still needed worker bees, which was the only reason they hadn't killed them all. Someone needed to take out the trash and scrub the floors. The pompous fucks weren't going to do it themselves. From what Samson had said, the headquarters hired more citizens than any other BHF city. It was not only the largest, but it also housed most, if not all, gifted individuals. The thought of people with gifts whoring themselves out to BHF made me sick.

It didn't take long for me to find the access point I'd been looking for, and I hadn't seen a single soul. If my calculations were correct, sunrise was a few hours away, which meant citizens were fast asleep.

The southeast entrance was used primarily by the guards. Samson had said they used the hangar door to move their trucks and supplies, and it was the point of entry and exit when they went on patrol. I found the section I'd been looking for and waited in an alleyway two hundred yards from the entrance. I chanced on a connection with Elyanna, calling out to her with my mind. It was awkward when we first learned to communicate like this, but it worked. We'd been practicing communicating this way in the lodge and around Summit. We couldn't hold an entire conversation, but we were able to communicate simple things, like "I'm in the bedroom," "I'm on my way," or "I love you." I kept my mind open, shouting, basically hoping she'd respond. Nothing.

After thirty minutes or so of sitting around in the dark, a lone guard exited Federation City. He wore the usual black uniform all guards wore and had a large sack draped over his back. He scanned the area, then crept along the wall. I followed and watched him scurry into an alley.

Federation City started as a master-planned community located in the middle of the desert, bordering Arizona and California. While the community was being built, people had been buying up the land surrounding the massive community and started to build businesses to take advantage of the opportunity. Sure, the city had a long list of amenities to include retail; however, during the construction phases, the workers needed places to live and eat. Construction in this part of the country surged. Apartments, motels, restaurants, and shops were built alongside the walled-in community. As soon as the plague hit, businesses had been abandoned. As the plague progressed and people became frantic for health care and someplace safe to live, a new community was formed around the perimeter and became known as the citizen encampment.

I expected the squalid conditions and was prepared to deal with desperate individuals who would do anything for food and water. What bothered me most was that El and Becks had to pass through this. They wouldn't find friends in the citizen encampment unless, of course, El used her gift.

The guard went straight to what had been a strip mall, entered the building through a glass door, and wedged it open.

"Close that door!" someone hissed.

"Not a chance. It reeks in here. Let the fresh air in," the guard answered.

"Fine. Hurry this along. You have what I need."

I was about to spring out of my hiding spot when a scream cut through the night.

CHAPTER TWENTY-TWO

Becks

I leaned up against the wall, sitting cross-legged. Shelly laid her little head on one thigh, while her sister, Dana, laid her head on my other. I patted their too-thin backs as they dozed off. This was harder than I imagined. Sure, I knew we'd see some shit, but this cleaved my heart in two. These children were parentless. Their father had died of the plague, and their mother had disappeared, probably also dead. They had no other resources, and that awful truth would probably never change. Unless BHF was no longer in control.

There were so many emotions rolling through me. Anger with BHF. There weren't many children left in the world to begin with, and they couldn't be trusted with these little ones, who needed and deserved a proper upbringing.

My heart ached for my children. I missed them and worried for them every second of the day. And Johnny, too. Was he even alive? Of course, he was. He had to be. There was no other option. I couldn't imagine living this post-plague existence without him. Hawk would keep him safe. He always did. That was a heavy burden to place on a mortal man, but I was grasping for straws. We had no way to communicate with our community in Colorado. Do states even exist anymore? Probably not.

El must've missed her family, too. She didn't need to be here with me in this filthy gas station, having to witness these atrocities. She'd seen it all, traveling alone for so many years and then dealing with Luther, but having to do this shit over and over again had to suck. Or maybe she had thicker skin than me. That sounded about right. I couldn't stomach another day of this.

We'd come back for these four little ones after finding Julia; that was a guarantee. I knew El; she wouldn't leave these kids behind. If anything, she'd try her damnedest to find their mother. I was certain she had gathered information from Max. They'd spent most of the time sitting on the opposite side of the room, speaking in hushed whispers. Whatever they discussed wasn't meant for all ears. I respected that.

El had fallen asleep, and I wanted to give her more time to rest. She was a machine and hadn't slept much, even when I drove. Neither did I. We were both too keyed up.

I gently eased Shelly off my lap and did the same with Dana. I'd been sitting in the same position for hours and needed some air. Doing my best to remain quiet, I slowly stood and tiptoed to the open door to stretch my legs.

The sun had gone down hours ago, and it was still a hundred degrees. Why anyone would want to live here was insane.

I stretched my hands overhead and then moved off to the side of the gas station where the latrines were. There were two bathrooms, one for men and one for women, neither of which worked. The plumbing had been clogged for some time and there was no running water.

My gift with water wasn't useful for fighting enemies, but I could ensure the children had clean running water and a toilet that worked. It wasn't something I'd reveal, so I'd waited for them to fall asleep.

I sensed the water, which was deep underground, and had called it forward shortly after we arrived. I hadn't used the strength of my gift all in one go as that would have surely attracted attention. Water running through stagnant pipes was sure to bubble and groan as it came to the surface.

Keeping the door slightly ajar for light, I went into one bathroom and called forth my gift, filling the pipes with water, then turned on the faucet. Murky water sputtered and I allowed it to flow until the water ran clear. I filled the toilet tank with water, made sure it flushed, then moved on to the next bathroom and did the same thing.

Both bathrooms needed a good cleaning and the electrical needed to be looked at, but at least the kids would have a working bathroom until we could find them a better home.

"Becks?" a little voice called from the other side of the door.

"Hi, I didn't mean to wake you," I said to Shelly. "I fixed the bathrooms. You now have running water."

"Oh. Wow. How did you do that?"

"I'm a plumber," I lied. *A plumber? Really?*

"Can I try?"

"Of course." I moved off to the side and let the little girl in. "There's no light, so keep the door slightly open. I'll be right here, okay?"

"I'll be fast," the little girl said.

A shuffling noise had me glancing over my shoulder, only to be greeted with darkness.

Cold water splashed over my face. It was refreshing.

"You need a bath," a gruff male voice said. "You stink."

My body was doused with water. My gift welcomed the cool liquid like a loving embrace. I arched my back and sighed.

"What are you?" the sharp voice asked.

I blinked away the water droplets that had collected on my lashes. A BHF guard pointed a fire hose at me, with the spray on full blast.

I was supposed to be cowering from the onslaught of water. Ooops. I slumped, dropping to the concrete beneath my feet.

Where was I? The last thing I remembered was talking to Shelly outside of the bathroom and then darkness. I'd been taken?! Oh shit. El? Shelly? The rest of the kids?

Breathe, Becks. I peered at the guard. He caught my gaze, turned off the water, and then threw something at me. "Use soap. The shower head works," he ordered.

A bar of soap struck my shoulder. I realized then that I'd been stripped down to my underwear. Assholes. As much as I hated being ordered around, being stinky was the worst. I lathered my skin and hair, turned on the shower, and rinsed off the suds.

The tall man stared at me, his tattooed arms crossing his chest. The name tag on his uniform read *Crosby*. He had the stature of a professional football player, a shiny bald head, and a thick red beard. His eyes roved my body appraisingly. It was flattering. I squashed that thought and flung the soap back at him, hitting him in the face.

"Oww. That was mean." He grimaced. "Towels are here, and a change of clothes. Hurry, we need to move."

I stepped in the direction of where he'd indicated and glanced around, relieved I didn't have any gawkers. My hands shook as I toweled off. I was so out of my element. *Think of Julia, Becks. Find her and return home.*

Crosby had the decency to turn his back while I changed into clean, dry underwear and slipped on the standard guard uniform.

"Time to go," he said as I was lacing my boots.

I narrowed my gaze at him, thinking through my options. I wasn't a fighter like El, and I had no idea how to use my gift for violent purposes. But perhaps I could run? Where, Becks? Crosby took the decision away from me by pointing a gun at my face.

"Don't make me use this," he said.

I followed his orders, unsure of what to say or do. If El were here, this asshole would be eating out of her palm. On the other side of the shower area was a hallway lined with lockers. The opposite wall was lined with a weapons cage. Good to know. The room beyond that was an open space with a dozen tables and chairs. Save for a handful of guards drinking coffee, it was empty. We passed countless closed doors with name placards on them, which meant nothing to me. We continued walking, making so many twists and turns that I lost track of directions.

"Where are you taking me?" I asked.

"Don't worry about it; we'll be there soon enough." He opened another door and ushered me inside. The room resembled a receiving area. A man stood behind a counter, a glass separating him from me and the guard, the only occupants in the room. He slid open a window and addressed Crosby.

"Where are you taking her?" another guard asked my escort.

"The Premiere Loop," he replied.

The other guard looked me over and said, "I'll call it in." A buzzer sounded, and we exited through double doors, revealing Federation City.

My mouth hung open. The sun hadn't risen, so I'd assumed only a few hours had passed since I was taken from the gas station. The glass roof began to close, accompanied by a humming noise that filled the night.

"Cooling system. They close the roof a couple hours before sunlight to keep it cool in here," the guard said. "Stop gaping and pick up the pace."

I was about to deliver a nasty retort, but the scenery was too hard to ignore. As far as the eye could see, there were box-like building structures of varying sizes, with vines crawling the walls. Gray pavers lined the streets, and potted plants and flowers were everywhere. It was pretty, clean, and relatively quiet.

Crosby continued leading me through the city for some time until we came to three circular buildings. He waved his hand, motioning for me to enter the building through a sliding glass door, and led me down a corridor and into an elevator.

"Stop staring; it's weird." I stood against the wall farthest from the guard.

"You're beautiful."

I gave him a scathing look over my shoulder. "I'm married."

"Is he still alive?"

"Of course. Why wouldn't he be?" I asked, offended by his question.

He shrugged. "Guess I shouldn't feel bad for doing this then."

"Doing what?"

The elevator door opened, and two burly men dressed in scrubs gripped my arms. I kicked and punched the two men, which did nothing.

"Just found this one in the citizens area posing as a guard," the guard told a woman who appeared in the hallway holding a clipboard.

Her eyes widened. "Sedate her!" the woman ordered.

"Wait. What is this place?" I shouted at the guard.

"Where you're meant to be gifted, lady," he replied as the orderlies hauled me away, kicking and screaming.

CHAPTER TWENTY-THREE

Elyanna

As soon as the gray-haired woman stuck her head out of the bus window, I used my gift. Her thoughts were chaotic. Images flitted through her mind in rapid succession. It was like watching a PowerPoint presentation on speed.

"Max, what did I tell you about wandering around late at night?" she scolded the kid.

"Sorry, Mrs. Brown," Max replied.

"Here, have some tea, and then go home." Mrs. Brown motioned for us to sit.

The first three rows of the bus were intact. The seats in the middle of the bus had been replaced with a table and a couple of boxes which were being used as shelves. A plastic see-through shower curtain sectioned off the rear of the bus.

"Tea?" Mrs. Brown fired up a two-burner propane stove and began boiling some water, while Max stayed close by my side.

"No tea for me, thank you. I'm looking for someone. Max said you might be able to help," I said.

"You refuse my hospitality and ask for help?" The woman scowled. "Rude."

Something pinched the back of my arm. I flinched.

"Sorry, El. I have to. It's my job. And my sisters come first," Max whispered.

"You did good, boy. Take your payment and get," Mrs. Brown's voice sounded muffled.

I tried to access my gift, but the ground hit me in the face.

A scream woke me. My body felt sluggish, and my mind was muddled. The damn kid had drugged me and probably did the same to Becks. In truth, I wasn't even mad at him. I would have done the same for my sister.

The woman screamed again. I wobbled as I stood, and braced a hand on the wall while I took in the dimly lit, ten by ten space. There was another cot across from the one I was seated on. Chipped yellowish paint coated the walls, and there was a small window on the door. I tried the door, which was locked. Fuckers put me in a cell.

There was a scuffle outside. I reached out with my gift and found a woman in despair. Her thoughts were jumbled but it was obvious she'd been hurt.

Shh . . . sleep now, I pushed the thought into her mind and withdrew.

Elyanna! Hudson's voice screamed in my head.

Hudson? I fell to my knees with relief. *You're alive.*

I'm here, babe. Are you hurt? Where are you?

A flurry of thoughts came from my husband. I couldn't understand him, but knowing he was near calmed my nerves.

I focused my thoughts and did my best to assure Hudson that I was okay. His mind quieted, and then he said to hold on.

The doorknob to my cell jiggled. I laid down on the cot with my back to the door. I focused on the guard entering the room, except it wasn't a guard.

"Time to go," the male voice said. I latched onto his thoughts and didn't like what I found. He was a citizen. He and a few of the leaders in the community were offering women to BHF as human chattels. The women weren't being given to the guards to work for BHF; they were being given to the guards to use for personal pleasure. It was the post-plague sex trade.

The citizen held a gun to my back while he led me to meet a

BHF guard. I rifled through his mind, searching for clues that might shed some light on what had happened to Becks or Cynthia, Max's mom. There was nothing about Becks, but Max's mom was one of the first women they traded to the BHF guards. Cynthia had given her body willingly, and in exchange, the leader of the citizens promised to provide for her four children. Their leader was Mrs. Brown.

Shit.

The citizen led me down a corridor to an alleyway. We continued our promenade through the citizen encampment until we came to a strip mall.

El! I see you. Hudson shouted in my mind. A flash of movement to my right caught my eye.

Stay hidden, I told him.

The citizen walked me through a door, where a BHF guard waited.

"About time," the guard said. "Wow. This one is hot. Where'd you find her?"

"She came to us," the citizen told him.

"Here's your payment." The guard kicked a large sack that had been sitting on the floor.

"You mean our first payment. We expect another drop-off in a week," the citizen said.

"A deal is a deal. I won't forget. This one will be well worth it." The guard leered at me.

The citizen took the bag and exited, leaving me with the guard.

Hudson, the citizen is coming out. Take him out for me, will you? I said telepathically.

Anything for you, baby. You good in there?

Yes, I'll wait for you.

I disconnected my gift from Hudson and focused on the guard in front of me. I searched the guard's mind, gathering information about the city. He licked his lips and began unbuckling his pants.

"My husband is going to kill you." I stepped to my right, circling him. He mirrored my movements, putting his back to the door.

"I don't see a husband here," the guard leered.

Just as he dropped his pants, Hudson walked through the door, took two long strides, and snapped his neck. My husband stepped over the dead guard and closed the distance between us.

The pit in my belly that had formed when I'd watched the helicopter drop from the sky filled with love, relief, and desire at the sight of him.

Our bodies collided, and our lips fused together. We were naked in minutes, our clothes thrown haphazardly on the dirty floor.

Hudson hoisted me into his arms and propped me on a counter. I spread my legs wide, desperate to feel him inside me. He plunged into my wet center. I hung onto his broad shoulders, gouging my nails into his flesh.

He held a firm grip on my hips. His rough thrusts had me crying out his name.

"I thought you were dead," I said against his lips.

"I'm here, El."

"Don't ever leave me, Hudson." I locked my ankles behind his back, melding our bodies together.

"Never," he promised.

My breathing came in rough, shallow pants. Our foreheads pressed together. I gazed into his emerald eyes as my climax burst through me. Hudson's hips jerked wildly as he chased his own release. A flood of warmth filled my depths as he came with an unrestrained growl.

I held onto him, burrowing my face into the crook of his neck for a long moment, savoring the thrum of his pulse and the warmth of his skin.

"Hey." Hudson drew away to look at my face. "What's wrong, peaches? Why are you crying?"

"I thought you were dead," I stammered.

He swiped away my tears with the pad of his thumb. "Shh, don't cry. I'm here."

"I can't, Hudson. I could before, but I can't anymore." The waterworks were on full blast.

Hudson kissed each eye. "Can't what, babe?"

"I can't live this crazy life without you. Won't."

He crushed me to his chest. "Nothing in this fucked-up world would keep me away from you."

I sobbed into his chest, comforted by his words, even though it was a promise I couldn't hold him to.

CHAPTER TWENTY-FOUR

Roman

I*'ve got eyes on El,* Hawk stated over the radio.

No Becks.

Shit. Becks and El had gotten separated. I shifted from foot to foot, clenching and unclenching my hands.

I was ninety-five percent healed. That's what I kept telling myself. My dry skin itched. I swung my arms back and forth and bent my legs, wincing as my skin cracked with each movement. My range of motion was good which meant I could tolerate the discomfort. I glanced around the area, ensuring I was alone, and called on my gift. My fire pooled in my hands, and the warmth felt good. I was back.

Waiting drove me mad. I could leave. But where would I go? Follow the direction Hudson took, or Xavi? Neither option was good.

I sat on the hood of the truck. A sharp whistle whizzed past me. A dart landed on the ground to my left. I dove and hid behind the truck. Bullets peppered the vehicle. Shit.

Taking fire!

I shouted into the comms device and aimed my weapon in the direction of where the bullets had come from. The shots kept coming. I retaliated, firing blindly. The truck was Swiss cheese, glass was shattered, and the tires were shot out.

The gunfire ceased. I remained hidden and peered over the hood. Three men, dressed in threadbare clothes, approached, weapons out. I fired my weapon, taking them out. A bullet lodged into the truck, scantly missing my head. I ran for cover. Bullets followed every step. I swerved, then dove behind a dumpster.

Shots were coming at me from all directions. I'd have to unleash my gift; there was no other option. I called on my fire. Groans and thuds had me peering over the dumpster. One by one, my assailants fell to their deaths; an invisible force sliced their necks and shot them in the head.

A second later, cold metal was pressed against my temple.

"Knock it off, Xavi." I brushed the invisible metal away.

He appeared in front of me. "I think you meant to say, thank you for saving your ass."

I gave him a dry look. "I had it under control."

"Sure you did." He strolled over to the prone bodies and shot them in the head. "Just making sure."

I got a closer look at the bodies and scratched my head. "Citizens and BHF guards. Are they working together now?"

"Nah. I'm guessing the citizens saw you skulking around in the dark and opened fire. BHF heard the ruckus, found you, and decided to join the fray," Xavi answered.

I shrugged. Easy guess. "Did you find anything interesting?"

He shook his head. "No sign of El or Becks. I got a good look at the guard area. The place is massive and crowded. I'm guessing they all live in one section. I was tailing a couple of guards, gathering information, when I got Hawk's report. I followed them and then got your cry for help. You're welcome."

He bowed.

"Fuck you. It wasn't a cry for help. I was letting you and Hawk know, so you wouldn't return to the same spot."

"Sure. Whatever you need to tell yourself to make you feel better. It's okay to admit that you need help sometimes. It's part of recovery. From you know . . . melting your skin off."

"Christ, you're an asshole."

"Takes one to know one." He strolled away like he didn't have a care in the world. "You coming?"

"Where? Hawk found El. They should be back."

"To find my sister, selfish prick."

"I . . . I didn't mean it like that. Of course, we'll go after Becks. El might have some important information. We should wait."

"Fine. You can wait here. I'll go rescue my sister." He took two steps away from me and then dropped to the ground.

I rushed to his fallen body and dragged him to the side. A dart stuck out of his chest. I whipped around and shot a guard sneaking up behind me. Something struck my thigh. Ahhh shit. Footsteps approached. A dozen guards were coming toward me. I tilted my head and realized the dart hadn't pierced my skin. I palmed the granola bar Chef had loaded us up with before we left. More guards came into view. There were too many to take out unless I wanted to burn down the entire encampment. I pretended I'd been hit, listed to the side, and murmured into the mic.

The guards dragged my body and Xavi's into Federation City. Of course, the fuckers didn't carry me or use a stretcher. It was excruciating. My raw skin felt like it was being raked over a grater as we crossed the asphalt into the gates.

"Two of them? Are there more?" someone asked.

"Not out there," another guard answered.

"Are they gifted?" the first voice asked.

"Doubt it. They used weapons against us. They'd taken out several guards using guns. If they had gifts, they would have used them."

"Alright, take them into the holding cells. We'll question them in the morning when they wake."

We were carted off into the holding area, which was decent, to be fair. Clean tiled floors, two single-sized beds topped with a fluffy pillow, and a wool blanket. A wall separated a sink and toilet. The guards placed me and Xavier in the same room. Big mistake. It took four of them to bring us in, and one drew the short straw and had to lock up. As soon as the other three left, I pounced and put him in a sleeper hold.

Depending on what they'd given Xavi, it would take hours for him to wake up. We didn't have that much time. They'd come looking for the missing guard before he woke.

I searched the guard's pockets and found smelling salts. I pocketed his other valuables: a gun, extra ammo, and a radio. I'd left my comms device on the ground, not wanting them to connect me to El and Hawk. Once done with my pilfering, I trussed up the guard with his handcuffs, used the facilities, and checked out my injuries. The skin that had been healing was now aggravated and seeping blood from being dragged across the pavement, but that was the extent of it. No time to baby my wounds.

Xavi was still out. I watched the aggravating man for a beat, reluctant to wake him. He was such a wise ass. Annoying as fuck. And yet, he did save my bacon. If he hadn't shown up when he did, I would have annihilated the city with my fire or ended up dead. I placed the bottle of smelling salts under his nose. Xavi woke up swinging and clocked me with a right hook. I grasped his hands and pushed him down on the bed.

"Xavier! It's me. Roman. Calm down; you're safe-ish," I said.

"Roman? Get off me!" He shoved me, and I stood. "Where are we?"

"In a jail cell." I motioned toward the guard with my hand.

"So, why are we sitting here?"

"I was waiting for you to wake up. Asshole. I could have left you behind."

"Am I supposed to thank you?" he snarked.

I ignored the jibe and opened the door. I peeked outside and said, "Clear."

"He's still alive." Xavi kicked the guard's foot.

"So? He's handcuffed and won't be able to get out."

"Not good enough." Xavier leaned over and twisted the guy's neck.

My mouth hung open. He shrugged, then pushed past me. "You coming, or are you going to stand there catching flies with your trap hanging open?"

I glared at him, thinking of creative ways to shut his smart mouth. *Punch to the face or dick down his throat? Whoa! Where the hell did that come from Roman?* I shook my head dislodging the lewd thought from my brain.

He stopped at the corner. "Wait here."

He went invisible. I waited. Nothing happened. I peered around the corner; no one was there. I stepped forward. A guard's body was flung into the corridor. He got up and raised his weapon. I tackled the guard from behind and knocked him out. Another body dropped beside me, blood dripping from his temple. Xavier reappeared.

"Do you have something against killing people?"

I gave him a dry look, then snapped the guard's neck.

"Better. Let's move them into that room." He dragged a fallen guard. "Listen, I can use my gift to conceal both of us, but that takes a lot of energy from me, and it won't last long. We should be able to get through this place quickly and undetected. I'm hoping we don't have to kill every guard we come across, but they will soon realize their prisoners are missing. I don't want to leave anything to chance."

I nodded, picked up the other guard, and followed him. The room we'd placed the guards in was a storage closet. We took their weapons and kept moving. We came upon a half-dozen guards on our way to the main entrance that would lead to the city. We gathered as much information as we could and killed them all.

It was brutal, and I liked it. Xavier and I moved in sync. We developed a natural rhythm, as though we'd worked side-by-side for years. He lunged, and I ducked. He stabbed, and I punched.

"This is fun." Xavi slammed his fist into a guard's gut. The guy doubled over, and I stabbed my dagger through his neck.

"You shouldn't sound so happy about killing people," I muttered.

"Like you're not having a good time," he chided.

A chuckle escaped me even though I'd just stabbed a guy to death.

"This way," Xavier said, jogging down a long corridor.

"How do you know your way around?" I asked.

"I came through here before I saved your ass."

"I saved your ass, too. We're even," I huffed.

"Being in love means not keeping score," he said, his pretty blue eyes searching my face.

Pretty blue eyes? What is wrong with me?

"Oh, we're in love now? I don't remember us being in like," I retorted.

Just as we came to a corner, his hand slammed against my chest and pushed me against a wall. He held up four fingers.

Fuck.

Xavi used his gift and disappeared. I rounded the corner as two men were being knocked into the wall by an invisible force. They flailed helplessly while Xavi's laughter rang through the air. The man was in his element.

I slammed my fist into someone's face, knocking him out cold. Another man swung his knife. I stepped back as the blade sliced through my T-shirt. I drop-kicked the guard. He stumbled to the ground and lost his hold on his knife, which sailed through the air and landed in his buddy's chest. At least that one wasn't on me. I pulled out the weapon and plunged it into his throat.

Once again, we dragged dead bodies into a vacant room. We were leaving trails of blood everywhere. We had to get out of this place quickly.

"You look like shit," Xavier quipped.

My shirt was torn, and I was covered in blood. I grimaced. Everything ached, especially my back.

"You say the sweetest things," I snarked.

"What can I say? I'm a true romantic. We need to find you something else to wear." He pointed at my shirt. "That will attract too much attention."

We both glanced at the dead guards. I wasn't above wearing a dead man's clothes, except they were just as bloody. We exited the room and tried every door until we came down a hallway, which Xavier had said was the barracks.

"Risk running around the main part of the city like this or risk going through the barracks? Or I can use my gift, but . . . we'd have to hold hands," he mocked.

"Pass on hand holding. Let's try a couple of doors."

I moved past him, stopping at every door. Listening before knocking.

"Psst." My gaze flicked toward the sound.

Xavi was on the other end of the hallway, waving at me.

I ground my teeth. The ass could have just started with that. I caught up to him and entered a room that slept two. Split the room in half, and they mirrored each other. There were duplicates of everything—two beds, nightstands, drawers, lamps—even the closet space was identical.

We rummaged through the closet and drawers until I found a shirt that fit.

Tugging my T-shirt off my back made me grind my teeth. I could feel the skin that had been healing splitting apart.

Xavier took in a sharp breath. "That must be painful. Did Jeff give you anything?"

"Yeah," I reached into my pocket at pulled out the ointment. In front of a mirror, I glanced at my back and winced. Yep, I'd definitely re-injured my skin. I squirted some medicine on my fingers and stretched as far as I could.

"Give me that." Xavier snagged the tube from my hand. "Turn around; you're making it worse."

I did as instructed. Xavi's hands were warm and surprisingly gentle as he spread the ointment over my wounds. He was being careful, and for once, he hadn't uttered a single smart-assed comment. My stomach felt weird and fluttery. I frowned at my reflection and noticed Xavi's face. There was something in his gaze. Concern. Admiration. He moved in front of me and began applying more medication to my shoulders. Then my arms. Then my chest.

The conversation between him and Hawk replayed in my head. If not mistaken, Xavier was a closet bisexual. A spark of something strange flared inside me. I'd always been attracted to Xavi. Even before I'd moved in with El and Hawk. He was a wise ass and a total asshole to El, but he had a swagger to him that drew me in.

My breathing became shallow as Xavi's heated gaze followed his hands as they traveled down my torso. Blood rushed to my dick, and I bit the inside of my cheek praying he didn't notice.

Xavi's fingers stopped at the waistband of my pants. "Are you injured . . . everywhere?" His eyes met mine.

I shook my head. My voice caught in my throat.

A commotion down the hall had us separating and I shrugged on a T-shirt. With the trail of bodies and blood we left behind, it was only a matter of time before we'd get caught. I shoved my bloodied garments under the bed and then we peeked out the door before exiting.

"What's all the fuss?" Xavi asked a guard.

"There's blood everywhere. Search the other rooms," the guard said.

I opened the door that had the four dead guards. "Nothing here. Check down the hall." The guards passed us. Once they were out of sight, we went in the other direction.

Xavi led me through a door that opened into the Federation City. I stopped and gaped.

"Hey." He nudged me forward. "No time."

I followed him as he walked briskly through the center like he owned the place. He made a sharp turn and headed straight toward a building.

"Where are you going?" I asked.

"I overheard the guards say this area was rarely used. We can lay low until . . ." He stopped short.

"Mom?"

A short woman with gray hair tripped over her own feet. Xavier caught the woman he had called mother before she hit the ground.

CHAPTER TWENTY-FIVE

Hudson

"I love you, Elyanna." I placed a light kiss on her lips, then her nose, then her forehead. "But we need to get moving."

She nodded.

As much as I hated to withdraw from her, I pulled out, mourning the absence of her warmth. I kissed her shoulder, then began picking up our clothes from the floor, shaking them out before handing her hers.

It took me two minutes to get my clothes on, and then I helped El get dressed. She hopped off the counter and leaned on me as she slid one leg into her panties, then the other. I kissed the floral pattern tattoo on her thigh before she shimmied into her jeans. Once she was fully clothed, I kneeled before her and rested my head against her belly. She gently raked her finger through my hair, eliciting a soft moan from me.

I love you so much.

"I love you, too," she whispered.

I smiled against her stomach, knowing she was connected with me.

"I wish we had more time for a proper reunion." Her voice was wistful.

"We don't?" I stood, crushing her to my chest.

She smiled at me and tip-toed to kiss my chin. "Later. First, we need to rescue Julia and Becks."

"Julia is at the farm," I told her.

She blinked at me in surprise.

I told her about Xavi returning to the farm after killing Dr. Carla.

"Thank God. We were at a BHF station when we heard about Dr. Carla; they didn't know who had killed her or who had taken Julia, so we decided to come here since we were a few hours away."

"Smart move. What happened to Becks?"

She'd told me about the four kids they'd run into and how the kid had taken her to an older woman who was supposed to have helped her. The kid stuck a needle into her arm, and she woke up in a cell.

"Anything from the citizen I just killed, or that guy?" I tipped my head at the guard dead on the floor.

"Nothing on Becks. The older woman, Mrs. Brown, Max had called her; I couldn't get anything from her either. Her thoughts were scattered. I'm guessing early dementia. The only thing I know for sure is that I was supposed to be handed over to BHF to be their sex slave. They take women to their barracks, and she's passed around for their pleasure. There are a lot of men in there and not many women. I'm guessing Cynthia, Max's mother, is a sex worker. We'll find her there."

My jaw clenched. The thought of the guards using her as a sex slave angered me to the point where my gift was bubbling at the surface.

"Hudson? Calm, love. I'm here." She stroked my arms. "Rein in your gift."

The counters were rumbling, and the debris on the floor levitated. I clamped down on my gift.

"Let's not separate from one another again," I told her, then winced.

Taking fire, Roman's sharp voice pierced the comms device in my ear.

"Shit. Roman is in trouble."

We exited the store and hustled to the other side of the citizen territory, stopping only once to gather the bag the guard had given the citizen as payment for El. The encampment surrounding Federation City was vast. By the time we made it back to where I'd instructed

Roman to stay, he was gone, and the truck was riddled with bullet holes.

I tried both Xavier and Roman, but neither answered.

A flash of worry crossed over El's features.

"Don't worry. We'll find them."

She nodded. "Yes. Yes, we will."

"We still have a few hours before sunlight. I imagine this area will be swarming with BHF come morning."

"That would be correct. According to the guard, he had planned to keep me to himself since his shift started in the afternoon."

"Babe, you may want to leave out some of the details," I told her.

She squeezed my arm and continued.

"They head out in shifts. The first one is at sunrise. Some look for workers among the citizens. They open the main entrance and have people line up and choose at random. And then other guards patrol the area. Apparently, that is a shit job because those guards deal with the rebels encroaching on their territory. They do this like clockwork. And of course, there are guards in Federation City and some place called The Loop. The guard didn't know much about it, which was weird. The only thing I could tell from his thoughts was that only select guards got that gig. It was considered a promotion even though, according to rumors, there aren't many altercations going on in there."

"If you were meant to be a sex worker, what did they do with Becks?" I asked.

"I don't know. And that scares me. We have the sack of goodies. I can find my way back to Mrs. Brown's place. I may not be able to use my gift on her, though."

"It's okay; I have ways of making people talk." I winked.

El led the way to Mrs. Brown's bus. We paused behind it, sticking to the shadows. El looked off into the distance. I scanned the area for threats while she used her gift. A moment later, she tilted her head and furrowed her brow.

She tipped her chin and led me away from the bus, down a lane sectioned off with boxes, tents, shopping carts, and other random items. We came upon an RV. El held up two fingers. I nodded. A moment later, two men exited the RV. They both placed their weapons on the ground and held their hands above their heads.

Her gift was the coolest. I patted down both men and removed their weapons. I then guided them back into the RV and cuffed them together.

El waited outside for me with the sack we'd taken from the guard. My sweet little wife was trying to lift it when I returned to her side.

"Here, sweetheart, let me do the heavy lifting."

She giggled. "By all means, muscle man."

El and I entered the RV to find both men docile, like little lambs.

"Tell us everything you know about the trade agreements between your encampment and BHF," El asked out loud.

Both men were co-leaders of the citizenship encampment. Mrs. Brown, being the eldest, made most of the decisions, while these men were the muscle. With El's gift, they confessed their sins. They had two arrangements with BHF guards. One was with the southeast gate, where El had been taken. The other arrangement was between the citizens and the main gate, where men and women were offered up or sold for experimentation. That was where they'd sent Becks.

El shifted uncomfortably in her seat. The news was not good. If they'd conducted experiments on Becks, they'd learn about her gifts, and that meant rescuing her had become much harder. If I had to guess, I'd bet she'd been taken to the elusive Loop.

The easiest route would be to take the southeast entrance, but Becks had been taken through the main gate earlier that evening. And there was a possibility she'd still be in a holding cell. It was risky. According to our informants, come sunrise, there would be triple the number of patrols roaming the citizen encampment. Inside, we'd be going through the most populated section of the guard sector, where the soldiers lived. It wasn't ideal, but we were running out of time.

El had decided to leave the citizens alive for now. She wiped any traces of our presence from their minds and made them think they'd gotten the supplies from the guards as planned.

We hurried back to the main gate and knocked on a door they'd said would be answered by guards who were in on their trade agreement. El used her gift on the guard, who answered the door. He welcomed us into his domain like a tour guide, giving us directions and highlighting places to avoid.

El took point, using her gift on everyone we passed. The guard sector was stationed along the entire perimeter of Federation City. The sector was heavily populated, which made sense. The area was a combination of training areas, workout facilities, a rec center, barracks, a cafeteria, meeting rooms, and an armory. From what I could tell, unless the guards were out patrolling, they weren't allowed beyond the sector. And that meant there were guards everywhere. In the initial twenty minutes of going through the place, we passed dozens of guards, all of whom let us pass. With the tour guide's directions, we found the holding area, which was empty. There was no sign of Becks, Xavi, or Roman. We continued moving through the guard sector. Guards spoke animatedly down one hallway, and men began moving through with a determined focus. It was a frenzy. My spidey senses were on full alert and I was concerned for my wife. She'd been using her gift for a while now, yet she pushed on as we continued to the exit. She was forcing herself. It was too much. She would need a break soon.

Out of nowhere, at least fifty guards ran by us as though we weren't even there. After they passed, El tugged on my hand and led me into a storage closet.

She leaned on my chest. "Hudson. I . . . I can't go on."

Even in the dim light, I could see that her skin was pale and she was trembling.

"Talk to me, babe, what's wrong?"

"I can't use my gift. There are just too many. It's overwhelming. They're frantic. Something happened. There are dead guards, and they're trying to find the culprit."

Dead guards meant Xavier had gotten hold of them. I could only hope he and Roman were okay. For now, my focus was on El.

I held her close. "It's okay, babe. The exit is close. Close your gift, and I'll lead us out of here, okay?"

She regarded me with watery eyes and nodded. Shit. We'd gone through a lot dealing with Luther; we lived in the woods for days, and she had never looked so fragile. I was worried, but the only way through was to move forward.

"Do you have a balaclava on you?" I asked.

She drew the black fabric out of her pocket and slipped on the mask.

"Stay on my heels. Hand here. Move with me." I placed her hand on the waistband of my trousers. She snaked her fingers through my belt loop.

I peered out the door. All clear. "Here we go."

I followed the exit signs, ducking into doors or alcoves when we needed them. It was slow going, but eventually, we made it out of the guard station into the infamous center of BHF headquarters.

Federation City didn't disappoint. It was exactly what I had imagined the green master-planned community to look like. The streets were clean and narrow, made for pedestrian traffic only. There were smart bike and scooter rental stations everywhere. The buildings thus far were low, single-story, with an occasional two-story, which I had to assume were residential.

I wasn't sure where I was going. Luckily, it was still dark out, and most residents were still asleep. The businesses were also closed. Thirty feet to my left was a staircase leading to a water fountain surrounded by a grassy knoll. I headed up the stairs to get a better view of the area.

A low whistle from behind caught my attention. Xavier released his gift and appeared against the building. Thank fuck.

I led El to him.

"How did you find us?" I asked.

"I'm looking for a place to hide," he said. His gaze landed on Elyanna. She pulled off her balaclava and leaned against me.

"Hey." Xavier tipped her chin to face him. "Are you okay?"

"Ghost." She sighed. "I'm fine. We need to find Becks."

He frowned. "Follow me."

CHAPTER TWENTY-SIX

Xavier

I stared at the woman that my sister and I buried pre-plague. This couldn't be.

"Mom?" I caught her before she hit the ground.

"Xavier?!" She embraced me. "What are you doing here?" Where's your sister?"

"We buried you," I said.

"It's a long story. We can't talk about that right now. Not here. Where is Rebecca? Is she here?"

"That's why I'm here. She was taken. Mom, I don't understand. Why are you here? How are you still alive?"

"No, no, no. This is not a safe place for you or your sister. I tried to keep you away from him."

"From who?" I snarled. My patience wearing thin.

"You must hide. Stay away from the Premiere Loop. Stay away from the hospital. Every dwelling ending in 23 is vacant. To unlock the door, enter 29547. It's a code the engineers used to make sure everything was working properly when Federation City was built. It still works. Find 1123 at midnight tonight; I will meet you there. For now, find a place to hide. Come sunrise, this place will be crawling with city dwellers, and you two . . . stand out." She looked at Roman, then me, and smiled. "Freshen up. You two will attract unwanted attention."

"Mom . . ." I began and she held up a hand cutting me off.

"Shh. Three guards are approaching. Use your gift. Hide. I'll find Becks. Your friend has already been seen. He will have to remain with me."

I called on my gift and peered around Roman's broad frame. Three guards were heading straight toward us.

"Go, Xavier. I'll explain at midnight," she said in a hushed tone and then faced the three guards.

"More guards? I only require one escort. He'll do," she told them.

"I'm sorry, ma'am. May I see your identification?" One guard asked as my mother held out her arm and showed him a wristband. The guard unclipped a contraption attached to his belt and scanned the wristband. Interesting.

I pressed against Roman's back and whispered, "I'll be right behind you."

He shook his head.

The guards caught his movement and eyed him. My mother walked past them, forcing them to follow her and turn their backs on Roman.

"Ma'am, we must insist," another guard said. He glanced over his shoulder at Roman. "We have some issues in the guard sector. We need all guards to report back to their stations."

My mother said something to him, keeping all three guards occupied.

"Go Xavi. I will find 1123 at midnight. Find our woman and your sister," Roman muttered.

I remained pressed against his back. He leaned into me. His muscular body was hard and strong against mine. My deviant side wanted to come out to play. I brushed my nose down the side of his neck. His breath hitched. His body responded to me earlier while I applied the medication to his skin. And now . . . I was curious if his cock was swollen. I snaked my hand over his torso. It was a major breach of boundaries, but I didn't care and from the way his ass pressed into my crotch, he didn't either. I wanted more.

Rome placed his hand over mine, stopping me from reaching further. "Later," he growled under his breath.

"Did you have something to add, Dennison?" a guard asked.

Dennison? Oh, right, he'd changed into someone else's uniform.

"No. Let me escort her to . . ." Rome replied.

"No. Report back to your station. I'll take the doctor myself," the guard interrupted before he could finish.

Roman turned his head, his lips nearly connecting with mine. "Go, Xavi." He stepped away from me.

I watched Roman walk away. Two guards flanked him, while the remaining guard guided my mother in the opposite direction.

For a split second, I didn't know where to go. I wanted to go after Roman. Curiosity piqued, and I wanted to explore what had transpired between us. It was unchartered territory, but a part of me craved his touch and I wanted to leap. The sexy fire-starter glanced over his shoulder and shook his head.

Fine. I followed my mother for a time as she and the other guard traversed through the built city. I should have been paying attention to my surroundings, but the conversation had been more enlightening.

"Has anyone new been brought in?" my mother asked.

"Not that I am aware, ma'am."

"What's all the fuss about at the guard sector?" she pressed.

"Umm . . . I probably shouldn't talk about this."

She stopped and placed a hand over her chest, as though he had insulted her. Her mannerisms were so similar to Becks' that it hurt to watch. "Do you think I'm a lowly employee, Adams? I will find out eventually."

"Well, no, ma'am. I meant no offense. Ummm . . . We found dead soldiers in the sector. We're trying to keep this from getting out. No one wants a visit from the Godfather."

She gave him a sympathetic look and patted his arm. "I under-stand." She resumed walking.

The guard sniffed his armpit, then sniffed the air. "Do you smell that? It smells like a citizen and blood. It's in my nose."

I didn't need to sniff. I reeked. It had been days since I last show-ered; even the change of clothing didn't make a difference. That was the thing with my gift. I was invisible to the eye, but scents and sounds would give me away.

Mom laughed. "Oh Adams, I think you've spent too much time on the other side of the wall. Come on, let's get to the hospital. I prefer not to pass the Premier Loop. It's a farther walk, but as you know, the Godfather is always watching. And you don't want to be near that man. Stay away. Far away."

Somehow, I knew she had said the last part for my benefit. My mother. The woman who had supposedly died of an aneurysm before the plague.

My military unit, which included Johnny, my sister's husband, was in Europe on deployment. Becks had come to visit us in Berlin when we'd gotten the news. By the time we returned to the States, Mom's body had been cremated. My sister and I had a funeral service and we'd been grieving over losing her since. And now my mother was walking right in front of me. I couldn't deal with all the emotions and questions swirling through me. Was my father alive, too? What the hell happened? Midnight at 1123 couldn't come fast enough. What a total mind-fuck.

The area I stood in had to have been the business section of the city. There were shops of every kind and restaurants, and I even passed a couple of bars. The cleanliness and perfection of it all irritated me. BHF had all of this, and they still came after us, the lowly rebels living in the country. We just wanted to be left alone. Live simple lives; raise our children. In comparison to how the citizens lived on the other side of the wall, we lived like royalty. In truth, we hadn't enjoyed our lives as much as we should have. We were always preparing for war because the fuckers kept attacking.

Hawk was always on pins and needles. Poor dude fought so hard to keep us safe, and with everything we had in place, BHF was still able to ruin our home and take our women and children. The very thought of it made me want to go on a killing rampage again.

Killing all those guards was not a smart move on my part. My deviant side was warring between wanting to kill and how my body responded to being around Roman. Random kills should have slaked my darkness, but Roman was killing right alongside me. It was violent, brutal, and seductive. It made me want to explore more of him. I couldn't do it. Shouldn't. The thrill of having his nakedness against mine sent thrilling sensations through me, making me want him all the more. A part of me knew it was the off-limits slash taboo situation that tugged on my deviant nature. It wasn't going to be a long-term situation. I never had one of those with another man. All of my experiences with male lovers were shallow one-nighters. That would be hella awkward since he lived with my love. Yeah, my heart was all Elyanna. Maybe Roman and I could have a friends-with-benefits kind of situation? How would he feel about that? More importantly, how would Elyanna feel? Would that be okay with her? I doubt she'd be okay with me fucking random dudes. That would be cheating and so much worse. Hawk would surely kill me if I did that.

A tall figure dressed in a BHF guard uniform stood upon a platform overlooking the retail area. Hawk. I whistled. His gaze darted around. He couldn't see me. And I couldn't reveal myself. Something peered around his back. Elyanna.

I jogged up the stairs, then released my gift as I came up behind them while sticking to the shadows.

"How did you find us?" Hawk asked with a low tone.

"I was looking for a place to hide." My gaze landed on Elyanna as she pulled off her balaclava. I drew in a sharp intake of breath. "Hey, are you okay?"

"Xavi," she sighed. "I'm fine. We need to find Becks."

Her skin was pale, and there were dark circles under her eyes. She wasn't fine. Not even in the slightest.

"Follow me."

I randomly chose a direction and led them toward a row of townhomes. At Unit 2323, I crossed my fingers and tapped in the code my mother had given me.

It opened. Exhaling a sigh of relief, I held the door while El and Hawk entered. "We should be safe here. The city will be swarming with people during the day. We need to lay low."

Hawk nodded, and Elyanna slumped to the floor, clutching her temples. I gaped at Hawk. Concern etched over his face as he kneeled at her side.

"Peaches, when was the last time you ate?" he asked.

She shrugged. "Don't remember."

Her voice sounded so weak and tired, it broke my heart.

"I'll find some food and . . ." Hawk started.

"No, I'll get the provisions. Invisible man, remember? Take care of her," I told him and went back the way we came.

The sun hadn't risen yet, so the stores were still closed. I chanced the code my mother had given me and silently thanked her as the door to a department store clicked open. It was a clothing store, much like the old Macy's, pre-plague. I grabbed a gym bag in the men's section and began stuffing it with jeans, T-shirts, socks, and briefs that would fit me, Hawk, and Roman. On the other side of the store, I found the women's department and came to a stop. What size did El wear? She was slightly smaller than my sister, so I guessed. My sister was a four; El had to be a two. I picked up a pair of jeans in size two. Then I found a tank, a T-shirt, and socks. I came upon the lingerie department and grinned. Didn't hurt to have sexy undies.

After my shopping spree, I exited the store and went to a grocery store next. A few people were there, preparing for the day. I wasn't worried, since I was still invisible. I just needed to be mindful of maintaining a smell-safe distance. I grabbed a reusable shopping bag and started loading it up with juices and fruit. The smell of freshly baked bread hit my nostrils, and my stomach let out an unholy growl. I followed the delectable scent to the baked goods section, where a woman was unloading trays of goodies onto a counter. I waited until she returned to the back of the store and loaded my bag with foil-wrapped packets of breakfast croissants, muffins, and a loaf of bread. I got a jar of peanut butter and decided that was enough for now. On my way out, I found the toiletry aisle and added essentials to the bag.

A few minutes later, my knees buckled, and my hands began to tremble. I paused on the sidewalk and drew deep breaths into my lungs. I'd pushed too far with my gift. How long had it been? I couldn't even guess. I'd been using it off and on for hours. I was out in the open, and the lightening sky above signaled the new day had arrived. I pushed with my gift, panting with every step, until I reached the apartment. I dropped everything on the floor, grabbed a bottle of green juice, and took a swig. It was earthy and oddly refreshing.

I followed the sound of running water and found Hawk and Elyanna in the shower. The glass door gave me the perfect view of the naked couple. They were a beautiful sight. El's soft curves were pressed against Hawk's hard muscles. His large hands roamed over her body as water sluiced over their skin. She tipped her head giving him access to her lips, their tongues meeting in a sensual dance. He rolled a hard nipple between his fingertips, his hard cock pressed against her belly. Desire stirred in my stomach making my dick tent my pants. I should have given them privacy, but I couldn't look away. They were the epitome of love and sensuality, and I wanted to be right there with them.

"You coming in?" Hudson's gaze met mine.

I cleared my throat. "In a minute."

El smiled and I reached in, handing them the juice, then went to get the bag of toiletries and clothes.

They were still in the same position when I returned. El's cheek pressed against Hawk's chest. He was massaging her shoulders. I shrugged off my clothes, grabbed the shampoo, conditioner, and soap, and joined them in the shower. I gave Hawk the soap, squirted a dollop of shampoo into my palm, and massaged it into El's scalp. She groaned. I kissed her on the shoulder and heard her moan my name.

Hawk was busy soaping her skin while I rinsed her hair and added conditioner to her long locks. Her hair had gotten so long the ends touched her ass. I trailed my fingers over her curves, then took the soap from Hawk.

While the conditioner soaked into her hair, I quickly lathered my body and hair, then rinsed. As far as I was concerned, I was clean.

Elyanna was, too, but Hawk and I weren't done pampering our woman. It was like we'd done this shower dance before. I captured her lips with mine, while Hawk ran the bar of soap up and down her legs and between her thighs. She released a breathy moan. I cupped her ass, then ran my fingers down her crack to her pussy where Hawk was massaging her clit. Our digits connected, and we probed her entrance. El hooked a leg around Hawk's hip and leaned her head on my shoulder.

She wanted us. We wanted her.

Warning. Water usage limit ninety-eight percent. Automatic shut off in one minute.

The three of us startled. A digital display above the shower head showed a timer countdown.

"Damn it," El growled.

We laughed and then got out of the shower. Elyanna, now cleaned and a little worked up, was still weak and pale. She took a couple of steps and staggered.

Hawk wrapped her in a towel, scooped her into his arms, and took her to the bedroom. I chastised myself for taking advantage of her while her body was weakened from lack of sleep or food. Or maybe it was using her gift. It was probably all of the above, considering I hadn't felt very strong myself. That was the difference with men. We were always in the mood. If blood rushed to our cocks, we were ready to go.

I brought the bag full of clothes and food to the room.

"You need to eat, El," Hawk said.

"Not hungry," she said, crawling to the pillow.

"Oh no, you don't. Eat, peaches. At least a little bit." He positioned himself behind her, forcing her to sit up, placing her back against his chest.

I passed out breakfast croissants. Hawk was working on his third, while El had declared she was full after eating only a half. He gave her a questioning glance and then shrugged. I didn't like it either, but it wasn't like we could shove food down her throat.

El gulped down some juice and wiped her mouth with the back of her hand. "Where'd you find celery juice?" she asked. Her weak-sounding voice screamed exhaustion.

"Is that what this is? It's good. I like it. Um, the grocery store and the department store for clothes."

"Thank you, Ghost." She gave me a small smile.

I crawled up to her and kissed her cheek. "You're welcome, love. Get some sleep."

She rolled over Hawk's leg and smooshed her face into the pillow. Seconds later, she was out.

"Thanks, Xavi. You saved our asses." Hawk's gaze lingered on El for a brief moment, then he faced me. "Tell me everything."

CHAPTER TWENTY-SEVEN

Elyanna

A puff of wind blew a tendril of hair onto my face, tickling my nose. I brushed the strands away only for them to be blown back. After the third swipe, my eyes snapped open, and I was ready to smack the offensive snorer. I disentangled myself from the limbs wrapped around me, to find Ghost, sleeping peacefully and snoring like a freight train. Relief replaced annoyance. He was here with me and Hudson, and he hadn't threatened to kill me once. I pecked the tip of his nose, then quietly got out of bed.

I left my men asleep, pulled on a T-shirt that was lying on the edge of the bed, and went to explore the apartment. Upon closer inspection, it wasn't an apartment. It was a loft. I'd been so out of it when we arrived that I hadn't paid attention to the space at all.

The minimalist design gave it a pre-plague, modern feel, and the plastic-covered furnishings and empty bookshelves indicated it was vacant.

The same light-colored hardwood flooring flowed from the loft slash bedroom area upstairs down a flight of stairs, which led to the open-plan living room. The taupe color scheme and high ceilings made the space seem bright and airy, despite the dim lighting. I padded across the thick, shaggy, throw rug and passed the L-shaped sofa to peer out of the bay window near the front door. I gently separated two slats of the wooden blinds. Sunlight reflected off a window pane in the building opposite the manicured lawn between the buildings. There were picnic tables and barbecue pits strategically placed along the empty courtyard. It had been nearing dawn when we arrived. I glanced at my watch and panicked. Becks had been on her own for hours.

Reluctantly, I peeled away the lock I'd placed on my gift. Buzzing overwhelmed my senses. I slammed my gift shut and slumped to the floor.

Damn it. We needed to rescue Becks. Roman was missing, and I was useless. I propped my elbows on my knees and rubbed my knuckles over my brows. There was a reason why I stayed away from the cities. Too many people in a small area.

Hillside was the largest and most populated rebellion community, with a little over two hundred people spread out over fifty-plus miles. I had no issues leaving my gift open while strolling around there. Here in Federation City, there had to be thousands of people clustered within a twenty-mile radius. It was too much. If I didn't keep my gift closed, I'd go mad.

I rose to my feet and decided to tour the kitchen. The refrigerator was cold, and in it were glass bottles of orange and celery juice, along with apples and breakfast croissants. More groceries were neatly placed on the counter. Xavi's pilfering and Hudson's orderly organization skills.

I'd practiced with my gift at the rebellion encampments and had gotten stronger. But I hadn't had the opportunity to practice among so many people. It was overwhelming. I just couldn't. Dread stirred in the pit of my stomach. Who was I without my gift? How would I survive? Before self-doubt could swallow me whole, I decided to continue my tour.

Under the stairs, I found a bathroom and a storage closet, which were stocked with a few towels and paper goods. Interesting. I wondered what they used this unit for.

On my way back to the bedroom, I grabbed more celery juice. Hudson and Xavi slept like the dead. Women's clothing was laid carefully over a chair near the bed, and my sword was propped beside it. I found my size jeans, a tank top, and sexy lingerie. Of course, Xavi would pick out lingerie. I stifled a giggle and went into the bathroom to get dressed.

The ensuite had the same color scheme as the rest of the loft. There was a LED panel on the wall that illuminated with a wave of my hand. Very modern. I helped myself to the toiletries left on the counter, then slipped on the lingerie. The delicate fabric made me feel feminine and sexy. For a moment, I could forget we were in the middle of enemy territory.

I knelt on the bed and gazed at my men. Hudson was on his back with an arm covering half his face. Xavi was on his side, a pillow between his legs, still snoring away. Hudson was alive. Xavier was back. My heart was full. Something I'd thought impossible since Axel had passed. It was odd seeing them together without their friend. He'd be missed forever. I placed a hand over my chest and closed my eyes.

When I reopened my eyes, Hudson was staring at me. "Come here," he said in a gravelly voice.

I slid against the hard ridges of his muscular form into his waiting embrace.

He pressed a kiss on my forehead. "You okay?" he murmured.

I wasn't fine, but he didn't need to know that. I answered him with kisses on his neck, along the stubble on his jaw, and up to his lips. He positioned me to straddle his waist. I ground myself against his hardening length. Hudson ran his large, calloused hands down my back and cupped my ass. I swirled my tongue through his mouth. His fingers slipped under my lacy undergarments, finding my wet center. He strummed my clit, drawing a primal moan from my lips. I reached between us, searching for his cock. The thick, velvety flesh throbbed in my palm. Our kisses grew hungry. Impatient.

Hudson smacked my ass and growled. I yelped in surprise, waking Xavi. His heated gaze roamed over me and Hudson. I sat up, riding Hudson's finger while reaching for Ghost. He grasped my hand and kissed a trail from my fingertips to my neck, then slid the straps of my bodysuit down my shoulders and palmed my breasts. I tipped my head back, reveling in the sensual assault on my body. Hudson pushed my bottoms to the side and dipped his finger into my pleasure hole. My body trembled in response as I nearly came undone.

"Not yet, baby girl," Xavi said.

Hudson withdrew his fingers.

"No. Don't stop," I begged.

"Patience, babe." Hudson sat upright and pressed his lips to mine, while Xavi shuffled off the bed.

"You two are so fucking sexy." Ghost nipped at my ear. He hooked my jaw between his fingers and angled my face away from Hawk, stealing my kisses.

I hooked an arm around Ghost's neck, deepening our kiss. Hudson's mouth latched onto my nipple, and his teeth grazed the sensitive flesh. My skin felt feverish and tingly all over.

"I need you inside me." I rasped. "Both of you."

"Not yet. I want you on all fours," Hudson ordered.

I got on my hands and knees.

"Good girl. Take Xavi into your mouth."

I opened wide and flicked my tongue over Xavi's crown. He groaned, then pushed his cock deep into my mouth until he hit the back of my throat. Tears welled in my eyes. Ghost gripped the back of my head and pumped his hips.

Hudson groaned. "Beautiful. So fucking hot. Spread your legs for me." He tapped the inside of my thighs. I felt his warm, wet tongue slide between my folds. I gripped Ghost's thighs, my throat contracting over his tip.

"Fuck." Ghost drew a sharp breath. "Feels so fucking good."

He pumped into my mouth with deep, long thrusts, then pulled out.

"I don't want to come yet." His lips found mine. His voice was desperate with desire. "I want both of us to fuck you at the same time."

Hudson bit my butt cheek, then said, "Climb on my cock, baby."

He rolled onto his back while Ghost helped me straddle Hudson's cock.

I impaled myself over Hawk's length, my pussy stretching to take in his girth. I folded over him to fasten our lips together. Ghost's fingers trailed my pussy lips while Hawk was deep inside me. I rolled my hips, eager for more.

"Hold on." Hudson gripped my ass.

Ghost reached for a bottle that was sitting on the nightstand, popped the lid, and squirted a clear, gel-like substance on his hand. Where he'd found lube was a mystery.

His lubed fingers probed my pussy, then slipped in. The intrusion was too much, but it felt so good. And I wanted more. I moaned while Hudson moaned with me.

"More, Ghost."

He slipped in another finger.

"Yes!" I cried.

"Ready for more?" Ghost whispered.

"Yes! I want you, Ghost. I want your cock."

He withdrew his fingers and then prodded my entrance with his tip. I tensed.

"Relax, El." Hudson cupped my face. His tongue swirled in my mouth.

Ghost nudged into my entrance, stretching me. His big, lubed-up cock found purchase and slid in. Sharp pain accompanied the pleasure.

"Oh my god," I gasped. I was full. Too full. I was being split in two.

"Breathe, babe," Hudson said with his lips against mine.

Ghost plunged deeper, sheathing himself to the hilt. He nipped at my shoulder, pausing for a moment. "Fuck, this is better than my dreams." His mouth found mine and Hudson's. Tongues swirled together. Ghost slowly slid out, then slid back in. Each thrust sent electrical tingles through every nerve ending.

I began panting. Ghost picked up the pace.

"So fucking good," Hudson purred.

My pussy clenched around my men, drawing a deep moan from both of them.

"That's it, baby girl. Come for us." Ghost pounded into me, rocking me over Hudson's cock. The friction of having them both inside me made me wild with need.

Our bodies were slick with sweat. Heady moans filled the room.

"I love you guys. So fucking much." My eyes rolled back in my head, and my climax overtook my body, drowning me in pure pleasure. It felt like I passed out, but my men were there. And they weren't done.

"Don't you dare stop," Hudson groaned.

Xavi responded by slamming into me with deep, brutal thrusts over and over again. It was too much and still not enough. I'd been waiting for Xavier to return to us for so long, I didn't want this moment to end.

I groaned, my words nonsensical as my pussy tightened again. Another orgasm crept up on me.

"That's it, baby. One more time." Ghost slapped my ass. The sting of his palm sent me over the edge. I rocked my hips and bit down on Hudson's shoulder as we came together.

Ghost draped his body over mine, while I lay limp over Hudson. We lay there for a moment. I could hardly breathe, but I didn't want them to move. That moment was everything, and I wanted to savor every second. Discomfort, be damned.

Hawk tapped Ghost's shoulder. "Off."

Ghost grumbled, then slipped out and settled beside us.

Hudson rolled us over, pinning me under him. "Are you okay?" he asked.

I nodded.

He kissed me deeply, then released me. His absence made me shiver. Ghost filled the void, pulling me into his arms. He whispered endearing words, and I closed my eyes.

CHAPTER TWENTY-EIGHT

Hudson

A smile stretched across my face as I watched them sleep soundly wrapped in each other's arms. For a while there I wasn't sure if Xavi'd ever find his way back into our lives. I returned to the bed with a warm washcloth to clean up my wife. Aftercare was one of my specialties; I loved taking care of her. El murmured, "I love you," and rolled over. I placed the washcloth on the nightstand and snuggled into her back.

Sleep didn't come though. I lay there listening to El and Xavi breathe. We had a long way home.

After Xavier told me about running into his mother, tension had perched on my shoulders like a pet monkey. An unwanted pet monkey. I glanced at my watch, anxious to get home. We had eleven hours until midnight.

Earlier, while Xavi and El slept, I'd decided to explore FC and find Unit 1123. I wanted to check out the town and make sure the meeting spot wasn't a trap. Xavi had given me the universal code, but I didn't need it. There was a key under the mat that granted me access. The unoccupied unit was larger than the loft. I imagined they used it as a meeting spot. For what? I didn't have the answer yet.

I explored Federation City for a good hour. It was my nature to map out my surroundings especially when in enemy territory. The sky above the dome shone bright blue. It had to have been a hundred degrees out there, but it was a cool seventy-two in the city. It was an extraordinary engineering feat to cool a place of this size. Whoever designed it thought of everything. The layout was well developed. The guard sector was on the perimeter, a good line of defense from intruders. I passed a farm which was one of three. It was tiny in comparison to pre-plague farms, but enough to accommodate the city's population. Clusters of residential buildings and businesses were scattered throughout the community. My exploration revealed a lot of the city, and yet I hadn't covered half.

From what I could piece together, the sun was their main source of power. Forty percent of the retractable roof was solar panels and there were more panels in a nearby field. Made sense since Arizona was sunny three hundred days out of the year. The state had always had water rights to the Colorado River which was still the case. With so much of the population gone, who was going to argue with them? The people who engineered the city had put limits on water usage, hence the timer that had gone off during our shower earlier. The alert made us pump the brakes on our amorous activities. El was barely standing and Xavi wasn't much better either. I should have known better.

I strolled around the business sector, where the stores and restaurants were. People were shopping and dining as though the end of the world hadn't happened. There were brand-name stores, a movie theater replaying pre-plague movies, and sports events. The bars and restaurants had a steady crowd. I spotted a delivery guy wheeling a dolly and followed him to a loading dock area. Sticking to the shadows, I learned that deliveries were brought in from their warehouse sector located along the border between Arizona and California.

We had traversed from Florida to Colorado when the plague hit. Colorado was a risky choice and one I wouldn't have chosen if not for Axel's gift. God, I missed that man.

The news at the time reported the population on the west coast had been decimated. The plague had started in Los Angeles and it spread like wildfire. Mexico and the bordering states, Nevada and Oregon tried to block California residents from entering but by then it was too late. California fell first, then Mexico. Once the plague infil-trated all those tourists in Nevada, the rest of the world was fucked.

I shook off thoughts of the past and continued to process what I'd learned during my recon.

As far as I could tell, there weren't surveillance cameras in the retail area or around the residences. I could have been wrong but if that was the case, we would have been tossed in a cell by now or dead. That thought made me uneasy, and I glanced toward the stairwell which could be seen from the bed.

The dwelling Xavi had chosen was not within sight of the business sector. It was surrounded by other townhomes and there was a community garden area out front. Guards strolled through the retail sector, but they seemed to steer clear of the residences. I had checked the units beside ours and those seemed to be vacant as well. And I hadn't seen people when I left the loft or when I returned after my exploration.

"Stop," Xavier muttered.

My eyes snapped open. His eyes were closed. Elyanna was nestled between us, her face buried in his neck.

Xavi opened one eye. "Your thinking is hurting my brain."

"You can't hear my thoughts." I kept my voice low.

"No, I can't. You're projecting."

"I am not."

He smiled. "What's on your mind?"

"Just replaying what I learned while I was exploring."

"You went out?" Xavier asked, raising his voice.

Elyanna rolled onto her back. Xavi moved her hair from her face, while I rubbed her belly. She sighed.

"You went out?" Xavi repeated in a whispered tone.

"Yeah, needed to check things out."

"And?"

I told him what I found.

"Interesting. Time is it?" He hooked El's leg over his hip and began rubbing her inner thigh. Fucker.

"Sun's still up."

"So, we still have time, then." He pressed his lips to her shoulder.

"Do you think of anything else?"

"I haven't been laid in months," he retorted.

"Whose fault is that?"

"Fuck off. As if you're not hard again."

He was right. My wife kept me perpetually hard. Watching her suck off Xavi, and take us both at the same time, made me feel like a pubescent teen.

Still, my wife's health and well-being always came before my raging hard-on. Something was up with her gift and I'd wanted her to talk to me about it before she fell asleep earlier. And now . . . Fuck me, I was painfully hard and wanted to sink my dick into her warm, tight cunt.

Xavi's tongue slid along the sensitive tendons on her neck. He nipped and sucked. Elyanna didn't move.

I was about to push him away from her, when she tilted her head, granting him access. Xavi grinned. Cheeky fucker.

She moaned and the scent of her arousal filled the air. I ran my fingers between her legs, happy to find her slit wet and ready. With a light touch, I stroked between her pussy lips.

"You're welcome," Xavi whispered.

I bit the inside of my cheek, ignored the asshat, and continued pleasuring my wife.

CHAPTER TWENTY-NINE

Elyanna

Physically speaking, my body felt pretty darn good. I was well-rested and fed, and my lady parts were tender from my men's attention. My gift, on the other hand, was freaking me out. I'd tried accessing it after round two of our love-making session and had to slam it closed immediately. Thoughts from thousands of residents roared through my brain.

At twilight, Ghost announced, "I am going to bust Roman out of the guard sector."

"Wait. I thought you said he was meeting us at midnight."

"Yes, I did. And yes, that's what he told me. But I think it might be best if I brought him back here. He can regroup, change, and then we can go to 1123 together."

"I don't like the idea of us splitting up," I told him.

"I'll be okay, El. And I'll bring your fly back safely," he said.

"Bug. He's my firebug," I replied.

"Fly, bug, same difference." He pecked my cheek.

"If you're not back in one hour, we're coming after you." Hudson shook his hand.

Xavi nodded and exited the loft.

I stared at the door for a beat, worry prickling my skin.

"They'll be okay. If there's one thing your Ghost is good at, it's these clandestine missions. If we knew where Becks was, he'd be able to go in and rescue her himself with no problems." Hudson steered me away from the kitchen to sit on the rug in the living room.

We'd decided to stay off the plastic-covered chairs as much as possible. Hudson was a bit anal-retentive with things, generally speaking, so the areas that we did use were organized and clean. When we left, we'd leave no trace of our presence.

"I have full confidence in him and his gift. But the last time he went off alone . . ." I couldn't finish my sentence. I didn't want to think about what Luther had done to him the last time we had a mission and had gotten separated. Ghost had just re-entered our lives after being away for almost two years. Losing him again would kill me.

"I know, babe. I know. I don't like it either, but he is familiar with the guard sector. Like you, he's had time to recuperate. I suspect his gift is at a hundred percent now."

Hudson and I sat cross-legged, facing each other. His knees brushed against mine, and he grasped my hand.

"Speaking of gifts, talk to me. What's going on?"

For a second, I couldn't say anything. I hated to admit that my gift was short-circuiting on me at a time when I needed it most. Maybe I should just stay behind and let the men do the rescuing.

I bit my lower lip, trying to find the right words.

"Hey." He pulled my lip free from my teeth. "I can't help if you won't talk to me."

I blew out a huff of breath. "I don't know how to control it. There are too many people here for me to filter out."

"How did you do it before? When you lived in Texas?"

"It manifested after Julia died. It sucked. I thought I was going crazy, or I was going to die from a migraine. I stayed away from densely populated areas. The neighborhood we'd lived in was a small community and managing that was a bear. I meditated a lot and slowly began to quiet the buzzing. Now I feel like there are thousands of bees living in my brain. I can shut it down completely, but once I open it, it's like a bomb has gone off in my brain."

"I understand." He nodded. "With my gift, I trained to layer it. To move multiple things simultaneously. For you, I think it might be the opposite. You need to peel back the layers."

"How can I manage that? We don't have time."

"How about we give it a go? See if you can filter out everyone else and focus on me."

He grasped my hands.

"If it's too much, El, shut it down."

"Okay. I can do this." I could at least try.

I closed my eyes and opened my gift. The thoughts of a thousand people pierced my mind. It felt like there was a bomb made from a million hot, sharp needle points stabbing the inside of my brain. My breath came in ragged pants. I clutched my temples, as a blinding light flashed over my retinas.

"Enough! Shut it down, El!"

I closed my gift and fell limp in his arms.

He held me close. "I got you. You're okay, Elyanna. Don't cry. It's over. You don't have to do that again."

I sobbed and held onto my husband, allowing the wicked migraine to drown me.

Soothing warmth ran up and down my spine, then settled at the base of my neck. I surrendered to the sensation, allowing the pain to leave my body.

Warm, pillowy lips kissed my cheek, then my lips.

"Bug?" I croaked, blinking one eye open. "Ghost found you." I wanted to throw my arms around him, but I couldn't get my body to move.

"I'm here, beautiful." Bug kissed me again. "I'm going to roll you over and massage your head, okay?"

I murmured a yes, and he gently turned my body. The throbbing in my head persisted, making me grimace. I squeezed my eyes together, willing the pain to cease.

Bug ran his heated palms along my shoulders and then to the back of my neck. He cradled my head, his fingers perfectly placed along the ridge of the occipital bone. I let my head relax in his hands. He held me in that position, allowing the natural heat he produced to seep into my tense muscles. He moved his deft fingers to massage my scalp and temples. Roman's magical hands made my migraine disappear.

"Thank you," I sighed.

He pressed his lips against my forehead. "Better?"

"Much." I cupped his face and brought his lips to mine. He tasted of mint and spice. My tongue dove into his mouth and swirled with his.

He pulled away. "Not now, Elyanna. Soon. But this is not the right time."

He was right, but I couldn't hide my disappointment.

He got into bed and pulled me into his arms. I realized then that he'd been sitting on a chair while my body was lying sideways on the mattress.

"You have magic hands," I told him.

He chuckled. "I'm glad you're feeling better."

"I thought you were dead." My voice cracked. "We saw the helicopter go down."

He rubbed small circles on my back. "It was a close call. Thoughts of you kept me alive."

Bug rolled, bringing us face to face, and pressed our foreheads together. "I'm sorry for what I said. I'm sorry for leaving. You are my heart, my everything. Forgive me, Elyanna. Let me come home."

I wanted him to come home. I didn't want him to leave in the first place. But my love for him wouldn't be enough.

"Roman," I sighed. "I love you. We love you. You deserve to be happy and live a full-filling life. We can't give you that."

"You can. And you have. Life with you, Hawk, and Axel is fulfilling. You're my family and I was wrong to think otherwise. Yes, I'll admit I've had sexual fantasies which included you and Hawk. Everyone has fantasies, right? Not acting on those fantasies doesn't diminish my love for all of you. It doesn't make my life with you less. I am content. And I'm sorry it took nearly dying to realize how much I love you. How much I need you. Don't send me away."

Doubt lingered at the back of my head but hope for a happy future together rang louder. We'd just gotten Xavi back, and without Roman, our family would be fractured again. No, it had to work.

I hugged him tightly and whispered. "Promise you'll tell me the minute things change. Promise we'll talk and always be open with one another."

"I won't change my mind. And, yes, I promise to tell you everything."

"Even the fantasies?" I whispered. The thought of Rome and Hudson together had me clenching my thighs.

He draped my leg over his hip and pressed his hard cock against my belly. "Even the fantasies."

Maybe we couldn't act out his fantasies but talking about them would be fun for both of us.

Our lips locked in a hungry kiss. My fingers trailed down his neck to his muscular back and the uneven skin. I sat upright, worry drowning lust.

"Are you okay?" I asked, taking in his scarred flesh.

"I'm fine. They put me in a cell last night and forgot about me, which was good. I slept until Xavi got me out. It doesn't hurt. Bummer about my hair though. I was growing it out for you." He ran his hand over his now bald scalp.

"Firebug." I sighed. "I don't care about your hair. I care about you." I rolled him over inspecting his flesh and gently kissed the marred peeling skin. It looked like he was recovering from a nasty sunburn. It appeared to be a minor thing, but it wasn't. It was everywhere, which meant it had to be excruciatingly painful when it happened.

My heart hurt at the sight of him. Roman was a beautiful man with smooth, tanned skin that highlighted every ridge of his muscular body. The fire had left traces of burned flesh on the back of his body. Arms, shoulders, legs, and all. I swallowed past the lump in my throat and gently rolled him over. The front of his body was the same. Tears pricked the back of my eyes. I kissed him everywhere, my heart aching. The agony he must've gone through. And yet, he suffered through it and came to rescue me and Becks.

"I love you, Roman." My voice hitched.

"Hey, come here," Rome drew me in to lay flat against his chest. I buried my face in the crook of his neck, hiding my tears. "I'm fine, Elyanna. I'm healed."

"You nearly died."

"But didn't."

"And you drove fifteen hours to save me and Becks."

He cupped my face and gazed into my eyes. "Elyanna, I will walk through the fire, and kick its ass, every single time to save you."

CHAPTER THIRTY

Elyanna

R ome and I lay in bed talking, caressing, holding each other close. There was no sex involved, and yet it was our most intimate moment. I'd never felt so connected or loved by my firebug.

Footsteps thumped on the staircase, indicating our slight reprieve was at its end.

The mattress dipped and Hudson sat beside me, then pulled me in for a deep kiss. "You scared me. Are you okay?"

"I'm fine, thanks to Firebug. Where's Ghost?"

Xavier plopped on the bed. "Did you miss me?"

I smiled. "Always." *Been missing you for the last two years.*

"I suppose we should get going," I said.

Ghost and Bug looked at Hudson.

"Elyanna, this will be a brief, what-to-do-next meeting. Maybe you should rest," Hudson stated.

"I may not have access to my gift, but I'm still useful. My sassy stick is right there," I replied.

"We're meeting my mom, El. Sassy won't be needed for this meeting," Xavi told me.

"No. I'm coming with," I replied.

"Beautiful, please rest. A migraine is not something to take lightly. We can handle this meetup, and we'll return right after." Roman ran his hands up and down my arm.

"No. If anything, this is exactly the type of meetup I should be going to. If it's just a meeting, I won't need my gift to manipulate minds." I crawled out of bed and began getting dressed. "Do we have a plan, or are we just going to show up?"

"Elyanna." Hudson gave me a stern stare.

"No, Hudson. Unless you're planning to chain me up again, I am going with you to Unit 1123."

Thirty minutes later, we were on our way to meet Xavier's mother. I was anxious to meet the woman who had raised my best friend, and my . . . I wasn't sure what Xavier was to me. Boyfriend and lover seemed insignificant. Was he my husband? Hmm . . . I considered Hudson my husband because he was the father of my son, and we'd been inseparable since he rescued me from Luther. It became easier to refer to him as my husband. The thought of including him and Roman in that mix made me smile.

We arrived at Unit 1123 five minutes before midnight. Xavier used his gift and entered the house first. Once he gave us the all-clear, I went in and hid, while Hudson and Roman remained outside until Xavi's mom arrived.

At the precise time, Xavi's mother entered the apartment. She ushered her son into an office that was located near the back door. Xavi followed, and I moved closer, my presence concealed by the dimly lit home.

She wasn't what I expected. Honestly, I didn't know what to expect, since the twins had been adopted. Neither of them talked about their parents much and I assumed they had died because of the plague.

Their mother was tiny, at four feet eleven, with snow-white, straight hair that touched her shoulders. Her blue eyes were framed by thick glasses, which sat atop a pointy nose, and her lab coat fit snugly around her curves. A part of me wanted to use my gift and dive into her head, but I was afraid. I didn't want to fall apart with another migraine. My men wouldn't be able to concentrate on anything else if I was unwell.

I waited in the shadows and listened.

"I'm so happy to see you," she said.

"Did you find Becks?" Ghost asked, ignoring the pleasantries.

"No," she said, shaking her head. "She wasn't brought to the hospital. The only logical place is the Premiere Loop."

She patted the bag that hung over her shoulder. "I brought a few things. A map. With your gift, you'll be able to go in undetected."

Hudson strolled in, his eyes wary.

Xavi's mom, startled, placing a hand on her chest. "Oh! Hawk?! It's good to see you. I'm glad you're still alive." She wrapped her arms around his waist.

"It's good to see you, too, Mrs. Cole. I wanted to make sure you weren't followed."

"It's fine. I understand. And I go by Patrice, now. Patrice Sanders. Here, let's get to it." She moved to a desk and began taking papers out of her bag.

I couldn't see what she was showing them, so I listened while keeping my eyes trained on the front door.

"Mom, how are you still alive?" Xavi asked.

She released a resigned sigh.

"After your father's heart attack, I began to notice odd things. I was being followed. As you know, your father and I assumed different identities when we left the project that was studying gifted genes. We were fine for many, many years. It wasn't until Luther Weiss started the development of the virus that our presence was detected. We may have told too many people about the plague before it began. Someone posted what we'd told them on a social media platform, and then the word spread. We knew it was only a matter of time before they visited us. The stress was too much for your father. Once he passed, I was afraid they'd come after me. So to keep you and your sister safe, I devised a plan to fake my death and start anew. It worked until the plague hit and BHF took over. I helped the people I could, but there

was only so much I could do on the outside. I volunteered as a doctor."
She paused. Her gaze flicked between Xavi and Hudson.

"They don't know who the real me is. They don't know about my
involvement with the original project all those years ago," she
whispered.

"Well, that's risky as fuck," Xavier muttered.

"Language!" she admonished.

He gave her a sheepish look.

"The risks are exponentially higher here. You need to find your
sister and get out. I brought a map to show you the layout and what
you need to avoid."

My men listened to Patrice as she pointed things out on her map.
I'd been hiding behind a pillar. I could see into the office and had a
glimpse of the front door via a mirror that hung on the wall in the
entryway. It wasn't the best option, but I could see if the door opened
and still hear the conversation.

It seemed as though there were a lot of don'ts we had to deal with.
We'd need to find either guard uniforms that were different from the
black clothing they wore while patrolling or scrubs. We also needed a
keycard. We'd have to take someone out for that. And of course, the
Premiere Loop was the only place in Federation City that had
surveillance cameras.

Patrice continued talking when I caught a slight shimmer in the
reflection. I blinked rapidly and focused on the mirror again, and sure
enough, the straight-edged entryway table had a slight curve to it. The
same type of waver Hudson had shown me which gave away Xavier's
stalking. Shit.

I glanced back at the office, confirming my Ghost was still talking
with his mother, then pulled my knife out of my boot and threw it at
the door.

Ooof!

The knife stuck into something invisible, which then shimmered
into a man. I'd already stepped out of my hiding place, sword drawn. I
thrust my sassy stick into the air, pivoted, sliced a figure eight, and cut
through the skin. Another man shimmered into view. He aimed his

gun. I sliced his hand. Blood spurted everywhere. His eyes widened, and then he screamed. I sank my sword into his throat, killing him on the spot and cutting off his screech.

The other man slumped against the door, clutching at the dagger sticking out of his shoulder. I held my blade under his chin.

"You need to start talking," I said.

CHAPTER THIRTY-ONE

Hudson

Hot damn, she was fast. There was a faint whir of something moving through the air and then a groan. By the time we stepped out of the office, Elyanna was at the front door, slicing and stabbing. Two men appeared. One with a knife sticking out of his shoulder. The other man had slices across his abdomen, and his trigger hand had a deep gash. He began to scream, and El jammed her sword through his windpipe.

Fuuucckk.

"That was so freaking hot," Xavier whispered.

"Sure was." I crossed the room to help my lethal wife with our new hostage, leaving Xavi to deal with his mother.

I hooked her jaw with my fingers, tipped her face to mine, and laid a wet kiss on her lips.

"I'll take over from here, babe," I told her.

"Wait! Don't kill me, please. I can help," the guy stammered. He pulled the knife from his shoulder and handed it to me. The wound began to heal.

"You've got some explaining to do." I hauled our hostage into the office, patted his pockets, and tied him to the office chair using duct tape Xavi had pilfered from somewhere.

One of the things I loved about my invisible friend was his forward-thinking. When he had gone into the guard sector to bring Roman back, he'd filled the gym bag he'd gotten from the clothing store and got us essentials, including more ammunition, weapons, and handy things like duct tape.

"You don't have to tie me," the man said. "I'm not a threat. My only ability is healing. I'll tell you whatever you want to know."

Xavier and his mother went to the main bedroom and closed the door.

"Are we expecting more of you?" El asked.

"No. Just me and Kyle. I'm Blake," he said.

Elyanna stepped closer to me. "Should I check on Xavier and his mom?"

I tore a piece of tape and placed it on Blake's mouth. "Give them a minute. I'll check on Rome. This guy isn't going anywhere."

Roman was hiding behind the hedges that separated Unit 1123 from the neighbor's courtyard. I whistled, and he came toward me. I motioned for him to come inside just as Xavi and his mother exited the bedroom. His mother looked pale.

"Mom, this is Elyanna. She's um . . ." Xavi glanced at me, and I nodded. "Our wife. Babe, this is mom," Xavi said.

"Nice to meet you." El extended her hand. "Apologies for that." El waved toward the dead body.

"Oh, it's fine. It was unexpected. You have skills." Patrice weakly shook my wife's hand.

I placed my hand on the small of El's back and guided her to the office, where we crammed in, surrounding Blake. Roman tore the duct tape off his mouth.

"Explain yourself, Blake," I told our hostage.

"We were following Patrice," Blake started.

Xavi's mother gasped. "Why me?"

"The guard who escorted you this morning said you were with another guard when they found you. The guard was an unknown, so they put him in a cell. Following you was a precaution." He swallowed hard. "Kyle was my partner for these runs. We, the gifted, have shifts. And this was our night to do patrols."

"Gifted shifts?" I asked.

He nodded. "Whenever there are odd reports like what happened in the guard sector, the gifted are sent to patrol the city. It rarely happens, but this time I was on the list as well as Kyle."

"What are your and Kyle's abilities?"

"I'm a healer. And he has . . . had invisibility with the added benefit of walking through walls."

"Fucking wicked," Xavi murmured.

"If you can heal, shouldn't you heal your friend?" Roman asked.

"Oh no, he's dead. I can't bring back the dead. Okay, maybe I can. I've never tried. And no, I don't want to try now. Kyle was kind of a dick."

"Tell us about the other gifted. How many are there? What are their abilities?" El asked.

"Forty-one, seven are women. We all have different gifts; I don't know them all. I can get you that information. I do admin work mostly and have access to the database."

"Why would someone who has healing abilities be doing admin work?" Xavi asked.

"Oh, I'm not allowed to heal the regulars. My gift is to be used on Pure Bloods only. I help the women with their enhancement."

El's eyes widened. "Enhancement? What the fuck is that?"

Blake cleared his throat. "Umm . . . Gifted people go through the enhancement stage. It increases our powers. Like Kyle. He was born with invisibility; the enhancement gave him the ability to walk through walls. I haven't been through it yet. I've witnessed it. It can be lethal. Most make it out alive with my help. For women, after the enhancement, they go through the insemination phase. The goal is to increase the gifted population. It's not so bad. The gifted women are pampered during all of it."

Shit.

"My daughter was taken last night. Have you seen her? Dark hair, brown eyes. She's very beautiful." Patrice asked.

"No, usually they tell me if someone new comes in." Blake shook his head. "Is she gifted? Are you gifted?"

"Not important," Xavier growled. "We need a way in."

"I can't get all of you in dressed like that. You won't blend."

I exchanged a look with Xavier. We'd do the disguises and keep our gifts under wraps.

Since Patrice's access to Federation City was limited, she wasn't needed for the rest of the evening. She gave us a little more information about the city, wished us good luck, and then went home. She couldn't corroborate Blake's story, so we were stuck trusting him. It was risky and the only option we had. He could have been leading us into an elaborate trap.

If El's gift wasn't on the fritz, it'd be easier to cut through the bullshit. At least Xavi was on our side. He'd be able to use his gift, which was nearly as good as El's, in this situation. For the time being, we followed Blake around Federation City, leaving his dead partner in Unit 1123.

An hour later, we were outfitted in new clothes. Blake had access to a boutique that had suits for men and dresses for women, which would allow us to blend in with the crowd. We'd either pass for gifted or one of the elite members of society.

According to our accomplice, there were a few after-hours places the residents would frequent. Becks could have been taken to one of the venues to work. With the population being more male-dominant, attractive women were forced into the sex trade. That seemed to be an ongoing theme in Federation City. If she had revealed her gift, then they would have brought her into The Premiere Loop, where Blake said they would put her through the enhancement process. He insisted he would have known if Becks had been brought in.

"Approximately two thousand people live here. As you can imagine, most of those people are or were pre-plague uber-wealthy. To keep people entertained, Jamboree Court has restaurants, nightclubs, bars, and music venues. At this hour, there will only be two places open. Humans will be there, and it will be crowded. Sometimes we gifted individuals are allowed to go out and oh my god." Blake stopped talking and ogled at Elyanna as she sauntered out of the dressing room.

My wife was always gorgeous, even when wearing yoga pants and one of my hoodies. To blend in with the crowd, she wore a bronze, sparkly gown that fit her like a glove. The cut was low in front, accentuating her full breasts, and the floor-length fabric hugged her round, perky ass. Her golden hair fell down her back in soft waves, and all that walking in the desert sun had tanned her beautiful skin, making her hazel eyes pop. My heart stopped in my chest as she strolled toward us. My cock was instantly hard.

I crossed the room and crushed our lips together.

"We need a minute," I growled, then nuzzled my wife's neck.

El moaned.

"We don't have time. Can it wait? I mean, damn. I get it. But if you want your friend back before things go sideways, you may want to get a move on," Blake told us.

"He's right, Hawk." El drew away and then kissed me again.

I hiked her dress up to her waist and hoisted her into my arms.

"That is so freaking hot," Xavier groaned.

Roman cleared his throat. "If you don't stop, we're just going to sit here and watch."

"Later, Hawk." My wife tipped her head back as I found her nipple with my teeth. She yanked my hair back and kissed me. "We need to go, Hudson."

She left feathery kisses all over my face and wiggled out of my grasp.

I groaned as she straightened her dress.

"Later, husband." She gave me a wistful smile.

"Fine." I adjusted myself and grabbed her hand. The men in the room stared at us.

"Well?" I asked. "Let's go."

"Uh . . . yeah. A couple of things. We don't use currency here. This is how we keep track of credits." He held up wristbands. "You need to wear these, or you'll stand out. Two belong to Kyle, and two are mine. Please don't go crazy if you're using mine." Blake rubbed the back of his neck.

"What are we doing with Kyle?" Roman asked.

"I will handle it once you four are in the club. I have someone in waste management who owes me a favor. He will dispose of the body and clean up," Blake told us.

"You are rather resourceful, Blake. Why is that?" El eyed the healer.

"I need a favor. I do this for you. And you . . ." He paused and looked at each of us. "Take out the Godfather."

"The who?" Roman asked.

"Later. I'll tell you about him after we get out of Jamboree." He motioned for us to follow him.

Damn it all to hell. I knew the Godfather was going to come up eventually. I scrubbed a hand down my face.

"Hey," El pressed her womanly curves against my side. "Let's get Becks, then we'll deal with the Godfather."

I nodded, then pressed my lips to her forehead.

CHAPTER THIRTY-TWO

Xavier

Jamboree Court was an entertainment district straight out of the pre-plague era. It was lively, and people were laughing and drinking. I hadn't paid any attention to the name of the bar we were walking through; for all I knew, it could have been called Beautiful People because it seemed like this was where all the beauties had come to roost. And that made me hate the fucking place. It reminded me of high school, where all of the cool kids gathered in cliques. I wasn't the scrawny weakling I had been, but the scene brought up uncomfortable memories.

Hawk, Roman, and Elyanna fit right in. Both men wore suits that highlighted their broad shoulders and trim waists. Roman's white button-down was open, revealing his dark, muscled chest. Hawk had that chiseled face and bright green eyes, which drew in the gaze. As captivating as those men were, they paled in comparison to Elyanna. Our woman stole the show. Men and women craned their necks as she gracefully sauntered through the crowd, head held high, her gaze scanning the crowd.

Blake led us through the crowd of beautiful people. Hawk and Roman flanked El protectively, as they always did, and I brought up the rear. The farther we got into the club, the more scantily dressed the workers became. Men and women were practically nude, holding placards as though they were part of the menu.

Elyanna glanced over her shoulder and extended her hand. I wasn't sure why she'd done it, but I appreciated the gesture. *That's right, fuckers, the most beautiful woman in the place was with me.* My posture straightened as I grasped her hand, and she pressed her body into my side. The feel of her curves sent shivers through me. I'd been sporting a semi ever since Hawk's and El's passionate display. I'd have a rough time keeping my cock to myself.

Focus, Xavi. Find Becks.

"New girls are brought upstairs," Blake shouted over the loud music. "I'll see you there. Blend in."

Blake disappeared into the crowd. Hawk gave me a curt nod, which was my cue. El cupped my face and brought my lips to hers.

"Hurry back, Ghost," she said against my lips.

I deepened our kiss, swiping my tongue through her mouth, then let her go, noting the flush in her cheeks.

"See you soon." I found a dark corner to disappear into and then re-emerged, concealed by my gift.

I'd never heard of someone else with the invisibility gift. It was a bummer I couldn't talk to the guy, especially about the walking-through-walls thing. Then again, I liked being the only invisible person.

I found Blake speaking with a man who looked like a familiar baseball player from the pre-plague era. The more I paid attention to the crowd, the more faces I recognized. It shouldn't have been surprising. The plague affected all types of people, regardless of their financial status. However, people with wealth did get premium health care, and from the looks of Federation City, it had to have cost a fortune to create the place.

Blake moved through the crowd and stopped to speak with another man. I followed them to a booth in the corner.

"Time to pay up, Don. I need a clean-up at 1123," Blake said.

"Who is it?"

"You'll see when you get there," Blake replied.

"Kyle. We're finally rid of that freak. That invisibility gift is fucked up. He was always skulking in the shadows, feeling up men and women." Don shuddered.

I took offense to the way he trashed my gift, but since he was getting rid of a dead guy, I'd let him go.

"Tonight," Blake said.

"I'm leaving right now, and after this, we're even." Don strode away from the table.

Blake walked through the crowd, and I tailed him the entire time as he made small talk. He did seem to have a fair amount of acquaintances, making me wonder what was up with this Godfather dude. My mother had warned me to stay away, but she hadn't said much beyond that.

Blake made his way upstairs, which was a strip club. Women and men were on raised dais' wearing absolutely nothing. Some were dancing; most just stood there, waiting for the highest bidder. I glanced around for Becks and didn't see her on the stage. Thank God.

Blake found his way to Roman's side. El and Hawk were nowhere to be seen.

I pressed against Roman's back and snaked my hand around his torso. "Hawk and El?" I asked, speaking into his ear.

He tipped his chin toward a hallway covered by a gauzy curtain, and then he placed his hand over mine and moved our hands down to his hard cock. I squeezed his erection and ground my length against his ass.

All the sexual stimuli had us going insane.

Blake bumped into us, causing me to stumble backward. Asshole.

"I'm going to find El," I told Roman while Blake chattered on about something.

On the other side of the gauzy curtain was a long hallway with five doors on each side. I peered into the first room on my right and got a glimpse of four dudes creating a pelvis-to-ass train. Damn. It had been a long time since I'd been a part of one of those.

In the second room, Hawk was leaning against a velvet couch with El on her knees between his legs.

"Close the fucking door, Xavi," Hudson growled.

My sister hadn't been outside; perhaps she was in one of the rooms.

I needed to hurry the hot couple along and get back to work. I snuck inside, closed the door, and released my gift.

I kneeled behind Elyanna and drank in her naked body with my gaze. She was a goddess, with her ass up in the air and her mouth full of dick. The glittery heels she wore were a nice touch. I grabbed a fistful of her hair and pulled her away from Hawk's cock, then kissed her. She tasted like wine and dick. Fucking delicious.

Hawk nudged me with his foot.

"Suck, baby." I guided her face to Hawk's cock.

My cock was painfully hard, I didn't waste another second. I ran my finger down her crack and probed the puckered hole. She moaned over Hawk's cock. I spread her cheeks and licked her ass while fingering her cunt. She rode my digits, bucking back and forth. I smeared her juices, then scanned the area. There had to be lube somewhere.

"Climb on my cock," Hudson rasped.

El released him with a wet pop and stood. I guided her to mount him, facing me. Her legs were positioned on either side of his. I gripped his shaft and threaded his thick cock into her tight hole while licking her clit.

"Oh fuck, I'm going to come." She slid down on his cock slowly, her body quivering.

I continued my assault on her swollen clit. She braced her hands on my shoulders and began working her hips. I licked and sucked, my tongue flicking over her folds and gliding over Hawk's shaft. He probably didn't appreciate me taking such liberties, but I didn't care, and he didn't kick me in the nuts. I took that as a good sign.

"Fuck that feels fucking good," Hawk grunted. His praise made the deviant side of me swell with pride.

"Fuck her mouth, Xavi," Hawk demanded.

Hell yes.

I stood and slid my cock down her throat while Hawk pumped into her from below. Elyanna was a slobbering, sweaty mess as she took everything Hawk and I were giving her. She gripped my thighs and swallowed my length. Hawk slapped her ass with both hands. El lost it.

Her nails dug into my skin, and her throat constricted over my tip. I followed her over the edge.

"Swallow all of it," I growled as ropes of hot cum shot down her throat. My body was still sputtering from my release when she was pulled away from me.

Hawk, the beast of a man, stood with her in his arms, his cock still seated in her juicy center. He placed her on the sofa and railed her from behind. Watching him fuck her was a work of art. They were masculine and feminine perfection, wrapped in a glow of pure love. They were my everything.

El reached for me. I leaned in, locking our lips. Her mouth was coated with my seed. I savored the taste of her combined with mine.

Hawk found his release, and he wrought another climax out of Elyanna. Her chest heaved with every breath. Hawk crumpled over El's back; his lips found ours.

El muttered a complaint as we released her.

"Take a minute, babe." Hawk kissed her shoulders. "Xavi and I will check the rooms."

I grunted. My friend was right. I tucked myself back into my trousers, while Hawk did the same. The door opened.

Hudson unleashed his gift and knocked the intruder to the floor.

"God damn it, Rome," Hawk growled.

The fire-starter shook off the hit and slowly stood. El was at his side, still gloriously naked, except for the heels. Damn. We were so bringing those home.

"Are you okay?" she asked, kissing the side of his face.

"Fine," he said, his half-hooded eyes drinking in her nakedness. "Do you want a break?"

She smiled brightly. "No, not yet."

He drew her in for a heated kiss and carried her back to the chair, his hands cupping her ass.

Hawk froze in place, while I sat back to enjoy the show.

Roman laid El on the sofa beside me and began kissing a trail from her mouth to her navel, while shrugging out of his coat. I was fucking hard again.

He glared at me and Hawk. "Don't you two have somewhere to be?

Becks is not outside. I didn't check the other rooms. I assume neither have you."

He began kissing her pussy, which was dripping with Hawk's cum. Fuucck.

Hawk kissed El. "I love you," he told her, then glanced at Rome. "Take care of her. We'll be back."

Damn it. I kissed El and followed Hawk out, letting the fire-starter and mind-bender have their moment.

Before exiting, I watched as Roman pulled out his big dick. The cheeky fucker winked at me, then went back to eating our woman.

CHAPTER THIRTY-THREE

Roman

Wearing nothing but those sexy heels, Elyanna was absolute perfection. And I loved her more than anyone I had ever loved before. Hawk and Xavi were fantasy and physical desire. With El, it was everything: fiery passion and undying love.

"I love you, Elyanna," I told her. My lips were covered with her release and her men. I wasn't sure who, but I'd gotten a mouthful of someone's seed mixed with hers, and it was so fucking good.

"I love you," she replied as I slid into her tight center.

Her cunt squeezed my cock. Fully sheathed into her depths, I paused and remembered to breathe. With Xavi constantly teasing me, watching Hawk and El nearly ravage each other at the boutique, and all the flesh in the club, I was wound up. I wouldn't last long, which I'd hoped wasn't disappointing for El. She'd just been double-teamed by two huge dicks, and I didn't want to deliver a sub-par performance.

"You feel so good," she mewled. Her words and the way she rolled her hips made me forget my insecurities.

"You like this. Being fucked all night by three big cocks." I nipped at her ear.

"Yes," she groaned. Her pussy tightened even harder.

"You're so fucking wet, so tight. Better than my dreams." I dug my heels into the floor, driving my cock deeper and harder into her core.

"When we get home, I want you to take all three of us at the same time. Would you like that? A cock in every hole?" I rasped.

"Fuck yes," she cried out.

God damn, this woman owned me. I wanted to wear her skin. Wear her pussy around my cock twenty-four seven.

"What else would you like, baby?" I asked.

She pressed our foreheads together, rocking her hips to match my thrusts.

"Will you . . ." she paused.

"Tell me what you want, babe. I'll do anything for you."

"Would you suck Xavi's cock while fucking me?" she breathed.

"Is that what you want?"

"Is that okay?" she asked, her voice unsure.

"Fuck yes. I'll suck and fuck him anytime you want," I replied without hesitation.

She was perfect. And mine. I drove into her body, my sac tightening with the need to explode. My thrusts became wild and erratic. My climax was right there, testing my restraint.

She arched her back and came for me. Thank fuck. I couldn't hold back, my orgasm shot out of me like a geyser. My hips bucked, pushing my seed deeper into her channel until I had nothing left.

For a moment, I lay on top of her, panting, sweat trickling down my back. I was in heaven until my insecurities reared their ugly heads, making me second-guess what she said. Did she mean it? Was she taunting me?

Her thumb glided against my forehead. "Hey."

I looked into her hazel eyes. "I won't force you or Xavi to do anything you don't want to. If it feels right, great. No matter what, I love you both."

"You're perfect in every way, Elyanna." I gave her a lingering kiss.

Reluctantly, I released her and said, "We should find the others."

She nodded. We dressed quickly and slipped out of the room. A woman had been waiting outside the door, presumably to clean up the mess we'd made and prep it for the next horny couple.

El stopped the woman and asked, "Is there a woman's room or locker room nearby?"

"Oh, you must be new. Well, you will be very popular. The women's powder room is out this way. Enter the last door on your right. It is unmarked, but here, take this key card to get in. One of the other girls forgot it after her last— " She paused, then waved her hand at the room. "Orgy?"

El laughed. "I seemed to have lost mine also."

"It happens. See you around."

We found Hawk and Xavi where I left Blake. El told them she was heading to the women's bathroom. "Maybe Becks is in there." Hawk nodded, and we followed her to the unmarked door and guarded it while she went in.

"Have fun?" Xavi asked, wiggling his eyebrows at me.

"You are so immature," I replied.

"Yeah, he is," Hawk added.

"So you guys . . . um, share?" Blake asked.

Hawk glared. His kink was watching his wife with other men, and yet he was really picky about who. I couldn't blame him. Hell, I wouldn't want to share if I could. But my own demons were a thing that made it impossible for me to be territorial. I couldn't very well put limitations on her if I wanted dick every now and then. It couldn't be random hookups, though. Hawk was not into sucking cocks. Xavi clearly was. But what would that mean? Were we going to be exclusive dudes? I wasn't sure, and really, it didn't matter. All I wanted was to be in El's life. And if that meant being with her and only her, hell yes, she was worth it. And the dirty fantasy talk was a bonus.

"Just asking. I'm not trying to insert myself into your . . . pod," Blake said.

"Don't overthink it, Fly." Xavi nudged my arm.

"What did you call me?" I scowled.

"Fly. Fire fly," he replied.

"The name is Roman," I told him. "Only Elyanna can have a nickname for me. And it's not Fly."

"Oooh!" He covered his mouth. "Did I hit a nerve? I thought shooting your wad would make you lighten up."

"I am going to scorch your ass," I threatened.

"Aww, have you been thinking about my ass? Again? Oh Roman, you naughty boy." He glanced at my crotch. "It's okay; I've been thinking about yours, too."

Damn him. His smart mouth was annoying as all hell, and yet he managed to make me hard again. It was confusing. But fuck him if he thought he'd get the last word.

I stepped into his space and said in a low tone, "Keep it up. That smart mouth of yours is going to get a good dicking."

Elyanna exited the powder room. I moved away from Xavier, who was speechless and pulled El into my arms.

"Hi," she smiled at me.

"Anything?" Hawk asked.

"No. Not in there, and no one has seen anyone new. And this," she waved behind her. "Is the women's dressing room for both clubs. There's another access door. I checked it out; she wasn't in there either."

"How'd you get through there so quickly?" Xavi asked.

"The room is small and one big orgy. No one resembled her in the slightest," El replied.

"Okay, that means the Premiere Loop," Hudson stated.

"Now?" Blake asked.

"Now," we said.

We left Jamboree Court and made our way toward the Premiere Loop, which was comprised of three circular buildings connected via long corridors.

"Where's the boutique from here?" El asked.

We'd left our bags and her sword in a hiding spot near the retail district.

"That way." Blake pointed to our left. "Did you need something?" he asked her.

"We need our gear," Hudson replied. "How far is it?"

"Twenty minutes," Blake glanced at El. "Maybe longer. We should head that way. It's not like we can get past security in the Loop anyway. The surveillance office is on the ground floor in a soundproof room with no windows. They can see people walking through the doors, but you can't see through the glass."

"Why would the surveillance room need to be soundproof?" I asked.

"I was told the original design was for someone with supersonic senses. They used it to test his abilities." Blake answered. "I'm not sure when or why things changed, but it is now the surveillance room."

"Interesting," Hawk muttered.

"Do you have a way in?" El eyed the healer.

"Umm . . . sure. They have retina recognition for gifted individuals. But I'm not allowed after hours. No one is. I figure you guys had a trick to break in, which is why you're so keen," he replied.

El gave him an exasperated glare. He was trying to get us to divulge our secrets. Not going to happen. We paused at a corner near the entrance to the Loop.

"We'll split up. Blake, you guide Roman and me back to the retail area. Xavi and El will remain here," Hudson said.

"I'll go with Blake. I'm the one who hid the stuff," Xavi volunteered.

"Take Roman with you," Hudson offered.

"I don't need a babysitter," Xavi scoffed.

"No, but you can't carry all that stuff by yourself," I told him.

"I did it before," he argued.

"Why are you being an asshole?" I crossed my arms over my chest.

"Why are you . . ."

"Stop!" Elyanna cut us off. She faced Blake. "How many security guards?"

"After hours, there should only be two, maybe three, in the surveillance room. There might be a couple of patrols in the women's section," the healer answered.

"All of you go with Blake. I'll go make new friends," she told us.

"No," Hawk, Xavi, and I said simultaneously.

"How do you expect to get past the guards?" Blake asked.

"The fine art of womanly persuasion." She sauntered off, putting an extra sway to her hips.

Hudson and I went after her. Blake tried to follow, but Xavi pulled him back.

"Wait, Elyanna," Hudson called out.

She turned.

"You can't go in alone," I said.

She glanced behind me, then said in a soft voice. "I can, and I will. I need to try my gift. I'm hoping the soundproof room will allow me to use my gift and get some information from the guards."

"I appreciate what you're trying to do, babe." Hudson shook his head. "I'm not leaving you here by yourself."

"Me neither," I added.

"Fine. Someone stay with me. Or both of you."

"Hudson will stay. He can use his gift to block out yours. That way, when you break into the guard's mind, he won't be affected, and he won't hinder whatever you need to do," I told them.

"Are you sure you don't mind?" El asked.

I smiled. "Not at all, beautiful. Hawk will keep you safe."

"Don't forget my sassy stick." She kissed the corner of my mouth, then stepped away.

Hawk and I bumped fists, and then he followed after her.

CHAPTER THIRTY-FOUR

Elyanna

Hudson grabbed my arm and steered me to a dark corner. "Elyanna, wait up. Let's come up with a plan."

"Hey, what's wrong?" He brought me to a halt and peered at me.

"Everything. I hate not having access to my gift, and my feet are killing me," I pouted. Fucking heels. It'd been years since I last wore stilettos. I never liked them pre-plague, and I hated them even more now. It didn't help that we'd been walking around for an hour, maybe more. Granted, I'd spent a lot of that time on my back or on my knees, but still, walking around in heels was pure torture.

"Those heels look fucking hot, especially without the dress." He ran a hand down my butt.

I glared at him.

He stifled a chuckle, then cleared his throat. "You can take off the heels, peaches."

"Don't you dare laugh, Hudson." I glared at my husband.

"I wish I could make it better, love. But going in there is not the answer." He pointed to the circular building behind us.

"Hudson, we need answers. Blake isn't being completely honest. I want to rescue Becks and go home to Axel. How about I try my gift? If it takes longer than fifteen minutes, you can come in and rescue me," I told him.

"Have you forgotten who you're married to?" He clenched his jaw. "The answer is no. We go in together."

"No, I go in alone. They won't allow me to enter if you're looming. I need to get in there, close the door, and use my gift. If all goes as I hope, in less than fifteen minutes the door will open, and you can join me."

He crossed his arms over his chest and glared. I mimicked his posture.

"Fine. Five minutes, come on." He grasped my hand, and we entered the building together. The surveillance room was straight ahead.

I faced Hudson. "We're being watched. You have to act like you're mad at me and then walk away. I'm going to act weepy, and the guards will let me in. Five minutes."

"I am mad at you. Five minutes," Hudson snarled and stomped off.

He was either a really good actor or he was truly mad at me.

A door opened.

Alright, Elyanna, time for Scene II, Act I.

Doing my best damsel in distress performance, I stumbled toward the door. "Can you help me?" I sniffled.

"Are you all right, Miss?" A man in his early forties approached.

"Can I come in? I just need to sit and rest for a moment. My boyfriend is upset. I don't want to wait here all by myself." I placed my hand on his arm and pleaded with watery eyes.

"Of course, you sweet little thing." He guided me into the surveillance office and then shut the door.

As soon as the doors closed, there was a sucking noise, and my ears popped as all outside sounds were cut off.

"Oh, this is nice." I sat in the nearest office chair, sighing in relief to be off my feet. I accessed my gift. The low buzz of two minds surrounded me.

"You're really beautiful," the second guard said to me.

The other guard watched me as I crossed my legs. "Your boyfriend seems like a real asshole."

"Thank you for being so kind and letting me rest for a moment," I said in an innocent tone.

Both men watched me with heated gazes that roamed the length of my body.

I didn't need my gift to know what they were thinking, nor did I need it to get them to do what I wanted. Still, I latched onto the thoughts of the two men in the room and began weaving a tale into their psyches.

It had taken me three minutes to make them forget my presence while they continued with their monotonous duties of watching multiple screens. While they were busy, I closed off my gift and opened the door.

Hudson was right outside, and he crept into the room.

I shut the door behind him and opened my gift again, sighing with relief. For a moment, I was worried the guards were going to realize they were enthralled.

Hudson rolled one of the office chairs to the corner and sat. The guards paid no attention to him. My husband winked.

I focused on the guards and had them tell me in detail about the Loop. There were three circular buildings connected to one another via covered walkways on the surface level and connecting tunnels underground, forming a circular loop. The first two buildings were identical in design and five stories high. The third building, hidden from street view, was two stories and had a domed roof.

The first building we entered was dedicated to the security department on the ground level and had five floors of administrative offices.

Building two was where the gifted women lived. The guards said there were seven women, and all were sequestered there. The first two floors were medical, the third was their recreation floor, the fourth was residences, and the fifth floor was the Godfather's office. I'd asked them if the women ever left the Loop, and neither had witnessed them leaving aside from training in building three.

The third building had only two floors. One was a gym, and the other was a medical facility. The center of the building was an arena, thus the dome roof. All gifted individuals were required to report seven days a week for various training exercises. The surveillance cameras on the fitness level were active, but they revealed nothing. No one was there. The guards did point out that there were no cameras in the dome area. There was a viewing room, which they showed us on the screens, and occasionally they'd get a glimpse of what was happening when the gifted trained.

"Wow, gifted individuals," I said, my voice coated with awe. "I wonder what kind of gifts they have."

"Oh, we have all that information here." Terry, the guard who let me in, pulled a binder from the file cabinet beside his desk. "We have all their stats. The gifted are like royalty here. Only gifted and staff with priority clearance are allowed here. It is our job to keep up-to-date information on all of them."

"Can I see it?" I smiled.

"Of course." The guard handed me his sacred binder.

"You're one of us now," the other guard added.

"I feel so special." I beamed and began leafing through the binder. I wonder if they would notice that this was missing. This was information worth studying. "Do the men live here?"

"No, they live with the Godfather. He has the estate on the far east side of the city," Terry said.

That was surprising.

"I thought the Godfather spent all his time here. He seems so important." I handed the binder to Hawk.

"He's here at sunrise until midnight," Lee, the other guard, told me.

I glanced at the clock. We had two hours.

"Can I see where the women live?" I asked.

"Sure. I can show the common areas." Terry tapped a few buttons on his keyboard, and he pointed to a screen that showed the corridor that led from the first circle to the second.

"That's just a hallway." Disappointment laced my words.

"Hold on, darling; it gets more interesting. Sort of." He tapped his keyboard again, and the screen flashed, showing a typical medical office waiting room. There was a counter in the middle of the space. A guard had his boots propped on the desk while focusing on a computer screen. The camera panned around the room showing two guards lounging on the plush seats in the waiting area.

"How do I get their job?" I muttered.

The guards laughed. "We all take turns. There's always two here and three patrolling," Lee offered.

"I'm not sure why they need us. It's not like the women are going anywhere. They have a nice life up there."

"It must be horrible to live there and never be allowed outdoors or to experience the city. Why is that?" I asked.

"Oh, we don't ask those kinds of questions. All we know is that they have a nice garden." Terry pointed to the screen showing the bottom floor of the building. He pressed a few keys, and another image flashed on the screen. "This is floor three; there's a gym, a spa, a salon, and an indoor pool."

"Has there been anyone new?" I asked.

"Yeah, earlier. Female. She should be in her suite resting, living the life." Lee laughed.

"And what do the suites look like?" I prodded.

"We can't see that floor or the Godfather's floor," Lee replied.

Of course.

Hudson tapped me on the arm with the binder. I took it and looked at the page he earmarked. Blake Patton. Age twenty-nine. Gift: Healer.

"Have you guys met any of the gifted?"

"Oh yeah."

"Some," Lee added. "Most are assholes."

"All are assholes." Terry corrected.

"How about this guy? He looks like an asshole." I showed them Blake's picture.

"Total asshole. He was just here whining about having to do patrol duty after working his shift."

"Shift? Is he a security guard?"

"No. He's a healer. See." He tapped the area where his gift was stated in black and white. Ass.

"He was here healing people?" I asked.

"Sort of. He's in charge of working with the women. He probably had to work on the new gifted that was brought in."

Fucking liar.

Terry and Lee proceeded to tell me more about the Premiere Loop. I got them to give me one of their security top clearance key cards that would allow us to have access everywhere in the buildings. And I had them shut off the cameras for the corridors leading to building two and the elevators. I'd prompted them to turn them back on when the Godfather arrived. We had less than ninety minutes left.

As soon as they'd done as I asked, I had them take a little nap just as a knock sounded on the door.

"If Blake is out there, I'm going to shoot him in the face," Hudson growled.

I placed a hand on his elbow. "Maybe just knock him out for now. We may need his help with Becks."

"You have a point. Ready?"

I nodded and shut off my gift. We exited the surveillance office and were greeted by Ghost and Bug, but not Blake.

"Your firebug knocked him out. He's in the closet." Xavier pointed to a door over his shoulder.

"He was irritating me." Roman held out my sword.

I grasped my sassy stick and brought it close to my chest for a hug.

"Clothes are in here." Roman tapped a duffel bag.

Hudson and I changed quickly while telling them what we learned.

"Let's search the Godfather's residence first." Hudson grabbed the bag and placed the binder in it.

We hustled to the second building and went straight to the fifth floor.

"Why are we doing this first?" I asked.

"Intel," my three men replied at the same time.

The security key card got us into the Godfather's office.

"Was there anything in the binder about him?" I asked Hudson.

"No."

The office was a grand fishbowl. It was an open space with floor-to-ceiling windows. On the far wall, there was a view of the garden below, while the other wall showcased the city. Stepping out of the elevators to our right, there was a stained glass wall, which led deeper into the office. To the left, an ornate desk sat in the middle of the marble flooring. Large leather sofas surrounded a glass coffee table. It was masculine and OCD-organized.

"This place is huge," Ghost said.

"What are we looking for exactly?" I asked.

"Anything suspicious," Hudson replied.

I wandered down a hallway while peeking into the rooms. There was nothing to note, a bedroom which looked like it was never used. A small spotless kitchen with a round glass breakfast table. The only space that looked as though it had been frequently used was the conference room. I perused the documents hung on the wall taking note of the many pictures of children. My heart stuttered in my chest as I came across a picture of a young boy with familiar green eyes.

"Hudson!" I called out.

A moment later Hawk, Rome, and Xavi were standing beside me.

"Mother fucker," Hudson snarled.

Rome gasped.

"Son of a bitch, Hawk. You still have the same smug grin," Xavier stated.

I glared in his direction, and he shrugged. "It's true."

"These are all of my classmates," Hudson stated, ignoring Xavi.

"Look at this, guys," Rome said. "This must be his war room."

The three of us turned our heads to see Bug looking at something on the conference table.

"Shit, this is a map of our home. Gator Springs, Briar Penitentiary and Royal Summit," Xavi pointed out.

"Hillside is here," Hudson added.

I perused some of the papers near the map. "This looks like plans. Attack plans. He's been sending his guards to our homes continuously. I don't like this, Hudson. Why does he have pictures of you as a child? What is all this?"

"It's okay, babe. We knew he was the one sending the troops after us. Now we have proof and his battle plans." Hudson pulled me into a hug. "We're running out of time. We only have one key card, so Roman, you read up on all this stuff. I'll take El and Xavi to the fourth floor and come back for you."

We went down one flight of stairs to the residences.

"I'll be back in fifteen minutes. Stay close to Xavi." Hudson pecked my forehead, and he ran back to the fifth floor.

Xavi grabbed my hand, and we began searching the women's quarters. A cloying floral scent assaulted my nostrils as soon as we entered the residential area. The double doors opened to a main room, which looked like any pre-plague living room. Cream-colored sofas faced a large flat-screen television. Crystal vases filled with purple flowers were everywhere. It was meant to be elegant, yet it felt staged and uninviting. The kitchen was spotless, as though it had never been used. A part of me wanted to peer into the cabinets to see if they were empty.

We moved past the kitchen and ventured down a hallway. We opened several doors that contained sleeping women. Xavi used his gift so that we could get a closer look. None of them were Becks.

We searched the ensuite bathrooms and every room and came up empty.

In the last room, I heard a familiar rattle of metal clinking together. I froze mid-step, squeezing Ghost's hand. We stepped closer to the sleeping woman. She rolled over on her bed, causing the metal to rattle again. I raised my shaky hand and drew back her comforter to reveal the woman's shackled ankle. I grit my teeth and followed the chain, which hung off the bed, and went into the bathroom. Rage bubbled in my gut.

Ghost placed a hand on my waist and guided me back the way we'd come.

In some ways, I wanted to confirm if the others were chained as well and decided against it. It wasn't something I wanted to witness, and there was nothing we could have done to release them. I made a silent vow to unchain these women and followed Xavi back to the Godfather's office.

"That didn't take long," Rome said as we entered.

"What are we going to do with this?" I asked, waving a hand at the maps and attack plans.

"Nothing. I need more time to study this stuff but taking them is too risky. No Becks?" Hudson replied.

"We need to check the first two floors; that's where the women get their enhancements. There are three guards there." I moved toward the picture of Hudson as a child. It made me think of my son and I hated the idea of the Godfather having it.

"Leave it, El. He'll know we were here and we're not in a position to take him on. Yet." Hudson tugged on my elbow.

"But," I began to argue.

"No buts, babe. We need to find Becks and get out of here" Hudson insisted, leading me out of the room.

"I'll take point." Ghost led the way downstairs.

CHAPTER THIRTY-FIVE

Elyanna

We took the stairs and waited while Xavi entered the medical office to create a diversion. Keeping the door slightly ajar, I heard a noise from down the hall. The guards got off their asses to check out the noise, and my men snuck up behind them and knocked them out. While the guards were being handled, I went searching for Becks.

I found her in the second stark white room I'd entered. She was in bed, eyes closed with an IV hooked up to her vein, and thankfully not chained. "In here!" I called out.

"Becks!" I patted her cheek.

"El?!" She blinked rapidly.

I pulled her in for a fierce hug, her skin icy. "Let's get you out of here. How are you feeling?"

"Tired. Dying to go home." Her voice was weak.

"Yeah, me too. We need you to change." I told her just as Xavi stormed in with the duffel bag.

The twins hugged. I pulled the extra uniform out of the bag. No shoes. Damn it.

"Xavi, search the closet for shoes. I'll help Becks get dressed."

Xavi ran circles around the room, searching for footwear.

"Did you find Julia?" she asked.

"Didn't need to. Your brother rescued her from Dr. Carla and took her to the farm. He met up with Hudson and Roman, and they found me. Then we found you. I wish we had gotten here sooner."

"You found me," Beck said. "I was so scared. But you came for me."

"Of course I did. I would never leave you behind." I buttoned her cargo pants, then helped her with a tank top.

"Shoes," Xavi shoved them into my arms.

I slipped socks on Becks' feet, then boots, which thankfully fit.

"Wait till you find out who I ran into here," Xavi told his sister.

"Hey Becks. Great to see you. We gotta run. We want to be out of this city before sunrise," Hudson told us.

"I'm ready," Becks said.

I grasped her hand, and we followed Hudson's lead.

"What are we going to do with the guards?" I asked as we passed the front desk.

"We took care of it," Roman answered.

The five of us squeezed into the elevator. Becks shivered beside me. I wrapped an arm around her.

She returned the hug and hung on. Xavi came and wrapped us in a group hug.

We filed out of the elevator and made our way to the nearest exit. I was directionally challenged in Federation City, so I relied on the men to lead us to safety. After running for a good what felt like thirty minutes, we came to a warehouse docking area.

"I found this while you and Xavi recuperated. It's a shipping and receiving area. I was hoping to find a truck here that we could drive out of here." He glanced around the loading dock. "I guess we're walking. Stay out of sight."

The rest of us hugged the wall. Hudson pressed a lever, and the bay doors rolled upwards. Beyond it, the desert sky was a silvery blue. Dawn was fast approaching. We'd just made it.

"Ladies, pull back the hair and put on the helmets. The guard shack is to the right. We're doing a foot patrol if anyone asks," Hudson told us.

Becks and I did as we were told. Hair up, helmets on. It was as good of a disguise as any. The one guard on duty was sleeping. We strolled right past him to an open road, which Hudson surmised was the route that would take trucks to and from the warehouse sector located in California.

We stayed on the open road for a time and then Hudson led us through what I assumed was the outskirts of the citizens encampment. The pace he'd set was a steady jog. The temperatures increased as the sun rose, and my back was soon coated with sweat. Becks wasn't faring well either. We took off our helmets, earning us a glare from my husband. I shrugged. It wasn't just the desert heat; Becks was putting off some weird vibes. I tapped her shoulder and almost flinched. Despite the desert heat and our steady jog, her skin was cool and flushed.

"Are you feeling okay?" I placed a hand over her forehead. No fever, clammy skin.

"I'm getting tired. It's fine; I can keep going," she insisted.

Hudson and Xavi were several feet ahead. Roman behind us.

I opened my gift, grateful to be away from the thousands of minds, and sent a message telepathically to my husband.

We need to slow down.

He glanced over his shoulder and slowed to a fast walk.

Becks linked her arm with mine, and we kept going.

We had been walking for over an hour, skirting the edge of the citizens encampment, when Becks began to stumble. My three men were in front of us, looking for a vehicle. Using my gift, I shouted for Hudson.

He whipped his head as I guided Becks to sit on the sidewalk.

"We need a place to rest," I told him.

"There's a strip mall a few miles ahead," he replied.

With my gaze, I pleaded with him. He nodded. Xavi sat beside his twin, pulled her into his arms, and carried her. My heart clenched.

Something was wrong with my best friend, and I wasn't sure if rest was going to cut it.

"Hudson, we need to find help. Something is seriously wrong with her," I said.

"Shit. We should've made Blake come with us." He looked back the way we came. "Come on, babe, let's catch up."

"Hey," he called out. Xavi slowed down. "I'm going back to get Blake. Head to the strip mall. I'll be back as soon as I can."

His hand cupped the back of my neck, and his lips claimed mine. "I love you. Stay safe."

"Love you, too. Come back to me." I watched him jog toward Federation City.

"Hawk! Wait up." Xavi pressed his chest against my back and wrapped his arms around my middle. "I love you. Take care of my sister."

He ran to catch up to Hudson. I turned to see Roman carrying Becks toward the strip mall.

CHAPTER THIRTY-SIX
Hudson

"You should stay with your sister," I told Xavi when he caught up with me.

"You'll need my gift to bring Blake back," he replied.

"I was just going to point a gun to his head and walk him right out." I snorted.

We laughed and picked up the pace. It was about seven miles to the docking area. Instead of taking the circuitous route to avoid the citizens, we ran straight through and made it in half the time.

The sun had just risen, and there were a few people moving about the city. We had maybe another thirty minutes before the masses would descend on the Premiere Loop, where a good amount of the population reported for work. Not to mention the gifted.

Upon entering the building, a guard stopped us. "New recruits. Finally. I hope you're more reliable than the last lot." His nostrils flared, and he scrunched his face. "Geez, did you two run all the way from the Citizen Encampment? Hit the showers before changing into your new uniforms. Let's get your IDs."

He opened the door to the surveillance room. The two guards El had used her gift on were standing to leave as two others took their place.

"Hey, Mullins." Terry, one of the guards from the night shift, greeted the guard. "Slow night, as usual."

"Oh, hey, new recruits from the patrol. Are there any women down there?" Lee, the other guard I remembered from the night before, asked.

"A few," Xavier responded.

"You guys have all the best benefits," Lee replied.

"What, no ladies here?" Xavi asked.

"Only the gifted. And don't even think about it. The Godfather will hang you by your tongue if you try anything," the guard who had let us in said to me and Xavi. "Is he in?" he asked the guards.

"Arrived a few minutes ago. He's having breakfast with the ladies." Terry tipped his chin to the screen.

I glanced at the screen. My stomach clenched as the familiar man moved around a dining table and sat between two women dressed in hospital gowns. There were seven women at the table, and three of them were heavily pregnant.

"They're pregnant," I murmured.

"Yep. If the rumors are correct, they're all his," Mullins replied. "Here are your temporary cards. Human resources and locker rooms are on the second floor. I'll call Jacobsen and tell him you're on your way."

Xavi and I exited the surveillance room.

"They're expecting us on the second floor. Let's get that done quick and head back."

Xavi nodded.

In under seven minutes, we spoke with Jacobsen, got our schedule, new uniforms, plus extras, because these things came in handy.

We ran back down to the first floor, ducked into the storage closet where Blake was trussed up in the corner.

We untied his legs and got him moving, keeping his arms and mouth secure with duct tape. Xavi's gift concealed them both, and they walked out of the building in front of me.

"Hey you!" a voice shouted behind us. "Recruit?!"

I nearly lashed out with my gift but tempered the urge.

"Keep going, Xavi. I'll catch up," I muttered, then turned to face the guard, who was fast approaching.

"Where's the other guy?" Mullins asked.

"Took off. We're not training until tomorrow," I told him.

"Well, since you're still here, you're starting now. We're short-staffed. Come on. You should take a quick shower."

What was with these people and body odor? Did we stink that badly? I suppose we did considering we ran several miles in one hundred-degree heat.

I shrugged and followed Mullins into the building. We took the elevator to the second floor, where he ushered me to the locker rooms. I had to keep up appearances in the Premiere Loop, so I took a quick shower and dressed in the new uniform, which was exactly like the other except it was charcoal gray instead of black.

A part of me wanted to snap the guy's neck and return to my wife. Leaving a dead body on the second floor would have sounded the alarm, and that wasn't ideal. I needed to give Xavi time to get away. And to be honest, I was curious about the entire operation. The gifted individuals were expected, and I'd hoped to see them train.

Mullins gave me a tour of the first circle. Unlike the other buildings, the first was nothing to note. Workers arrived and began their day. None of them gave us a second glance. Before we moved on to buildings two and three, Mullins handed me a binder, exactly like the one I had taken the night before.

"You'll need to familiarize yourself with this information. The gifted are granted special privileges, and the Godfather wants us to steer clear of them. We are not to speak with these individuals for any reason. Basically, give them a wide berth."

"Why?" I asked.

"The Godfather wants them to focus on their training," he replied.

That didn't make much sense to me, but I wasn't going to press for more.

He led me to the third building, which was the designated area for the gifted men. At first glance, the training floor looked like any fitness facility; there were weights, treadmills, spin bikes, a rowing machine, and a locker room, which led to an Olympic-sized pool. I wasn't impressed until we went to the arena.

"The gifted spend a lot of time in here," Mullins said as we entered through steel double doors.

I released a low whistle, gazing at the dome ceiling. "Wow. What do they do in here?"

"Train. Basically, they use their gifts against one another. We don't have surveillance in here, but we do have surveillance of the viewing room." He pointed to a window along one of the walls. "Sometimes you'll be able to see what they're doing. We should go; they'll be starting soon."

We went through the corridor toward the women's section and up to the floor, where we had found Becks. We stayed in the lobby area, where Mullins had instructed me that this was as far as guards went.

"Seems odd that we are here working as security guards, and we're not allowed in most areas." I watched Mullins for a reaction.

He rubbed a hand down his face. "Yeah. Those are the rules. And honestly, the gifted don't need security. Our job is to make sure other people, regulars like ourselves, don't enter."

I almost scoffed, considering the guards hadn't done their job last night, and so far, Mullins hadn't either. He was literally taking the leader of one of the Rebellion factions on a tour.

"Hold right there soldier," a male voice called out.

I kept my facial expression neutral and allowed Mullins to respond while I slowly turned to face the man I'd hoped to run into. Alexi and I had stayed in touch over the years. He looked the same, except the tattoos that had started on his forearms were now covering his biceps and his neck.

There were a handful of men in the gifted binder I recognized from school. We all had our separate issues with the headmaster, and it made me very curious as to why they were serving him now.

"Where are you headed?" Alexi asked.

"New recruit. Showing him the ropes," Mullins replied.

"Good, I could use some help moving some things around. Come on, newbie." Alexi motioned.

I wanted to laugh. Alexi's gift was superhuman strength. He didn't need help moving anything. It was in the binder; I'd seen it myself. Mullins either didn't remember or he didn't read the darn thing.

"Sure. After you're done, report back to the surveillance room. Good luck." Mullins scurried away. Maybe he did read Alexi's profile and wanted to get far away from the man.

I shrugged and followed my old schoolmate. We walked for some time in silence until we reached the underground corridor between buildings three and one.

"I can't believe you're here, man. Why?" Alexi asked, then wrapped me in a bear hug.

"I was going to ask you the same thing. The last I heard, you were staying away from the old headmaster." I patted his back and stepped back to get a good look at my friend.

He nodded. "Yeah, we dodged him for a time. My wife got caught by the patrols. So we voluntarily came in to save her, and now we're stuck."

"Okay, wait. That was way too much info all at once. Strong Russian man is stuck in here? And *we* volunteered? Who's we? And you're married? Who the hell would marry you?" I smirked.

"Fuck off." He chuckled. "My wife and her other mates. There are four of us. What's your story?"

"Rescue mission. Long story. Who else is here? Anyone else from school?" I asked.

"There are two of us. Three, including you."

That was not true. I'd glanced at the binder containing profiles of the gifted and had recognized a half dozen of them. He noticed the questioning look on my face.

"Your binder is full of shit. The Godfather experiments on us as much as he does on humans. The others perished during the enhancement period. There are only thirty-two of us left, and eight are women. The binder didn't include Dani, which is good. He's holding her because of us." He ushered me back to the main floor. "Don't let the Godfather catch you. He'll figure out a way to hold you hostage. If you're looking to put an end to him . . . I'm with you. This place is not what it seems. I'm on patrol duty this evening and will check in with you later."

"What's his deal? How is he keeping you stuck here?" I asked before he walked away.

"He's keeping my wife hostage," Alexi said with a low breath as he went toward the training center.

Shit. The Godfather was keeping the women as hostages, and the men were willing to do anything to keep them safe, even if it meant kowtowing to that asshole. I understood Alexi's reluctance to leave. Hell, I wouldn't leave El behind either.

A group of gifted people should have been able to overpower the Godfather with ease. The headmaster was a telekinetic like me. I had gotten stronger, but even at full strength, I couldn't stand against a dozen gifted hostages, let alone thirty. I was missing something, something big. A part of me wanted to find out what that was. The other part wanted to return to El.

I reached the doorway that led to the first building and had decided to leave the loop behind to find my wife. We could deal with the situation here another time together.

A voice from my past called my name and made me stumble.

"Hudson Pierce, all grown up. I was hoping you'd find me."

I turned to face my former headmaster, now known as The Godfather. Seeing him through adult eyes gave me a new perspective. He was sporting a head full of white hair. He was tall, but a few inches shorter than me. His narrow shoulders and lithe frame made him seem scrawny. And the deep scowl etched on his pale face made him look constipated. The man that haunted my childhood memories was no longer intimidating. I met his glare with a stern gaze of my own and rolled my shoulders.

Bring it, old man.

CHAPTER THIRTY-SEVEN
Xavier

Blake didn't give me any trouble as we walked through Federation City and found our way to the shipping and receiving dock. I hadn't expected him to, considering his hands were tied behind his back and his mouth gagged, but after Dr. Carla's betrayal, I didn't trust anyone.

In the shipping and receiving area, I went straight to the first SUV, where two men were about to enter. I shoved Blake into the back of a truck and slid into the back seat. The guards were too busy shooting the bull and hadn't noticed us at all. They got in and proceeded to drive past the security gate.

As soon as we had driven a couple miles from BHF headquarters, I stabbed the passenger in the neck, then pressed my gun on the driver's temple.

"Pull over," I ordered.

The man cried and screamed incoherent things but did as I asked.

"Put your weapons on the dashboard and get out of the truck."

"Don't kill me. I have children," he stammered while putting his gun and a knife on the dashboard.

I exited the vehicle, keeping my gun trained on him the entire time, then made him get out of the car. He begged for his life, and I responded by shooting him in the face. I didn't have time to waste. I got behind the wheel, leaving the guard's dead body behind. The other guard was bleeding out in the passenger seat, but there was no time to deal with him. I needed to get Blake to Becks yesterday.

I brought the truck to a screeching halt in the parking lot. Roman's hulking frame came out of a door that had been a mattress store. He gave me a curt nod and followed me to the back of the vehicle, where Blake was waiting.

The man was shaking and sweating profusely. His eyes widened as I dragged him into the store.

El was sitting beside my sister's prone form and her gaze locked with mine. A flash of relief crossed her face. Then she looked over my shoulder.

"He was detained as a new security guard in the Loop. I'm sure he's fine," I told her.

She nodded, then got up and pushed a plastic chair beside the bed.

I shoved Blake into the seat and ripped off the duct tape.

"Heal my sister," I snarled.

"What the hell? Are you gifted? Are you all gifted?" His gaze darted around the room.

"Focus, Blake," El said. "She needs help. We rescued her from the Loop. Something's wrong, and I don't know what."

"You got her out of the women's ward?" Blake asked.

"No more questions. Do your thing?" I drew back my fist.

"Ghost." El placed a firm hand on my bicep. "Don't. We need his help."

"Please, Blake," she pleaded with the healer.

He raised his bound wrists.

In one swift move, El withdrew her sword and sliced through the duct tape.

Blake blanched. "Umm, okay, tell me where you found her."

While Elyanna patiently told him what he wanted to know, Blake placed his hands on my sister's forehead and closed his eyes.

After a moment, he paused and faced Elyanna.

"Uh, there's only so much I can do" he started.

"Fucking liar," I spat.

"I'm not lying! My abilities can only do so much. She was given an enhancement serum, and her body is rejecting it. Long story short, it's attacking her cells. My gift can keep it at bay for a while. For her to live, she needs a counter-serum. It's something they created that will neutralize any adverse effects. Without it, there's not much I can do."

"You fucking liar." I grabbed Blake by the throat and squeezed.

"Ghost!" Elyanna tried pulling me away from Blake. "Let go, Ghost. We need him."

"He's trying to send us back to Federation City," I growled.

"Please, Ghost."

Strong arms encircled my neck. "Let. Go." Roman's voice was low and menacing.

Blake sputtered as I released him. Elyanna was there, patting his back.

I paced, trying to calm down.

"Do what you can, Blake, please," Elyanna told him, then she faced me. "Ghost, a word, please."

I followed her out of the store, expecting a tongue-lashing. Instead, she wrapped her arms around me and buried her face in my chest. The anger and worry left me as I held her close.

A moment too soon, she stepped away. "Ghost. I umm . . . I would never do anything to hurt you. I hope you know that, but I need you to do your invisible thing. I don't trust Blake. I have to use my gift to get the truth. I'm stressed, so my control is tenuous at the moment. So when I open my gift, every mind in there will be accessible to me. I can try to shield everyone except Blake, but I can't make any guarantees. After what happened with Luther, I don't want you to feel threatened by me, okay?"

Her request floored me. She was trying to protect me after the damage Luther had done. He had really done a number on me, and for nearly two years, I thought it was all her doing. Maybe I did have it wrong to begin with. I felt like shit.

"Of course, El." My voice was gravelly. "Anything you need."

I called on my gift and followed her into the store.

Elyanna sat at the foot of the bed and spoke with Blake.

"Blake, this is Becks. She . . ." her voice hitched. "She's my soul sister. I am begging you to do everything you can to save her."

"Elyanna, I would if I could."

"Okay. Help me understand. Talk me through this again."

A few days ago, while El and I were in the woods, I noticed a strange sensation in my head when she used her gift. My immediate reaction was defensive. I threatened her and made her shut it off. As I watched her work, I was curious, so I released my gift to see if I'd notice El's presence in my head. And fuck me, I did.

Luther's had left a lasting impression in my mind. With his gift, it felt like he was rooting around in my head with a million hot, sharp daggers, and every thought I'd had of El since had the same searing pain. Elyanna's gift was soft, like a gentle, cool breeze.

I studied Blake's face as he spoke about the enhancement procedure. He went on and on about what they did and how they proceeded to take care of women during and after. He didn't grimace; he didn't wince. He showed zero discomfort, and yet I knew she was extracting information from his mind.

"After the procedure, they are monitored closely. My role is to step in while this part is happening to ease the discomfort," Blake said.

"Have you seen this happen before?" El asked.

He nodded. "A couple years ago. We lost two gifted. Since the counter-serum has been introduced, we've had nearly a hundred percent success rate. My role is to ease this process. I can help the body adapt during the enhancement. This serum is foreign. Unnatural. My gift can heal wounds, stop bleeding, and help cells become healthier. This is beyond my abilities."

"Should we take her back?" El asked.

"No. I don't advise it. The trek all this way on foot must have done a number on her immune system. She is having a difficult time fighting this on her own."

"Why did you tell us that you hadn't seen her?" There was an edge to El's voice.

"I hadn't. I swear. I showed up for my shift and was told I wasn't needed until after my patrol with Kyle. I had tried to argue because I hated patrols and hated Kyle. Usually they wait to administer these things, but the Godfather is anxious to keep things going. There's some rebellion encampment he wanted to pursue."

"Tell me about the counter-serum. Where to find it and what it's called. Everything."

Blake talked for at least fifteen minutes. He gave us a whole bunch of details, which I tried to remember.

"How long does she have?"

Blake breathed deeply. "Twenty-four hours at most."

Elyanna's face paled. "Keep her alive, Blake. I'm going to get what you need."

Just when I thought that was it and we were on our way, Roman shouted, "We got company."

CHAPTER THIRTY-EIGHT

Elyanna

"How long does she have?" I asked Blake.

"Twenty-four hours at most," the healer replied.

His words felt like a kick to the teeth. "Keep her alive, Blake. I'm going to get what you need."

Roman shouted, "We got company."

I set a sense of urgency in Blake's mind to keep Becks alive and withdrew my gift.

"How far, Roman?" I asked.

"Two minutes. They're pulling into the driveway. I can drop them before they get out of the truck." Roman sighted his weapon.

"No," I told him. "Let them come."

I opened my gift again and latched onto the guard's minds, asking them to come in.

"Hi," I said, greeting guards Tillotson and Gruber. "Thank you for reporting for duty. Your assignment is simple: keep this man and this woman alive. You will not leave their side until I return. Do you have radio communications with headquarters?"

The guards nodded.

"Call them and tell them you haven't found the missing vehicle and will be continuing your search," I told them.

Gruber did as I asked and then handed me the radio.

"No one gets in unless they know my name," I told the guards. They nodded and stood guard.

I released their minds and then spoke to Ghost and Bug. "Can one of you check the trucks for food or water?"

"On it," they replied.

I went to sit next to Blake and Becks.

"How's she doing?" I asked Blake.

"Same. If you get the meds, I will save her, El. I promise."

Bug and Ghost returned with jugs of water and enough canned goods to feed the four of them until we returned. I nodded at them gratefully, then moved closer to Becks.

Pressing my forehead to hers I opened my gift to speak into her mind.

Becks, it's me, El. Hang on for me, for Julia, Jonah, Aaron, and Johnny. Please. I am going to get the medicine needed to help you, but you need to hold on. I won't be long. I promise. Stay alive, Becks. I need you.

I stood woodenly and trudged to the door. My heart weighed a thousand pounds.

"Blake." I stopped at the doorway and glanced at him over my shoulder. "What kind of powers does the Godfather have?"

"All powers. He absorbs powers from the pure bloods around him."

All? Blake's words rocked me. How was that even possible?

"I can stay behind and watch them, El," Roman said, breaking my thought train.

"No. I need you, Bug." I moved to the passenger door of the car Ghost had driven but was steered away.

"That one is already occupied," Ghost told me. I gazed through the window and saw a man sitting in the passenger seat with his throat sliced.

"I didn't have time to dispose of the body," Ghost shrugged.

"There's Premiere Loop uniforms in here." Ghost tapped a gym bag as we settled into the truck Gruber and Tillotson had driven.

My men thought of everything. While he drove, Roman and I changed.

"Eat, Elyanna." From the back seat, Roman handed me a granola bar and a bottle of water. I wolfed down the bar, and he handed me an apple. I ate that, too, then chugged the water.

"What's the plan?" He tapped my shoulder with another snack bar.

I shook my head. "I'll use my gift." I wasn't sure how I was going to manage that. It was easier being so far away from the Citizen Encampment and Federation City. Going into the hornet's nest was going to kick my ass. There were no options.

"I can find the serum, El." Ghost offered. His fingers tapped anxiously on the steering wheel.

"I know you can, Ghost. This one will take both of us. We don't have time," I replied.

"Didn't Blake say twenty-four hours?" Bug asked.

"That's what I heard; was there something more?" Ghost glanced at me.

"He did. But he's like us. Our powers are not infinite. There is no way he'll be able to continue healing her for that long."

Ghost stomped on the gas pedal.

"How are you doing with your powers, El?"

I didn't respond to Roman's question. He got the hint and began kneading my shoulders, then he stopped.

"Recline the seat" he said.

I did, and for the next five minutes, he used his magic hands to ease away the tension that had been throbbing at my temples.

"Guard gate in two minutes," Ghost said.

"I'm going to use my powers to get us through; act casual. The story is, we need to refuel and restock, then we're back out for a supply drop-off."

"Hey man" Ghost greeted the guard. "Can you have this refueled and restocked?"

The guard looked at a clipboard, then looked at me and Ghost. He peered into the backseat at Roman, all while I weaved the story into his mind that we were indeed on the manifest and to do as asked.

A second later, he called another guard. "This vehicle needs a refuel and restock right away."

The other man nodded and waved us in.

"Follow him," the guard said.

I breathed a sigh of relief. One down.

I used my gift on the next man and asked for a minute to gather my bearings. There were maybe fifty guards within a mile radius, going about their day. On a normal day, this was a piece of cake with my gift. It wasn't a normal day. My stress levels were heightened with Hudson somewhere in the Loop and Becks hanging on by a thread. I didn't have the elegant finesse I'd honed with my gift, but I would make it work. Buzzing mad hornets in my head, be damned.

"What can we do, El, to make this easier on you?" Ghost asked.

"Save your gift, Ghost. I will use mine to get us to the Loop. Once there, we're separating. One of us will search the first floor of Building Two. The other will take the second floor. Bug, I need you to find Hudson and get him out of that building. Ready?" I said to both of them.

They both looked at me. "Are you?" Bug quirked an eyebrow.

"I will soldier through this and save Becks." My voice filled with determination.

The three of us exited the car, and I led the way. Getting through the docking area was easier than I thought. I'd used Hudson's advice and peeled away at the voices that bombarded me.

Entering Federation City was an entirely different story. The first five steps nearly brought me to my knees. I braced a hand on Bug's elbow and blinked back tears.

Don't you dare cry, Elyanna. Don't do it. I bit the inside of my cheek and pushed forward. I used my gift to compel every person who glanced in our direction, erasing our presence from their minds. The pressure in my head increased and sweat coated my back.

"Almost there," Ghost urged.

Almost there was more like an eternity later. As we approached the building, I said, "Ghost, your turn."

We waltzed into the first building with zero problems. Ghost used his gift to conceal himself and me while telling Roman where to go. We went down a set of stairs, which eased the pressure on my mind. I leaned against the wall and placed my hands on my knees, panting for air.

"Where are we?" I asked.

"Underground corridor. It must be sealed," Ghost told us.

"Thank you; this helps."

"El, I don't like this. This is taking a toll on you, and it's freaking me the fuck out." Bug kneeled in front of me.

"I got this Bug, we're almost there. Let's keep going. When we get to the stairway, I need a second to reach Hudson. Once I have his location, you will find him. Then Ghost and I will head to Building Two. We'll meet back here. Ghost, if you find the serum, get back to Becks. Don't wait for me. Worst-case scenario, I will find Unit 2323."

"I won't leave you here," Ghost said.

"Yes, you will. You have to. I will survive this, Ghost. Trust me." I started toward the stairwell.

"Me first." Ghost moved in front of me and opened the door; he disappeared, and I felt his hand tug on mine.

At the top of the well, I opened my gift. A tidal wave of thoughts slammed into me so hard my knees buckled. I gritted my teeth and used my gift to call Hudson.

Hudson! We're in the Loop. Where are you?

El? Stay away.

Damn it, Hawk. I don't have time to argue. Where are you?

I'm in a cell, lower corridor, building three.

Roman's coming.

Panic swept through my mind. Everyone in the loop went into a flurry of mayhem. I dropped to my knees.

"Something's happening. Hudson is in a cell in the lower corridors of Building Three. Go, Roman."

"I don't want to leave you like this," Roman protested.

"Bug, please. Bring Hudson back to me," I pleaded.

"Really? You're giving me the puppy dog eyes? Damnit, El." He kissed the top of my head and ran off.

"El, wait downstairs," Xavi growled.

"No." I braced my hand on his arm and stood. "Use your gift to conceal us, please."

He did. As we got closer to Building Two, people were hurrying past us to get to the second floor.

"Go upstairs, Ghost. I'll be fine down here. There are fewer people," I told him.

"El. Please don't make me leave you." He held me close.

"For Becks. For our sister. Please."

"Fuck, El." He squeezed me harder. "Technically, she's my sister, making her your sister-in-law."

He winked, then ran upstairs.

CHAPTER THIRTY-NINE

Hudson

My former headmaster gave me a once-over with narrowed eyes. "Maybe your power has grown, too."

"Come, let me show you around. You must be hungry." He led me to the cafeteria.

The smell of bacon hit my nostrils, making my stomach roar. A couple of men were at the buffet station, piling their plates with eggs, bacon, and pancakes.

"Please help yourself. I just ate, but I'll sit with you while you have some breakfast. I could use a cup of coffee. Eat Hudson. People on the other side of Federation City can hear your stomach growling. And I don't poison my gifted."

I narrowed my eyes at him, refusing to take the bait.

"Fine. I will serve you myself." He went to the buffet line, pointed at the bacon, and piled some on a plate. He gestured to the eggs and added them to the plate, then pointed to the potatoes. I shook my head.

He placed the plate of food on a table and motioned for me to sit. I glanced at the other men who were seated a few tables away and watched them eat. One guy gave me a stiff nod. So it wasn't poison.

I sat. I ate. I was starving. The Godfather eyed me while sipping his coffee and hadn't uttered a word.

After breakfast, he led me down an empty corridor. Static electricity glided over my skin. A similar thing had happened the last time I'd seen the headmaster, and it made me wonder if he was assessing me with his power.

"Stronger, indeed. And more disciplined. Excellent. Follow me, Hudson. I'm sure you're dying to see your schoolmates."

He strolled away, two men flanking him. I crossed my arms over my chest and froze, testing to see what he'd do.

With his telekinetic power, he slammed me into the wall and laughed. "You're an adult, not a child. Stop being insolent. Do as I say, or I shall rip you to shreds."

He released his powers. I stood gingerly and dusted myself off. He was strong, but I was stronger. And I was no longer a little boy.

Both of his guards walked through the doorway that led to the training facility I had just toured. I called on my powers and slammed the door shut, leaving me and the Godfather alone in the corridor. I used my power wrapped an invisible force around his neck and held him against the door. His guards pounded on the door.

The Godfather gasped for air, kicking his legs.

"You're right. I am no longer a child. Show some fucking respect."

The door was blown off its hinges and crashed to the floor with the Godfather under it. The two guards rushed into the hallway, stomping on the fallen door. One guard had flames floating above his palms. The other flexed his muscles, and his skin turned a metallic silver. The door crushed under his weight. The Godfather groaned.

"Where is he?" the metal man growled.

I couldn't help it. I laughed my ass off. The two guards looked at me like I'd lost my mind, and that only made me laugh harder. The two idiots stood on the broken door, completely unaware that they'd been standing on their boss's body, crushing him to death.

It took them a hot minute to realize what they'd done.

I should have ended it all right then but fuck me. It was funny as shit.

The Godfather stood, straightened his suit, and glared at me. His guards groveled at his side. The Godfather muttered something that sounded like a tongue-lashing, while I couldn't get the giggles under control. His narrowed gaze shifted to me, then back to his guards. He didn't know whether to kill them or me.

Finally, he shouted. "Enough, Hudson. You've had your fun."

He turned toward his guards. "Leave, both of you."

I gave them a double thumbs up. The metal man returned the gesture while the fire-starter walked away with his tail tucked between his legs.

"Defy me again, Hudson—"

"Or what? You don't scare me anymore, Headmaster Neville. If it weren't for the comedy act, I could have killed you and your two guards."

"Don't underestimate me. Come on. I'll show you around and bring you into the fold. You need to change out of that ridiculous uniform first. My personal guards don't wear rags." He stormed off.

I followed, regretting my actions. I should have just killed the man, and we would have been done with BHF. Now I needed another shot. And somehow, I knew I'd have one.

He led me to the training area of the gym, where I was asked politely to change into gifted training gear: joggers, a t-shirt, and running shoes. When I emerged from the bathroom five minutes later, Neville motioned for me to follow him into the fitness area, where several gifted men were working out.

"Alexi?!" I called my old friend, who was on a treadmill. He glanced over his shoulder, then came to greet me.

"Play along, my friend," I muttered while giving him a bro hug.

"Hudson?!!" Over my shoulder, a man approached me. It took me a moment to recognize him.

"Hey, Monty. It's been a long time." I shook the speedster's hand.

"No shit. Good to see you, man," Montgomery said.

"Reunion's over, Hudson. I have more to show you." The Godfather tapped his foot on the floor.

"Neville's showing me around. I'll catch you guys later," I said.

I shook hands with both men, then followed the Godfather

through the second floor and down a set of stairs to the underground corridor. Fine with me.

We ended up in a room that was much like the rooms I'd spent lots of time in as a kid. It was a twenty x twenty box with three white walls. The fourth wall beside the door had a large, one-way glass window. As a boy, I'd practiced my gift for hours while the headmaster and staff gave their instructions and observed. The door closed behind me. With my gift, I latched onto the locking mechanism, keeping it unlocked.

"Let's get down to business, Hudson." The Godfather's voice came through a speaker located in the far right corner of the room. "Why are you here?"

"Why don't you come in here and talk to me man-to-man? Scared?" I smirked.

"Don't make this difficult, Hudson."

"Or what? You'll gas me, like you did when I was twelve. You do remember what happened when you tried that last time?"

Silence.

I sat in that room, glancing at the clock every few minutes. It was times like these that I had to trust in Elyanna's power and resourcefulness to survive. She would; she was tough. That fact didn't make it any easier to be away from her. At the fifteen-minute mark, I was ready to make my move.

The fire-starter opened the door, carrying a glass pitcher of ice water and an empty cup. The Godfather right behind him. The fire-starter put the glass and pitcher on the table in front of me and then moved to stand in the corner.

"You know I'm not stupid enough to fall for that trick, right?" I raised my eyebrow at Neville.

"I'm not interested in poisoning you, Hudson. If that's what I wanted to do, I would have done it already. You're more useful to me alive." He sat across from me, folding his hands on the table.

"What makes you think I have any interest in helping you?"

"Because you're here. And everyone has a weakness. Either way, help me, or I will kill the people you care about. Like Alexi and Monty and whoever else you consider a friend. Simple."

I laughed.

The Godfather sneered at me; his face flushed, and then the room began to get warmer and then hot.

I tipped my head to the side. The Godfather's hands were clenched into tight balls, and veins popped on his neck. Very interesting.

Sweat streamed down my face, and my back was drenched. It was easily over one hundred degrees and getting hotter.

The fire-starter slumped against the wall, and deep lines creased his brow. Motherfucker was siphoning the fire-starter power. How is this possible?

Two hundred degrees and climbing.

"You will do as I say, Hudson," the Godfather said through clenched teeth.

I gave him a dramatic eye roll. It was hot as fuck, but the way I saw it, he'd have to burn all three of us alive, and I was pretty sure that's not what he wanted. He wanted me to be impressed by the fact that he was somehow channeling the guard's power. Curious? Yes. Impressed? Not really.

A loud banging on the door broke the Godfather's concentration.

"I told you not to disturb me!" he snarled.

The knocking continued.

Hudson! We're in the Loop. Where are you? Elyanna's voice cut through my thoughts. I fought my facial muscles to keep my expression neutral.

El? Stay away, I replied with a thought.

Damn it, Hawk. I don't have time to argue. Where are you?

The desperation in her voice gave me pause. She was struggling and I didn't want to make things harder for her.

I'm in a cell, lower corridor, Building Three.

Roman's coming, she said.

Dammit.

The door swung open, revealing metal man. "Godfather, there's an emergency in the female ward."

"Take care of it! I'm busy." His narrowed gaze was fixed on me.

"It's . . . It's one of the mothers. She's going into labor."

The Godfather sprang out of his chair. "Why didn't you start with that?! Don't just stand there; let's move."

Both guards followed him out the door, and just before it closed, something stung my forearm. I pulled a syringe out of my arm. This can't be good.

The Godfather casually leaned on the doorframe. "That was an enhancement serum. Lethal without a counter-drug. You were always an arrogant little shit. But I am smarter, stronger, and have more experience. You will bend to my will, Hudson. Or you can die here. Think about it. I have a baby to deliver."

Aww shit.

CHAPTER FORTY

Xavier

Damn that beautiful, stubborn woman. I stormed up the stairs to the second floor, which was like Grand Central Station. People hurried through the halls as though they had an earth-shattering emergency. Dodging the crowd made my search much slower. Patience, Xavi.

The second floor of the women's building had a half-dozen exam rooms, all with various medical equipment. I recognized an MRI machine in one; the drawers were empty. In another room, there was an ultrasound machine. I was about to search the cabinets when the door knocked into me. I bit the inside of my cheek to stifle my yelp. The nurses unplugged the machine and wheeled it out the door. The cabinets were empty, so I moved on to the next room and the next. I searched each exam room, and aside from bags of IV solutions, there was no serum, not even needles.

At the end of the hall, there was a single door to my left and an open double door to my right, where people were scrambling to get in. I chose the left, which was locked. Of course.

I followed the crowd and entered the double doors, weaving through the packed room while scanning each person for something—anything that would help me get into the locked door across the hall. A woman's scream had me pause mid-step. The crowd gathered by a glass window. There were too many people for me to get close so I hung back. There were three rows of chairs, all unoccupied. I stood on one chair and saw what the fuss was all about.

Beyond the glass window, a pregnant woman was lying on a hospital bed. Sheets covered most of her body except her feet, which were propped in stirrups. Medical staff hovered about doing medical things. The most interesting thing to note were the six women sitting on chairs on the opposite side of the room. They wore hospital gowns, and their ankles were shackled. An older man walked in wearing scrubs. The women linked their hands together.

The crowd observing gasped.

I couldn't wrap my brain around what I was seeing. The woman was obviously in labor, and the others, I wasn't sure. Were they forced to be in the same room? Why were they shackled? We'd witnessed the chains around their feet while they were asleep, which was barbaric, but I imagined they hadn't wanted them to escape at night. And now? Were they forced to watch the delivery?

A jingle of metal caught my attention. A burly man to my right had a thick wad of keys dangling from his belt loop. There were so many keys that he'd notice the absence of the weight in seconds. Fuck it, I had wasted too much time as it was. I took a deep breath and made my move.

The minute I unhooked the keys from his belt loop, the guard moved his hand to brush his hip. Someone bumped into him, causing him to raise his hand instead. I stepped backward, glancing behind me as I made my way to the door, one slow step at a time.

As soon as I cleared the double doors, I ran across the hall. There were a dozen keys, which took me a few minutes to get through. The lock clicked just as the man I'd stolen the keys from exited the room. He kept his eyes on the ground as he moved through the hallway in search of his keys.

I exhaled and entered the storeroom. Fucking finally. They'd kept everything under lock and key. I stifled a groan and began sorting through the keys again. After unlocking the cabinets, I stuffed the bag with anything I thought might be helpful. Syringes, gauze pads, and sedatives. Finally, in the refrigerated section, I found what I was looking for. There were several rows of stuff. I recalled Blake stating he needed the bottles labeled SX series and not the TR bottles. The top four rows had bottles of enhancement serum marked TR. The counter-serum was on the bottom two rows. And there were two distinct serums. Shit. I took a half-dozen of both each. I did a quick perusal of the area and found a laminated sheet with what seemed to be perti-nent information, and I decided to take a half dozen TR bottles also. You just never know.

Satisfied with what I'd found, I exited the storage and threw the keys on the floor in one of the exam rooms, just as the woman in labor let out another gut-wrenching scream.

ROMAN

Leaving Elyanna when she was obviously not okay was literally fucking painful. I hated walking away from her and only did so because staying would have made things harder for her. I couldn't block her gift from my mind like Hawk could. She'd pick up on my stress, and that was the last thing she needed.

The underground corridor that linked the buildings together was empty. I made it to the next building quickly and ran up the stairs, only to realize I was in the wrong place. Damn tunnels had no signage, which I suppose was on purpose.

I went back underground and jogged down the long hallway. The Loop itself was the biggest set of buildings we'd come across in Federa-tion City. It didn't seem that large on the surface, but underground, the tunnels were spread over several miles, with approximately two and a half miles between each building. I lost thirty minutes going to the wrong building and had to double time to the next set of stairs.

At the end of the tunnel was a set of stairs. I went up, found myself in Building Three, crossed the hall, and went down another set of stairs. Fucking loop. The ground level was connected by a seamless walkway—no stairs, no doors—just a hallway that led from one building to the next in one continuous loop. The tunnels weren't as simple. There was a solid wall between the corridor and the next building. To get into the building, you had to take the stairwell. To get back into it, you had to cross the hall on the ground level and take the stairs down.

The reasoning behind the design was lost on me until I found myself in the corridor, which was under Building Three. Per Xavi's explanation, there was a training facility in Building Three for the gifted. Underneath, it was something much more sinister. It was a dungeon with steel doors, all of which were locked. After passing several steel doors, the aesthetic changed. White walls greeted me, while fluorescent lighting buzzed overhead. I passed a viewing window and a standard door, which I was about to open, until a crash in the distance had me slowing to a brisk walk. A set of booted feet was being dragged into one of the rooms. I drew my weapon and approached warily.

Three feet from the doorway, something slammed into my face, knocking me to the ground. I called on my fire.

"Fuck, Rome," Hawk said. "I almost killed you!"

I extinguished the flames in my palms and accepted Hawk's hand.

"Where's El?" he asked.

"Building Two. Do we need to do something about that?" I tipped my head to the room he'd just exited.

"No, he'll take a nap for a while. He's a fire-starter just like you," Hawk told me.

Curious, I backpedaled and peered into the room. The guy was scrawny and unimpressive looking. I shrugged.

"This way. I just came from that direction," I explained.

"No wonder it took you so long," Hawk smirked.

I glared at the telekinetic. Yep, I got lost, and I wasn't about to admit it.

"What happened? Why'd you guys come back?" he asked.

"Blake needs some sort of counter-drug to heal Becks. They've given her the enhancement serum, and she's reacting to it. Without it, she won't survive."

"Shit. Is El okay?"

I shook my head. "She's been using her gift, and it's kicking her ass. She's stubborn. Like you."

We hustled to Building Two and went up to the ground level, which was a serene garden. It was a nice touch, considering the place seemed to be nothing short of a women's prison.

Two men dressed in scrubs came out of the elevator. "It can't be down here," one man said.

"I checked every room," the other replied.

They searched the garden, eyes on the ground.

I ushered Hawk into the stairwell, which led underground.

"What floor is she on?" Hawk asked.

I had to think about it. Xavi was taking one floor; she was taking the other. Which one? "First floor," I said.

"We're on the first floor," he retorted.

"This is ground level. There are five," I replied.

The door opened and closed. Hawk and I waited.

"Knock it off, Ghost," Hawk snarled.

"I forgot to release my gift. Elyanna?" He appeared beside us.

I almost flinched. His gift was something.

"She's not here yet," I replied.

We all glanced at our watches. Everyone in Gator wore watches, which was more or less the correct time. We hadn't bothered with daylight savings time or time zone changes like we had pre-plague. Those things didn't matter. All that mattered was that we were in sync, and at that moment, Elyanna had been gone for an hour, give or take a few minutes.

"Fuck," Hawk snarled.

"Did you get what you needed?" I asked.

Xavi tapped a bag. "And then some."

"Let me see," Hawk asked.

Xavi pulled out a piece of laminated paper. "This seemed important, but I haven't read it. There were two counter-serums. I wasn't sure which was which."

Hawk paused to read the paper. I peered into the bag, which seemed to be more than what we needed for Becks. Better to be prepared.

"Let's go after her," I said.

"I agree. Hawk?" Xavi and I glanced at Hawk, who was studying the laminated piece of paper with his brows furrowed.

After a long, dramatic pause, Hawk finally spoke, "I had a run-in with the Godfather. He shot me with this stuff."

CHAPTER FORTY-ONE

Elyanna

I stumbled into the first room and fell to the ground. It seemed as though there was no one but me on the first floor, still, the buzzing minds of the city were pressing on me. My gift was kicking my ass.

Breathe, El. You can do this. I stayed on the ground and focused, shutting out the thoughts of people who were closest to me. I decided against shutting them out completely since it was overwhelmingly harder every time I reopened my gift. Instead, I gritted my teeth and got the buzzing to a manageable level. It wasn't perfect, but the pain was a dull ache instead of a full-on migraine. I rose and forced one foot in front of the other. My movements were sluggish, and according to my watch, I'd spent nearly twenty minutes on the floor. Shit. I searched the drawers and cabinets of the first exam room and moved on. There were twelve rooms, and I found normal medical things: rubbing alcohol, thermometers, and blood pressure cuffs. They even had tampons, condoms, ibuprofen, aspirin, and even prenatal vitamins. I popped a few tablets of Ibuprofen, hoping it would help with the headache, and kept going. I searched the storage area. IV solution, lube, more gauze, bandages, and tongue depressors. No serums of any sort. God dammit. I even searched the bathroom, used the latrine, and decided to head back to meet with my men.

The main door opened, followed by footsteps. "Check every room," a male voice said.

I latched onto two minds with my gift.

You didn't find what you were looking for here. Turn around and leave.

The men did as I asked. It was a simple command that should have been child's play for me. Instead, I braced a hand on the wall as I staggered to the exit. Fuck, fuck, fuck.

My vision was spotty, and my breathing ragged. I crumpled to my knees and began to crawl.

"I got you." A warm set of arms helped me off the floor and helped me walk.

"Becks?" I asked the female voice.

"Dani," she replied. "I've been waiting for you."

Dani helped me through a door to a darkened room. She was holding me up, and I could not focus my gift to get a read on her mind. Shit. Feebly, I reached behind my back to grasp my sassy stick. She pushed my hand down and placed me on a bed. I rolled over.

"Oh my," she said. "I knew this would happen, but I didn't expect this."

She propped me up against her and pressed something to my lips. Cool liquid entered my mouth. It was heavenly. I gulped the water, then choked.

"Slowly," she said.

I drank more water and croaked my thanks, then slumped on the mattress.

Dani straddled my waist, and then a sharp sting ran across my face. I blinked rapidly.

Smack.

My eyes widened as Dani came into view.

"I need you to focus. Do you need another slap?" Her voice was firm yet sympathetic.

For some reason, two slaps seemed to make it possible for me to focus on the woman in front of me.

I shook my head and eyed the pretty freckled girl sitting astride my waist. Her wavy auburn hair hung past her breasts, the tips skimming her protruding belly.

"I need your help. We all need your help." She settled her weight on top of me.

"Who are you? Where are we?? And do you mind getting off me?"

She giggled as she scooted off me, remaining close.

"Dani. In my room. And I need your help. Your turn. What's your name?"

"Elyanna. I don't think I'm in a position to help you." I rubbed my temples.

She lay on her side, next to me, and angled my face to meet hers.

"Elyanna. That's pretty. And yes, you can. You need to push through this. You can do this. I know you can."

"You don't understand. Being around so many people is overwhelming me."

"I know. Sort of. It has something to do with your gift. I saw it. Saw you. You can get through this."

"What are you?"

She scooted closer and pressed her lips against my ear. "I'm a seer. I saw this moment. Believe in yourself, Elyanna. You can do this."

She leaned back and regarded me with kind, turquoise eyes. "My gift is never wrong. You will get your shit together even if I have to kick your ass to do it."

Well, shit. I swallowed hard. "Ok, seer. Tell me about your visions."

Dani scrambled off the bed and moved to the corner of the room to rummage through an armoire.

I sat up and winced.

"Fight it, Elyanna. Tell those voices to shut the fuck up," Dani said with her head still in the closet.

I smirked; she was a bit of a bitch, and I immediately liked her.

There was a pitcher beside the cup, which was full, so I refilled the cup and drank. I was on my second cup when she returned to the bed with a beautiful Louis Vuitton tote. I gaped.

"Beautiful, isn't it? I was a purse whore before the plague." She ran her hand over the leather, then proceeded to withdraw a notebook.

All doubts about Dani's abilities vanished as she opened the book.

Tears streamed down my face. Her sketches reminded me of the countless pages we'd packed from Axel's home in Gator Springs High. Hudson framed a few of them and hung them in the lodge. A lump formed in my throat.

"Sorry." I wiped my face with the back of my hand.

She handed me a tissue.

"I'm a mess. First the voices in my head, and now . . . I'm an emotional wreck." I sobbed.

"You loved a seer. Is he . . ." Her voice faltered. "Don't answer that. I can already guess."

I blew my nose. "Okay, okay." I steadied my breath, told the voices to shut the fuck up, and gave Dani my attention. "Talk to me."

She patted my hand. "It's okay," she murmured.

"First, you need to find my men. They will gather the forces, and we'll make our stand here," She pointed to a drawing.

I angled my head to peer at the picture she had drawn. It was detailed. I had only been there once, and my voice caught in my throat.

"Are you sure?" I asked.

"Elyanna, my gift is never wrong. I've had it all my life."

"How are you here unsupervised? How come you're not chained like the others? You seem to have the freedom to come and go." I searched her face which up until that point had been passive.

"Two reasons. First. Health care." Her expression darkened. "Hard to take care of yourself and a growing baby when you're always on the run. I've had complications. I was taken to the hospital first until my men showed up. Once the staff discovered I carry a baby with gifted genes, I was moved here. The Godfather knows I won't run. I need them."

Shit.

"Are you and the baby okay?" I asked.

"We are now." She rubbed her belly. "The Godfather won't hesitate to lock me up once the baby comes."

"We won't let that happen," I said reassuringly. "What's the other reason?"

"They don't know about my seer gift," she whispered. "They think

I just read auras. The Godfather wants my baby because my men are all gifted. And only my men know that I am double-gifted," she replied.

"Reading auras is a gift?"

"Yes. I made a living balancing chakras."

I choked on my laugh, then cleared my throat. "Spit went down the wrong pipe."

She gave me a dry look, then smiled. "I knew I'd like you."

"Okay, so, how do I find your men?"

"Well, the men have training shifts. Luca and Clemmons aren't morning people, so they come in in the afternoon. Alexi and Monty are early risers, so they should be here now. However, they often have patrols in the city. They work in pairs: Luca and Alexi, Clemmons and Steel, Monty and Kyle."

Ah fuck. Kyle was the invisible guy I ran through with my sassy stick. Please tell me there was more than one.

"Six men, huh? That's a lot." Even I could hear the weirdness in my voice.

"No!" She shook her head. "I only have four. Steel and Kyle aren't mine. And Kyle is . . . ewww. Patrols go out in teams, and Monty got stuck with him."

My shoulders relaxed.

"Why? Did you?" She pointed at my sword.

"If the Kyle you are speaking of is the invisible guy, then yes. I did."

"Nice." She raised her hand for a high-five.

I slapped my palm against hers.

"I have a friend to save first." I rose from the bed, surprised at my steadiness.

"No. You can't. This is where you need to go. Unit 3023." She tapped on her book.

"Becks needs me. I need to get her medicine or she'll die."

"No, have someone else do it. You need to rest before the big showdown tonight." She said. "My men know about my vision of you and I meeting. They're expecting a blonde woman carrying my note-book. They won't believe anyone else. The Godfather will have the city locked down as soon as he finds out his prisoner is no longer in his cell."

She showed me a picture of a room with a man standing, pulling at his hair while standing over a body lying at his feet.

"I'm assuming the prisoner was one of yours," she added.

Hudson broke free.

"Do you know where they keep the counter-serums for the enhancement procedure?" I asked.

"Upstairs in the storage room," she replied.

"Okay, anything else I need to know?"

She flipped to another page in the notebook and tapped on it.

I glanced at the drawing. The picture was of her hunched over, clutching her stomach, with a digital clock on the wall. I glanced at the clock on her bedside table, then looked at the picture again.

"This is the delivery room upstairs. You have less than twelve hours. If the Godfather is still alive when I go into labor, I'm fucked. He will learn of my gift, take my child, and he will rally the gifted to come after you and your family."

"Great. No pressure, then." I rubbed my temples.

"You can do this, Elyanna." She stuffed the notebook into her Louis and handed it to me.

"How? You just told me your gifts are never wrong."

"I didn't see the after part; that was just a likely assumption." She shrugged. "Think about it. If your husband gets away, the Godfather will be pissed, and he won't stop."

She wasn't wrong about that. Fight through my gift, make sure Ghost finds the serum for Becks, find Dani's four men, and defeat the Godfather all within twelve hours or so. No sweat. I synced my watch with hers and hugged her.

"I believe in you, Elyanna. You can do this," Dani called out as I exited her room.

CHAPTER FORTY-TWO

Elyanna

The onslaught of thoughts hadn't left me. I managed to ignore it for a while when I'd been speaking with Dani, but as soon as the main door opened, it hit me like a tsunami, making me gasp for breath. God damn it! I forced my feet to move as fast as I could toward the stairway that led to the underground tunnels.

I heard my men's voices as soon as I closed the door. The buzzing was muted underground, and I was grateful for the reprieve.

My men fell silent as soon as they saw me. They wore identical expressions of fear and worry.

I must look as bad as I feel.

They rushed me at the same time. Three large muscular forms closed in on me. I soaked up their strength and love for a precious second, then pushed them away.

"I'm fine." I lied. "We need to move."

"You are not fine," Bug growled.

"Let's get you out of here." Ghost gripped my hand.

Hudson hoisted me in his arms. "Christ, El. You're pushing too hard. Close off your gift. Now."

"Stop Hudson. Put me down," I said.

"No."

"We need to go separately. I met a seer."

Hudson paused. "Tell us everything as we walk toward the exit."

He didn't set me down; instead, he set a quick pace, nearly jogging, with Ghost and Bug beside him. I told them about Dani.

Before I finished my tale, we reached the staircase to Building One.

"Stop, Hudson. Please. Set me down so we can plan."

He set me on my feet, a deep line formed between his brows.

I ignored him.

"This is what she saw." I pulled out the book and showed them the end scene with us confronting the Godfather. "And this is our time-line." I showed them the picture of Dani going into labor.

"How does this line up?" Roman asked. "If he's in the retail sector, and she's in there?"

"Exactly. He's not there. Usually, he is at every birth. He'll be distracted, wanting to get back to the Loop around this time. And look here." I pointed to the end scene picture and pointed out a clock in the entertainment sector.

"Same time. I remember the bell tower with the clock." Ghost said.

"You guys need to get back to Becks now," I told them. "I'm going to find the husbands. Alexi and three others."

"No," they said simultaneously.

"We don't have time to argue," I protested.

"El, you can barely stand," Roman said.

"We're not leaving you here. You come with us to give Becks her meds, and we'll come back together," Ghost added.

"No," I argued.

"Fine, we'll separate. El and I will stay here. I know Alexi. Xavi, Roman, go save Becks," Hudson said.

"No, Hudson, I cannot rely on my gift to hide you and me while we're walking through Federation City. I am not strong enough," I told him.

"You don't have to be. Dressed like this, people will think I'm one of the gifted. Shield yourself; we'll get you some street clothes and find Unit 3023 together. End of story." Hudson took the bag out of my hands.

"Let's sync our watches with El's," he added.

They adjusted their watches to match mine.

"Xavi, serums, please." Hudson opened the Louis Vuitton bag, and Xavi deposited a couple of syringes and bottles of serum. "Thanks. Use your gift to get El out of this building. Follow us out. Once we're clear of the Loop, go and save Becks."

"Got it." Ghost crushed me into his chest. "I'll be back as soon as Blake tells me Becks is on the mend."

I wriggled free of his hold. "No, you can't look." I showed him the picture again. "This looks like Becks to me."

The resemblance was undeniable. So were the sketches of Bug, Blake, Ghost, and Hudson. I wasn't in the picture.

"Where are you?" Hudson asked.

I flipped the page, which showed me hiding at the entrance of Jamboree Court. The hostess stand was behind me, and I was staring in the direction of the square, where everyone else was.

"Dani told me my role is to stay hidden as long as possible. I am not supposed to get close to the Godfather, or he'll use my gift against everyone."

"Wait, what? He's a mind-bender also?" Roman asked.

"When Blake said he has all gifts, I thought that was bullshit." Ghost scratched his chin.

"Maybe not all gifts, but he has telekinesis and fire. I witnessed it," Hudson added.

"He's a siphon. He can siphon gifts from Pure Bloods when he's around them for a while. He needs thirty minutes to assimilate someone's powers. Dani said her interaction with him is always under twenty, and he has never suspected who she truly is. He thinks Dani reads auras, so he hasn't given her much time. He just wants her baby. As far as the others, he keeps them close. The men live in his mansion, and we all know what the situation is like for the women," I told them.

"Shit. Let's move. Xavi, once Becks is ready, you'll find us in 2323."

Roman gave me a smooch, and then he and Hudson took the stairs. Ghost grabbed my hand, and his gift washed over both of us. With his gift shielding him, I couldn't hear his thoughts even while holding his hand. Everyone else came in loud and clear.

The buzzing bombarded my senses. My knees buckled. Ghost helped me stay upright. Ahead of us, a guard approached Hudson and Roman. I panicked and latched onto the guard's mind.

"Oh, my mistake. You're good to go. Have a great day." The guard turned on his heel and went back to the surveillance office.

Hudson and Roman continued out the door with Ghost and I on their heels.

Hudson and I separated from Ghost and Bug.

"Let's get you to safety, baby." Hudson grasped my arm.

I wanted to insist on finding the husbands, but Federation City was bustling. I'd exceeded my limit and was about to pass out. Still, I pushed, using my gift to conceal me from sight. People wouldn't notice me at all. I followed Hudson blindly, focusing on people passing by.

We came to a familiar retail section near the loft. I tugged on Hudson's arm. "Hawk, if we need provisions, we should get them now."

"What? No. You need to rest."

"And you need to stay hidden. The Godfather will lock the city down as soon as he realizes you're gone," I told him.

He cursed and veered toward a grocery store. I pulled a wristband out of my pocket. "This is Kyle's. And I have Blake's also."

Hudson took the band, and we began adding things to a shopping basket. Food items, a couple of T-shirts, and lots of celery juice. Five minutes later, we were out of the store and on our way to the loft.

Hudson punched in the code and opened the door. I stumbled in and shut off my gift.

"Here, babe, drink," he said, pressing the bottle of juice to my lips.

I shut down my gift and guzzled. "I need to figure this out, Hudson." I wiped my mouth with the back of my hand.

"You will, Elyanna. I believe in you," he assured me.

Everyone seemed to believe in me, and I wasn't convinced.

"I know you're tired, but you need to eat. Here." He handed me a banana.

My hands shook as I tried peeling the fruit. He took it gently, peeled it, and placed it back in my palms.

"I'm going to start a bath for you; finish that." He caressed my cheek.

I ate and drank until he returned.

He didn't usher me into the bathroom; instead, he opened the bag and pulled out a piece of paper, a syringe, and a bottle. He read the paper, looked at his watch, and checked his pulse. He fiddled with his watch and put everything back in the bag.

"What's going on?" I asked.

"Nothing for you to worry about." He picked me up.

"Liar. Don't make me use my gift, Hudson. Tell me."

"The godfather stabbed me with a needle filled with the enhancement serum."

The banana and celery juice in my belly churned.

"I'll be fine, peaches. Xavi got enough serums for both me and Becks. The paper I was reading has basic instructions. The serum I have is the one they use for male patients. There are time intervals, so I have another two hours before I need to take anything. I've already set my alarm."

"You should go to Blake, Hudson. He can help you. I'll be fine here." He placed me on the bathroom counter and began unlacing my boots. I pulled off my top and unbuttoned my jeans.

"Xavi will bring him back after Becks is cared for. Her need is more dire. She'd been injected almost a day ago. For me, it's been barely two hours. I'll monitor my heart rate. If it falls below normal or I feel odd, I'll give myself a shot. And who knows, maybe I won't need it." He helped me shimmy out of my panties.

"I don't like this, Hudson. How can you be sure it was the same serum that is listed on that stupid paper?" I stepped out of my pants and panties.

"I kept the syringe. I don't know what it will do to my powers, but I have the counter-serum. No need to worry." He steadied me while I stepped into the tub.

I sank into the warm water. The bubbles were a nice touch, but I hadn't felt relaxed. Worry over my husband and my best friend shrouded my thoughts.

Hudson kissed the top of my head and moved to leave.

"Stay. Please," I pleaded.

"I'll be right back. I'm just getting us some juice."

I watched him walk out of the bathroom, my heart heavy with concern.

CHAPTER FORTY-THREE

Xavier

A pit in my stomach bloomed as I watched Hudson and Elyanna walk away. El was pale, her body trembling. She was unwell, and I had no idea how to help her. Roman gazed at them, the lines etched on his forehead deeper. Leaving them behind was hard on both of us, but I had my sister to save, too.

"You can stay," I offered.

Roman shook his head. "No. Hawk will take care of her. Stick to the plan. Let's go."

We were both in BHF uniforms, so we were able to move through the city easily enough. Time was a luxury we didn't have, so walking leisurely was out of the question, and running through the city would attract unwanted attention.

I called on my gift and grasped Roman's hand. We ran through Federation City, our hands linked together. His skin was hot in mine, his palms were heavy and calloused. So unlike El's delicate feminine fingers. As much as I enjoyed teasing the fire-starter, this contact was different. It wasn't an unpleasant feeling. As soon as the thought entered my mind, Roman tried to wiggle his hand free. I held on tighter.

"You don't . . ." he began.

"Shh. Keep quiet," I cut him off.

Handholding was more intimate than sex in my book. If I had to guess, Rome felt the same way. I didn't care about his comfort issues. I wasn't trying to force things between us. Time wasn't on our side and I was torn between saving my sister and taking care of El. As much as I appreciated my invisibility gift, it'd be much cooler to be in two places at once. I wondered if such a thing existed.

We were both out of breath by the time we reached the shipping and receiving area. I released my gift and Roman's hand. In our uniforms, we had no issues as we got into the truck. I got behind the wheel and turned the ignition just as Roman hopped into the passenger seat.

I didn't waste another second and drove toward the security gate.

"Get ready to shoot anyone who dares to stop us," I muttered and pulled out the pistol holstered at my waist.

The same guard El had coerced with her powers was still at the gate. He glanced at me with a quirked eyebrow, looked at his clipboard, and then trained his gaze on me. "Oh, right, I remember you. Go ahead."

As soon as we were out of sight of FC, I stomped on the gas. Worry clawed at my spine. I glanced at my watch. We were cutting it close where Becks was concerned. It had taken us longer to get the serums. Our efforts were not in vain. Every minute at the Loop was eye-opening. If the intel Elyanna had gotten from the seer was correct, we could end the war between BHF and the Rebels tonight.

I side-glanced Roman. His knee bounced nervously, and his lips were pressed into a thin line. I didn't have any comforting words to offer, so I remained silent.

His gaze landed on me, and I focused on the road. "They'll be okay. They have to be."

"Of course they will. Why wouldn't they be?" I snapped.

Okay, that was uncalled for. He was probably saying comforting words out loud to appease his own anxiety. And my response was to be a dick about things.

"Just worried. She's struggling," he murmured. His voice sounded . . . vulnerable.

"Don't mind me," I said. "I'm stressed."

I sped around a corner, causing the heavy SUV to tilt a bit.

He gripped the arm rest between us. "Um . . . Yep. We're both worried. We won't be able to help anyone if we wind up dead."

"At least you didn't waste the last two years being a dick to the woman you love," I retorted. I had a lot of making up to do where Elyanna was concerned. The desert flew by as I floored the gas pedal.

"You'll be able to make it up to her," he told me. "If we don't end up in a car wreck."

I clenched the steering wheel and took another turn at breakneck speed.

His big palm covered mine. "Do you want to talk about it?"

"Talk about what?" I asked, bewildered equally by his question and his hand on mine.

"About this. You and me," his voice low.

"Uh . . . there's nothing," I stammered. His hand remained where it was and I loosened my hold on the wheel, appreciating the contact. What the hell was happening? Sure, I liked flirting with the man, and pushing his buttons. But this . . . this was different.

"There's nothing between us or nothing to talk about?" he asked.

His question made my head spin. I eased up on the gas pedal.

"I'm in love with Elyanna," I said.

"I love her, too," he replied while running a thumb across my knuckles. "I'm man enough to admit there's more than just something between you and I. And I'm looking forward to exploring whatever this is. Later, when El and Becks are safe."

He removed his hand from mine. The absence of him was sorely missed. I didn't like it. At all. I reached for his hand, linking our fingers together and floored the gas pedal.

"We have a wife, son, Hudson and each other," Rome added. "We can have it all, Xavi. Everything we've been wanting."

Soft lips brushed the back of my hand. I stole a glance at the firebug.

"If you're going to speed like a maniac, keep both hands on the wheel. I'd like to survive this journey with you." He gently placed my hand on the steering wheel.

My stomach did a weird flip flop thing and the grin on my face was too big to hide. I settled for punching the gas pedal again and shook my head, trying to focus.

At some point, I needed to stop and recuperate. I'd been using my gift steadily for the last few hours. If I didn't rest soon, my body would give out on me. I glanced at my watch again. My plan was to get Becks on her feet and haul ass back to the city within the hour. That was the best-case scenario, considering we had no idea how long the counter-serum would take to work.

I took another turn, causing the tires to screech. Roman braced his hands on the dashboard and glared in my direction.

The strip mall where we'd left Becks and Blake was a mile up ahead.

Roman released an audible sigh. I smirked, but I didn't dare slow our approach.

He reached for the bag loaded with the serums and jumped out of the SUV before I put the vehicle in park.

I hurried into the mattress store behind Rome. The flutter of hope and happiness from his words fizzled to ash and were replaced with a paralyzing fear that stopped me in my tracks. My sister was sheet white, and a sheen of sweat covered her face. Her lips were bluish, and her breathing was labored.

Roman was barking out orders. Blake was shuffling through the bag. And I stood there, my mouth hanging open.

My sister was tough as nails. Tougher than I'd ever been. She was smart, beautiful, and didn't take any shit. She used to stand up to bullies for me when we were in school. My sister was the muscle. And I was the awkward, weakling brother. She was my hero. Rebecca had always remained the one constant in my life, no matter what life threw at me. I had to admit that there were times I'd taken her for granted. Especially after Luther. She'd tried repeatedly to draw me out of the darkness I wallowed in. I had been content to allow my dark side to take over, refusing to talk to her about it. I pushed her away countless times. And she stayed by my side. I couldn't imagine life without her.

"Xavi!" Roman shouted.

I blinked several times and finally found my legs.

"This is perfect. But . . ." Blake trailed off. "She should have been given these serums at regular intervals. Since she's missed a couple doses, I'm giving her the full lot. This may shock her system. You'll need to hold her down."

"Hang on, Becks. I got you." I settled on the mattress beside her and held down her shoulders, while Roman moved to the foot of the bed to hold down her legs.

Blake plunged a needle filled with a pinkish liquid into her vein.

Nothing happened. The room was silent. I loosened my hold.

"Is it . . ." Roman started to say.

Becks' body began to convulse.

"Hold her down!" Blake instructed while he placed a hand over her heart. He closed his eyes, and his hand glowed with power. The luminescent shimmer flowed through Becks' body, blooming outward from her chest.

Blake worked his magic for what felt like an eternity. The spasms seized, and the glow continued traveling through her body. Becks' skin returned to its normal color, her breathing evened, and her heart rate steadied.

After several minutes, the glow vanished, and Blake released her. His shoulders slumped; and sweat beaded his temples. He was tapped out.

"She'll make it." His voice was weary. "I'm not sure what it will do to her powers, but she'll live."

"Thank you," I said, my gaze fixed on Becks. She was sleeping soundly.

"How long?" Roman asked. "I'm not rushing the process, but we have to get back before the Godfather shuts down the city."

Roman told Blake the story, while I made myself comfortable beside my sister since the other two guards were already asleep on the only two mattresses in the place. So much for keeping watch.

"We should be able to move in an hour or two." I heard Blake say, "I'm exhausted."

"Me too," I said. "What's with your protection?" I jerked my thumb toward the two sleeping guards.

"I told them to get some rest. They pulled a twenty-four-hour shift and weren't being helpful," Blake answered.

I nodded. "Rest, Blake. One hour, then we're out of here."

CHAPTER FORTY-FOUR

Hudson

While we sat in the bathtub, I all but force-fed Elyanna. She was wiped out. I thought the last time we were in this place was bad. This was ten times worse. Her body was so weak, she hardly had the energy to chew. I was able to get some food into her system and lots of juice. Then I tucked her in bed.

I watched her sleep for a while and decided to risk leaving her alone. I laid her sword beside her on the bed and exited the apartment with the intention of finding the unit Dani had mentioned to El. It was a long shot considering they were probably still at the training center, but I'd hoped to find one of the seer's men and relay the news El had obtained.

It had taken longer than expected to reach Unit 3023. The location was farther from the retail sectors and Jamboree Court. And the homes nearby were custom designs, with manicured lawns and wrought iron fences. There seemed to be a lot more foot traffic in the vicinity, which made me hesitate.

I scanned the neighborhood before approaching the unit and slowly made my way to the front door. Like the loft we were in, I was able to use the generic code to unlock the door. The empty home was a single-family dwelling. Two stories, with a master suite downstairs and three bedrooms upstairs. Alexi and his friends must have used it as a meeting space. My search of the residence revealed nothing untoward, so I moved on to gather more provisions.

To ensure we blended in with the locals, I went to a clothing store and gathered more items for El, Becks, and the other guys, plus more food. It was midday, and there were a lot more people in the retail sector milling about. The shops, restaurants, and bars were busier than they had been the day before. It made me wonder if it was the weekend. But then again, there were people reporting to work in the Loop. Maybe the Loop was a seven-days-a-week kind of operation. I wasn't sure. What I was sure of was how sickening it all was. People in FC were living comfortable lives, while the people who lived outside of its walls were living in squalor, begging BHF for scraps. Fuckers.

An hour later, I returned to El, who was still asleep. I glanced at the time again. I had another hour before I needed to take the counter-serum. I double-checked the info sheet regarding the protocols. There wasn't much to it. The serums were labeled, which was fortunate for my purpose considering none of the ingredients were familiar to me. Where was Dr. Jeff when I really needed the brainiac? I checked my vitals and began using my powers to do simple things like move items around the loft. Standing next to the bed, I could see the bags I'd left on the floor near the front door. Using my telekinesis powers, I brought the bags to the bedroom area and began unpacking the items and placing them on hangers in the closet. My power was as it had always been. To test things further, I focused on the king-sized bed and levitated it a foot above the ground. Easy. I added the armchair and the nightstands. No sweat. I placed the furniture on the ground gently so as not to disturb my wife. She didn't move an inch.

I focused on the front door and secured the lock. From my vantage point, I couldn't see the kitchen. Typically, I had to see what I wanted to move. I'd tried several times in the past to no avail. The serum was supposed to enhance powers, and so I thought, why not?

I closed my eyes, picturing where the refrigerator was and the celery juice Elyanna loved so much. I had to admit, it was pretty good. Using memory recall, I opened the fridge, picked up the bottle of juice, and imagined it floating up the stairs and into my hands.

I wasn't sure how long I'd been standing there. My powers didn't feel different, and for the most part, it felt as if I wasn't using them all.

Something cold brushed against my arm, making me jump out of my skin. Thanks to my quick reflexes, I caught the bottle before it hit the floor. Well, shit.

I checked my vitals again, just to be sure, then gulped down the juice. Thirty minutes left. Maybe I didn't need the counter-serum. Nah. Better to take it to be sure. Or not. I couldn't decide.

In the end, I nestled next to El, her body warm and soft. She repositioned herself, bringing her body to lie directly on top of me, like a human blanket. Smiling, I dozed off.

"Hudson?" El's voice sounded far away. "Hawk, baby."

I groaned and rolled over.

"Hawk!" She nudged my shoulder. "Your alarm is going off."

I reached under the pillow with my right hand to hit the off button on my watch, then rolled, curling my body against El's, her back to my chest.

My hand snaked under the t-shirt she'd been wearing and found her breasts. I began rolling her nipples between my fingers. El sighed and arched into me.

Every inch of Elyanna's beautiful body was imprinted in my mind. Despite having my eyes closed and my brain foggy with sleep, my body moved instinctually, caressing her skin and tantalizing her into a frenzy. A soft moan escaped her lips as she pushed her ass into my crotch, where my swollen length was seeking her entrance.

My lips brushed against her shoulder, and El angled her head, giving me access to her neck. I suckled the sensitive skin. El moaned and moved my hand from her breast to her pussy. She shoved my finger into her slick opening while grinding her clit into the heel of my palm.

I loved how responsive she was to my touch. Always wet and so fucking tight. My wife chased her orgasm. Gyrating her hips with wild abandon. I slipped in another finger. Her body tightened. Her moans were louder, and her breathing came in pants.

My cock wanted in her cunt . . . or her ass. I wanted to fill every hole. I bit on her shoulder, waiting my turn while El fucked my hand until her body spasmed and juices soaked my fingers.

I smeared her cum all over her pussy and back entrance, then shoved my boxers down and nudged my crown into her cunt while working a finger into her ass. El gasped and spread her knees apart. I slid my cock into her warm, wet hole with a guttural moan and slowly pushed my finger deeper into her ass.

She cried out my name, pleading for more. My wife loved dick, and I loved giving it to her. Watching Xavi fuck her from behind while taking my cock in her mouth made my dick ache. The need to come strong and powerful. Not yet, too soon. I wanted to make her come again and again. I wanted to fuck her ass.

With that thought, I slid my other arm under her torso and found her clit. I removed my cock from her cunt. She was so wet. Her juices coated my shaft; we didn't need lube. I worked my tip into her ass.

I rolled her onto her stomach and propped her ass into the air while pushing my shaft past the tight ring of muscles.

Ffffuckk. I growled and buried my cock to the hilt.

El's face was buried into the pillow, and her moans muffled. She pushed her ass back against my cock and rocked her hips.

"That's it, baby. Fuck my cock." I gripped her hips as she moved back and forth over my shaft.

"Babe," I breathed through clenched teeth, my release close. I draped my body over hers and slid my arm under her body, seeking her clit. Her fingers were already there, rubbing furiously over the swollen nub.

I pushed her hand away and replaced it with my own. I slithered a digit into her hot cunt and pressed my palm against her swollen nub.

"Yes," she cried.

I pumped my hips, I couldn't hold off any longer. "Come for me."

Covered in sweat, I drove deeper into her ass and lost control. My dick sputtered. Jets of cum shot into her. I kept thrusting until El arched her back, her muscles tightening around my fingers and my cock.

I crumpled on top of her, crushing her with my body weight. I was spent.

Aftercare was my specialty, yet I didn't have it in me. I rolled onto my back. El snuggled to my side.

"Hawk," her voice sleepy. "Your skin is hot."

My eyes snapped open, and I checked the time. Shit. "Up, peaches." I drew away from her and swung my legs off the side of the bed.

"Everything okay?" She rested her chin on my shoulder.

I nodded. "Yep." Sort of. We'd slept for two hours straight. I put a hand over my forehead. Slight fever. Pulse normal. Deep breath in. Exhale slowly.

El had moved away from me and grabbed the info sheet. "How long, Hudson?"

"A little over two hours."

She placed her palm on my forehead, then grabbed the syringe I'd already prepped. "Arm please?"

I placed my forearm on her thigh and watched as she administered the shot. Her golden locks draped over her torso, effectively covering her nipples but not enough to conceal the swell of her breasts. The ends trailed down past her lower abdomen, brushing her mound.

"You're gorgeous, Elyanna," I said.

She pricked my arm, a shy smile gracing her lips. "Are you having a fever dream?"

"No, I'm not." I leaned in to peck her lips. "I love you."

"I love you, too. How do you feel?" she asked.

"Good. A little tired. My powers are different," I told her.

Her brow furrowed. "Different how?"

"Let me show you." I cradled her to me as I lay back on the mattress, all while using my gift to turn on the faucet, grab a washcloth, and run the towel under warm water.

"Um, is something supposed to happen?"

"I'm working on it."

A moment later, the damp cloth floated toward us, and I let it hover over the bed. "Impressed?" I asked.

She caught sight of the cloth and sat up. "What the what?"

I snagged the cloth and began wiping between her legs and her crack. I used the other side to clean my dick, then sent the towel back to the bathroom.

Elyanna gaped. Her gaze darted between me and the bathroom. "Are you feeling okay?" She caressed my face, feeling my temperature, then her delicate fingers traveled to my neck while she checked my pulse.

"Seems so. The others will be back soon. I'll have the healer check me over." I laid back on the mattress, bringing El down with me.

She straddled my waist and pressed our foreheads together. "I love you, Hudson. Don't leave me."

"I'm not going anywhere, El."

"Promise me."

Liquid dropped onto my face. I caught the dribble with the tip of my tongue. Salty.

"Don't cry, baby." I swiped her tears with the pad of my thumb.

"Promise me, Hudson."

"I promise."

She sealed her lips to mine. Her mouth was hot, desperate, and possessive. As was always the case with my wife, blood rushed to my cock. Moisture from her core pooled on my abs. I let her take what she wanted as she impaled herself on my cock and rode me until we both collapsed from another orgasm.

CHAPTER FORTY-FIVE

Becks

I'd recognize the sound of the freight train rumbling through the room anywhere. I tilted my head to my left and found my twin lying on his back, an arm draped over his eyes. He was always a loud snorer. That was the one thing that irked me about my twin. At that moment, I wasn't even slightly annoyed. I was . . . relieved.

"Becks?" an unfamiliar voice came from my right.

A slight man with light brown hair and eyes was seated beside the bed.

"I'm Blake," he said. "Are you feeling okay? You must be thirsty."

He reached toward the floor and picked up a bottle of water, then handed it to me.

"Thanks," I said, my voice gravelly.

"Your friends brought me here to help you. I'm a healer," Blake explained. "You needed a counter-serum for the serum you were given at the Loop."

"The Loop?" I asked.

He explained the facility I'd been taken to and the state he found me in.

"I gave you a huge dose of the counter-serum and did some healing.

You should be fine. Do you mind if I check your pulse and your temperature?"

I nodded. He placed his hands on my wrists. His fingertips glowed, and the light flowed into my skin. I felt a cool rush flow through me for a beat, and then the sensation and light vanished.

"Vitals look good. We've been out for more than three hours. Your brother wanted to leave hours ago, but I couldn't wake him," he added.

Roman entered the room at that moment.

"Glad to see you're feeling better, Rebecca," Bug stated.

"Call me Becks, Bug." I gulped the rest of the water.

Roman rifled through a bag sitting at the foot of the bed and handed me another bottle of water along with a snack bar. I inhaled the bar and chugged the water. "How long?" I asked.

"Half a day," Roman replied. "Hey!" He gave my brother's leg a good thwack.

Xavi startled awake. "Becks?"

"I'm here. I'm fine."

He rubbed his eyes, then leaned in for a hug. "I was worried," he murmured. "We have to get to El."

He shot up to his feet and checked his watch. "Shit. Did we sleep for four hours?"

"You slept for four hours," Roman corrected. "We tried waking you. I would have been more insistent at the two-hour mark, but Becks wasn't ready to be moved."

My twin glanced at me and nodded. "You good?"

I nodded. "I just need to pee."

Roman jutted his chin toward a door located at the back, which led to an alleyway behind the store. I did my business and went back to find the guys waiting at the front door.

"Who are these guys?" I waved at the two guards sleeping on mattresses.

"They were supposed to be our protection. I gave them a sedative," Blake told us. "Let them sleep. They can find their way back on their own."

I shrugged and followed my brother to the SUV. He filled me in on what El had found at the Loop and our plan going forward. He was excited about the prospect of ending the war between the Rebels and BHF. A spark of hope lit inside me. All of this—even being away from my family—would be worth it if we could end it here and now.

"So, um . . . I ran into Mom," Xavi stated.

"No, you didn't. That's impossible, Xavier."

"I did too. Ask Fly."

"Who?" I arched my brow.

"Bug, Fly, same difference."

I couldn't hide my grin as I turned to face Roman in the backseat.

"I've asked him many times to stop calling me that." He shook his head. "As far as your mother, she's about four-ten. Shoulder-length hair. Cornflower blue eyes and wears thick glasses. And goes by the name of Patrice. She was very helpful."

"Mom?" I faced Xavi. He nodded. "How?"

As he told me the story, something in me began to bubble over. Anguish. I was angry at the woman for lying to us. For hiding. I mourned her daily. I missed her presence in my life profoundly. I longed for her guidance, her reassuring words, and her shoulder to lean on. I'd been on vacation in Europe when she passed and hadn't had a chance to say goodbye. The guilt I'd carried all these years for nothing. She was alive the entire time. How could she abandon us like this? After all this time? We knew as children that our parents were in hiding, but to fake her death after my father had just died? Why wouldn't she confide in me? We were close . . . or so I thought.

What the hell, Mom?

"Are you doing this?" Xavi asked.

I ignored him, fuming over my mother's lies. She knew how devastated I was after my father had passed. She was the one who encouraged me to take a vacation while Xavi and Johnny were deployed. She'd probably done that on purpose. Dammit. I was such a naive asshole.

Years had passed, and she didn't even try to reach out. She could have come with us to Gator Springs. We would have kept her safe.

"Becks. You need to calm down," Blake said.

That set me off.

"Calm down! Fuck you. I am calm. I just found out the mother I'd buried is still alive. This whole time! Who the fuck are you to tell me to calm down?!"

"Sis." Xavi placed a shaky hand on my arm. "Your powers are doing something weird."

I looked at him. He was shivering, and his breath was coming out in puffs. The truck windows had a coat of fog. Blake and Roman were both shivering. I didn't understand.

I glanced at my skin, which was pale and almost blueish. I started to panic. Shards of ice formed on my fingertips.

"What's wrong with me?" I tried to open the door, but the handle broke off.

"Rome, can you counter the frost?" my brother asked.

"I don't know." Roman's teeth chattered.

"Do it! Or we'll freeze to death!" Xavi urged. "Becks, sis. Please relax. Deep breaths. Think of Jules, Jonah, and Aaron. Think of home."

I was hyperventilating.

"Becks!" Xavi shouted.

He was turning blue. So were the other men. No. This can't be.

"Please." Xavi's eyelids looked heavy.

I closed my eyes and thought of my husband and children. *Mommy's coming home. I won't leave you like my mom left me.* I continued breathing.

"Shit. That was close," Xavi groaned. He tried the ignition. Nothing happened. "Frozen engine. Rome?"

"Yep. Let me um . . . try to warm things up in here first."

The interior of the vehicle was like sitting in a sub-zero freezer. I tried pushing the door again.

"Don't force it," Xavi warned. "It's frozen. It will break."

Warm air flowed through the SUV.

"Faster, Roman," Xavi barked.

"No, I don't want to burn you all alive. Give me a minute." Roman concentrated on his gift.

"Holy shit. You guys are powerful," Blake muttered.

The vehicle warmed. "Try a window," Roman said.

"Can't turn on the engine," Xavi replied.

"I'm sorry," I said. "I don't know what's happened to me."

"I'm guessing the enhancement allows your water manipulation abilities to now include ice formation," Blake offered.

Son of a bitch.

"Try a door," Bug said.

Xavi opened the door, allowing a whoosh of hot desert air in.

Roman and Blake stepped out. I climbed over the seat and exited through the driver's side. Water dripped as the ice covering the SUV melted. Xavi popped the hood and whistled.

"We might have to walk." He scratched his head.

I peered over his shoulder and gasped. The engine block was frozen.

CHAPTER FORTY-SIX

Roman

I stared at the SUV's engine in disbelief. One minute Xavi was talking about seeing his mother again, and the next thing I knew, the SUV rolled to a stop and a winter storm blew into the car. Unlike the other men present, I hadn't felt it at first. The windows fogged, the air coming out of the air conditioning vents iced over, and Blake, who had been sitting next to me, began to shiver.

My inner fire kept my body warm for a time without me having to think about it. Becks' power was strong. And I was speechless. It took me a moment to conjure up the power to warm my body. By then, I was also shivering.

The desert heat was rapidly melting the ice, but it would take a while.

"Go, get a head start. I'll use my power to speed up the melting process," I told the others.

"Why don't we just wait while you do your thing?" Xavi asked.

"Because I might blow up the engine. I won't be able to protect all of you from the explosion. I'll do what I can and pick you up. Stay on the main road; we've got several miles to go."

On foot, it would take hours to reach FC. Hopefully I could salvage the frozen engine without blowing myself up, and we could get back to Elyanna.

Xavi didn't waste any time. He got a duffle bag out of the SUV and said, "You heard the man. Let's get out of the blast zone." He ushered his sister and Blake to get moving.

"Good luck, man. Don't blow yourself up, or El will be pissed." Xavi nudged my shoulder.

I grunted in response and called on my fire. I used a slow, steady stream of heat, melting the outer components first. It was a slow-going process to which I was not accustomed. My natural instinct was to release my fire in blasts filled with rage. This was taxing on my patience.

After thirty minutes, I tried the engine. It didn't work. I kept at it, the slow burn leaving a mass of water enough to fill a kiddie pool. An hour later, the engine finally turned over. I put the SUV in gear and drove down the street. It didn't take long for me to find the trio.

Xavi opened the driver's door. "Move," he told me.

I arched my brow.

"The guards will recognize me more than you. Move."

"You could ask nicely," I muttered.

"Let me drive, honey. You sit back and relax," he chimed in a mock falsetto.

"You're such an asshole." I got into the back seat.

Minutes later, the guard waved us through without a question. Xavi parked in the usual spot and looked over at his sister.

"Stay in the car, Becks. I'll come around and lead us to Hawk and El."

"I want to see Mom," she argued.

"I don't know where she is," he replied when opening her door.

"I do," Blake said. "She lives in the area where the other hospital staff lives. Unit 501."

We glared at him.

"I was on patrol, remember? Kyle and I followed her."

"Right," I said, then looked at Becks. "I think that visit will have to wait, Becks. We shouldn't separate."

I exited the car.

"Please, Xavi. I need to see her," Becks begged her brother.

He scrubbed a hand through his hair. "Fine. One hour."

"I can take her," Blake offered.

"No," Xavi and I said simultaneously.

"You lead, Becks and I will be right behind you. You won't see us. So don't turn around or talk," Xavi told the healer, then pulled out a knife from his boot. "I will gut you if you do anything stupid."

"One hour, Becks." I pulled her in for a hug. "El will be worried about you."

She hugged me back.

"I'll see you guys at 2323." I nodded at the two men and went to find El.

I was still in my guard uniform, the charcoal gray one that was the uniform designated for the Loop guards. No one paid any attention to me. It seemed safe enough, and yet I took a circuitous route to the loft instead of going straight to it, just in case someone was watching me.

Thirty-five minutes later, I arrived at the loft. It was quiet. Food items sat neatly organized on the kitchen counter. Hawk.

His eyes snapped open as I approached the bedroom area. I leaned over him and brushed strands of hair away from El's face. She slept soundly, and her skin tone had returned to its normal hue. I placed a lingering kiss on her forehead.

"Others?" Hawk whispered.

"Becks wanted to see her mother. They should be back within the hour," I explained, then told him Blake was taking them to her place.

"What? She might not even be there."

I shrugged. "Becks was freaking out about it, and her powers are . . . different."

Hawk groaned.

"Rest. I'm going to take a quick shower. We still have a few more hours before sundown." I strolled to the bathroom and took a quick shower.

I didn't have clean clothes. What we did have was in the bag Xavi took with him, and even then, I wasn't sure there was anything in it that would fit me. I wrapped a towel around my waist and noticed the closet door was open. There were several items of clothing. I picked out a pair of boxers and settled on the bed beside Hawk. El laid directly on top of him.

I smiled. I'd seen them sleep in that same position often. The urge to steal her away from him was strong. I wanted to embrace her but wouldn't disturb her slumber. Lord knew we all needed our strength if we were going to go up against the Godfather. I laced my fingers with hers and closed my eyes.

It didn't take long for her to notice my presence. She curled her body against mine and buried her face in my neck. I held her close, allowing sleep to take me.

———

Elyanna's moans woke me. She was on her back between me and Hudson, one leg draped over my torso, the other draped over his. Xavi was between her legs, feasting on her pussy.

Droplets of water dripped from his hair onto her pelvis. Her nipples stood in stiff peaks. A large hand massaged her tits. I glanced to my left and caught Hawk's green-eyed gaze. He kissed a path from El's neck to her lips.

I shoved my hand in my boxers to palm my swollen cock and began sucking her neck. She hooked an arm around me and then turned to give me her lips. The taste of Hawk was still on her tongue.

I smeared my precum over my head and squeezed. God this woman. These men. Every time I tried to be gentlemanly about the relationship, I was thrown into an ocean of lust. And I wasn't complaining about it one bit.

Xavi crawled up her body and angled her face away from mine, stealing her kisses.

"I want to watch you get fucked, baby," he said to her.

She responded with a low moan and reached for my cock. Xavier noticed.

"You want Rome's big dick, don't you?" Xavi groaned.

El rolled on her side and pressed her butt into my cock. I took that as a yes.

I tugged off my boxers and lined up with her wet heat. She hooked an arm around my neck while her lips were locked with Hawk's.

Xavi sat on his heels at the foot of the bed. Hawk brought her leg over his torso, granting me access. I sucked her neck and threaded my dick into her cunt.

Her walls squeezed my length as I slipped in. I took my time, savoring her tightness.

"Angel." I gasped. "Your pussy feels perfect around my cock," I said with a restrained breath. I'd been lusting after her—after them—for over a year. Being with them like this was even better than my wildest dreams.

I pumped into her with slow, languid strokes, wanting to draw out the moment as long as I could.

Elyanna groaned my name.

"Fuck, that's hot," Xavi's voice said, deep and husky.

Hawk was kissing her neck and pinching her nipples.

I continued moving my hips in and out. Something smooth and wet flicked over my shaft every time I withdrew from El's pussy. Xavi was between her legs, licking her clit, running his tongue over my cock in the process. The sensation lit every nerve ending on fire.

My thrusts became more and more erratic. The thought of his tongue on my length, while buried deep inside El, made me wild. My balls drew up tight. Xavi suck the heavy sacks, and I lost it.

My climax erupted. My spend coated her walls and my breath came in ragged pants. Xavi was just getting started.

I pulled out of El's tight pussy only to be swallowed up by Xavi's hot mouth. Fffuck. Being with them like this was pure heaven. They fucking owned me. I didn't think I had anything left in but my cock sputtered as he took my length. He groaned around me like I was the most delicious thing he'd ever tasted, and then he released me and fixed his lips to El's drenched cunt.

"Give me his seed, baby," he told her. "Let it drip into my mouth."

"Oh my god," she gasped.

"That's it, El. Just like that." Xavi feasted on her cunt while she released my cum into his mouth.

It was filthy and so hot. My dick hardened again.

My lips collided with El's in a feverish kiss while Hawk guided her hand over his cock, stroking it furiously.

Xavi groaned and slurped as he ate her out, then shot up abruptly. "My turn." He slid his cock into her, pumped a few times, and then came with a harsh grunt.

"My turn," Hawk sat up, a feral glint in his green eyes.

He positioned her on all fours and growled. "Suck them off, babe."

El propped herself up on her elbows and licked her lips as she gazed at my cock and Xavi's. I brought my tip to her mouth, while Xavi did the same.

"I fucking love you." Hawk bit her neck, then slammed into her, making her body jerk. His thrusts were rough, and she loved it. She groaned around our dicks, her tongue flicking over our crowns. Saliva dripped down her chin. She took my length to the back of her throat, then popped off, and then did the same to Xavi.

Fuck, she was good at this.

Hawk spanked her ass, and she dug her nails into my thighs. I gripped my cock and stroked. Xavi did the same.

Hawk worked a punishing pace and unleashed. El came with him, and Xavi and I followed soon after, coming all over her face.

She was covered with sweat and cum, and she looked magnificent. "I love you," I whispered in her ear, then removed a pillow case to wipe her face. She gave me a lazy smile and slouched on the mattress.

Hawk draped his body over hers, holding her close. Xavi disappeared into the bathroom. I heard the water running, and he returned moments later with a bottle of green juice.

"Drink, El," Xavi said.

Hawk sat on his heels and brought El to rest on his thighs. God, they were beautiful. Sated. In love. I kissed her belly as she pulled a deep drink of juice. She ran her nails on my scalp and handed the juice to Hawk.

"Bath is ready," Xavi announced, his gaze fixed on where El and Hawk were still joined.

Hawk gripped her hips and slowly raised her off his semi-hard cock. Xavi sucked in a deep breath. I couldn't peel my eyes away.

His cock gleamed with her cum. I licked my lips just as Xavi muttered, "What I wouldn't give to lick her cum off of you right now."

El tipped her head back onto Hawk's shoulder. He kissed her jaw and said, "That was the third orgasm I've had in less than five hours. I'm done."

"I just wanted to taste it," Xavi muttered.

"Sure you did." He climbed off the bed and carried El to the bathroom. "Next time," Hawk said over his shoulder.

Fucking tease.

CHAPTER FORTY-SEVEN

Elyanna

"**B**ecks!" I rushed downstairs to meet my best friend as she entered the loft with Blake following behind her.

I flung my arms around her and squeezed. "How are you feeling?"

"I'm . . . I don't know." Her eyes got misty.

I steered her to the plastic-covered couch, and she leaned on my shoulder. My men hovered, and I waved them away.

Xavi sat next to his sister and draped an arm over her shoulders.

"Can I get a minute with El?" she asked him.

Ghost nodded and moved toward the door.

"Great to see you, Becks," Hudson said to her, then faced me. "We're going to do a recon."

"No, have Blake do some healing first," I told him and gave Blake a pleading look.

"You look fine, Hudson, but better safe than sorry. It will only take a minute. Roman told me about your run-in with the Godfather. Have you taken any counter-serums?" Blake asked.

Hudson nodded and proceeded to tell him about his rise in temperature and the changes in his powers.

Blake placed his glowing, healing hands on my husband's wrists. A minute later, he said, "Huh?"

"Huh?" Hudson repeated.

"It seems like your body has assimilated the serum. Almost like that concoction was made specifically for you. Interesting. The men who had been given a full syringe experienced severe symptoms. You seem perfect," the healer stated.

"See, all good, peaches." Hudson kissed my temple and ushered the guys out the door, giving me and Becks privacy.

"Talk to me, Becks," I encouraged.

"Did Xavi not tell you? My powers are fucked up."

"No, he didn't say anything." We were busy doing sexy things, and I hadn't had a chance to ask. Oh my god, was she here the whole time, listening? My face heated.

Becks didn't mention it as she scooted away from me, covering her face with her hands.

"Look at me, Becks. Tell me what happened."

"I'm scared." Her voice was soft, barely above a whisper.

"It's okay. Whatever it is, we'll figure it out together."

Slowly, she brought her hands down.

My eyes went wide. Before I could neutralize my expression, she caught my reaction.

"It's awful, isn't it?" She sobbed, sort of. Her tears emerged like drops of crystal.

I wiped her face, catching the ice formations in my hands. They melted in my palm.

Holy shit.

"It's actually . . . kind of cool." I gave her a genuine smile.

"It is not! Look at my hands."

Each fingertip was a frozen point.

"Oh . . . well. That's different. I am sure we can figure this out somehow. What did Blake say? Your mother?"

"Blake said my vitals are fine, which means the serum has taken root. As far as my mother is concerned, she wasn't at her apartment."

"And Blake didn't mention what to do with your new powers? The others must do something to adjust."

"He said during and after the enhancement, the women stay at the Loop where they are monitored. The men undergo training in the arena."

"The Loop is not an option, so maybe you need to practice with your powers. That might give you better control," I offered.

"I froze the SUV." Her voice trembled.

"What?!" I screeched.

Becks proceeded to tell me about their journey from the mattress store to FC. My mouth hung open as she described what had happened in the interior of the SUV and the engine block.

"You iced a three thousand-pound vehicle while it was a hundred and twenty-five degrees outside?! That is bad ass." I was genuinely impressed.

"El! This is serious."

"I am serious. Come on, let's see what you got," I encouraged.

"Stop making fun of me," she snarled.

"I'm not, Becks. Let's play with this new power while we're in a safe place. It's just you and me. When you've used your power before, there was always water nearby. We can go into the bathroom." I stood and tugged on her hand.

She didn't budge.

"Becks! Come on! We have to face the Godfather soon. Let's do this so we can go home to our children."

That was enough motivation for her to get moving.

We went to the upstairs bathroom since the downstairs bathroom did not have a tub. First, we filled the sink with water. With one flick of her wrist, the water froze. I turned the faucet on and let the hot water run.

"Okay." I moved to the bathtub and turned on the water. "Instead of a full wrist flick, try one finger."

She glared.

"I'm thinking a smaller movement will yield smaller results," I said hopeful.

She rolled her eyes and did as I asked. Water arced from the faucet and froze midair.

"This is so cool. You're like Elsa." I grinned. "I think you just need to practice, Becks. That will give you better control."

"This isn't a Disney movie, Elyanna," she huffed.

I nodded. "I know. But when you have lemons, make lemonade. Right? We have some time before the big meet-up. You can practice making ice pops. And I could use some practice, too."

"What's wrong?" she asked.

I told her about my issues with my powers.

"Maybe we can sit this one out and let the guys save the day," she muttered.

"I wish that were the case. Let me show you something." I showed Becks the sketches from Dani and told her about my visit with the seer. She agreed that the woman in one of the drawings did look like her.

"Shit. Guess we can't let the guys have all the fun."

Becks set herself up on the kitchen counter to practice with her icy powers. It was impressive. She sat on the kitchen counter with cups and bowls filled with water. Her brows drew together as she tried controlling the icy flows.

On the other hand, I moved into the living room and pushed the plastic-covered seats to the side, which gave me twenty by forty square feet of space to run through sword drill exercises.

When I discovered my abilities, I worked with a sword master at a dojo in my city. The drills were exhausting, and they helped me filter the thoughts from my mind.

Twenty minutes in, my muscles were warm and my movements fluid. I slowly released the block on my powers, layer by layer. Every ten minutes, I released a layer, allowing thoughts to trickle through my mind. Fifteen minutes later, my men's thoughts bombarded my consciousness. I nearly stumbled. I ground my teeth and continued, swiping left diagonally, then right diagonally.

You got this, baby. Hudson's encouraging thoughts came through loud and clear. I kept going until the buzzing became too much. I crumpled to the floor, my body and mind exhausted.

My men rushed to my side.

"I'm okay," I breathed. "I'm good."

"I'll get you something to drink," Bug offered.

"And eat." Ghost pecked my forehead and followed him into the kitchen.

Hudson helped me to my feet and put me on the couch. "I found Alexi; he and the other guys will be here in about an hour. You have time to go upstairs and rest, baby."

"I just need a minute," I replied.

"Are you sure?"

"Yeah, let's get this over with. I want to see my son and get out of this desert."

CHAPTER FORTY-EIGHT

Hudson

After our sex fest, we got a couple hours of sleep. El could've used more rest, but that wasn't going to happen with three hot-blooded men hovering around her nakedness. I reminded them we weren't alone which prompted the guys out of the loft.

Blake separated from us, stating he needed to gather a few things. I shrugged him off and nodded to Xavier. We rounded the corner, and Xavi used his gift to tail the healer, just in case. He seemed like a nice guy and had proven helpful, but it was too soon to tell.

Roman and I proceeded to 3023. I went in while he remained outside. It wasn't even dark yet, and we still had plenty of time, so I wasn't hopeful.

Alexi was in the living room doing push-ups. My schoolmate didn't even flinch when I walked in on him.

"Your lack of security is astounding," I stated.

"Saw you coming," he said while holding in plank position.

"Are you trying to impress me? It's not working." I shrugged.

He laughed and came to a seated position.

"How'd you know I was coming?" I asked.

He pointed toward the ceiling. "Attic. This unit has the best view of the comings and goings. Thank God you showed up when you did. It was getting hot up there."

I laughed.

"Let's get down to business," I told him. "My wife ran into yours."

I pulled the sketch out of my pocket and retold the story of El meeting Dani.

"Finally. We've been waiting for months." Alexi sighed. "I'll gather the others. And you need to lay low; the Godfather knows that you aren't in the cells."

"Did the woman have her baby?" I asked.

"As of," he glanced at his watch. "Twenty-eight minutes ago, no. He'll remain in the Loop until the designated time. For now, you need to watch out for his minions, the guards, and the community as a whole."

"What's that supposed to mean?"

"It means once we take down the Godfather, which we will do, we will have an uprising. The residents here, in case you haven't noticed, bought their right to live in this fancy community. They are perfectly fine in their bubble."

"Shit. And the guards? Do you have a connection in the guard sector?"

He nodded. "That is a sticky situation. The man in charge of the guards is a Pure Blood. Has a weapons gift. We need to subdue him first before the Godfather tells him of your escape. Luca has made friends with the second-in-command. Former military colonel. Older guy, but he'll rally the guards under his rule once we take over."

I massaged the bridge of my nose. "Dammit. Alexi, all we want is to be left alone. The state of Federation City is of no concern to me or mine. Do you have a system in place? Do you have leaders here that will do the right thing?"

"We want the same. I want my child and wife to be free of his hold. We can maintain what we have here without him. We need help taking him down. He's powerful, Hudson. He's been able to siphon multiple powers at a time."

"For how long?"

"Not sure; he's been testing it regularly. If I had to guess twenty to sixty minutes."

"That's a long time, even at twenty. Why haven't you tried taking him down before? With all the Pure Bloods in this place, you should have been able to kill him years ago."

"Those who have tried are dead. Those of us who are alive have children and wives. It's an odd situation. The more time you spend around him, the easier it is for him to siphon your powers. The more he takes, the more it drains the Pure Blood. That's why he keeps the men living with him. It's a prison. He allows those with passive powers to roam freely for the most part. The others who are loyal to him have more privileges. On top of all that, he always has at least two Pure Blood guards with him at all times."

My throat felt dry. "Well, what the fuck are we supposed to do against all that?"

"Take him by surprise. He hasn't been around you all that much, so he won't be able to drain your power that easily. The rest of us can deal with his guards."

"Fuck, Alexi. This is a shitshow."

"I know, Hudson. I know. According to Dani's visions, the real power is the blonde. Keep her away from him and let her take him out."

"My wife, El."

"El. Dani never mentioned her powers. Whatever it is, she'll be the key."

The weight of the world settled on my shoulders as I exited 3023. Alexi and I came up with a plan to create a plan. We needed all of the players involved, and although we had time before the confrontation, it didn't seem like enough.

Roman and I ran into Xavi and Blake on our way back to the loft. Blake had an armful of bags.

"I need to change, and I'm starving. How you guys survive on snack bars and water is beyond me. I'll cook," the healer stated.

I raised my eyebrows.

"Listen, I realize you don't know me, and I haven't earned your trust yet, but you're stuck with me. I am not going home. I live with the Godfather. There is no way I'm going back there. He probably has scouts searching for me and Kyle as we speak. And I do not want to be found."

"He does," I said, leaving it at that. Alexi and someone named Steel were assigned that duty. He said Blake was good people. Kyle hadn't been. Elyanna took care of him, which was one less worry.

Elyanna was a different story. I wasn't sure how to help her with her gift. I couldn't imagine what it was like to have so many people stuck in her head. She was strong-willed, and if anyone could master it, it was her.

Back in the loft, Becks was sitting on the counter with frozen bowls of water, and El was in the living area waving around her sassy stick. I'd seen her practice sword drills countless times since we met, and this was different. Her jaw was clenched tight, and a sheen of sweat covered her furrowed brow. She was testing her gift, and we'd just invaded her senses with our inner dialogue.

You got this baby, I stated in my mind, hoping she got my words of encouragement. She pressed on. I motioned with my chin to the others, telling them to give her space. It was times like these that I wished I could teach them how to close off their minds to give her peace.

Blake went straight to the kitchen, while Rome, Xavi, and I watched El. As soon as she collapsed, we rushed to her side.

I held her steady, then placed her on the couch. "I found Alexi. He and the other guys will be here in about an hour. You have time to go upstairs and rest."

"I just need a minute." Her voice wavered, but I didn't mention it.

"Are you sure?"

"Yeah, let's get this over with. I want to see my son and get out of this desert."

She swayed on her feet, then said. "Maybe I should lie down."

I nodded and watched as she trudged upstairs. Xavi and Rome tried to get her to eat or drink, and she waved them off.

"She needs a minute." I scrubbed my hand through my hair.

Elyanna was never unsure or fragile. She always had a fierceness in her eyes, even when I had her chained to my floor. The self-doubt she shrouded herself in twisted me up inside. I hated seeing her suffer, and I hated it even more that the success of our mission to take down the Godfather rested on her shoulders.

Time to come up with a new plan, Hawk. Hell if I was going to let her take on this responsibility on her own. My goal was to get her home, even if that meant tearing this entire city to the fucking ground.

CHAPTER FORTY-NINE

Hudson

An hour or so later, Alexi and Luca arrived. Blake cooked an Asian stir-fry dish, which fed all of us. We ate, giving everyone a chance to get to know one another. El came down to join us for dinner while we went over the plan. Straight posture, chin held high, she put on a brave face, even though those of us who knew her knew she wasn't well.

"Give us a run-through of what we're dealing with," I said to Alexi.

He picked up the binder we'd taken from the surveillance office and began leafing through it, tearing the pages out and separating them. "I'll separate these into piles. Passive gifts are people we don't need to worry about. Loyal to the Godfather, here, and a separate pile for those that are no longer living. And the women, of course, since they won't be joining us."

Once done, he had a pile of papers and passed them around. "These are friendlies. We can count on them to help; get familiar with them."

El studied them for a moment while I peered over her shoulder. She'd taken a short nap and ate more than I'd seen her eat since we'd gotten to FC, so I was hopeful. I knew she'd be fine, still, I planned on shielding her as much as possible.

The stack of friendlies was thin—only six of them. Could be worse. I committed the faces to memory, and El passed on the papers.

"These are loyal to the Godfather. Let's call them loyalists." He handed us a thicker stack of papers.

There were about ten of them, all with powerful offensive gifts: lightning, fire, metal, and invisibility. I noted the name and removed Kyle's sheet from the stack. A weapons master . . . interesting. And the list went on.

"El, do you have that sketch?" I asked. "I remember the familiar faces, but I don't remember seeing anyone else."

"Yep, it's upstairs." She stood.

"I'll grab it, babe," Roman offered and shot up the stairs.

El settled on the cushion, leaning into me.

"We need to pay a visit to the guard sector first and subdue the weapons master," Alexi told us. "He often threatens the troops. We'll need to kill him before meeting up with the Godfather."

"What exactly does he do?" Xavi asked.

"He has an affinity for weapons. He can conjure a weapon with a thought. Whatever he needs in a fight appears in his hands, and then bam!" Luca said.

"He won't be easy to take down, which is why we haven't gone after him before," Alexi added. "Like the Godfather, he has amassed a slew of loyalists. We want to get rid of them before moving forward. Thus, we will not only have Emit to deal with; we'll have a dozen guards to take out before moving on to the Godfather."

I glanced at the time. We had a couple of hours to go. Shit. "We need to move. Now. We don't want a group of trigger-happy soldiers at our back when dealing with the Godfather."

"Guard uniforms or civilian clothes?" Roman asked, handing me the sketch.

I rubbed my jaw. The sketch didn't include anyone else. Dammit, this wasn't helpful.

"Guard uniforms for us. We'll go in first. Do either of you know where we'll find this Emit?"

"I'll guide you," Luca, the brainiac, offered. "I'm always in there helping with engineering issues and the like."

"Roman, Xavi, and I will go in with Luca. Alexi, you and the rest of your men will handle the guards," I said.

El faced me, her eyebrows raised.

"Stay here with Blake and Becks, babe. We'll handle this and come back this way when we're done." I ran a thumb down her cheek.

"Are you making me stay home because my gift is wonky?" she asked.

"Yes," Roman and Xavi said simultaneously.

"It'll be an easy gig. And we need you to save your gift for the head cheese," I added. "And maybe Blake can offer a healing."

She thought about it, then shrugged. "Couldn't hurt."

I donned a guard uniform, said a quick goodbye, and went to the guard sector to speak with the man running the place.

At the guard sector, we waltzed in with Luca in the lead. Luca was a brain child like Dr. Jeff. His specialty was engineering. He'd been involved with the initial architectural and engineering plans for Pleasanton, which became Federation City. He would be perfect to stick around and manage this place when we were gone.

The guards treated him with deference and eyed us as we passed. I noted a group of a dozen or so men sitting in a lounge area. The scowls on their faces and narrowed gazes told me they were certainly going to be a problem. Rome wore a passive expression, while Xavi and I smirked. Idiots.

We turned a corner and walked into the rec room. Large sofas filled the space along with game tables—ping pong, video games, and pool tables. On the far side of the room, a man stood in front of a big screen practicing his golf swing, his back turned toward us.

"Emit, I wanted to introduce . . ."

"No need for introductions." The curly haired man followed through with his swing, pivoted on his heel, and pointed the game controller at us. "I've been waiting for you."

"Duck!" I shouted just as bullets peppered the wall behind us. I dove behind a large sofa with Xavi beside me. I hurled the nearest video game at Emit.

Emit grunted but kept firing. Shit. Staying low to the ground, I ran to the other side of the room, getting away from the door.

I recalled everything I'd seen in the room via memory and began hurtling things to where I'd last seen him.

"How the fuck are you doing that?" Xavi huddled beside me.

Gunfire blared from outside the rec room.

"Shit. Cover me." Xavi ran.

I picked up a leather sectional and used it as a shield to cover him as he ran. He peeked out the door and fired his weapon. "Thanks man!" He shouted over his shoulder and gave me a thumbs up.

Ass.

I peered over the recliner I was crouched behind to see Luca's foot peeking out from behind a video game. Rome was a few feet to his left, behind another video game, firing off rounds.

Emit was on the opposite side of the room. In a split second, the automatic weapon in his hand morphed into a flame thrower. I tore it from his hands and flung it across the room while Rome pumped a couple of bullets in him.

Emit dropped to the floor, riddled with bullets.

I nodded at him and moved toward Xavi by the door. The battle raged on. I peeked around Xavi's frame and caught sight of a half dozen men aiming their weapons at us. I yanked the guns out of their hands with one pull of my power, then Xavi and Rome opened fire, taking them down.

"Cease fire!" Alexi's voice bellowed from the hallway.

He slowly waltzed in as we made our way out of the rec room. Alexi glanced over my shoulder, then nodded. Luca followed behind me, no worse for wear.

"The others?" I asked.

"Dead, all dead. The new man in charge wants a word."

I stepped out into the waiting area where the loyalists lay dead and moved into an office with Emit's name on the door.

"Hudson Pierce. I should have known." A bald man with faded tattoos crawling up his neck stepped from behind a large wooden desk to greet me.

I extended my hand to shake my former commander's hand. "Colonel Summers. Glad you're still around."

"Xavier, too." He shook Xavi's hand. "I should have known you guys would be together. So where's Axel?"

His question felt like a gut punch. Xavi stiffened, then cleared his throat. "Dead. I . . . uh. I killed him."

"It's not your fault, Xavi," I said in a firm voice. "We had a run-in with the Puppeteer," I explained to the colonel.

"I see. Definitely not your fault. Still, I'm sorry for your loss." He placed a firm hand on Xavi's shoulder and waited for Ghost to meet his gaze. "Not your fault, Xavier. I take it was you two who ended the Puppeteer?" Colonel asked.

"Our wife, actually," I said.

Colonel's eyes widened. "Wow. I can't wait to meet her. First, what shall we do with this mess you've brought to my doorstep?"

CHAPTER FIFTY

Elyanna

Blake sat across from me on the now plastic-free sofas. When Dani's husbands, Alexi and Luca, came over, the first thing they'd done was tear off the covering on the furniture, confidently stating the Godfather's reign would be over in a few hours.

I didn't care much, considering the plan was to be on our way home in the morning.

"May I?" Blake extended both hands toward me.

I mimicked him, outstretching my arms. He gently wrapped his fingers around my wrists, and a white glow emanated from his fingertips. Blake closed his eyes as I studied the healer's face. He had an amiable personality, which tracked with his healing gift. His bedside manner was gentle and kind. He was fit, and his good muscle tone told me he wasn't a lazy man, but he was no fighter. He had an attractive face and often wore an open expression, which made him seem honest and trustworthy. From what I could gather when I looked in his head, I knew he was as he appeared, an honest, trustworthy individual.

A slight warming sensation flowed under my skin for a minute. His eyes snapped open, and he smiled, then released my wrists. "You're fine, Elyanna; I think it's just stress. You should take it easy."

I frowned. "I've been resting, and I feel . . . good. Energized. Thank you."

"Anything else?" He eyed me.

"No. Should I be feeling something else?"

"Nope. Not at all. Becks, how about you? How are you feeling? Any luck with your powers?"

"No," she replied. "I'm frustrated. Can we go to my mom's? We still have time."

I glanced at my watch and shrugged. "Almost two hours to go. Is it far?"

The healer shook his head. "No, but I don't think that's wise. Your men will skin me alive if they find out you went gallivanting without them."

Becks and I looked at each other and started laughing.

"Come on, healer, dude. We're going to my mother's," Becks told him.

"But . . ."

"It's fine, Blake. I'll deal with my men if they fuss." I strolled toward the door.

He stayed seated, wringing his hands.

"It's fine, Blake. Either you come with us or we're going alone." I motioned toward the door.

Twenty minutes later, we were at Becks' mother's place. Patrice opened the door and pulled Becks in for a bear hug. Mother and daughter cried. And I was relieved to see real tears coming from Becks' eyes instead of the frozen ones.

"I'm so happy to see you, Rebecca. Come in. And hello, Elyanna." Patrice gave me a small smile.

"Hi. Do you remember Blake?" I waved at the healer as I entered her home.

She nodded and motioned for us to sit.

Patrice's home was a one-story, one-bedroom place. The decor had a coastal vibe, which reminded me of our cottage at the Summit, which Becks decorated for me.

"Please have a seat. This is my . . . friend. Wayne." Patrice glided her hand over the young man's shoulders. Wayne, from the looks of things, had to be a decade, maybe two, younger than her.

"You must be the daughter. Your mother has told me so much about you and your twin. Where is he?" Wayne smiled and extended his hand toward Becks. She ignored him.

"Mother? We have important things to discuss. Maybe your friend should leave," Becks growled.

"Rebecca! Don't be rude."

"It's okay, Patrice; I'm not offended in the least. We talked about this. We knew your children wouldn't be happy with us being together, considering our age difference." Wayne's glasses slid to the tip of his nose, and he pushed them back with his middle finger.

"I'm sorry, hon. My daughter has forgotten herself."

She leaned into him and pressed her forehead into his shoulder. The dark-haired man patted her back gently. Patrice straightened her posture and addressed us. "Can I get you anything? Tea, coffee. Wayne made the best pork chops. Or I can whip up . . . pancakes. You used to love those, Rebecca."

Patrice moved into the kitchen. Wayne followed closely behind her.

"Mom, we're not here for pancakes or pork chops. I need you to tell me what happened. Why did you fake your death? I grieved for you. So did Xavi! I was devastated. How could you do this to me? To us? Did you plan on leaving? Is that why you encouraged me to go to Europe? What about Dad?"

Becks' hands began to shake, and her fingertips frosted over.

"Are you okay? Sweetie, you need to calm down," Patrice said.

"I feel like I should go." Blake stood against the door.

"No!" Becks snapped. "Sit."

I patted the cushion next to me, and the healer ambled his way toward me.

"You have every right to be angry. I know this is a shock to you. I loved your father. But he passed away years ago, and I needed some-one. Wayne has been so kind. I need him."

"I needed you!" Becks began to pace.

The temperature in the room began to drop.

"Oh no. Not this again," Blake muttered.

I ran my hands up and down my arms to ward off the chill. Shit. "Becks?" I said in a gentle tone.

She glared at me. I pointed to her hands. "Shit," she muttered.

"Patrice, maybe something warm? Tea, perhaps?" I asked.

Becks sat on the couch beside me and laced our fingers together. Her hands were icy, but I didn't flinch. She was looking for support, and I would give it to her, even if that meant frostbite.

"Of course." Patrice busied herself in the kitchen.

"So, Wayne. What is it that you do?" I asked.

"I'm a physician also. I run the hospital," he said.

"I knew you looked familiar." Blake pinched my arm.

I yelped then glared at the healer. His eyes were round as he studied Wayne. Well, that wasn't a good sign.

"And I recognized you also, healer. I wonder, does the Godfather know what you're up to?" Wayne wrapped an arm around Patrice's shoulder and squeezed.

I stood and drew my sassy stick in a flash. "Step away," I snarled.

Wayne pulled a pistol from under the counter and pressed the barrel against Patrice's temple.

"Hey! Get that gun away from my mother!" Becks stood.

"I . . . I don't understand," Patrice stuttered.

"Did you think the Godfather didn't know who you were, Patrice? He's been watching you for a long time. He gave me implicit instructions to turn you in when this happened. It's been a long time coming." Wayne clapped a hand around her neck.

"Step the fuck away from her!" Becks shouted.

"Oh my, you are a powerful gifted. The Godfather has been waiting for you and your brother to show up. I thought it was a lost cause, but he was right."

Patrice began to cry. "How could you?"

"Easy. The Godfather made me an offer, and I took it. And now I get my freedom."

Blake stood. "You were caught with one of the gifted women, and the Godfather wanted to punish you. This was his offer."

"He killed Lissette. And he was going to kill me! I only did what any man would do." Wayne sneered.

"You asshole!" Patrice shoved him away from her.

"Don't make me, Patrice. You're expendable. And the Godfather is already on his way." He pulled some kind of device out of his pocket. "I've already activated the signal."

I was about to use my mind-reading abilities to fry the asshole's brain, consequences be damned, but Becks unleashed her gift.

A sharp, pointed, icy stake shot out of her fingertips and slammed into Wayne's throat. Blood poured from his wound. "Help me," he gurgled. A second later, he was on the floor.

"Oh my God! Rebecca, how did you do that? What happened to your gift?" Patrice stammered. "And why is it freezing in here?"

I was shivering, and so was Blake. Becks was a seething ice queen. She prowled into the kitchen with a predatory glint in her eyes.

"Rebecca!" Patrice shouted. "You are not yourself!"

Becks' narrowed gaze was fixed on her mother. "I. Want. Answers."

"Becks?" I approached my best friend slowly. "Becks? Hey." I waved a hand in front of her face.

She turned her icy gaze on me. I stood still, not wanting to antagonize her. After a pregnant pause, her gaze softened.

"Hi. You did good. I'm proud of you. But," my teeth chattered. "I'm freezing my ass off. Can you maybe take a deep breath?" I inhaled deeply and exhaled. "With me," I said, inhaled deeply once more, and let it out slowly. Becks followed my breathing pattern.

"El?" She stammered. "What did I do?" She looked at Wayne, who lay dead on the kitchen floor. "Did I just?"

Becks began to hyperventilate. "I ki . . . killed. I killed a man."

I shivered, and my breath came out in puffs. "It's okay. He was a bad man. You're not in trouble. But you need to control your gift."

"I . . . don't know how." Confusion and worry flashed over her features as she looked at her hands.

Blake moved from the couch. Becks' head whipped toward him, and another icy stake shot out, barely missing him.

"Becks! No! He's a friend," I told her.

Patrice pushed me aside and jabbed a needle into Becks' arm.

Becks gasped and then crumpled to the hardwood floor.

"What did you do?" I kneeled beside Becks and pulled out the syringe.

"It's a sedative. She was out of control. This was the only way," Patrice said, her hands shaking.

"Help me move her to the couch," I told her.

"What am I going to do with Wayne?" she asked.

"One thing at a time." We settled Becks on the couch. Blake rose to his feet.

"How long will this sedative last?" I asked.

"Several hours. I gave her a full dose." Patrice replied.

"Shit." I glanced at my watch. I had less than thirty minutes to get to Jamboree Court.

"The Godfather will be here soon. What was I thinking?" Patrice cried.

"He won't be coming. Not right away. He has more pressing matters to deal with. Is there somewhere nearby that is safe for you and Becks to wait?" I asked Patrice.

"Umm . . . no. Not really. There is an empty unit. It has no furniture, though, and there are a lot of neighbors." She replied.

"Scratch that idea. Blake, can you do something about this sedative?" I asked him.

"No. Sorry." He checked Becks' pulse. "She's fine. She's just asleep."

"I can try giving her something to wake her but it will take time, and she'll be groggy."

Great. Just fucking great. "I need to go. How far is Jamboree?"

"You can't go alone. I'll go with you," Blake offered.

"No, stay with Becks," I told him, then turned to Patrice. "Give Becks whatever you have to wake her. But only if it's safe. If not, sit tight."

"Where are you going?" Patrice asked.

"To liberate the Pure Bloods and the rest of this city from the Godfather."

CHAPTER FIFTY-ONE

Hudson

It'd taken a lot longer than expected to get Colonel Summers and the guard sector into the fold. We were able to question one of Emit's loyalists before he passed and learned the weapons master plan. The Godfather had ordered them to search the empty residential units for us and head to Jamboree Court. They were about to assemble teams when we arrived.

The Colonel had been my mentor in the military. There was something about the old man that made me want to listen and learn. He had the same effect on everyone around him which made him a great leader. The guards at BHF did as he asked without blinking.

Having their cooperation was one thing. The Colonel was concerned about the guards and loyalists that were out in the field. It was a delicate topic that could have gone either way. He'd decided to call the troops home and would detain them all until their allegiance could be ascertained. I didn't need to be there for that discussion, but that was how Colonel rolled. He made sure his men were well-informed and their opinions were taken into account. I appreciated his insight at the moment since we'd learned another group of soldiers were deployed to raid our homes. Colonel called them off, of course, and with their sophisticated radio systems, I was able to reach Hillside,

Gator, Briar Penitentiary, Royal Summit, and the farm. Thankfully, Johnny had been able to set up the comms system at the farm after I'd left. I wanted to hear my son's voice but he was already asleep and we were on a tight timeline.

We arrived at 2323 with thirty minutes before having to get to Jamboree. The loft was empty. El, Becks, and Blake were gone. Xavi found a scrawled note on the bathroom mirror.

Visiting Patrice. C u at JC.

"We need to go to my mother's. She's in 501," Xavi told us.

"That's on the other side of the city. It will take at least twenty to get there and another thirty to get to Jamboree," Luca chimed in.

I huffed out a breath. "We don't have time. I trust El to be at Jamboree as planned."

"She'll be there. Besides, she wasn't supposed to be with us at the confrontation. She was hiding in the background," Rome reminded me.

I nodded. "She'll be there. Let's head out."

Twenty minutes later, we arrived on the outskirts of the courtyard fronting Jamboree Court. The clock tower loomed above while people strolled into the nightclub venue. The rest of Alexi's crew were already waiting.

"They're on their way," Clemmons stated. The teleporter appeared out of thin air, startling me and Xavi. He chuckled.

"Quit, Clem," Luca said.

Alexi nudged my shoulder. To our far right, five gifted men sauntered into the courtyard. They fanned out, surveying the area.

I'd already committed the unfriendly adversaries to memory. The one I was most concerned with was there, which was disappointing. He had light brown hair and a freckly face. Thin and tall. He had the gift of flight, and I'd hoped he would sit this one out. Not because of his power, but because he was only seventeen years old.

There was the metal skin guy and fire-starter I'd met earlier. As well as one that was a speedster and someone called Cyclone, who could manipulate air.

"If I remember correctly, there was a siren and a stormbringer," I stated.

Luca nodded. "He's keeping them close. We'll circle around back and take care of them."

"Alright, let's deal with these guys. The more we can thin out the herd, the less we have to worry about when the Godfather comes around. Tranq the kid, though," I ordered.

Alexi and his crew took the left flank, while me, Rome, and Xavi took the right. A tranquilizer dart sped through the air, hitting the kid. I sighted my weapon and took out my second target. The man with the metal skin went down. Xavi took care of the speedster, while Rome dropped the fire-starter with a bullet.

As soon as the shots were fired, people went into a frenzy. I watched the crowd searching for Elyanna.

A moment later, the Godfather arrived, with the siren beside him. Shit. Where was Alexi? They were supposed to take him out. Before the Godfather could utter a single word, Rome fired his weapon taking out the siren.

I glanced in the direction Alexi was supposed to be.

Shit.

A cyclone surrounded Alexi, Clemmons, and Luca. They were trapped in a prison of torrential wind.

"Show yourself Hudson, or these civilians die at my feet," the Godfather shouted.

"Stay hidden," I told Rome and Xavi.

I strolled out of my hiding spot, hands in the air. I glanced at the hostess standing at the entrance of Jamboree. There was no sign of El. *Where are you babe?*

"Bring your friends," the Godfather ordered.

I kept walking, taking my time.

The Godfather aimed a pistol at the nearest patron and shot her in the head.

Asshole. I signaled for Xavi and Rome. The men caught up to me. We stopped at the edge of the courtyard, maintaining a safe distance of twenty-five feet. From what Alexi had said, the Godfather could siphon when he was within a five-foot radius and needed to be in your presence for thirty minutes. He'd already siphoned my power twice. I wasn't sure if he was still able to siphon from me. Alexi didn't have that answer either. The last thing we needed was for him to go invisible or siphon Rome's fire abilities.

"Let the civilians go, Neville," I said.

"No, I think we'll play a game. For every minute you make me wait, I take out an innocent." He raised his arms. Thunder roared, and lightning arced in the sky. The lightning streamed down and slammed into two civilians.

The crowd scattered. They were in panic mode, screaming and tripping over one another. The women were having the hardest time of it with their heels on. I almost felt sorry for them, but honestly, I didn't choose their footwear, and I had to focus.

I hurled a nearby planter and slammed it into the Godfather's direction. He stopped the potted plant mid-air. Shit. I pushed it against this power. The Godfather dug in his heels. People scattered. Gunfire blared around me. I trusted Rome and Xavi to have my back.

The ceramic pot split in half. The Godfather recovered quickly and sent streams of lightning into the courtyard, which was mostly cleared out except for a few fallen bodies. Some were dead. Most were too injured to get out of the way.

Rome moved past me. I tugged on his elbow and shook my head.

"We need to help."

"You won't be helpful if the Godfather gets a hold of your powers," I told him.

He growled and stepped back.

"Submit, Hudson!" the Godfather bellowed. It began to rain.

"I don't think so."

I hurled another ceramic planter. The Godfather blasted it with lightning.

"I have your mother. And your twin," he snarled, looking behind me.

"Fucking bastard!" Xavi raised his weapon and stepped forward, firing his weapon.

Lightning struck his chest. The electricity jolted his body, and then he fell to the ground, convulsing.

"No!" Rome hurled a fireball at the Godfather who dodged out of the way. The fire missed him by an inch and smacked into a sign, burning it to cinders, and revealing a man bowed over. Well, hello, Stormbringer.

Roman ran toward Xavi.

"Don't!" I shouted just as a bolt of lightning hit his back. Rome's body went ramrod straight. Sparks of electricity engulfed his body and then he crumpled to the ground.

Both of my friends were down. *Please still be alive.*

Fury rose within me. I began hurling everything I could find toward the stormbringer and the Godfather. Bricks, pavers, and chairs. The Godfather thwarted every hit, using my power against me.

Another strike of lightning flashed in front of my face, and the world went white.

CHAPTER FIFTY-TWO

Elyanna

"E l!" Blake shouted.

I turned but didn't slow. The healer ran to catch up with me. "Hey. You can't go alone. What about the seer's visions and stuff?"

"I don't have a choice, Blake. You and Becks not being at this showdown may change things, but I have to try."

"I'll come with you," he said.

"No. I need you to look after Becks. Maybe you can get there before it's too late. Go Blake, take care of Becks. Please," I told him and broke into a run.

"El! Wait! You're going the wrong way."

I stopped and looked at him. He pointed to the left. "Thanks!"

With my gift shut off, I ran down the paver-lined streets and began to wonder if Blake had steered me in the wrong direction The roads weaved around the city in a non-sensical pattern. And I'd been so focused on how things would change since Blake and Becks weren't going to be at Jamboree Court, that I hadn't paid any attention to my surroundings.

The sky overhead darkened, and thunder boomed in the distance. I followed the storm. Ten minutes later, I found myself at the edge of the courtyard.

Alexi and another man I wasn't familiar with were trapped in a whirlwind. A man stood five feet away, focusing on the cyclone.

I unsheathed my sword and sliced the Pure Blood's back as I ran past. Blood spurted from the gash. His knees buckled, and the cyclone disappeared. The wound was deep, but not fatal.

"Deal with him!" I shouted to Alexi and kept running.

A few feet away, Luca was being beaten bloody by something or someone zipping around him at blinding speed.

"Free me! Please. I can help him," another man was trussed up in ropes shouted.

I stopped to cut through the ropes. "I'm Monty. You must be El, Hudson's wife. I went to school with him," the dark-skinned man said.

"Where is he?" I asked.

"In the square. Go, I can untie the rest," Monty said.

I ran toward the square. Bodies were littered throughout the court-yard. Lightning arced overhead.

The Godfather stood near the entrance to Jamboree. Hudson and my three men were opposite him. I stopped in my tracks, remembering to stay a safe distance away from the Godfather who was controlling the storm.

Everything happened so fast.

Xavi shouted. "Fucking bastard!" He aimed his weapon and fired at the Godfather. Lightning hit him in the chest. His body convulsed on his way to the ground.

Roman ran toward him.

More lightning filled the square.

A jolt of electricity slammed into Roman's back.

A shower of lightning engulfed Hudson in a brilliant flash of white. Time stood still.

My three men writhed on the ground. I stumbled over my own feet. My heart stuttered in my chest. No! I was too late.

Maniacal laughter filled the air. The Godfather raised his arms once more and shot more bolts of lightning into my men.

He was killing them.

Hot rage ran through my veins. I opened my gift, welcoming the onslaught of thoughts from the thousands of people in Federation City. Instead of shutting them out, I soaked them in, allowing them into my mind, and focused on one person.

The chaotic thoughts from the Godfather flashed through my consciousness. I compartmentalized his knowledge and then pushed my power into his mind, forcing him to do my will.

Enough.

I prowled through the courtyard with single-minded focus.

The Godfather's lightning assault on my men ceased.

"You. You're the mind-bender. I've been waiting for you." The Godfather's hungry gaze roamed my body. "Come closer."

With my fists clenched at my sides I walked toward him, in slow measured steps.

"That's it. Just a little closer." He licked his lips.

"You want my power, is that it?"

"Yes, you have the most powerful gift of all. And you have no idea how to use it. Pity for you. Good for me. That's it; come to Daddy."

"You want what I got, Daddy?" I sneered. "You got it."

I unleashed my power, flooding his mind with every thought, and every voice from every person in Federation City. The Godfather clamped his hands to his temples and screamed.

"Feels good, doesn't it? All those thoughts swirling through your head."

"Stop! Stop! You need to control it." He dropped to his knees, his breathing ragged.

"Oh no, I can't stop now. I'm not nearly done." I pushed more of my power into his mind. Blood poured from his eyes and ears. He writhed on the ground, his face twisted with agony.

"Xavier!" someone shouted. The distraction caused my focus to waver as I saw Xavi's body twitch. The Godfather noticed and used that split second to blast me with a lightning bolt.

My body felt weightless for a moment and then my head hit something solid. The world went dark in an instant.

CHAPTER FIFTY-THREE

Hudson

Static electricity filled the air, making the small hairs on my arms stand. My old headmaster sent a shower of lightning at me. Instinctually, I rolled as the blinding white light impeded my vision. My body went tight, my ears rang, and everything felt numb. I couldn't move.

The Godfather's voice cut through the courtyard.

"That's it, come to Daddy."

Who the hell is the creep talking to?

My eyes darted to my left, where Elyanna was stalking toward him.

"Yes, you have the most powerful gift of all. And you have no idea how to use it. Pity for you. Good for me. That's it; come to Daddy,"the Godfather said to her.

"You want what I got, Daddy? You got it," she replied.

The Godfather screamed and clutched his temples.

I willed my body to move while El continued using her power against our enemy. He fell to his knees, screaming in agony. Blood streamed down his face and neck. *That's right, asshole. My wife is going to fuck your shit up.*

Electricity continued to course through me, making each movement jerky. I raised my head.

"Xavier!" a woman shrieked, distracting Elyanna.

Everything slowed.

Elyanna turned toward the voice. The Godfather used the distraction to recover and slammed a bolt of lightning into her body, throwing her a few feet into the air. Her head hit the pavers with a solid thud so loud I felt it.

Fury and despair propelled me forward. I rose to my feet and sent a blast of power into the Godfather, slamming him against the ground. He recovered quickly and hit me with a shot of lightning which brought me to my knees. I used my gift, pulling blocks of concrete and brick from the building and beating him with it. He was hunched over, still bleeding from his ears, eyes, and nose but the fucker would not go down.

A glint of metal overhead caught my eye. Using my gift, I yanked the bell from the tower. It clanged as it plummeted to the ground and landed on the headmaster. The heavy metal crushed his body with a satisfying crunch.

I forced my body forward, crawling on the hot pavers toward Elyanna. Each step painstakingly slow.

Please be okay. Please be okay.

I passed Patrice, who was fussing over Xavi, who was awake but seemed to be disoriented. Roman was still on the ground, his body motionless. *Sorry guys, El comes first.*

"Elyanna? Baby?" Her head lolled to the side. Her eyes were vacant. "Somebody help!!" Her T-shirt was burned, revealing a squiggly pattern of red and purple scorched skin above her left breast.

"Stay with me, baby. Alexi?! Blake?!" Where the hell was everyone? I felt for a pulse and panicked. I couldn't find it.

No, no, no. I was about to start compressions, but the burned flesh on her chest made me hesitate. Should I touch it? I wasn't sure. Sheer panic overwhelmed me; I couldn't think. I pressed my lips to hers and breathed into her mouth.

"Breathe, baby. Please." My cheeks were wet, and my eyes stung.

"Somebody help me!" I shouted.

"I'm here." Blake rushed to my side. "Shit. What happened?"

"Where the fuck were you?! You were supposed to be here!" I shoved the healer, causing him to stumble. He held up his hands.

"Hawk! Stop. Let him help," Becks said beside me.

"Save her!!" I begged.

I cradled El's head in my lap while the healer went to work. His hands glowed over the wound on her chest. Nothing happened.

"Do something!" I shouted.

The glow traveled from his hands to her body and then to mine.

"Hawk, you have to let her go while I work. Skin-to-skin contact is splitting my energies from her to you."

I laid her head gently on the ground and noticed the blood on my hands. A pit of dread formed in my stomach. "Her head. It's bleeding," I stammered.

"Fuck! Move." Blake shoved me aside. "Come on, Elyanna."

I sat there, begging every known god for mercy.

Her best friend sat there, sobbing. "Blake. Save her."

"You're not helping Rebecca," the healer snarled.

Becks swiped her cheeks then rushed to her brother. I should have checked on Rome, but I refused to leave El's side.

The courtyard buzzed with activity. My focus was solely on my wife, who had yet to wake up. Blake continued his healing, his face contorted with strain. *Please, El.*

Alexi and his crew had shown up. Someone said something about taking the others to the hospital. I ignored them all.

"Hawk, we need to move her to the hospital," Blake said. "Clem?! Clemmons!"

The teleporter appeared next to Blake.

"Take her to the hospital. She needs a CT," Blake told him.

"No!" I shouted. "You can't take her." I grasped her hand, refusing to let her go.

"We have to! I can't help her with my gift. I . . . I need help," Blake explained.

"Let them go, Hawk. We'll meet them at the hospital," Xavi said.

"Xavi?" I asked. When did he wake up?

"You need to get looked at. Rome has been taken. We need to go. Come on." Xavier tugged on my arm.

I glanced at El's unresponsive body. My heart filled with dread. I kissed her hand, nodded at Clem, and watched him disappear with my wife.

CHAPTER FIFTY-FOUR

Xavier

Everything ached. I struggled to raise my head; my vision was blurry. My mother called my name. Elyanna's beautiful hazel eyes met mine, and then she was gone.

A bright light struck her chest and sent her body flying several feet. I pretended I didn't hear the loud crack when her head hit the ground.

The bell rang. And then there was a squelch.

"Xavi?! Son? Oh my god! You're hurt. We need to get you to the hospital," my mother said.

I blinked at her for a few minutes while she fussed at me. *I'm fine; help Elyanna.* I thought the words, but they didn't come out of my mouth.

A dark figure crawled past me. I tilted my head, trying to figure out why the black sludge moving across the pavers looked familiar.

Another figure lay on the ground near me. The body was so still, as though frozen. I knew him, too, I thought, but I wasn't sure.

"Xavi? Hey, look at me."

Rebecca. Rebecca's my twin. Mom and Rebecca are here. Why are they here? What happened? Elyanna?

"I'm so confused." My voice was gravelly.

"Xavi, it's me, Becks," she said.

"I know who you are, Becks. What happened? Why are you here? Elyanna?"

"She was struck by lightning. Blake, the healer, is looking at her," she said.

"We need to take you to the hospital, Xavi," my mother added. She inspected my torso, which felt hot. She gasped.

"Your pulse is erratic but seems fine. We need to do a full exam," she continued.

"I'm fine. Help, Elyanna," I repeated.

"You're not fine, Xavi. You've got a wicked burn on your abdomen, and you seem confused. Let's get you to the hospital," Becks told me.

"No, El, first." I stood and staggered.

"We need to get her to the hospital also," Becks said.

I ignored my mother and sister and moved toward El. A man held her hand and refused to let her go. Hawk. Recognition hit. The events of the last few days flooded my brain. Shit. I scanned the courtyard and found Roman, still on the ground. Alexi beside him. The strong man picked up the fire-starter, carrying him bridal style, and deposited him onto a golf cart, which sped away.

"They're taking him to the hospital. It's not far," Alexi said. I looked behind me.

"You all need to get looked at. From the looks of things, all four of you were hit with a million volts of electricity," Alexi continued.

So he was talking to me. My brain was foggy; I couldn't keep up. I nodded.

Hawk hadn't let El go.

"Let them go, Hawk. We'll meet them at the hospital," I told the telekinetic.

"Xavi?" he asked, his brows furrowed.

"You need to get looked at. Rome has been taken to the hospital already. We need to go. Come on." I patted his shoulder.

Another golf cart stopped in front of us with Alexi behind the wheel. Hawk and I got on. My mother and sister were on another cart. Becks waved at me. "See you at the hospital," she said.

I noticed the chaotic scene around me. People were crying. Several bodies were lying on the pavement, covered with sheets. A couple of golf carts were speeding to and from Jamboree Court. The bell sat in the middle of the courtyard, and a limp hand poked from under the metal.

"Hudson tore the bell from its tower and smooshed the Godfather," Alexi explained as we drove past.

I glanced back at my friend. He was silent, his skin ashen except for the veiny red scorch mark that sprawled across his shoulder up to his neck. His shirt was a tattered mess. I looked down at my torso, noticing for the first time that I was in the same state of disarray.

If it weren't for the evidence of Hawk's handiwork with the bell, I would have said we had just gotten our asses kicked.

CHAPTER FIFTY-FIVE

Hudson

N early one week had passed since we confronted the Godfather, and Elyanna, the love of my life, remained unresponsive. She'd been in a coma, and there was nothing the doctors or the gifted healer could do to help. "Her vitals are stable," they said. "She's in a deep sleep. Her body is recuperating from all the stress," Blake, the healer, told us.

Dr. Jeff arrived two days ago, and even he hadn't been able to solve the puzzle. It was beyond frustrating to have the most brilliant minds and the most sophisticated medical facilities and technology and yet feel so helpless. *Please, God, send my wife a lifeline.*

"Hawk? We need all of you downstairs." Colonel Summers stood in the doorway of our hospital suite. "The residents are causing a fuss."

"We don't give a shit about the residents or this fucking city," Xavier announced.

Ghost was right. We didn't. We wouldn't be in this damn hospital if it weren't for this damn city.

"If you're there, we'll diffuse this situation in minutes without casualties," Summers added. "Please."

"Go." Rome wheeled himself into the room. "Both of you. I'll stay with her." His shirt was drenched with sweat.

The fire-starter had taken a lightning bolt to his spine, leaving a wicked scar across his back. Thanks to the sophisticated technology at Federation Hospital and Blake's healing abilities, they were able to save his life. At first, it seemed like he'd be paralyzed. Thanks to his gifted body's ability to heal itself and Blake's powers, he slowly regained feeling, starting with his upper body and then lower. The day before, he had been able to stand on his own and had taken a few assisted steps. He continued physical therapy, and we were all confident that it was only a matter of time before he'd be back to his old self.

I glanced at Xavier. He rolled his eyes. "Fine." He pecked El's cheek and exited the room.

Aside from the scar Xavier had on his torso, his injuries from being attacked by lightning weren't physical. His were psychological, which was worse. He berated himself constantly for the way he treated El after the incident with Luther. He was desperate to make amends and afraid he wouldn't have the chance. There were two sides to the invisible man I had come to love and accept: the deviant who loved to kill without remorse and the fun-loving man most people knew. The Xavier that was present was one of utter depression. Between El's condition and Rome's, Xavi wasn't himself. Of course, he never shared what was going on in his head, so there wasn't much I could do to help him except be present whenever he needed me.

And he did. When El hadn't woken up on day two, he snuck into bed with me in the middle of the night. Rome was paralyzed. El was unresponsive, and I was the only warm body available. I gave him a questioning glance as he slid under the covers.

"It's not a sex thing, Hawk. I just need to be close. I'd get in bed with either one of them, but . . ." He choked up as he tried to explain himself.

"Do you want to talk about it?" I asked.

He just shook his head and made himself comfortable beside me.

"Don't hog the covers," I said, trying to lighten the mood.

He'd been sleeping with me ever since, and I had to admit, his presence was welcome. I wasn't dealing with the situation much better than he was. El was everything. She was a remarkable woman, and although I'd seen her struggle with her gift days before, seeing her in bed weak, pale, and her body completely still tore me to shreds. The only saving grace I had was Axel.

Dr. Jeff came to the desert with Johnny, who piloted the chopper. They brought Axel and Julia with them. My son was not dealing with his mother's situation well. We'd hoped his presence might bring Elyanna back, but that didn't work, and my kid felt it. He had never been a whiny baby, and it made me question my parenting skills. Maybe he shouldn't have seen her this way. Maybe we'd left him for too long. He was only a year old. I didn't have the answers. I was doing the best I could with what I had to work with.

I moved to El's bedside and brushed my lips against hers. *We'll be right back. Please be awake when I return.* She didn't respond.

Like Xavier, I hadn't sustained any serious injuries after our confrontation with the Godfather. I was sporting a gnarly scar from being hit by lightning. Mine was right under my collarbone and ran up to the side of my neck. Elyanna had a matching scar above her left breast. It was like the four of us went out and got matching tattoos. Not tattoos; no, these were raised scars of puckered pink and white flesh. We had been branded by fire. I gently kissed El's scar. *Please wake up, baby.*

I squeezed Rome's shoulder as I exited the suite and found Xavi and Summers standing near the elevators. "Stairs," I said.

"I'm too old for that shit," Summers snorted. "See you downstairs."

I passed the elevators and took the emergency exit with Xavi right behind me. We didn't speak as we descended to the ground floor. The walk cleared my head. And I was grateful Xavi wasn't in the mood to be chatty, yet grateful for his presence.

Federation Hospital was comprised of two separate, five-story buildings. One wing was for the residents. We learned there was a team of scientists and doctors there that had been studying the plague and the vaccines given to the residents. I was certain there was nefarious bullshit going on in there, but that was of no concern to me at the moment. Dr. Jeff would be all over that shit after he figured out how to help Elyanna. She was his priority.

We were in the second building of the hospital, which was dedicated to the gifted Pure Bloods and their children. With our ability to heal, gifted adults didn't need much medical care, and if they did, that could be administered at the Loop.

The first two floors of the gifted wing were where the Pure Blood children lived and went to school. There was a daycare facility and a dormitory with twenty-four-seven staff. All twelve of the children in the dormitory had gifted mothers whom they never got a chance to meet until a few days ago. The Godfather had attended each delivery and ensured the infant was then taken from the Loop and brought to the hospital. The only positive about the horrific situation was that children were well cared for and cherished. Nothing replaced a mother's love, though. It was heartwarming and bittersweet to witness their reunion when El was lying in bed, being fed nutrients via an IV.

Anger and frustration seeped out of me as I shoved the door, which led to the ground floor of the hospital.

Alexi and Colonel Summers had taken control of Federation City. The first thing Alexi had done was unchain the women in the Loop and reunite them with their children. Summers had called a cease-fire on all attacks on rebel communities, and slowly the guards on patrol were making their way back to FC.

There were a couple of gifted individuals who had decided to leave. According to Alexi, they had been loyal to the Godfather. Alexi had given them the choice to stay and live in peace or leave. They left. I imagined they'd return to FC in the future. Hopefully, it would be a peaceful reunion.

They hosted a town hall meeting, which had been met with a lot of resistance from the residents. This was expected, considering they'd paid a lot of money to live in post-plague luxury. The biggest contention was about allowing the people from the citizen encampment to move in. I didn't give a shit. As soon as El woke, we were going home.

The park in front of the hospital was packed with people. Fan-fucking-tastic. Guards were policing the crowd. Alexi was speaking into a bullhorn, trying to speak over the obvious discontent.

"Can you believe this shit?" Xavi muttered. He rolled his neck, a feral glint in his eyes.

"Easy, Ghost. We can't go on a killing rampage." I draped an arm around his shoulders and patted his chest.

He exhaled.

A car horn blared as the vehicle was driven onto the manicured grass. People jumped out of the way, clearing a path for the candy-apple green vehicle. It was a fancy sports car from the pre-plague era, which at the time must've cost a million bucks. Now it was fucking worthless.

A brazen couple stepped out of the car, dripping with gold and diamonds. Fucking assholes. They sauntered toward Alexi, screaming about how they were taking over.

"This is our city!" the man shouted. The crowd behind him cheered.

"We freed you from the tyrant that ruled this place," Alexi responded.

"That tyrant kept us safe. All you've done was bring us death," the woman added.

The people roared in response.

"We refuse to let those degenerates from the citizen encampment into our sanctuary!" The man pumped his fist. The people were incensed.

I stood beside Summers, with Xavi close behind me.

"I've had enough of this," I said.

Alexi extended the bullhorn toward me. I waved it away.

I called on my power and levitated the fancy car off the ground. People screamed and darted out of the way. I raised the vehicle twenty feet in the air, flipped it over, and slammed it into the ground. Metal crunched and glass sprayed the grass.

"Go back to your fancy homes and abide by the new laws. Or you can leave," Summers told the crowd.

To add insult to injury, Alexi strode to the car, picked it up, and smashed it into a ball of metal.

Xavi let out a gut-roaring laugh. I joined him.

The crowd dispersed, tails tucked between their legs.

Xavi and I said strode away, leaving Summers and Alexi to deal with their people, while we went to check on Ax. My son didn't like being away from us at all, but I'd insisted, and so did Becks. The kid couldn't stay in a hospital room all day waiting for his mother to wake.

I heard Axel wailing as we approached the daycare. He was fussy. Again. As we got closer, I noticed Becks bouncing him in her arms. His chubby face was red and streaked with tears. Poor little dude.

She saw us enter, and relief flashed over her face. Ax saw me and outstretched his little arms.

"Dada!" he sniffled.

I cradled my son to my chest and squeezed. Xavi kissed his head.

"He's been fussy. He keeps saying, 'Mommy, wake'." Becks told us.

"Mommy, wake, da-da," Ax repeated.

"Okay, buddy, let's go check on her." I kissed his cheek.

"Thanks, Becks," Xavi said to his sister.

"Come get me if something changes." She waved and went back to the other children.

We took the elevator back to the suite. Rome's head rested on the side of El's bed, their fingers linked together.

"Uncle Bug," Ax said.

Rome raised his head and gave him a crooked smile. "Hey, Bubba."

"Momma wake."

Rome frowned, then backed his wheelchair away from El's bed. I took his place at her side and gently laid Ax on her chest.

"I'm gonna shower." Rome wheeled into the ensuite bathroom.

"You need a hand?" Xavi offered. Before we killed the Godfather, those words would have been laced with lust and innuendo. Now, Xavi was honestly just being helpful. It was sad.

"Sure," Rome replied. No lust or innuendo in his response either. The wheelchair was too big to fit into the bathroom and the fire-starter wasn't above asking for help when he needed it.

I pressed a kiss on Elyanna's lips. "Ax is here, baby. Please wake up."

Ax climbed up to his mother's face and kissed her eyes. "Wake up, momma."

The little man had sad eyes. My heart lurched, and my knees buckled. I managed to move a plastic chair under my ass before falling to the floor.

"Come back to us, Elyanna." The pain in my voice was evident and my eyes burned with unshed tears.

Sometime later, I heard my wife's sweet voice. She was speaking with our son, who was speaking in full, coherent sentences. It was a dream, of course. Ax was able to form words and have a baby-talk conversation. The voices in my dream gave me comfort, and so I lay there, eyes closed, and continued to listen.

"I missed you, baby boy," she told him.

"Missed you too, momma. Let's go home now," he replied.

"Soon. We have to wake your daddies."

Her nails stroked my scalp. I sighed.

"Daddy!" Ax slapped my face.

"Hey buddy," I rasped, blinking sleep from my eyes. The curtains were wide open, revealing a silvery sky. Shit, how long was I out? Xavi was in our bed, asleep, with Rome next to him.

"Hudson," El said.

My sleep fog vanished, and I whipped my head to the right to find my wife's gorgeous hazel eyes staring back at me.

CHAPTER FIFTY-SIX

Elyanna

THREE MONTHS LATER

W e'd stayed in FC for several weeks after I'd woken. Dr. Jeff administered countless exams before releasing me from the hospital and deeming me fit for travel. While undergoing medical testing, my men were helping Alexi and Summers organize the city. They didn't relish being involved in politics, but it was necessary. After a few labored discussions, the new leaders of what was now called Freedom City and its residents came to an amicable resolution.

We'd accomplished a lot of good while at FC. In addition to releasing the gifted women at the Loop and reuniting them with their children, we found Cynthia, who had been working at Jamboree Court. We reunited her with her children—the four siblings we met at the citizen's encampment. Max and his three sisters were overjoyed to see their mom again. Summers had given her a job in the guard sector, and he found the family an apartment.

Dani, the seer, had a healthy baby girl. They moved into Unit 3023 with her husbands, who were all pitching in to organize Freedom City.

Another happy ending we had cause to celebrate was between

Becks, Xavi, and their mother. They mended their differences, which was a relief for all. Patrice had her reasons, which I could understand. There wasn't much a woman wouldn't sacrifice to keep her children safe. It may not have been the best choice, but the twins agreed to put it behind them and move forward. And Becks had other pressing matters to deal with. It had taken weeks for her to control her amplified powers. She worked with some of the other gifted in the training dome at the Loop. It wasn't her nature to be a lethal killer, but she could easily defend herself in any situation. I was so proud of her.

My control over my mind-bending abilities was better than ever. At first, I didn't even notice the difference until Rome asked about my powers a full day after I'd woken. I was able to silence the thoughts of thousands with ease, and my range increased. I could pick out a mind from miles away. I'd been able to talk to Hudson in clear, concise sentences from opposite ends of the city. Who's to say why? I imagined it had to do with being struck by lightning. Or maybe it was the concussion.

Hudson hadn't experienced any adverse side effects from the serum, however, his gift was more powerful than before, which was amazing and unsettling at the same time. It wasn't just being able to move things without seeing them; his range was farther, and it didn't matter how heavy the object was. I was worried. But the medical team, comprised of Dr. Jeff and Blake, swore to me he was fine.

Hudson had also mentioned hearing our son's voice in his head while I was in a coma. I'd heard it as well and thought it was just a dream. The news had everyone on edge. Axel was just a toddler, and having a mind-bending gift at that age was a bit terrifying. My son hadn't exhibited any abilities since, and thus, the best we could do was sit and wait.

Dr. Jeff took a special interest in everything the scientists were doing at FC. Once I passed his medical exams to his liking, he spent every waking hour gathering information, studying samples, and conducting multiple tests on practically every gifted person who had been put through the enhancement procedure. For a minute, I'd been worried that he'd choose to stay, but he was eager to return home with us. He loaded himself up with plenty of data to study, and we brought home more gadgets for him to continue his quest for knowledge.

With the new regime taking over and working the other communities into the fold, the list of things to do in Freedom City was crazy long. Thankfully, once the infrastructure was in place, my men decided the rest was up to the people who wanted to remain. Communication protocols were put into place, and we left knowing that the city was a new ally.

Before leaving, my men had commandeered two RVs and a couple of trucks from Freedom City's massive pool of surplus. BHF had hoarded everything they could get their hands on, and most of it was just wasting away. The RV's, I learned, were tour buses belonging to a famous, pre-plague, pop-star living in the city. After Hudson and Alexi smashed up someone's Lamborghini, the pop star didn't complain. It wasn't like she was going on tour anyway, and the only reason we'd taken the large vehicles was because we brought a few residents with us and a whole mass of supplies that would last a lifetime.

We'd taken a short road trip to the warehouse sector along the California and Arizona border. We had gotten backup generators, tools for Xavi's garage, weapons for Hudson's collection, medical gear, and equipment for Dr. Jeff. Roman loaded up fishing and hunting gear. Becks and I picked up essentials for the Summit, including kitchen tools for Chef Loretta, books and learning tools and supplies for the school, as well as clothing items for ourselves and our families.

Several gifted individuals came home with us, as well as Patrice and Blake. Freedom City was undergoing changes that would make living there a dream, however, some of the gifted had expressed their desire to start fresh. I couldn't blame them, they'd been traumatized by the Godfather's regime.

By the time we returned to Royal Summit, the main building had already been repaired from the damage sustained when we were attacked. Residents from Gator High, Briar Penitentiary, and Hillside had helped to rebuild. It was their way of showing support and saying thanks for ending the relentless attacks we had encountered over the years.

We knew it wasn't completely over, though. There were a couple of gifted individuals, who left FC and many guards on patrol or at BHF stations across the country who were loyal to the Godfather. Even with him gone, his loyalists still believed rebels were evil. That was another problem for the men to deal with when the time came.

My men weren't worried, and neither was I. We no longer needed to hide our gifts. The residents at FC were fearful, but that was appropriate considering the display of power they'd witnessed at Jamboree Court. Some of the residents in our communities were afraid of us: the telekinetic, the fire-starter, the invisible man, and me, the mind-bender. I didn't care anymore. It was freeing to be out in the open. And fuck them all if they feared us because we're different. My family was back together; we were healthy and stronger than ever. We'd face our adversaries together. For now, we'd enjoy peace while it lasted. After the torment we endured, we deserved it.

It wasn't until a week after I'd wakened that Rome had fully recovered. The lightning had hit him in the spine, nearly severing his body's central communication system. If it weren't for Blake's healing abilities combined with Rome's accelerated healing gifts he may have not survived. Poor firebug. First the helicopter crash and then a lethal dose of lightning. His body had worked overtime to heal and thankfully he did. The scars were there though. We all had them which was a testament to what we'd been through.

Xavi no longer harbored any hateful thoughts toward me. We had long conversations about what he described as his deviant nature. My heart ached after hearing about him being bullied as a teen. The teen years were confusing for most, and his experience left deep emotional scars. Luther's meddling had brought his inner turmoil to the surface. I assured him that he no longer needed to hide his wild side. He would always have a streak of defiance in him and the need to unleash dark desires, which I was okay with. He was hesitant about it all, stating he was afraid he'd scare me away. I promised I wouldn't run as long as we communicated. It was the best I could do because, truthfully, it was his burden to carry. Somehow, he would need to find a way to meld the two parts of him together. Easier said than done, considering how my being comatose made him feel vulnerable. It was still a work in progress.

From the moment I'd met Hudson, I knew he was something special. His unwavering dedication to us, his fierce protection, and his loving touch brought me more happiness than I ever thought possible. After everything he'd done to keep me and his people safe, I was relieved to see him finally relax and enjoy the home and family he had fought so hard to build.

Warm fingers brushed my knee, bringing me out of my musings. Xavi's face was nestled between my breasts with one of my legs wrapped around his torso. Roman was on the other side of him, reaching for me. While Hudson's chest was pressed against my back with his hand on my belly, protectively cradling the little one growing in my womb. I released a contented sigh, feeling truly blessed. Our family was safe and growing. My son was in his room sleeping soundly. And I had the love of three men, each one vital to my life and happiness: Roman, my adoring shadow; Xavier, my wild, passionate ghost; and Hudson, my unwavering protector. They all owned a piece of my heart, and I theirs.

The road to earning our freedom was not easy. We faced challenges that tested us to our very core. Lives were lost. A lot of blood was shed. But through it all, we stayed together, united by our love and determination to create a better life for ourselves and our families. We survived insurmountable odds, solidifying our bond and making us stronger than ever. Together, we would confront whatever the future threw our way.

THE END

THE PLAYERS

These characters make an appearance in books one and/or book two. Special abilities are italicized.

Elyanna Gray: *Mind-bender*, Mother of one - Axel

Hudson (Hawk) Pierce: *Telekinetic*

Axel Davis: *Seer*

Xavier (Xavi) Cole: *Invisibility*

Roman (Bug) Borgia: *Fire-starter*

Rebecca (Becks) Salinas: *Affinity for Water*, El's best friend, Xavier's sister, Mother of three - Aaron, Jonah, and Julia

Johnny Salinas: Becks' husband

Doctor Jeff: *Brainiac*

Loretta: Chef at Royal Summit

Doctor Carla: Psychologist

Luther (Puppeteer): *Mind-bender*

Samson: Guard at Hillside Rebellion

Sheridan: Guard at Hillside Rebellion

Patrice Sanders: Doctor, Scientist, Mother of two - Xavi and Becks

Godfather: *Villain*

Blake: *Healer*

Kyle: *Invisibility*

Dani: *Seer*
Alexi: *Strength*
Monty: *Speed*
Clemmons: *Teleportation*
Luca: *Brainiac*
Colonel Summers: Guard at Federation City

A NOTE FROM THE AUTHOR

Feedback Request

Thank you for choosing Elyanna's story! I hope you enjoyed it. Please leave a review as I'd greatly appreciate your feedback. As a new author I am whole heartedly interested in what my readers have to say. Your feedback helps me hone my craft and publish books you'll enjoy reading. Connect with me on my website at: genaviecastle.com

ALSO BY GENAVIE CASTLE

The Kenzie Chronicles - Series Complete

Fae Magic

Fae Blood

Fae Bonds

Fae Chaos

Banished, An Elemental Kingdom Novel

Pure Blood Duet - Series Complete

Chained, Book One

Unchained, Book Two

The Sentinel Series

Nightmare Girl

Book Two & Three - available in 2025

Made in the USA
Columbia, SC
15 October 2024

44248087R00183